RAVEN'S RIDGE

A MAX BLAKE MYSTERY

WILLIAM FLORENCE

WILDBLUE
PRESS

WildBluePress.com

RAVEN'S RIDGE published by:
WILDBLUE PRESS
P.O. Box 102440
Denver, Colorado 80250

Publisher Disclaimer: Any opinions, statements of fact or fiction, descriptions, dialogue, and citations found in this book were provided by the author, and are solely those of the author. The publisher makes no claim as to their veracity or accuracy, and assumes no liability for the content.

WILDBLUE PRESS is registered at the U.S. Patent and Trademark Offices.

ISBN 978-1-947290-73-0 Trade Paperback
ISBN 978-1-947290-72-3 eBook

Interior Formatting/Book Cover Design by Elijah Toten
www.totencreative.com

ALSO BY WILLIAM FLORENCE:

The Max Blake Mystery series ...

Raptor's Ridge
Misery Ridge
Faraway Ridge
Snowfall Ridge
Emerald Ridge
Emerald Ridge
Melia Ridge

The Max Blake Western series ...

The Killing Trail
Trail of Revenge
Trail to Redemption
Trail to Dead Man's Gulch
Trail from Crooked River

ACKNOWLEDGMENTS:

My gratitude is once again extended to Jennifer Guyor Jowett, Lori Kronser, and Chuck Goodrich, first readers and editors extraordinaire, for their critique of the evolving manuscript; and to Aoife Barry, Limerick journalist, and Jim Malloy with the Garda Press & Public Relations Office *in Dublin, for their help with the structure of the Irish police force; to Ashley Butler, Rowena Carenen, Elijah Toten, and Steve Jackson of WildBlue Press, for their help, expertise, advice during the production of* Raven's Ridge; *and to a variety of friends, Doc Strand and Michael J. Parker and Bill Kohlmeyer among them, who once again served up their names to the cause.* Molto grazie di tutto.

A grateful acknowledgement also is offered to the late William Hughes Mearns for two stanzas from his poem Antigonish, *and to the late Irish poet Seán Ó Ríordáin and his beautiful masterwork* Cúl an Tí, *a line of which is used for the Chapter 49 title. I urge readers to research the poem, which is easily found online. The translation:* **Where chaos is the heart of rule**

To my pal Willy Boy – and what a good boy he is ...

... and for Mitts, good soldier that he was, a feisty full-time job who kept me company through the bulk of the writing of Raven's Ridge

CAST OF PRIMARY CHARACTERS

THE PORT SIDE OF
THE ATLANTIC

Bill Kohlmeyer: Chief of police of Oregon's capital city

Fredo Fierro: Max and Caeli's friend and client

Elmore and Leonard: Fierro Enterprises employees/bodyguards

Michael J. Parker: Max and Caeil's attorney

Dr. Floyd Strand: Max's medical adviser

Joan Shedd: Bunratty Castle visitor and robbery victim

THE STARBOARD SIDE
OF THE ATLANTIC

Max Blake: Private detective; retired college professor and former reporter

Caeli: Max's fiancée, also a former reporter

Mitts and Koko: Caeli's rescue cats

Detective Sergeant Alan "Spud" Phelan: Avid reader and Limerick copper

DCI Thomas Óg McNeill: Limerick office of the Guards

DCI Declan Abbot: Limerick office of the Guards

Chief Superintendent David Sheehan: head of the Limerick division of the Guards

District Detective Superintendent James Ryne: Overlord, western division of the Guards

Frog One/Jean-Claude Daimallier: Global terrorist

Mister Denmark/Lance Corporal McMahon: former sniper, amateur hypnotist

Kathleen MacAmhlaoibh: Quick-change artist

Liam Gallacher: G2 branch operative

Danny O'Herlihy: Gallacher's driver/bodyguard

Ian and Gavin: G2 agents

Aedan O'Duinn: Computer guru/techie

The Four Magi: Unexpected visitors

"Oh, all kinds of lunacy happens in Ireland – all kinds of lunacy."
– *Anjelica Huston*

"There's nothing so bad that it couldn't be worse."
–*Irish proverb*

PROLOGUE

JOURNEYS HOME

He was patient. You had to give him that.

He'd spent years and never came close to being caught, or even suspected – until now.

Right now he was concerned, although … *well, first things first*.

Here are a few other facts to chew on.

He was generous, in his own mind, anyway. He didn't care who he showered his attention on: the rich and the unassuming, those nearing their golden years and those about to flower, men and women of varied shapes and sizes and hues … all were acceptable targets, so long as they provided a hint of something valuable.

Women especially. He'd been hurt by women in his distant past, and he relished every opportunity for payback.

A fat wallet, a luxury watch, a shiny ring with precious stones, a studded broach or necklace or glittering bracelet, earrings that sparkled and shimmered: Whenever something caught his considerable eye, he was hooked and, when conditions were right, made it his own.

He enjoyed the hunt, even now … even with this secondary mission, which he'd undertaken as a lark, little more than something to keep his mind off the dark days. But he remained forever on the prowl for other prey, other marks, other distractions.

Four years earlier, when he was still in the unit, deep inside the great expanse of Mideast desert, he'd described himself as the least bigoted man on the planet. His mates scoffed, knowing well his predilections. But he assured them with sound logic.

"It's true, lads," he'd said. "I'm happy enough to steal – trinket or life – from anyone, regardless of race, color, creed, or place of origin."

The line, with many variations, always generated a laugh.

But he wasn't joking, even as he grinned at his comrades with eyes that were dark and brooding and mesmerizing but that somehow managed to conceal the poison in his soul.

Steal? Sure. He couldn't help himself.

Kill? Absolutely – with glee, relishing his sniper's role with such enthusiasm that even the seasoned officers who appreciated his lack of conscience and prodigious talent with an L96 rifle grew concerned about the type of man they'd nurtured, day after day, during the height of the conflict.

A few of them, though their fears were never shared with their overlords, wondered about the type of man they would someday return to the land of supposed peace and tranquility, a place where the sounds of burping gunfire and belching explosions could be heard only on the telly or the movie screen at the local bijou. These were the same 3- and 4-star lifers who'd huddled in the aftermath of a particularly vicious skirmish, almost two years to the day they'd first turned him loose, and abruptly decided that he should be sent home ahead of his deployment's scheduled end – for his own good, of course.

What he might unleash on the unsuspecting throngs back in the corridors of civilization was a subject they didn't dare dwell on beyond the few minutes they'd taken to agree on expediting his same-day departure. Then again, their decision was made easier because he wasn't British at all but Irish – a hard-bitten commoner who couldn't be trusted ... not for long.

The orders came as a shock that he only fully recognized when he was duly escorted to the plane and determined that everyone on board the noisy military transport was an easy target for a man with his extensive skills.

I'll have to set my own missions now ...

He returned to that thought, many times.

He'd come away from the conflict without a scratch, as those who are born under the right alignment of stars and karma and the serendipitous nature of war so often do. Even his head was in decent working order, at least initially: no misgivings about his role whatsoever – and damn few veterans of the Middle East mess, regardless of uniform, could say that to a shrink or their best friend or lover with a straight face.

Then again, he didn't have friends, and he bought his lovers when the need arose.

He settled in London for a time, choosing to avoid the familiar places and faces of his ancestral home, fortunate that his boyhood life on the road, once he'd bolted the orphanage and the vicious nuns for good, had taught him to disguise his accent and to adopt a variety of personas. He recognized that he was being watched by the military brass, but he could deal with that inconvenience because he understood how they thought and what they looked for – and also what they expected of him.

He gave them nothing of value in return, playing the game and the role of a good soldier who'd made his peace and was happy to return to one of the great touchstones of Western culture.

He enjoyed the city because it offered sights and sounds and a feeling of euphoria that nothing in Ireland could match – not even Dublin. He relished the vibrant energy, the varying judgmental filters of the natives, the fluctuating languages that were spoken by the many thousands of daily visitors who bustled about with cameras and cell phones at the ready. He had an ear for dialects, and he also appreciated the overwhelming security of the place, which was something of a misnomer when he considered where he'd just been.

And what he was up to, of course.

"It's all good, despite the bloody CCTV cameras on every street, ever corner, every shopfront," he'd grumble from time to time, always to himself, when he was in the middle of some enterprise that was best hidden from the world. But he was adept at avoiding security nonsense anyway.

And, what the hell, he'd tell himself, once the generals had given up their half-hearted, conscience-driven attempts to monitor his activities, ensuring that his adjustment to civilian life was uneventful, he recognized that he could go anywhere, do anything, and hide his actions amid the daily bustle of the place with impunity.

Once he'd adequately adjusted to his new hunting grounds, he fell back into old habits, stealing when the urge was too great to resist and killing for sport ... just to keep his hand in the game.

When media attention began to grow, as it inevitably did, he abandoned London for Paris, then Berlin, and was soon on to Rome and then Athens. He gave it up entirely for six months, spending time on Crete and later on Rhodes, where he enjoyed wandering the Street of Knights and wondering about its history and what it must have been like to strike the unsuspecting with a knife, a piece of metal, a rock, even a fist, centuries into the past.

"No DNA, no fingerprints, no cameras, no social media posting photographs across the internet, no coppers with full-auto weapons ... absolutely bloody brilliant," he'd mutter.

He was troubled for a spell, more than a year on, by an onset of dreams that frequently erupted into splitting headaches. His tour in the desert began cycling through his head on an endless loop, and he speculated about how much time he'd lost and sank into a lingering depression.

As the dark images jumped into his head with surprising ferocity, his body would deflate, like air gushing from a slashed balloon. He would sink into the nearest chair or bed and collapse inwardly, his shoulders slouching and contracting, his fists clenching in and out, and blood would rush to his neck and face and scalp, attacking his extremities with the force of sharp needles repeatedly jabbed into his skin. He would visibly shudder and will his eyes to remain sealed. But the mere act of clamping down, holding on, caused such excruciating pain that he was compelled to muffle the unbidden cries by clinching his mouth shut with such savagery that his lips would bleed.

He couldn't predict how long the onslaught of melancholy would last: minutes and hours when he was fortunate. But sometimes the feeling would go on for days and long, weary nights. All he knew for certain was that when the fear came and gripped him and held him tight, a vice around his still-beating heart, he understood the emptiness of space and time and the heavens and the enormity of the vast darkness and the chilling depths of the soul and, finally, the places where no one should visit, even in dreams.

Places like the orphanage.

Places like the desert.

He eventually took up chess, fell into regular seaside games with a couple of ex-pats and even a local fisherman who was terrible but amenable, and thoroughly enjoyed himself for a time, drawing on his considerable savings.

But the yearnings, the urges, proved too strong, and he shook off the shackles of nightmares for good.

He never let on about his humble beginnings, the early abandonment, his time on the road with gypsies and tinkers, his initial efforts at bending the will of strangers to spend money they didn't have on games of chance or trinkets they didn't need, or on the tricks of memory and manipulation that allowed him to peek into their own hidden dreams, reaching inside to snatch what he wanted.

The time that he spent in the sunny Mediterranean was a revelation, opening some corridors to light, closing others to moody darkness. Still, he suspected, deep in his heart, that the inactivity he so wanted to enjoy was slowly killing him, like the constant dripping of a leaky faucet.

He also found that he missed the thrill of the hunt – the tedious days of heat and rain and wind and coming to know your opponent, and then the glorious takedown, when a just and forgiving god was something that you read about or heard of only in the knuckle- and ass-walloping classrooms of his youth.

Mostly, he enjoyed looking into his victims' eyes when the realization struck that this was their final day on Earth, that all of their expectations and aspirations were gone in the flick of a knife blade, that nothing they did would stay the hand of the executioner.

He wandered north: Tirana, Bari, Naples, Rome, Barcelona, Marseille, Paris again, then Brussels, Amsterdam, and back to London. He never remained in place long enough to be noticed, and he was forever cautious, alert, ready.

But the tug of his native island and his roots called to him, as did the thought of revenge on those who'd taken away his military career and, years earlier, had repeatedly abused him when he was but a boy with nothing to protect himself but his own small fists.

"I'll get 'em all," he'd muttered while drinking on the mail boat that took him from London's Euston Station to Holyhead,

Wales, in the dead of night and then on to Dun Laogharie and Dublin's Pearse Station.

And on this night, at least, the gods were listening.

A chance meeting with Frenchman Jean-Claude Daimallier and his beautiful traveling companion, an Irishwoman named Kathleen MacAmhlaoibh, with skin so white and eyes so green and hair so red that he was reminded of a rainbow, would provide him with an opportunity to get back at damn near everyone.

Or at least, that was his hope once the magnitude of their plans and proposal fully sunk in. He hated most women – that much was true. But Kathleen was a strident charmer, and he was ready for something new, something different, something … *challenging*.

What he didn't plan for was an unexpected encounter with Caeli Brown.

ONE

ANOTHER DAY IN PARADISE

I don't recall what I was doing, exactly, when the doorbell first chimed and then reverberated throughout our Irish estate on the River Shannon, west of Limerick.

Earlier that morning I'd chatted briefly with Caeli before she left for the city to run some errands. I'd also enjoyed a piece of toast and a second cup of Earl Grey while trying to finish a crossword puzzle that I'd worked, off and on, for two days and, if memory serves, grabbed the Nikon at one point to shoot photos of a gaggle of gliding geese riding low across the great expanse of water that fronts our home.

At least I wasn't in my bathrobe.

Hell, I'd even snuggled into a new pair of slippers that had come winging their way across the Atlantic, thanks to L.L. Bean's mail order magic. At this stage of the morning, I was ready to greet the world – or at least an unexpected visitor.

Mitts, Caeli's 26-pound Maine Coon, still skittish from our recent move from Oregon to the wilds of Ireland's west coast, bolted at the doorbell's chime, his multi-toed front paws churning madly across the hardwood as he sought shelter.

While the big guy, an unapologetic 'fraidy-cat, scrambled his retreat, Koko, Caeli's midnight black longhair feline who is half Mitty's size and constantly exhibits five-plus times the courage, purred her way to the door to greet the chime-ringer.

I mentally ran through the usual prattle – *too early for the post; we aren't expecting workers today so far as I know; we've been here too long for neighbors to drop by with a welcome gift* – and even muttered aloud ("Who the hell can this be?" were my exact words) before pointing a finger at Mitts, who was cowering in the corner under one of the parlor chairs, with an accusatory line ("Big Fat Mitty, the Big Fat Coward") and opened the door with a flourish.

I wasn't expecting a copper, the Irish term of endearment for the constabulary, and my surprise at seeing the youngish man with a police ID in hand must have been evident. I'm terrible at poker and worse at showcasing the necessary deadpan look.

"Max Blake," he said as I opened the door a foot or so, careful to lodge my left foot squarely at its base to prevent a forceful entry while keeping Koko from bolting.

It wasn't a question, although I responded in like manner.

"Yes," I said, only slightly distracted as Koko curled around my leg and eyed the opening longingly. She'd recently discovered that a world of opportunity awaited her on the outside, one that included bevies of birds and warrens of mice in the far-flung fields surrounding the estate, and longed to bolt for greater hunting opportunities than the inside of our home provided.

"You are Max Blake then, the college professor and author and, dare I say it, private detective," he persisted with another statement.

"That's right," I said and managed to read the name on his warrant card, which serves as an ID badge, similar to the shield American police officers present when they arrive unannounced. "Officer Phelan, I see. How may I help you?"

"It's actually Detective Sergeant Phelan, and I wonder if I could have a minute. It's important, I guess you'd say."

It hit me then, a blacksmith's hammer crashing into an anvil.

God – something's happened to Caeli, I instantly thought in a rising panic.

"Why are you here? What is it? Tell me she's OK," I said, blurting the words in the rat-a-tat fashion of a wildly firing machine gun.

"If by *she* ya mean Caeli Brown, I've no knowledge whatsoever of either her health or whereabouts," Phelan said quickly, holding up a hand as though warding off evil spells or the verbal bullets I'd fired. "I'm not here on official assignment, Professor Blake – I trust it's all right to call ye that – and, in fact, if my superiors knew the nature of this visit, my guess is they'd be disappointed, with me and in me."

He smiled, displaying a rack of solid white teeth and eyes that sparkled with sincerity. But I wasn't remotely relieved at Phelan's rambling stream-of-consciousness attempt at assurance that my fiancée was all right … *to the best of his knowledge.*

I wondered where I'd left my cell phone, thinking that I could call Caeli to determine her current status. But I didn't have it on me, and I couldn't for the life of me recall where I'd last placed the damn thing.

"So how do you know about Caeli – and me, for that matter, if you're not here to deliver bad news?" I managed in the next breath, buying time. "What's this all about, exactly?"

"I've read yer books, ya see. All of 'em," he said, straightening his shoulders to demonstrate his prowess with the written word. "I've greatly enjoyed 'em all and must say I'm impressed with yer adventures. Imagine me surprise when a computer check indicated yer recent move to Ireland and this very estate, which puts ya in me own back yard … a remarkable coincidence, considerin' the idea I'm in need of assistance and, well, here ye are, close enough for me to swing by and introduce meself and see if ya might be available."

If he'd rehearsed the spiel, he couldn't have delivered it more effectively, given the fact that I'd left him standing, warrant card in hand, at the entrance to the estate while gently nudging Koko away from the narrow opening to the outside world.

I bent down, grabbed the cat, ignored for the most part her wiggling and verbal protests, and allowed the door to swing open.

"Where are my manners?" I said, though still rattled at the thought that something might've happened to Caeli. "Won't you come in, DS … what did you say your name was again?"

"Phelan, sir,"

"Right. DS Phelan. Sorry. Would you be kind enough to come inside? I'll offer up the American equivalent of putting the kettle on and serving you tea so you'll at least be comfortable while explaining what brings you here."

He laughed as he entered, reaching out a hand to ruffle Koko's thick patch of between-the-ears fur, a gesture she's not fond of even when Caeli attempts it – and Koko allows Caeli great latitude. She rewarded him with a throaty growl that produced another laugh as he pulled his hand back in surprise.

"And this feisty little beastie would be Kokopelli," he said, without seeking acknowledgement. "You've described both of yer cats in the books, which is how I recognize the wee charmer. I take it I won't see cowardly Mitts today?"

I was damn near floored by his familiarity and offered up an appraising eye that he couldn't easily miss or dismiss.

"Maybe if you check under a bed or sofa – or that chair," I said, pointing a finger toward Mitty's current hiding spot.

"Ah – the big bloke with the extra toes. Nice to meet ya, Mitts," he said, calling out the last line.

He got nothing in return but a nasty glare, one that proclaimed a clear message (*Get the hell out of my house*), and he again laughed heartily.

"Get on with that look then," he said to Mitts. But he focused on me once more with this: "You could call that cat Balor of the Evil Eye, now that yer livin' in Ireland. It's *Balor Birugderc* in the Irish, if yer interested."

"I'll let Caeli know," I said. "He's her cat, after all."

He seemed to accept this and smiled easily, a task at which he apparently excelled.

He was in his late 30s, I guessed, modestly tall, in decent shape (though he sported the makings of a potential Guinness gut), with light hair that defied specific color identification. He was dressed as you'd guess a police detective would present himself: off-the-rack gray suit that was a touch ill-fitting and shoes that had taken a mud bath during the past couple of days and had yet to be set right again. He could hold a grin far longer than I'm comfortable in doing, and his teeth were his own and straight enough (*even* is a decent description) – not something you saw every day in our new homeland.

"I take it yer good wife's not at home then?" he asked.

Technically, Caeli is my fiancée and not yet my wife (the date was drawing ever nearer), although I didn't see a reason to correct a man I didn't know, let alone the reason why he'd called at this early hour.

"She's not, which is why I'd thought you'd shown up, unannounced and scaring the bejabbers out of me," I said, striving for friendly and not quite delivering, judging by the look on his face. "I was certain something had happened."

I checked my pockets again, wondering whether I'd somehow missed my cell phone during the initial search.

"No – nothing a'tall like that. And I'm sad to hear she's not at home. I was so lookin' forward to meetin' her. Again, Professor Blake, I'm sorry to catch ya unawares like this," he said. "I figured I could strike a couple birds at once and come out to meet ye and yer bride – I'm a big fan, ya see – and to perhaps ask for yer help on a matter of some … well, let's call it a matter of discretion."

He smiled.

I frowned.

"It's all a bit strange – don't you think?" I said, seeing as how we were well on and I still had no idea what he wanted. "Come into the kitchen and we'll see what's on your mind, DS Phelan, while I try to locate my phone. How's that?"

"I'd rather you called me Spud," he said. "But tea sounds lovely."

"Good. We'll start there. As to first names, let's see how the rest of this goes before we swear out a blood oath or exchange mobile numbers and email addresses and favorite movie lines, or directors, and whether your given name is actually Alan."

"But of course it is," he said. "That one, at least, is easily solved."

It didn't take extraordinary powers to determine that much. Most everyone in Ireland with the first name of Alan is generally always called Spud.

I'll confess that I discreetly checked for a holstered weapon as he walked with me into the kitchen, though I knew that members of the Irish constabulary don't normally carry a firearm during the routine discharge of daily duties. Of the many differences between my native country and newly adopted home, I found this fact to be among the most odd and counterproductive, particularly if you found yourself in a tight spot and needed an officer's protection.

Suffice it to say that Caeli and I have been in enough tight spots to know that all too well.

"Earl Grey or Lucky Irish Breakfast?" I asked after fishing a cup from the appropriate cupboard. I was still having difficulty remembering where Caeli had decided to stash our various dishes and glasses and whatnot and had to open two different cabinet doors before finding the correct location.

"Lucky Irish Breakfast? Jaysus, man – what's that then?" he asked, laughing.

"It's described as a Pot o' Gold in every cup," I said.

"Sure it is – a Yank's brand. Orson Welles," he said. "I'm a big fan, though mostly of his smaller films. I find *Citizen Kane* exceptional, of course – how can you not? But it's overplayed, especially at festivals and college courses, where the lecturer drones on about how fabulous it is with the lighting and weird angles and low ceilings – surely you'd agree. As to tea, whatever yer having's fine."

"Right," I said, temporarily ignoring his take on movie directors and great films; I'd opened the door, after all. "Earl Grey then. I'd offer a slice of raspberry red velvet cake on the side, but I'm afraid someone polished it off days back, and nobody's gotten 'round to whipping up another."

"Ah, lovely," he said. "You can actually get yer wife to cook then?"

"Caeli's a grand cook. Her sherry trifle is as good as you'll find anywhere in Ireland. But she doesn't do raspberry red velvet cake. That delicacy is my specialty."

"So you were the one to polish it off."

"Not me – that was Caeli. Still, it falls to me to produce another, and your visit serves as a reminder. Would you like a splash of something extra in your tea? We've a bottle of Power's about."

"It's a bit early for me, but help yerself."

I found myself amused at the back and forth, at least initially, and decided to play along, just to see where it would lead.

"Right. John Ford. Still not ready for a blood oath, though."

"Don't tell me ya like Ford because of *The Quiet Man*."

"I won't, though I like the film a great deal – especially when they run it on St. Patrick's Day in the States each year," I said.

"Ford did *The Searchers*, which is reason enough to call him my favorite director."

He smiled easily while I filled the empty cup with tap water and placed it inside the microwave, setting the timer for 2 minutes and change.

"That serves as a Yank's teakettle then?" he asked.

"It does. It may not hold with tradition, but it's far quicker in a pinch."

"What happens when that thing gives up the ghost?"

"Gives up the ghost?" I repeated, surprised at the concept.

"Sure. You know – clanks out, expires, stops workin' entirely. They do that, ya know."

"In that unlikely event, I supposed we'd buy a new microwave."

"And what would ye be after doin' for tea in the meantime, eh? Tell me that."

"We'd boil water on the stove."

"But you've just admitted ya don't have a proper kettle."

His logic was impressive.

"No worries. It's working today, and all is right with the world," I said.

"Sure it 'tis, and I'm delighted for yer hospitality," he said. "I'll also admit, in general, I think ya have to be a Yank to appreciate cups of tea that come from ovens – and Western movies in general. We don't have the landscape for it over here."

"For ovens or Westerns?"

"Yer havin' a bit of a go at me," he said. "In case ya didn't know, the Irish call the contraption a *oigheann micreathonnach*."

"We're back to microwaves, I take it. Lovely."

"Sure, 'tis. You can drop that in one of yer books, professor. No charge for the suggestion."

"You're a fount of knowledge, DS Phelan," I said. "I'd spell that with a U, by the way."

"Fount or Phelan?"

"Definitely fount."

"Good on ya. I've never cared for being a font of anything, especially a Wide Latin or an Ariel Black."

"You know your fonts then. I'm partial to Times Roman and Cambria – the first for text and the second for headlines," I said, mentally admiring the acuity of the man's mind and his ability to switch from one arcane point to the next with a dexterity that reminded me of a couple of Irish professors I'd had at University College Dublin back in the day. "You'll spot it in all my books."

He nodded but didn't reply this time, and I wondered whether he was finding the conversation as offbeat as I'd been – and yeah, I recognized that I was contributing to the craziness, *just to see what makes him tick.*

Damn strange, I thought.

Then, a moment later, I tried another line of attack.

"I read somewhere that Pierce Brosnan grew up playing cowboys and Indians when he wasn't serving mass or fishing the River Boyne in Navan. If he liked Westerns, DS Phelan, why not you?"

"Pierce Brosnan's a hundred years older 'n me. Besides, he hardly qualifies as a genuine Irishman," he said. "He was James bloody Bond, after all. Last I looked, Bond's a Brit. Then again, ever been to Navan?"

"I know where it is," I said. "North of Dublin – off the M3. But I've never spent time there."

"If ya had, you wouldn't be after mentionin' Pierce Brosnan as quintessential Irish with a basic understandin' of Western movies."

This time, I couldn't tell whether he was putting me on.

Maybe he has a fondness for extending conversations, I considered – something I could relate to easily enough.

The microwave dinged, and I removed the cup and set it down in front of my guest before offering three types of sweeteners in case he had a preference.

"We might have English Breakfast kicking about, but I wouldn't be so bold as to dig it out unless you insisted and, now that I think about it, confess to being surprised I even admitted to having it in the house at all," I said. "You must be one of those coppers who naturally gets people to spill what they know without force or coercion."

"Like that great American CIA pastime of waterboardin', ya mean?" he said. "Yer wife likes it then?"

"Waterboarding? Not that I'm aware."

"English Breakfast."

"Ah. No, but a friend does, which is why … sorry, but what's this all about anyway?"

I'd realized that Caeli was now overdue and was struck with a sudden suspicion that Phelan's roundabout discussion was some kind of odd Irish tradition for breaking bad news to unsuspecting foreigners.

He seemed surprised that I'd switched gears so suddenly, which prompted me to explain the detour.

"Here's the deal, DS Phelan/Call Me Spud. I'm happy enough to make a cup of tea and pass along pleasantries and engage in what might be called inane banter, and even to parse logical reasons for supporting John Ford over Orson Welles, if you insist – and I like Orson's work a great deal," I said. "But I'm curious as to why you're here, exactly, and how you seem to know so much about me, and Caeli, and the cats, and our being here in Ireland … all of it."

"Shall I start at the beginning then?" he asked.

"Yeah. I'd appreciate it."

He splashed a packet of sugar into his tea, I forked over a spoon after fishing one from the silverware drawer (which I found on the second try), and he eventually stirred the concoction with the bag held in his left hand, dripping over the cup.

"Pitch it in the sink," I suggested.

"Grand. All right, from the beginning then," he said. "I read yer book *Emerald Ridge*, which I enjoyed immensely, by the way, despite the ghastly accent ya gave to Caeli's uncle the archbishop, and then ordered a copy of …"

"Hang on. Caeli's Uncle Jack sounds exactly the way he was presented," I said, interrupting. "The man may have been a one-time muckety-muck, as refined a churcher as you're likely to meet, even here in this citadel of Catholicism. But he sounds like a Dublin dock-worker when he feels the strain of the world on his shoulders – and during that time, Jack was under a great deal of pressure."

"All right – fair enough," he said. "Ya didn't make up the part of his still being alive, right? Because I've got to tell ya, it was big news at the time of his death, here and all over Ireland."

"The truth shall set ye free," I said, holding up my hand as though swearing an oath.

He muttered something, perhaps "I'll be damned," before launching in again.

"Anyway, I read the book and picked up a copy of the next one, *Melia Ridge*, because to my way o' thinking, I had to get the rest of the story. I enjoyed that, then went back to yer first case, which ye called *Raptor's Ridge*, I think, and read the rest of 'em through in little more than a fortnight. I'll admit I was hooked, or at least interested to press on, and was only too happy to learn ye were locating into me own back yard."

"I don't recall providing an exact location of the estate we inherited in either book," I said.

"And you'll recall I'm a detective sergeant with the Guards and have access to all manner of records, plus sundry information yer average bloke would never get at – even if he'd a hankering to do so, even if he'd read yer books recountin' assorted cases and adventures. Or should I call 'em capers? That was a word of contention in *Melia Ridge*, I think, between you and yer bodyguard, the one ya call Leonard. I'd like to meet him one day – along with Elmore."

"You've a surprisingly good memory," I said, making a mental note to reconsider just how much information I wanted to pack into subsequent cases that could be turned into books. "If it's an autograph you're after, you have a roundabout way of asking for …"

"No-no – that's not what brought me out here, though an autograph would be lovely … one from the both of ya, in fact. But it's not that – delightful as it'd be. It's just that, well, the books were my entry into yer world, Professor Blake, and I feel as though I know ya after reading 'em."

Flattery, apparently, will get you another question.

"All right then, DS Phelan. Alan. Spud. Whatever. What is it exactly that you want from me? I'm happy to provide it if it's in my wheelhouse, which is more or less a baseball expression and may not easily translate. Let's see. If it's in my …"

"I get it – thanks," he said. "I'd like to talk a bit regardin' a case I'm workin' – or at least workin' 'round. In Yank-speak, yer a famous private eye, after all, and I'd be remiss in me duties of servin' the good people of Ireland if I didn't come a'knockin' to ask. Truth is, I was hopin' I could enlist both you and yer wife. But because Mrs. Blake isn't currently at home, maybe I can at least start with you and see where that takes me … if anywhere a'tall."

"Only if you concede that John Ford's body of work is more impressive than Orson's," I said. "Do that and you can tell me what's on your mind. No guarantees of interest or investment, mind you, but I'd be happy to hear you out."

I got the big smile again – evenly spaced teeth and all.

"I'll concede as much without forsakin' me own principles," he said. "Ford made many great pictures and won six Oscars, if memory serves adequately … and it does. By sheer volume, Ford's work is more impressive by far. Still, that doesn't make him my favorite director. I trust ya understand."

"I do, and I agree with the assessment. You're a principled man. Tell me about this case that's brought you all the way out here."

"Ah, but that's just it, ya see. The case is the thing wherein I'll catch the conscience of the professor."

A Shakespearean reference now, on top of everything else. This guy is good, I thought.

I liked Spud Phelan – even back then, when he first entered our lives.

TWO

BUNRATTY'S MISFORTUNE

He was smooth and glib and well-rounded, to be sure: *Likeable* came to mind. And it never hurts to play the flattery card, especially where the books that I write based on our more interesting cases come into play – just like the one you're now holding. DS Phelan was growing on me, all right, especially when he mentioned an intriguing Irish tourist locale as the focus of his attention.

"Let's jump ahead to Bunratty Castle," he said. "You know it, I'd guess – being a Yank an' all. What ya don't know – the stuff you'll never read in the newspapers, ya see – is this: Many people, yer own countrymen among 'em, are being scammed there, day after day – not by the operators, mind ya, nor the staff, most all of whom are wonderful. But skullduggery's afoot, to be sure, Professor Blake, and me own force is lookin' the other way. It's up to the likes of you, I'm thinkin', to get to the bottom o' things."

I'll admit to being intrigued. Bunratty, which began its life in 970 A.D. as a Viking trading camp, is one of the major tourist draws in the west of Ireland, attracting visitors from around the world. The 15th Century tower house and its various iterations, situated close to Shannon's busy international airport and a few miles northwest of Limerick, has a storied past that includes centuries of bloodshed, violence, warfare, and anarchy – a terrific enticement for tourists anxious to explore the shenanigans of their ancestors.

The fortress we know today is the fourth castle on the site, dating to 1425 A.D. Its builder was Miccon Sioda MacNamara, likely the chieftain of *Clann Cuilein*. A cycle of abandonment, destruction, and rebuilding followed until 1956, when what was left of the structure was purchased and restored to its current condition.

Bunratty's contemporary overlords, the Shannon Heritage organization, offer a nightly medieval banquet that has operated since 1963, featuring performers in elaborate period costumes. You eat with your fingers, just like it was done 600 years ago, and drink mead while the servers, who also provide the entertainment, partake in mostly period song and dance and genial mischief suited for family consumption.

Nearby Bunratty Folk Park, an open-air museum with 30-plus period buildings also operated by Shannon Heritage, helps support the local economy, drawing many thousands of visitors and employing large numbers of Irish artists and artisans.

I was curious about the details of the scam, of course. We've visited many times and keep it high on our list of places to take company who come to see us. Doc and Barb Strand were with us the last time we'd been there, short weeks previous, when they flew in to determine how we were faring. But given the nature of my discussion with DS Phelan, I decided to approach the topic in a round-about manner befitting my talkative Irish guest.

"What does me being a Yank have to do with knowing about Bunratty – scams or otherwise?" I asked. "I'd wager that everyone living here, along with most every visitor, be they tourists or on business, regardless of nationality, knows of the feasts at Bunratty, as well as something of the castle's history."

"That's it then?" he asked, his face registering mild surprise. "Yer interested in the Yank comment ahead of the scam? Or am I misreadin' the tea leaves?"

"Tea bags?"

"I don't think ye can read a tea bag – tell me I'm wrong," he replied in rapid-fire fashion. "Still … that's the best you've got?"

"No. I'm interested – at least enough to hear you out," I said. "But seeing as you brought up a Yank connection as though it were a magic elixir, I figured I'd start there and wait for you to spill it out … that or until Caeli gets back with a list of chores and I lose my curiosity entirely."

Where the hell is she anyway? I wondered.

He stared at me for a full five seconds, his eyes wide with feigned disbelief, before bursting into a hearty peal of sustained laughter that seemed to emanate from his core and grow in intensity. Six seconds, then 10 seconds more, and still he guffawed, staring at me as though I'd relayed the most ribald joke he'd ever heard.

Even Koko, who remained curious about our guest and had followed him into the kitchen, perked up from her perch on one of the nearby barstools that surround the spacious kitchen island.

He wiped at his eyes after a few additional seconds passed and clasped his hands, signaling, I suppose, that he'd milked the occasion for all it was worth.

"Ah, a good one, Professor Blake," he said. "Very good, indeed."

I was puzzled.

"I'm happy to oblige on cue," I said. "If only I knew the source of such profound amusement, I could bottle it and sell it at the Folk Park. Think of the opportunities. I could charge a couple of Euros per bottle and make my fortune."

The line was rewarded with a mega-watt smile.

"I suggest ya don't shortchange yer thinkin', money and time, on the venture," he said. "Keep in mind the gatherin' of supplies, bottles and labels and such, and the actual deliverin' of product … plus petrol for yer vehicle as you scurry to and fro. You'll need to account for that as well."

"Maybe I could convince Caeli to do that," I said, playing along, amused by the circuitous discussion though still wondering about his unexpected and prolonged laughter. "Or perhaps I could hire one of your overlords to undertake that burden and relieve you of whatever misery he causes."

He barked out a good-sized belly laugh, and this time his eyes told me that he wasn't feigning anything.

What a strange manner of man he is, I thought.

He eventually gathered himself, though it took some effort.

"You're a better man than me by half again if you can pull that off …"

But he let the thought drift away and turned serious.

"My superiors don't seem a'tall upset at the notion things are amiss at Bunratty, for reasons that are strictly political in nature and entirely self-servin', so far as I can tell," he said. "And I can't seem to … what's the American phrase?"

He paused, giving the impression that he was thinking mightily, and I was at a loss as to where he was going to even hint at a suggestion.

"It's an automotive reference, I'm thinkin', indicatin' an inability to make clear headway," he eventually said. "It's a phrase I'm sure a Yank would recognize."

"Talking with you is like working a crossword puzzle," I said. "Gain traction, maybe?"

His face broke into a genuine grin.

"Exactly. Ta – thanks for that. They won't let me pursue the matter a'tall, saying it's of little importance in the general scheme of things as to whether the odd Yank or Brit gets nicked by some poor beggar tryin' to make ends meet. I know it's all bollox, but what can ya do when blighters reign, eh?"

I found this revelation most odd, recognizing that bad publicity about a money-maker like Bunratty could wreak havoc on the economy, and tried to prime the pump for a better explanation.

"I'd expect the opposite. You'd think if word leaked of any funny-business out there, tourism in and around Bunratty would slow considerably, which would be bad for business," I suggested.

"Ah, but only if word was to get out," he said. "If no police reports are filed, ya see, the local lot of reporters, on the telly and the ones still scribblin' away, don't have a clue and, consequently, can't alert the gatherin' hordes."

"That's the way things stand now?"

He shook his head in agreement, looking glum.

"It's a bad bit o' business, 'tis," he said. "But me greater fear is someone'll get hurt, and then the whole thing'll collapse like a house of cards – or is it a deck?"

"Either way."

"Right. When that happens, and the whole lot of it blows up in the bloody media, which it inevitably will, all of Ireland'll look down their noses at us as incompetent eejits who didn't bother to pursue the truth, let alone address the grave injustice that's after bein' executed on all those blissfully unaware visitors, as well as the gullible."

His logic was spot-on, for as far as it went. I just needed to secure the details.

"So what you're saying is that your department's higher-ups refuse to let you pursue a legitimate investigation because they're afraid that an investigation will expose them as being incompetent for not pursuing an investigation in the first place."

I was the recipient this time of what amounted to an enormous grin.

"Nicely offered, professor. I knew I came for a reason."

But he'd left himself open once more.

"And you'll tell me how the scam works – correct?"

"Jaysus – thought I already did," he said.

"Not quite. So riddle me this, DS Phelan. If no one's supposed to know about whatever this is, how do you know about it?"

"I've an inside feed."

"I'm intrigued. Why not start by telling me everything, beginning with how it works?"

And yeah, he took his time.

"Sadly, it works beautifully," he said after another round of tea was poured. "Unsuspecting Bunratty visitors are flim-flammed into handin' over their valuables by a mesmerist who meets 'em, both inside and outside castle grounds, and whispers a lot of blarney about orphans and the infirm and those in need – or so I'm led to believe. Next thing ya know, wallets and purses are opened, money and valuables are gladly handed over, and afterward, only a fleetin' memory of what took place remains."

He paused, giving me a moment to either absorb what he'd said or to ask questions. I waved him on.

"Most of the victims, and I've been told this by a couple of coppers who have the know of things, are too embarrassed to make a report a'tall. Those that do try to explain are short on facts, descriptions, anything a'tall of value to aid an investigation. And reports, when they trickle in, are locked away to collect dust, or whatever it 'tis that unopened files gather in dark places."

"Why?"

"Nobody's talkin'. It's all, well, 'Hush up and keep yer bloody nose out of it and get back to yer work, boyo.' "

"Does that strike you as odd?"

"No. It strikes me as dangerous," he said. "But right now, I'm one man alone."

"CCTV cameras?"

"I'm told our man's too clever," he said. "But again, I don't have proper access."

I'd latched on to something else that he'd mentioned, of course.

"You used the word mesmerist – an odd choice by any measure. Elaborate."

"I can think of no other manner of lout who'd attempt such a daringly consistent ruse and leave no memory of its details behind," he said.

I had another thought.

"What about drugs? The effect you describe sounds like what you'd see from people under the influence of rohypnol or ketamine."

"Sure – the date-rape drugs," he said. "I've thought of that, true. But it's ruled as unlikely, given the time that transpires from start to finish, which is precious little."

I considered the scenario he'd painted, sipping my tea while keeping a wary eye on Koko, who in turn was keeping a suspicious eye on our visitor, as though ready to spring at any moment and force him to deliver sensible details.

"There's something you aren't telling me," I finally said. "Why do you care so much, especially when ordered to let it go? Why come out here to ask for my opinion … unless this is a ruse on your part. Maybe you're here to case the joint. Or maybe you really do want an autograph and are using this other scam as a … scam."

I'd tried to deliver that last part in jest, and Phelan, who was sharp, gave as good as he got.

"Ha. Ya caught me then, fair an' square," he said. "Sure, I'd be happy to take an autograph an' treasure it for a day or a week, maybe. But the simple truth is me Aunt Mary Elizabeth, me mother's own sister who lives in the States in a great house filled with cats of all stripes and a rich-as-god husband in or near

Boston, was relieved of her treasures by this scoundrel when she visited here short weeks before. It was herself who told me what'd happened in as much detail as she recalled over a couple of days of steady inquiry, all of which makes me think somethin' needs to be done – or at least somethin' more than the wankers above me think is warranted."

At last ...

"So your aunt lost something of sentimental value, which bothers her greatly – and you," I said.

"More than one item, I'm afraid, and it bothers me own sainted mother as much or more as it does me aunt," he said. "It's a family ring, ya see, an heirloom, handed down from four generations. Me mother and her sister share custody of the ring, with each of 'em wearin' it with great pride for a full year. They trade it off by makin' a trip to the other's home – in Boston and in Limerick – ensuring that, despite what life throws at 'em, they remain in touch across great distances."

He took a deep breath and sipped at his tea.

"It was me mother's turn this year ahead, and Mary Elizabeth had the ring with her – she hadn't yet turned it over, ya see. They do it in a sort of gifting ceremony, this time while the two of 'em were out to Bunratty. It's a silly thing, sure, but they enjoy the feast, even if they've done it a hundred times over. At one point, me aunt went off to the jacks, and when she returned ... well, the ring was gone, along with a splendid emerald broach, another heirloom though one that isn't passed between 'em, plus a diamond bracelet valued at more than I manage in a year, and all the foldin' money she carried."

He paused, allowing me a chance to jump in, but I again waved him ahead.

"When the theft was noticed, the two of 'em put on quite the show, at Bunratty and then afterward, with me," he said. "The details initially proved so elusive to me aunt that me mother called me out to the castle grounds to determine whatever I could – 'While the trail's still warm,' as she put it. They were desperate to find the ring, of course – it means that much. It's the reason I'm here. But by the time I arrived, the trail was more than cold. It was non-existent."

He looked glum as his eyes bounced around the room.

"The banquet was over, most of the guests had left the grounds, and the staff was too busy bustlin' about settin' this and that straight again to aid an off-duty copper with no warrant papers. Worse, those in charge were skeptical that a crime had been committed a'tall, which makes sense when ya consider their livelihood rests on runnin' an operation beyond reproach. And, I'll admit, me poor aunt was flustered and far less helpful than is normal, which isn't great even when she's operatin' with a fully charged battery."

He grabbed his tea cup, sipped, set it down, and stretched out an arm toward Koko, who was lingering nearby. She swatted his hand, hissed, jumped from her perch, and sashayed haughtily out of the kitchen.

"Quite the prissy one," he said.

"She gets it from Caeli," I said without thinking, then glanced around in the event that my longtime companion had snuck in the back door and was eavesdropping.

That's when I thought about the voice recording system, which I'd discovered was installed in the estate by its previous owner, Don Vincenzo Fierro. The damn thing kicks on every time voices are detected anywhere inside the house. I hadn't gotten 'round to disabling it, perhaps because I figured that if we ever ventured into another case and discussed it at home, the recordings would be useful for accuracy's sake – much as they've proven to be here.

Can't let Caeli hear that, I thought – which of course got me thinking about where she was.

"I do wonder what's keeping her," I said, speaking to myself, and began searching the kitchen area for my phone to check for a message.

"Judging by what I've read in your accounts, Professor Blake, your wife is more than capable of handling any emergency that presents itself," Phelan, who'd obviously heard me, offered up.

His assessment was correct, of course. But when I gave him a look reminding him to remember his place, he tossed his hands to the side and added, "Just sayin' …"

"I'd feel better if I heard from her – if only I could find the damned phone," I muttered.

Not surprisingly, I located it moments later, plugged into its charger – exactly where I'd left it the previous evening. When I didn't find a waiting message, either via text or email, my guest had a welcome suggestion.

"Why not ring her up and set yer mind right then, boyo?" he said.

"You're right. Give me a second."

I punched in Caeli's mobile number and waited as the blips and bleeps congealed and eventually produced a ringtone. But the call went directly to her voice mail, and I left a cheery message explaining that we had a guest and a potential case and asked her to call me when she got the chance.

"So you'll be after havin' a bit of a go at the case?" he asked once I'd severed the connection.

The question caught me off guard, and I scrambled to produce a reasonable reply.

"You'd call this a case, would you?"

"You wouldn't?"

"I'm not sure – not yet, anyway. Maybe. I'd like a further explanation of the one truly intriguing part," I said.

"Ah. That would be the bit about a mesmerist being the responsible party."

"Exactly. The whole thing seems far-fetched."

"How else do you explain what's happened – especially after the victims are left with so little to report?" he asked. "If it wasn't drugs, and me aunt wasn't drugged, that leaves a mesmerist as the logical explanation. Sure, it's a guess – but a good one, I think. Don't you?"

"Maybe. It might even be a good place to start – if, in fact, we were willing to take it on."

"Sounds like a big if."

"I'm an iffy kind of guy," I said.

He looked crestfallen.

"So yer not inclined to lend a hand?"

"I'll admit that I'm interested in your theory – from that single angle, anyway. The rest of it's just cops and robbers. But I'd have to talk it over with my partner and see if she's inclined to get involved. We've other things in the works. And we're retired, you know – or at least we're supposed to be retired and living in paradise."

"Ireland is hardly paradise, Professor Blake. It has the same bits and bumps and scrabble in the road as every other spot on the planet and, all bein' equal, is likely similar to what you found in the States – though with fewer serial killers, I'd wager, judgin' at least from yer case files in book form. Well, that and more stable management at the top."

"A silver lining then," I said, mustering up what I trusted would pass for a smile. "And sorry you've missed Caeli. She's running late – or at least later than I thought she'd be."

"You worry too much, professor. I'm sure she's fine," he said, and for some reason I believed him and set my worries aside – at least momentarily.

I figured that we were finished and was about to ask for his business card for contact purposes – just in case – when he provided an incentive to get me to bite at the apple that he'd tantalizingly dangled.

"There's a reward, ya know – for the ring and the brooch and bracelet, I mean … to be paid by the insurance company engaged by me mother and aunt to protect the family jewels. If yer seekin' a reason to help, beyond the notion of doin' good for the sake of it and helpin' a couple of old ladies along in their waning years, there's that."

"How much are we talking about – just to satisfy my curiosity?"

"Enough to make it worth yer while, unless yer sellin' more books than J.K. Rowling and Stephen King combined."

"Hardly."

"Good to know on the one hand – not so much on the other. But it's there, if and when ye decide to pester yer misses with this … proposal, for wont of a better term."

"Is that *wont*, with an O, or *want*, with an A?"

"Either way, so long as you agree."

"Are you going to pull out pictures of your mother and aunt and hit me with a guilt trip?" I asked him.

He produced his phone and began stabbing at its face, looking earnest and driven somehow.

"Never mind," I said. "I'll talk to Caeli when she gets back. We'll have time for family portraits and 20 questions if she's amenable."

"Thanks," he said, seeming to mean it. "Now … one more thing."

"The restroom's down the hall, on your …"

"I was thinking more of an autograph, if it's not too much trouble."

I've already told you: I liked this guy.

We shook hands a few minute later, with Koko hovering nearby, keeping a cautious eye on the would-be fur-ruffler and Mitts still cowering beneath a chair.

Getting involved in the case would be a simple enough amusement, it's true – or so I thought at the time. But the truth of the matter was that I was bored.

THREE

A SECOND POINT OF VIEW

Caeli was home within 10 minutes of DS Alan Phelan's departure. I figured that they must've passed each other on the road: Caeli in her red Range Rover with the heavy protective metal bars covering the grill, the Limerick copper in an aging Mini Cooper.

She entered the house carrying two bags of groceries and, seemingly charged with energy and a sense of purpose, set them on the counter for distribution and called for me.

"Can you give me a hand?" she said, unaware that I was in the study, already seeing what I could learn about Phelan through a cluster of social media sites, in addition to the official website of Limerick's *Garda Síochána* operation. "The Rover's stuffed, front and back both."

"I'm on it," I said and got up instantly. The best way to stay on Caeli's good side is to do what you're told and when you're told to do it.

I passed through the kitchen, gave her a quick kiss on the cheek as she was transferring a carton of eggs and a half-gallon of milk into the refrigerator, and headed out the door with a tantalizing prompt of things to come.

"We had a visitor while you were gone," I called.

"Oh. Were we expecting someone?"

"It was only the police. Hang on. I'll tell you about it."

She called out something that I didn't catch, but I figured that I at least had her interest.

I returned moments later with six additional bags of groceries, placed them on the counter, gave her a few seconds to press me about the police bait that I'd dangled, but headed out for another load when she remained busy rinsing fresh fruit at the sink. I then made a third trip, this time bringing in an additional five sacks of staples.

"Don't forget to check the rear," Caeli said. "I picked up potting soil and some flowers."

"Seeds or the real deal?" I asked.

"Do you think we have time for seeds to sprout – especially with what's taking place in a matter of days?"

"Right. Give me a minute. I'll tell you all about our unexpected guest. We might have a case on our hands."

"A case? A case of what?"

"A real, honest-to-god detective case," I said.

"Whoa – what's this? Hold on – I want to hear more," she said, although she was talking to my back because I already was moving through the door.

"You didn't hear me dangle the carrot about a police visit while you were out?" I asked, pausing momentarily.

"I did not – only that you'd hollered something. I figured it could wait, seeing as you were on a worthy mission."

"I must be slipping in my old age."

She glanced up from her work.

"Faster than you know. So what's going on? I thought we were retired."

I chose to ignore that last bit.

"Hang on. I'm prepared to tote potting soil and move crates of flowers to the front of the house, which is where I'm guessing you want them," I said. "What I have for you is a good story that requires time to tell properly."

"Yes – the flowers are for the front. For what it's worth, they come in flats, not crates. But I want to hear about this case, which must be tied to your unexpected visitor."

"Yup. One and the same. Give me a bit and I'll oblige over an iced tea before we dig in on the planting. Then again, I could always hire someone to do that for us."

"I tried. It's too late, and they never do it right anyway. Give me a clue," she insisted. "Then I'll give some thought to brewing tea."

"All good things in time, my dear. Do we have any mint?"

"I think so. I'll check," she said as she followed me outside, as much to indicate where the potting soil and flowers should be dropped off as to prod me with additional questions.

I managed to hold her off, though, and we got into the discussion 20 minutes later, after I'd unloaded and swept out the Range Rover and washed my hands while Caeli returned to the kitchen to stir up a pitcher of tea, which she soon brought out to the lengthy porch that overlooks our view of a magnificent stretch of the River Shannon.

Enjoying a glass of iced tea while viewing the great expanse of Ireland's grand waterway is a true pleasure.

"Let's have it," she said after filling two glasses and taking a seat.

I added a sprig of mint, a trick I recalled from my newspaper days (and one of the few habits I carry with any fondness from my time spent at that particular grindstone), and offered one to Caeli before launching in.

"Our visitor's name is Phelan, a detective sergeant with the Limerick Guards, representing not his department but rather himself and the interests of his mother and his mother's sister," I said. "He requires our help – craves it, in fact."

I paused, giving her the opportunity to shape the discussion in whatever manner she chose. Typically, she asked the two primary questions that most mattered.

"OK, so why not use his own skills or that of his department to do whatever it is that needs doing? And, just as importantly, how did he know to ask for our help?"

I saluted her instincts.

"The case, as Phelan outlines it, appears to be out of the scope of the *Garda's* considerable reach, for reasons he wasn't able to adequately explain," I said. "Better still, and you'll like this, he knows about us because he's read the *Ridge* books. That's what brought him here."

"He's read your books?"

"Every one of them, starting with *Emerald Ridge*, which led him to …"

"*Melia Ridge*, which apparently led him to the rest," she finished.

"Exactly. Taking the man at his word, he enjoyed them and also learned that we were his neighbors, essentially, or at least living in his back yard, prompting him to …"

"Yes – to pay us a visit. I get it, I guess. Sorry I missed him. I would have liked to question him on …"

"Wait. Let me guess. You wanted to learn what drove him here instead of handling the case himself. Yes?"

"Not a'tall. I would have asked whether he'd caught any grammatical miscues during his readings."

"Nice. If only I could get you to edit the manuscripts before I send them off …"

"Yes, well, sorry I missed him."

She rewarded me with a smile that let me know she was having fun.

"As am I. He seems to be a decent bloke," I said. "And he has work for us."

"So you've mentioned. What sort of work, exactly? You do remember we're busy here, right?"

"I do. But the man has asked for our help. How much do you know about the operation at Bunratty Castle?"

She glanced at me as though I'd lost my nose.

"We've been there, together – more than once. Recently, in fact, not long after we moved, with Doc and Barb. The food was good, as was the presentation. I'm not a big mead fan, but the wine was acceptable. And the singing was – how to best describe it? – spirited, I guess. Energetic. What am I missing that would prompt such a question?"

Gotta love Caeli, I thought.

"I'll tell you what he told me, and then you can determine whether you have an interest in pursuing this – with me, of course. As a team, just like the old days."

I laid out the details as Phelan explained them: his mother and aunt; the precious ring the two of them shared and annually traded; the circumstances on the day that it went missing, along with a couple of other adornments and cash; the theory of mesmerism as a thieving technique; the lack of interest from Limerick police authorities, which was fascinating in and of itself; and, of course, his comments about how he felt that he knew us from reading my accounts of our cases.

"He even knew Koko and Mitts by name when he came in and wasn't surprised that Mitty hid when the doorbell chimed," I said.

"Did he now?" Caeli asked, without amusement. "I've long wondered whether the detail you put into those books might get us in trouble one day."

I knew enough to shut up.

She followed up moments later, after a third sip of tea and a graceful finger's point toward a heron along the river bank, yards from where we sat.

"I recall mentioning, as you were busy toting groceries, that we were retired – a line you ignored," she said. "What's changed?"

"I don't know," I said, lamely upon reflection. "Don't you grow tired of … hell, planting flowers?"

She laughed, softly, if only for a couple of seconds.

"I've never enjoyed planting flowers, though I never get tired of looking at them once they bloom," she said.

She stared at the river for a moment, eventually rewarding my shaky patience with another question.

"Why do you want to get involved in this?" she asked.

It was a fair question.

"There's a reward for finding the ring and the other jewelry, from the insurance company," I said. "We could expect a significant finder's fee."

"You don't think we have enough money to see us through our golden years? Besides, we have Fredo to think of. He pays the freight, and he expects us to be there when he needs us."

Fredo Fierro is our lone client through an arrangement made with his father, the late Don Vincenzo Fierro. We earn a great deal of money for the advice we offer about his various enterprises around the world. His father's kindness to us and generosity in his will is the reason we're now living on the River Shannon.

"I don't see how we'd shortchange Freddy in any way by undertaking a local investigation into what essentially amounts to theft by hypnotic suggestion," I said. "We could donate the money to charity. God knows there's plenty of need."

"What about our wedding?" she asked, and this was the crux of her reservation. "It's just around the corner. A great many people are traveling a long way to be here, with any number of details still needing to be ironed out – flower-planting among them – and preparations that are pending, and …"

"… and perhaps Phelan and his mother and aunt can join us for the festivities, adding some local color," I suggested, interrupting with a point that I hoped she'd take seriously. "The incoming Americans might enjoy a chance to speak with honest-to-god natives because lord knows we don't qualify. Or at least I don't. Not yet – probably not ever."

"You're reaching, Max. In a good way, I suppose, but you're reaching."

I was surprised at her resistance but didn't say so.

At least she's not saying no …

I figured that I'd try one more angle.

"What about the thrill of the hunt? Don't you miss it?"

"I don't miss being shot at," she said quickly. "I don't miss being chased by crazed killers or lunatics in clerical robes or deranged psychopaths without a shred of conscience, or by revolutionaries with machine guns and agendas – even when they're related to me. I don't miss any of that."

"I hardly think we'll be pursued by revolutionaries with guns, let alone killers or narcissistic priests," I said, referencing our two most recent investigative efforts that centered on Caeli's Uncle Jack, the former archbishop of Armagh. "More likely, we'll discover a pickpocket, or a band of pickpockets, and will perform a public service for the good folks at Bunratty and the tourists who visit there. Who knows? If we do it right, we may even get our faces in the newspapers or on the telly."

She laughed again.

"You'd like that, would you?"

"Not me. But you may. The stories would focus on Caeli Brown, late of the USA, a true daughter of the Auld Sod, returned home to her native land just in time to help its citizens in their hour of need – a Local Gal Makes Good yarn in its truest sense. The spotlight can shine entirely on you, my dear. Whatever role I play will always be second fiddle to you."

"Nice try, Max," she said.

"Then why not give it a go for the sake of being a good neighbor?" I persisted, exposing the fact that I'd been bored stiff since our arrival in Ireland and was forever on the lookout for something to do besides snapping pictures and taking long hikes and cooking traditional Irish fare. "Our help was requested by a decent chap, judging from the little time we spent together. Besides, maybe his mum will add to the insurance reward by offering up her recipe for, I don't know, Guinness pound cake, or sherry trifle with almond slices, or …"

Her expression told me to shut up, and I smiled back and did exactly that.

"I already make the best Guinness pound cake and sherry trifle you're ever likely to taste, and you know it," she said.

I thought that was the end of it, but she surprised me again – a trait I adore.

"This is important to you – isn't it?" she asked.

I nodded but offered nothing in return.

"Then I guess it won't hurt to go out to Bunratty and take a look around – once the flowers are planted," she said. "Just know that I don't want to get wrapped up in an investigation that takes weeks to settle. We don't have weeks."

"Yes, dear."

"I mean it, Max."

"I know you do."

"All right then. We'll have a look around and let it go."

Yeah. You're likely thinking exactly what I'm thinking as I look back across the safety of time to relay this part of the story.

Should have left well enough alone.

FOUR

CONFLICTING MISSIONS

It's easy enough to determine how the initial planning for an investigation into the shenanigans taking place at Bunratty became enmeshed in our endeavors to ensure a stress-free wedding day, I suppose.

In a nutshell, and without divulging the cosmic recipe that holds the universe together, Caeli was fixated on our pending nuptials, to the exclusion of almost everything else.

Me? Not so much. I figured that my time would be better spent by helping DS Alan Phelan. It's not that I didn't give any thought to the wedding. I was actually looking forward to it; it had been far too long in the making. But it wasn't something that I wanted to dwell on for long, unlike Caeli, who was caught up in myriad details of her own exacting expectations regarding how perfect everything – and I mean *everything* – needed to be.

I didn't need everything to be perfect. I just wanted the day to come so that we could celebrate with our friends and get on with our lives together.

Standard stuff, I guess … one of the fundamental differences between the sexes. But it also was a point that I didn't want to debate – not with the number of commitments that Caeli was juggling.

Essentially, our trip to Bunratty was designed as little more than a reconnaissance foray, sticking a toe into the murky waters of what was purported to be transpiring there. If we spotted anything hinkey, we'd follow up by alerting the proper authorities. But first things first, which was a simple visit to get the lay of the land, given what we now knew.

As Caeli put it, "I know I've been pushing to get things done before the wedding. I also know these tasks don't come naturally to men in general, shocking as that seems. But it's equally true that all work and no play makes Max a …"

"… weary boy?" I suggested.

"Hardly. I was going to say … well, never mind. So long as this little side venture doesn't get in the way of anything important, I suppose we can spare a few hours while you keep your hand in the game."

"Just my hand?" I asked. "Not yours, too?"

"First things first. Besides, I'm expecting an easy afternoon, followed by a decent meal. And we'll have to make up the time lost."

"Right."

As I envisioned our effort, we'd attempt to gauge the potential for malefactor misadventure of any sort, from potential pickpockets working the grounds to parking lot smash-and-grabs to relatively easy restroom theft and, yes, even hypnotists selecting a likely candidate to rob through whispered words of devious deception.

I also figured that it would be wise to assess existing security in ways that we'd given little thought to during our previous castle visits, beyond the cursory sitting with a wall at our back, determining the closest exits, spotting those in the crowd who presented the greatest potential threat – just as we automatically do when we're out in public.

Caeli called for reservations, which is essential if you want to actually get inside the castle and enjoy the meal and general festivities. Our hunch was that tourists were the likeliest targets for the mesmerist, and he'd find plenty of them at the feast.

As is usual during the summer months, seats for the nightly extravaganza were booked well in advance, and she had to get creative. I'm not certain what strings were pulled or what she said to the telephone representative after abandoning online attempts to get us in, but we soon were approved for an evening of revelry, and with any luck some revelations, three days hence.

The lag provided us with the opportunity to plant flowers, trim bushes and shrubs, and dozens of similar tasks around the estate.

"It's perfect," Caeli said. "We've places to go and things to see and do" – her pet phrase of late for attending to the wedding.

But flowers and shrubs and bushes and whatnot were merely a start. The big day was steamrolling toward us, and Caeli's list grew longer by the hour. With her Uncle Jack out of the picture and out of our lives for good, we hoped, we still needed to make arrangements for a priest to perform the service, as well as locate and secure a reliable caterer for food, another for drinks, plus hire an Irish band, along with a team for cleanup afterward and god only knows what else she'd set her mind to.

She even wanted to hire authentic *ceili* dancers for both performing and providing lessons to those who'd had too much to drink and wanted to become adventuresome or otherwise immersed in the local traditions as the night wore on.

It's worth mentioning that all I wanted was to say "I do" with conviction, reward my bride with a meaningful kiss, hoist a glass to those who'd made the trip to help us celebrate our good fortune, and enjoy a bit of song and perhaps even a slow dance or two before calling it a night.

As Caeli is so fond of reminding me, how much can you expect at my age?

But that wasn't going to happen – or at least not that simply.

"We can't forget shuttles to and from the airport," she said while we were still working on the flower-planting. "A limo service would be good."

"Why not just rent a car or take a cab?"

"Can you imagine landing at PDX and renting a car to go into Salem?"

"Well, yeah," I said, apparently missing the point entirely. "That's exactly what I'd expect."

I got one of those looks that Caeli is adept at flashing during times of annoyance. This one was a doozie, a full-on version of *malocchio*, the Italian equivalent of the Evil Eye, at which she excels, even if she hails from 100 percent Irish stock.

"All right," I said, dropping a flower clump and raising my hands in mock surrender. "Leave it to me. I'll hire a limo company and keep it on standby throughout the weekend, even if I have to go to Dublin to make the arrangements."

"Good," she said, as though this declaration of responsibility was the only sensible approach. "Don't forget to tip the drivers in advance."

"It's now on my to-do list," I said, inserting conviction into the reply. "Anything else I can help with? I want to hold up my end of things."

She shot me a look of suspicion this time, but I swatted it away.

"I do," I said. "I mean that."

"Fine. But I won't know until I think of it, I suppose," she said, and you could almost see the wheels spinning as she thought through myriad problems that didn't exist and attempted to provide instantaneous solutions to all of them. "One thing's certain: We're running out of time. I'm not sure we'll get everything done before our guests arrive, let alone seeing to this investigation of yours."

Ouch, I thought.

"It shouldn't take us long," I said, thinking quickly. "We go to the castle and learn what we can about how things operate while enjoying the feast and entertainment. Then we come home. Hell, if we play our cards right, maybe we can spot some local talent and hire them to perform at the wedding – *uccidere due uccelli* and all that."

It didn't register.

"Killing two birds … in that other language I practice."

I got one of those looks again instead.

"It's unlikely that anyone performing at Bunratty gets a night off," she said, ignoring the rest of it. "But maybe we can get some ideas, or even recommendations. Good thinking."

I'd meant the comment as a reassuring aside only, but her response was classic testimony, I suppose, of where her head was at the time. Still, that prompted a suggestion that was ill-advised, now that I look at it afresh.

"Perhaps we should scale back on the whole thing – the wedding, I mean, not the investigation," I said, avoiding eye contact as I stuck another flower into the rich soil. "We'd initially talked about keeping things simple – far simpler than this is turning out to be, anyway."

The proposal was not received well.

"Just plant flowers and hire a limo service, Max," she said, more sharply than I think she realized.

I did my best to climb out of the other hole I'd just dug with a line of concession.

"And anything else you think of, right?"

"Exactly."

"OK, got it. Tell you what: As soon as we finish here, I'll start washing linens for the guest bedrooms – all 10 of them – and scrub out the toilets in the guest bathrooms. That should keep me busy."

She gave me the once-over again, testing to see whether I was sincere.

"You might want to wash your hands first, but yes … sounds good. I'll let you know what you can do once you finish," she said, which indicated that I'd passed momentary muster.

To my credit, I refrained from any mention of Bridezillas and a flagging sense of humor. But it's safe to add that from my perspective, at least, a night at Bunratty couldn't come fast enough.

For what it's worth, I washed my hands, along with the linens, and scrubbed out the toilets and cleaned the floors and sinks in the bathrooms and also managed a dozen other household tasks – after finishing the flower-planting and general lawn upkeep ahead of the wedding. I also mentally moved up the hiring of a housekeeper to the primary spot on my own list of things to get done – once the wedding was behind us, of course. As things now stood, Caeli wouldn't trust anyone but the two of us to tend to the tasks at hand … and she didn't really trust me, either.

That aside, I found a limo company and hired it for the entire date-appropriate weekend, as well as agreeing to a generous tip arrangement for the drivers so that no one using the service would have an out-of-pocket expense – just as Caeli had drawn it up.

Even better: What was designed as a quick phone call to Alan Phelan, letting him know that we were on the Bunratty job for at least one day, turned into a goldmine of recommendations and support for the tasks ahead.

"A wedding, is it?" he asked when I told him that we'd be going out to Bunratty to have a look-see between excursions to make our wedding plans come together. "I bloody well thought you'd already been hitched."

"Not quite," I said. "We're three weeks or so out and counting, with much to do in the meantime."

He was like Pavlov's salivating dog with his next line.

"What is it ya need then that ya haven't already accounted for? Maybe I can help in some small way."

"Be careful what you wish for," I said.

"Bring it on," he replied. "I may just surprise ya."

In short order, he recommended a *ceili* band that featured one of his cousins, a traditional jigs and reels band to provide the bulk of the entertainment that included a nephew and a niece, and caterers for food and drink as well as a set-up and clean-up crew – and yeah, these, too, contained members of the prodigious and enterprising Phelan clan.

"You're bucking for an invitation, you know. If all your recommendations pan out, you'll get one," I said after taking notes that included contact names and phone numbers and assurances that he'd call ahead to ensure that the various parties cleared their schedules and gave us their best rates and service.

"Ah, but that'd be lovely ... bloody brilliant," he said. "An invitation to what's sure to be the social event of the season in Limerick? I wouldn't miss it for anything. And I know just the gift to bring – somethin' ya desperately need. How many people can I bring along?"

"Forget the gift. In the States, at least, an invitation is usually extended to a person and a single guest. I'm tempted to ask how many women you know and can handle at any one time," I said with a laugh. "But help me pull this off without a hitch, mister, and I promise not to do a head-count when you stroll in."

"Done," he said. "How 'bout someone to perform the ceremony then? I'm sure yer intended had her heart set on having her uncle, the former archbishop, do the honors. If that's now off the table because of his ... well, because he's no longer in Ireland, maybe I can help there as well. An uncle on me *dadai's* side is a priest in good standin'. I'll bet he can be persuaded to do the honors."

"God, but you're a lifesaver, DS Phelan. I'll have to ..."

"Call me Spud."

"Spud. Right. Let me check with Caeli. She'll want to meet him first, but that's one more thing we can check off."

He turned serious for a moment, or at least more so than he had been.

"I must say ya seem to be waitin' right up to the last bloody minute to get this done, boyo. Given what I've read about yer penchant for planning ahead, I'm surprised."

"It didn't start out this way," I said. "Initially, all we wanted to do was invite a few friends and make a casual afternoon of it. The next thing you know, well …"

"Let me guess. Yer intended took over and left you bolloxed."

"You understand all too well."

"I do. And I'm happy to lend a hand to ease the burden," he said. "But more to the point, tell me I'll get a chance to meet the people I feel I already know from readin' yer books."

"There's a good chance you'll get your wish," I said. "Whether you'll thank me is another matter."

"Jaysus, but this is bloody grand. Let's see. Will the famous Fredo Fierro be after attending?"

"He will."

"Perfect. Who else? Tell me I'll get to see Elmore and Leonard and swap yarns with the pair of 'em."

That made me laugh.

"As Fredo's primary bodyguards, they'll no doubt make the trip, though each was extended a separate invitation, above and beyond their duties as Freddy's protectors. He'll likely bring additional bodyguards, giving Elmore and Leonard some time off to enjoy themselves, if they choose. Elmore will be happy to meet you and talk about … whatever. As for Leonard, I wouldn't count on much."

"Yes. I understand. He's prickly, as you've mentioned in print. Who else?"

I was impressed with his enthusiasm.

"Let's see. You'd know of Doc Strand, of course, and his wife, Barbara. Both have RSVP'd favorably. Michael Parker is coming, barring a last-minute court case, along with his secretary, Effie Smith. We've invited Mad Dog, and the last I heard he was planning to make the trip."

"The restaurant bloke, right?"

"One and the same."

"How about the chief police? Bill something or other … a name that's definitely not Irish."

"Yes. Bill Kohlmeyer and his wife, Skyla, are coming. It wouldn't be a party without them. Plus a number of longtime friends and neighbors who're dear to us, most all of whom were happy to say yes because it'll be their first visit to Ireland."

"It must be costin' a bloody fortune," he said.

I gave him the standard line, the one that's expected.

"What's a little money among friends?"

"Tell it to me aunt and mother," he said quickly. "They're anxious to see what ya think of the mess out to Bunratty and findin' their ring."

"I hope their expectations aren't too high," I said.

"High? High hardly covers it," he said. "When I told 'em two famous modern-day American Sherlocks were on the prowl, you'd think the heavens had parted and St. Patrick himself came thunderin' out from the clouds with smiles and blessings aplenty."

I laughed.

"No pressure, though – right?"

"Now that you've invited me to yer wedding? None a'tall," he said. "Here's one more I'll be happy to do, if ya like. I can bring along a few of the boys from the station house – friends, ya understand – to provide extra security for you and yer guests … at no cost, of course."

"I really don't think security will be necessary …"

"Are ye kiddin'? Don Fredo will be there, which could attract all manner of pests, perhaps even more than Elmore and Leonard can deal with," he said. "Besides, with two noted private detectives gettin' married, one of them a well-known writer, I wouldn't be surprised if every freeloader in Ireland decides to crash the proceedings. No, Professor Blake, it's me duty to stand ready with a contingent of Limerick's best – just in case."

You're likely thinking exactly what I was thinking at the time.

FIVE

CASING THE JOINT

Before we left for Bunratty, on a day that began as dreary and overcast with a sniff of rain but by early afternoon had turned into an Irish gem of blue skies and stacked white clouds, I stashed two sealed sets of plastic eating utensils from one of the fast food chains into my pocket.

The reason for this bit of foresight is no mystery if you want to enjoy the medieval feast, which is generally superb, and also retain your sense of dignity, which is not always so easy. For the uninitiated, the lone silverware setting you receive once seated at the banquet table is a knife for cutting meat. You're required to supply thumbs and fingers for everything else – either that or cheat and bring your own fork and spoon.

I'll confess that my days of eating most anything with my fingers (burgers and fried chicken not included) are long over, although Caeli swears that if you live long enough, everything you outgrew will eventually return.

We set out for the castle at 3 p.m. with Caeli driving the Range Rover, the same vehicle that Leonard secured during our trip to Ireland a year earlier to locate Caeli's uncle. The castle and adjoining Folk Park are 35 kilometers from our home, although the trip would be considerably shorter if it weren't for the River Shannon to our immediate north. You could probably even see the place from our property with a decent set of binoculars and a tower to stand on.

But with no bridge available, we're forced to travel south to the N69, heading for Clarina village, and follow it eastward toward Limerick, bypassing the turnoff for Dooradoyle, before joining the N18 and traveling north and then west after cruising under the Shannon via the 675-meter Limerick Tunnel, which equates to about seven football fields.

The fare for its use, €1.90 ($2.02 U.S. at the current exchange), got me thinking that we might want to purchase a frequent user's pass. When I made the suggestion to Caeli while extracting two bills as we approached the toll booth, she shot me a look that I instantly recognized because I've seen it often. It conveys, in effect: *I know you're up to something, mister. I'm just not sure what it is yet.*

"Are you suggesting we'll be visiting Bunratty on a regular basis?" she asked as she accepted the twin notes.

"Who knows? It's a great place to bring visitors, foreign and domestic," I said, striving for nonchalance. "A pass would save money and time."

"But that's not what you were thinking," Caeli said as she made the exchange and accelerated forward, dropping the change into the ashtray. "You were thinking – correct me if I'm wrong – that you could milk this Bunratty business for who knows how long, extending your hand in the game."

Yup. She doesn't miss much.

"Now that you bring it up, I like keeping my hand in the game," I said. "It helps keep me young."

I got another look, which is no surprise. I often get that very reaction and figured that it wouldn't hurt to offer assurances.

"Trust me. Everything's under control."

But this time I thought that I'd have to reach across the console and grab the steering wheel to ensure that we stayed in the appropriate lane as Caeli delivered a disdainful laugh while throwing her hands in the air.

"Nice try, Max," she said. "But I've been with you for far too long."

"And yet, here we are, living together in Ireland, just days away from the Big Day – and both of those momentous words are capitalized for emphasis."

"You're right," she said. "I still have time to back out or get my head examined … or both."

"Back out? I'm crushed, especially after all the work we've put in at the estate."

That's what she wanted to hear, apparently.

"I should thank you again for Alan Phelan and taking advantage of his contacts – and I don't mean that in a negative sense," she said. "We'd still be swimming upstream were it not for his help."

"You know what they say: It ain't what you know but who you know – or one of its many variants."

"I like the fake Mark Twain quote: It ain't what you don't know that gets you into trouble. It's what you know for sure that just ain't so."

"That quote is fake?"

"Just like your line about having everything under control."

We pulled into the Folk Park minutes later and lucked into a parking spot that provided us with an easy escape route should the world end during the festivities. That may seem odd to you, but it's standard operating procedure in our world – along with locating the exits to any room we enter and sitting with our backs to the wall in a public setting while scoping out potential threats.

I should add a line about firearms here.

In Oregon, both of us carried Walther P99 semi-auto handguns for protection. Given our line of work, it was the prudent thing to do.

In Ireland, we aren't afforded that luxury. The Irish have some of the most restrictive gun laws in Europe. Since 2009, the private possession of center-fire handguns is strictly *verboten*, although I'm told that some grandfathering was allowed for shooting competitions. Licenses are required for everything, long arms included, and must be updated every three years under stringent conditions. And the best you can do if you're deemed fit to qualify for a license is a single item: a lone shotgun for bird hunting, for example.

You can look it up if you want the details, which are myriad and microscopic in length and complexity.

Caeli's dual-citizenship allows us a single weapon at the estate. We also keep handy two expandable metal batons (sold by the Irish military to civilians for €40), though it's illegal to carry one for personal defense.

Yeah. Go figure. Essentially, you're on our own, although we both pack Swiss Army knives when we're out and about.

I'd added one additional line of defense, and I'll admit that it was a Hail Mary at best. I'd copied the sounds of gunfire on a CD – a short section of sustained fire from a 9mm handgun, featuring double- and triple-taps and longer bursts; a second section of rifle fire, again with various incarnations; and a third of full-auto/machine gun fire – and made three duplicates: one for the house, one for the Cadillac, and one for Caeli's Range Rover. As foolish as it sounds, my rationale is that it's the modern equivalent of the barking dog recordings that apartment dwellers in New York City made semi-famous.

For this venture, given what we were seeking, my thinking was that we might run into someone who didn't play by the rules should a confrontation occur. And this fact alone might be why Caeli has been reluctant for us to pursue our old trade since making the transition to Ireland, though I've never pressed her on it. In this instance, I was happy to have her squeeze out the time she'd agreed to devote to our current enterprise.

The Folk Park sits on 26 acres immediately adjacent to Bunratty Castle and features buildings that showcase Irish life as it existed more than a century ago. From farmhouses and cottages to a variety of shops – drapery, grocery, hardware, pottery, a working pub – set on streets recreated in striking detail, the park provides visitors with the opportunity to experience snippets of a time far removed from the incessant hustle of the internet and smartphones and earbuds connected to all manner of entertainment – some of which might even be entertaining.

We wandered the grounds for more than an hour, taking our time, enjoying ourselves while ducking in and out of the houses and shops and displays and watching some of the live demonstrations. But all the while we were on the lookout for someone who didn't belong and who we suspected would be wandering the place like a predator instead of an interested visitor or tourist.

"Statistically, we should look for single males in their early 30s," Caeli had said as we set out.

"If that's the case, let's find the pub, enjoy a pint, and see who drops in and fits the profile."

"That's actually a good thought, but let's walk a bit more," she said. "Maybe we'll spot something of interest."

In time, as our feet began to protest the uneven paths, the idea of a pint of stout or a glass of wine took on more appeal, and we eventually checked into P. MacNamara & Son and enjoyed the traditional fiddle and pipes music, with both of us nursing a Guinness. But the patrons we saw were tourists enjoying the day, many of them with packages of shop purchases placed randomly on the tables they sat at: homemade breads and baked goods, hard candies and sweet assortments, woolen items, candles – you get the idea.

I was tempted to have a go at a second pint. But Caeli reminded me that we still had the feast ahead of us, and she didn't think that stout would mix well with mead.

"Besides which, I don't want you falling asleep before the main course," she said.

"Good point."

So we wandered again, checking in at the school house and the doctor's home, picking up a temporary boost of energy at the sweet shop, enjoying the baked goods demonstration featuring strong-fingered, thick-shouldered women who'd give you a hell of a battle in an arm-wrestling match.

I visited with the wandering town constable for a bit, chatting him up about crime in the park, striving for casual while determining whether he'd seen anything that might be construed as unusual. Even though he plays the part, wearing a costume from days long past that includes a traditional helmet and wooden baton, I figured that he was in a better position to spot the ins and outs of what takes place at the park than most of the regulars.

"So it's the unusual yer interested in then?" he said, his intonation as thick as pudding. "Only the odd Yank, time and again, though most are with their families and on their better behavior. Otherwise, ye can only guess at what mischief they'd bring to the place – yerself included."

I couldn't tell whether he was serious or merely putting me on, and Caeli affected a convincing Dublin accent to nudge him along, which she can do with ease, and the two of them were soon commiserating at my expense.

The time for the feast was growing nearer, and we started for the castle after leaving the constable behind with smiles and handshakes when we spotted him – or I should report that Caeli spotted him and gave me a quick heads-up with an arm-poke to make sure I didn't miss it.

"Trouble, at your 10 o'clock," she said, speaking casually, as though talking about the weather. "Ball cap, sunglasses, tan windbreaker."

I made it a point to glance instead of stare, gaining an initial look that was little more than a brush-by, and my first reaction was general agreement.

"Yeah," I said. "He looks the part anyway."

"He's older than I imagined him," she said. "More seasoned, anyway."

"If he's our guy …"

Our suspect was chatting up a middle-aged woman who obviously came from money, judging by her overall appearance and trappings. The diamond bracelet she wore on her right wrist was sparkling in the sun with a radiance that reminded me of disco lights, but I didn't offer that observation for fear that Caeli would brand me as an oldster, stuck in the past.

The woman appeared to be enchanted with the attention that was being showered on her, although she was striking enough in her looks, clothing, and general presentation and had no doubt enjoyed plenty of male attention through the years. I glanced around for a spouse, companion, friend, paramour, someone/anyone who might be looking after her but spotted no likely contenders for the role, which was odd.

Then it dawned on me that perhaps our candidate was, in fact, with her from the start, and this was little more than an August/March relationship in full bloom.

"Maybe there's nothing to this," I suggested. "It seems damned fluky to find the guy on our first trip here."

"Sometimes luck's on your side," Caeli said.

"Still …"

But I didn't finish, and she shot me a look that conveyed far more than any words she might have selected.

"So what are you thinking?" I asked.

"Hard to say, exactly, but something's off. I don't like the way he's lingering …"

She let the words drift away, but she began walking toward the couple, who appeared to be earnestly conversing outside a pawnbroker's shop with the title of J. Brown on the overhead nameplate.

Given what we were looking for, the location seemed fitting.

"Maybe he's with her – her date or a lover," I said, lengthening my strides to keep up.

"Not a chance," she replied. "Look at her – then take a good look at him. There's something off. Trust me."

While the woman exuded wealth and sophistication, her companion demonstrated none of those traits. His classification, in fact, would be charted as seedy, scruffy … *predator*.

I was surprised when that last word jumped into my head, but not enough to dismiss it. Caeli was correct: Something was off.

She also was focused on her target, which is typical when she suspects that bad things are about to happen. I was more afraid about blowing our cover, just in case this wasn't our guy, and whispered that notion.

Caeli brushed it off.

"Let's get close enough to catch him in the act. Follow my lead."

Uh oh, I thought and began considering all of the recent wedding planning that had materialized from nowhere in the past few days. *That hasn't led to anything good.*

But I didn't say that aloud, either, and we quickly were within earshot of our mystery man and the diamond-bedecked woman who most likely was his prey.

SIX

A TASTE OF IRELAND

It was difficult to determine exactly what was taking place as we approached the seemingly mismatched twosome, although I suspected that Caeli already had her mind made up and was ready to step in, forcibly if necessary.

Yeah. I know. Wrong again.

I still wasn't fully convinced that the situation was anything more than an oddly paired couple having a friendly chat outside of a phony pawn shop in a fantasy setting north of Limerick. From what we knew then, it was a stretch to connect the man we were surreptitiously appraising with what had happened to Alan Phelan's aunt's heirloom ring days earlier.

Besides, I figured, *that took place inside the castle, not at the Folk Park.*

I was about to point that out when Caeli approached the shop and, by default, our suspicious couple, paused momentarily at the door, and turned toward me with a look of unmistakable impatience covering both her face and outward mannerisms.

But she didn't say a word, which I decided later might have broken the spell that Caeli figured was being woven around our supposed victim. Instead, she rolled her wrist over a few times with her hand extended, a classic *What's taking so long?* gesture.

I correctly determined that this was part of the act and, playing along, said nothing aloud, picked up my pace, and then held the door and followed her inside.

"I'm not certain our situation has improved," I whispered. "We can't exactly hear what's going on out there."

She pointed toward the window next to the entryway, which was open at the bottom by four inches or so, allowing occasional washes of fresh air to enter the shop. Fortunately for our cover, a handful of people milled about while the pawnbroker, so-called, was holding court behind a long counter at the back, explaining the process that people went through a hundred years into the past to hock their possessions and stay afloat during the hard times – and back then, in this part of Ireland, they were all hard times.

Caeli edged close to the window sill, determining whether she could overhear what was taking place immediately outside. It was a clever maneuver, allowing us – or at least allowing Caeli – to eavesdrop on the discussion without being noticed.

Trouble was, I couldn't see or hear a thing and am not known for my patience.

"What are they saying – can you tell?" I whispered once she'd settled in. "What's going on?"

"Hush," she replied, so quietly that the word barely registered. To make sure that I understood her intent, however, she waved me away with a flick of her hand.

Already getting ready for marriage, I thought.

And yeah, I didn't dare offer that, either.

Recognizing that I'd either have to force her aside or swing around to the other end of the window and risk being seen by our suspected target, I opted instead to start counting backward from 100 to see how far I would get before the situation changed. Marking time, I've found, is a useful endeavor in investigations.

I got to 67 when she nudged me.

"It's him. Let's go," she said, rising quickly. "Back my play – whatever it is."

The admission surprised me, and I couldn't stop myself from blurting out a question that seemed to make sense.

"You don't have a plan?"

She rewarded my concern with a sharp glance before pausing at the exit for a fleeting instant to ensure that her intent registered. Then she nodded at me a single time and, tugging at her sleeve, pushed the door open with more force than was necessary and, best of all, somehow managed to make it appear accidental when she bumped into the woman who was meekly listening to the guy in the sunglasses.

His ball cap, I noted, was dark blue and sported a large DK inside a white oval. It looked new, as if he'd worn it for the first time that day. What I spotted next was far more interesting. At some point after we'd entered the shop, the woman had removed the glittering diamond bracelet from her wrist and was now extending it toward her companion, as though handing it over for safe keeping.

Caeli got there first.

"Oh, I am so very sorry. Forgive me, please," she said, affecting her nicely tuned Dublin accent. She spoke loudly and reached out to steady the woman, grabbing her forearm in a clench that I figured, in retrospect, would leave a bruise the next day. "I can't believe I just did that to ye – I apologize a t'ousand times and more. Are ye all right then, ya poor dear? I'm so klutzy today – in too much of a hurry, I suppose, and just not after payin' near enough mind a'tall to where I'm goin'."

She paused her rambling apology abruptly and leaned in close to the woman, ensuring that their faces were inches apart. She released her death-lock grip and this time placed both of her hands on the woman's shoulders, turning her about so that she was no longer facing her equally startled, though clearly annoyed, companion.

He was about to enter the conversation – I could tell because he'd screwed his lips up indignantly and dropped his mouth half-open – but Caeli was again too quick.

"There now. Ya seem to be fine and no real harm done then," she said, beaming a full-wattage smile that conveyed – to my mind, anyway – sympathy and concern and even the idea that she could be trusted. "It's a good thing to see, it 'tis. T'ank the saints for that much, at least."

The bracelet that had seemed to be the primary focus of the increasingly vexed man in the sunglasses dropped to the ground as Caeli subtly shook the woman's thin shoulders, and I watched it fall as though in slow motion and reached for it no more than a second after it landed with a soft plop on the pavement.

"Oh, my – here ya go, then," I said, dusting off my own Dublin accent, which is generally reserved only for the direst of emergencies – or for following Caeli's lead, I guess. "Yer after droppin' this item of rare beauty … ya wouldn't want to lose that now."

I stood quickly, making a show of brushing off the bracelet and then briefly checking it for damage before handing it over to the startled woman, who by now seemed to register what was taking place.

"You certainly came out of nowhere," she said, addressing Caeli in what I took for an American accent originating somewhere in the Midwest: *Iowa*, I thought, *or Kansas.* "You startled me. And how in the world did you come by this?"

She'd just noticed the bracelet and glanced at her wrist and then gazed at the two of us with mounting suspicion, as though we were responsible for taking it from her during the encounter. I could envision an ugly scene to follow, with coppers summoned and accusations made and a situation that would amount to what passed for intent and our word vs. hers – and no doubt her companion would back up every notion that she supplied as well, which also didn't bode well, considering the fact that Caeli had used a pickpocket's maneuver to allow us in.

Geez. I'm going to have to drag DS Phelan into this mess, I thought.

But Caeli again saved the moment.

"Ya dropped it when I was such a clumsy cow and carelessly banged into ya whilst leavin' the shop and payin' no attention whatsoever to where I was about," she said. "Again, my apologies, though it seems no real harm's done. Surely yer all right despite me clumsiness."

The woman had her doubts, or at least she was adept at conveying them with a decided frown. But instead of pressing the point, she changed directions on us entirely when she looked about as though she'd misplaced another prized possession and had only just now noticed.

"Where did he go … that nice young man I was talking with?" she asked.

She glanced over Caeli's shoulder and then leaned around me to take a longer, deeper look. Caeli and I turned at the same time to determine why she couldn't see the man we'd been shielding her from, a man who'd been there short seconds previous, and discovered with dismay that he was, in fact, gone, as though he'd never been there at all.

"That's odd," she said softly. "I could have sworn …"

"Ah, but it's all right then – pay it no mind a'tall," Caeli said. "I'm delighted to see yer all right once more. Is there anything a'tall I can get ye, Miss …"

She waited for the woman to fill in the verbal blank and was rewarded an instant later.

"Mrs. Shedd, double D at the end," she said. "Call me Joan."

Caeli smiled brightly.

"Delighted, Joan. Me own name's Caeli, and this is Max."

It was apparent that Caeli wanted to press the woman for additional information about what had just happened. But she also wanted to determine exactly where our mystery man disappeared to – or, more to the point, she wanted me to find him.

"Are ya sure there's nothing I can get ya? Some water, maybe?" she said.

When Mrs. Shedd demurred, Caeli made a show of brushing off the polite refusal and brought me back into play.

"Max. Be a darlin' now and see if ye can find Joan a nice bottle o' water," she said. "Maybe the sun's gotten to her a bit. It's awfully bright, ya see, and will sneak up on ya if ye aren't careful, this bein' Ireland an' all."

"Straight off then," I said, ignoring Joan's repeated plea that she was fine. She continued to glance about, however, seeking the whereabouts of her companion who'd so effectively disappeared during Caeli's ploy to interrupt whatever he was up to – and apparently just in time.

I moved rapidly down the street, ostensibly to locate a shop that sold bottled water, all the while looking for the guy in the DK ball cap.

What I was going to do with him if, in fact, I could find him was another matter entirely, and I gave that some thought as I prowled about.

I can snap a picture and send it to DS Phelan, I thought, fumbling around in my pocket to ensure that I was carrying my phone. Fortunately, I'd taken it before we left, and I don't always remember to do that.

Satisfied with that plan, I checked behind the pawnbroker's shop, walked toward MacNamara's pub to see if my prey might have made his way there to locate another unsuspecting victim, and ducked down a couple of side streets, looking into the windows of the various shops I passed along the way, searching for a familiar face ... *or at least for a familiar hat.*

DK represents Denmark, I thought. *Maybe he's a Dane, or he's traveled there recently. Maybe he's a fan of something or someone from there – a soccer team, perhaps, or ... hell, Hans Christian Andersen.*

"Or maybe it's just a hat he picked for a disguise," I muttered.

I eventually located a gift shop offering visitor necessities, bottled water included. I purchased three and started back for the pawnbroker's, though I continued to search for the man we suspected of relieving rich women of their valuables through means that we didn't adequately understand.

But I struck out and had pretty much given up entirely, figuring that the guy either headed to the castle or had blown the place entirely, when he found me instead, moments later – a turnaround I hadn't considered. I was cruising through a lane filled with tourists exiting from a charter bus when a deliberate collision sent me off course. I dropped the water bottles and was forced to reach out to refrain from face-planting into the side of a building.

"Sorry, mate," he said, loudly enough to cover himself and his actions from the passers-by, most of whom were oblivious anyway. Then he moved in closer and grabbed me by the elbow, much as Caeli had done with Joan Shedd. He was behind me so that I couldn't see his face, and his fingers dug into the joint in a way that made me squelch a yip.

"I don't know what kind o' game the two of ya are playin' at, Yank, but I don't like it," he hissed, his voice low and throaty, decidedly menacing. He was pressed close enough to the back of my head that I could smell breath mints and a faint wisp of cologne. "Stay the fook away from me if ya know what's good for ya, boyo. I won't be after tellin' ya again."

He shoved me once more toward the building and was gone before I could do anything more than stop myself from crashing head-first into the drably painted wall.

I met Caeli and her new friend at the pawnbroker's minutes later, handing off the water bottles and conveying with a look and a nod to my partner that I had a story to tell, if only we could find a free minute.

Caeli had other ideas.

"Here ye are then, Max. Thanks for this, for the both of us," she said. "You'll be happy to know Joan is free and has a ticket for the feast. She's agreed to join us. Isn't that grand?"

We learned in short order as we strolled across the grounds toward the castle that Mrs. Shedd originally was from Missouri, had lived in Michigan and Wisconsin before moving West to California and then on to Idaho, and that her husband of more than 25 years, with two grown children between them, had abruptly left her a few months earlier.

"We were supposed to be here together, just the two of us, before … well, before he walked out without so much as a decent excuse, or even an apology. He just … left. It's a common enough tale, I suppose," she said, talking as if she'd provided the same explanation of her current status a hundred times over but still wasn't immune from the shock or the hurt. "It's just one I never thought would happen to me."

Caeli patted her back, and I remained silent, and both of us played our role.

I was torn about whether we should take Joan into our confidence about the situation that had brought us out to Bunratty on this day. But Caeli had decided in my absence to gain whatever information she could without spilling the whole tale. That meant, of course, that we remained on the hook to maintain our cover, accents included.

In Caeli's case, that doesn't present a problem. She's a natural, influenced by Irish speakers on both sides of her family. Caeli can more than hold her own in conversation with anyone from Dublin or Cork, or even from Belfast and Derry. She also speaks a bit of Irish, though her vocabulary is limited – something she intends to rectify.

I'm not so fortunate, nor verbally talented. I may have attended college in Ireland in my distant youth, but I'm far from gifted when it comes to affecting an accent and can hold my own only in brief bursts with practiced lines … or when I'm conversing with the distracted or, better yet, an unsuspecting American whose idea of an Irish brogue is what you'd hear in a Barry Fitzgerald movie.

Still, whatever I could manage on this day would have to be good enough to get us through the feast without giving ourselves away while slowly extracting what we could from unsuspecting Joan Shedd.

As the castle festivities got under way and Joan loosened up with a second glass of wine and the overall friendly ambience of the evening, I found myself enjoying the woman's company — enough so to hand over my plastic eating utensils when the time came to dig in. She explained that the bracelet that had almost gotten away was a gift from her children after their father's abrupt departure from their lives and that its sentimental value was worth far more than whatever amount they'd paid.

Still, from the looks of it, I suspected that they'd paid plenty.

She also dished as much as she was able about her male companion.

"I was just wandering the park, killing time, when he happened by," she said. "He seemed nice enough. He was very handsome, of course, and I'll admit that I was flattered at the attention … especially after, well, you can guess why, I suppose. The next thing I knew, you bumped into me, Caeli, and it seemed as if I awoke from an unpleasant dream."

She smiled, although her eyes seemed sad and distant.

"I wonder where he went off to in such a hurry," she muttered softly. "It's almost as if he wasn't there at all — almost as if I'd imagined the whole thing."

As we drove home that night, after seeing Joan Shedd to a waiting taxi that would take her to her hotel accommodations, I provided Caeli with the details about my unpleasant encounter with the mesmerist.

"He was strong — physically fit," I said. "He had me shoved into the wall and immobile before I could react. God — I must be getting old."

"It's finally starting to sink in," she said, though I could tell that she was concerned as I provided the particulars.

"Apparently. Worse, he called me a Yank straight off," I said. "He wasn't buying my accent — even if he likely bought yours."

"What was it that he said again, exactly?"

I repeated the two sentences that he'd whispered and described in detail the breath mints, his cologne (it reminded me of a barber shop), his voice, his accent, and the strength of his hands.

"He mentioned *mate* and *Yank* and *boyo* – correct?" she asked a moment after absorbing my observations.

"Yeah. The first and third were sentence-fillers, I think. The one that mattered was Yank."

"*Boyo* is an Irishism," she said. "And much as I hate to say it, you do sound like a Yank trying to mimic a native – no offense. You're good enough to fool the likes of Joan Shedd, but you won't fool a local, Max. It's something you'll have to work on."

"Tell me again why you went with an Irish accent when you banged into her."

"I thought it would give us cover from him," she said.

"Yeah, well, sorry I couldn't pull it off. But at least we've located the guy, which is fairly amazing considering the little time we've spent on this," I said. "All we need to do now is give Phelan a heads-up and leave the rest of it to him. He can check CCTV footage, given what we know and the time frames."

"Sure. Sounds good," Caeli said, but she seemed distracted. When I mentioned it, she acknowledged my concern with a nod.

Another minute passed, and I watched her with interest as she seemed to wrestle with the situation.

"He can ID us, you know. He got a better look at us than we did of him."

"That worries you?"

She didn't answer. But for much of the drive home, she looked into the rearview mirror for lengthy periods while varying the SUV's speed, especially after we'd passed through the Limerick Tunnel.

"You think we're being followed," I eventually said.

"I do," she replied, moments later. "I just can't say it with certainty."

She smiled at me, briefly, and seemed to let it go.

Even so, I began watching the road behind us with a zeal that I'd normally reserve for a full-out chase.

We arrived home uneventfully minutes later, and I didn't give the matter a second thought once we were inside the house and the security system was re-activated and the cats greeted Caeli with their usual affection and demands for food and attention.

It was another mistake I made that day.

SEVEN

THE CITY OF LIGHTS

[What follows was assembled from Interpol and CIA surveillance video and audio recordings, as well as grudgingly declassified reports.]

Paris at midnight could be frightening.

Innocent lovers who'd once embraced the City of Light were now its victims. The glorious landmarks of legend and song were the new Ground Zero. The anonymous street musician, the fastidious shopkeeper, the speeding bike messenger – all were potential terrorists, just as they were potential victims.

Jean-Claude Daimallier loved the new order of things.

What he couldn't tolerate was a lack of respect. And he could sense it now, quickening his pulse, at the other end of the connection.

"Conduisons audjourd'hui nos affaires en francais," Jean-Claude whispered into the telephone – a polite request to continue the discussion in French.

The Irish voice at the other end of the line was mocking.

"Je sauterais plutot de la Tour d'Eiffel," the man said in passable French, then repeated the phrase in lilting English: "I'd rather jump off the bloody Eiffel Tower."

"Be careful what you wish for," Jean-Claude offered in impeccable English, spoken with but a hint of accent. "It's possible a guardian angel will grant it."

"The angels've long since stopped listenin' to me, boyo," the Irishman said. "They've better things to concern themselves with than the salvation of me almighty soul – or yers."

"You Irish have a way with words," Jean-Claude replied, though the sarcasm in his voice was as thick as the cables that ran beneath the Irish Sea, making the long-distance connection possible. "You more than most."

"*Merci.*"

"And now you mock me."

"Mock? There's not a trace of *mock* in me words nor disrespect in me tone, laddie. Truth be told, I do little else but sing yer bloody praises to all who'll listen. Surely you feel it – don't ya, boyo?"

He waited, but no response was forthcoming.

"They say confession's good for the soul," the Irishman said.

"Enough of this," Jean-Claude snapped. "Where is she?"

The Irishman coughed out a laugh.

"Yer askin' me like I should bloody-well know the fookin' answer," he said. "Yer the one made the arrangements. I was on the outside, as usual – as per yer own bloody orders. Now it's caught up with ya at last. Sweet Jaysus, but there's a touch of irony in that."

When his words were met with silence, the Irishman persisted.

"Nothin' a'tall to say then, is it?"

"Too much is riding on this for your games," Jean-Claude said.

"Don't I know it then."

"Listen to me," the Frenchman hissed. "I'm tired of it. There's no time."

The Irishman laughed again.

"All the more reason to bid you *adieu, mon ami*. I'll tell her ya called. I'm sure she'll find it comfortin'. A good day to ya, boyo, if such a thing's possible in Paris."

The connection died. Jean-Claude stared at the receiver in disbelief before slamming it into its cradle and pushed through the door to the phone booth on a dark side street a mile from the *Arc De Triumph.*

He checked his wristwatch and shook his head in disgust. Cursing aloud in his own language, he began walking rapidly, unaware that he was being followed ... unaware that a small transmitter had been surreptitiously placed in the lining of his coat, days before.

Jean-Claude had been in touch with the Irishman for weeks. The method of contact varied: a disposable phone, a letter sent to General Delivery in care of Tomas Levet, a note pushed under the door of a room in a fleabag hot-pillow joint that he'd been forced to stay in for two nights, a slip of paper tacked to a laundromat cork board, a three-line advert in the classifieds section of *La Tribune*.

The Irishman was cautious and required careful handling.

The woman presented even more of a problem.

Jean-Claude took a cigarette from his shirt pocket and absently tamped it a dozen times or more on the lighter that he pulled from his sports jacket.

"I can kill him … blame it on the Americans," he muttered, loud enough to be picked up by the sensitive surveillance equipment.

"*J'espère que le bâtard pourrit dans l'enfer*," he whispered and then repeated the phrase in English: "I hope the no-good bastard rots in hell."

He glanced at the cigarette in disgust and threw it onto the cobbled streets.

The inexpensive flip-phone attached to his belt began to vibrate noisily, and he pulled it from its leather holster and snapped open the cover, refusing to break stride.

"*Oui?*" he snarled.

He listened for a few seconds, glanced at the darkened windows that lined a row of apartment buildings on the street, and grunted once, then again.

"Yes. I understand," he said a moment later. He snapped the phone shut, dropped it to the street, and forced all of his weight on the plastic cover, which shattered under the force. He stooped down and collected the pieces before continuing. Within minutes, he'd dropped the various remnants into trash bins and sewer grates, momentarily saving only the memory card and battery.

Later, he would dump the battery in a cigar box at his apartment.

He beat the memory card with a carpenter's hammer before pitching it into the Seine the following morning.

EIGHT

A BACK-DOOR SLIDER

I'd slept uneasily, dreaming of car chases on dark country roads, and awoke early the next morning with a headache that persisted despite a couple of pills and two cups of Earl Grey. Worse, I looked rumpled, even after my routine exercise regimen and a long shower and some extra time staring into the mirror, razor in hand and disappointment registered on my half-shaven face.

Who the hell is that guy? I wondered.

Caeli, who as usual looked radiant, breezed in and smiled.

"Staring at it and wishing otherwise won't hide the years, mister," she said as she rummaged through a drawer.

She sang the words in jest, but they registered.

"I used to know that guy in the glass," I said. "But it was awhile back, and he seems to have taken a turn for the worse."

"Nothing that hard work and a new bride won't cure – that and swearing off the mead," she said and brushed past, running her hand across my grizzled cheek.

"You missed a spot," she whispered.

"More like I missed a decade. What are we up to today? Anything fun and exciting?"

"If by fun and exciting you mean taking care of a dozen wedding incidentals, your wish is granted," she said. "Among other things, we need to arrange for tables and chairs, plus dishes and silverware and glasses and everything else we need that we don't have enough of now."

"So it's Wedding Prep 101, Part 57," I said. "The caterers don't take care of that sort of thing?"

"The caterers take care of food and drink. What to put the food on and the drink in is up to us."

Time spent on busy-work exercises had little appeal, and I began looking for an out that wouldn't force Caeli to conclude that I was ducking vital labors.

"I'll ask Alan Phelan if he knows anyone," I offered after once more swiping the razor against the grain of the decidedly gray sprouting whiskers. "I should talk with him anyway – provide a report on our findings from yesterday."

"Good idea," Caeli said. "Maybe he can save us a drive into Limerick. We could use that time to get after …"

"… a hundred other things on your to-do list," I said, finishing the thought. "I can hardly wait."

"That's good to hear, Max," Caeli said as she started toward the stairs, calling over her shoulder, effectively hiding any trace of sarcasm, which only highlighted her true meaning. "If you get started early enough, you might finish in time to enjoy supper. Where are you taking me?"

"Anywhere you like – and I love you, too," I called, enjoying the hit-and-run. But by then she was already gone.

My headache continued to send out steady reminders that mead, even in small doses, is a bad idea when I dialed Phelan's mobile phone minutes later and left a message. I thought about taking another pill but abandoned it as too soon from the time that I'd first raided the Tylenol bottle and made a mental note to add Extra Strength Bayer Plus to the shopping list.

By the time I'd dressed for the day's battle and was starting down the stairs, my phone chirped with Phelan's name attached to the screen.

"Alan – thanks for the reply," I said once he'd chimed in with a cheerful greeting. "I have news and a favor to ask in return. Where would you like to start?"

"Does the news concern me aunt's ring?"

"It does, although let me first ask a question," I said. "Whenever you mention the ring, you always indicate that it's your aunt's. During your visit here, you explained that the ring passes hands annually and belongs to both your aunt and mother. Why not call it your mother's ring instead of your aunt's?"

I know. This sort of query may not register at the top of your list. But it's the kind of thing that rings my chimes, which is why I asked.

"It's that old bit about possession being nine-tenths of the law," Phelan said. "Had the ring been nicked from me mother, ya see, I'd call it her ring rather than me aunt's."

"So it's timing."

"Exactly. And to answer yer question, let's go with news first and then the favor … but only if the news is good news and not bad news or what yer angry man in the White House calls fake news … whatever that might be."

He waited, perhaps hoping that I'd weigh in, but I let it go and spent a minute or so on what we'd done in preparation for our visit to the castle and surrounding grounds the previous day and narrowed in with specifics when I told him what we'd found.

"Caeli spotted him initially," I said. "How she managed it, considering the crowd, is a question you'll have to take up with her."

"All the more reason for me to meet this woman," he said.

"You'll get your chance soon enough. Back to your crook. When Caeli pointed him out, you could tell that he at least looked the part – reason enough to move in close and see if the stars aligned."

I told him next about our approach at the pawnbroker's shop, the quick duck inside once Caeli spotted the open window near the door, and her efforts to overhear the conversation between our mystery man and Joan Shedd, the unsuspecting American who'd come within a tantalizing whisper of handing over her valuables.

"What did Caeli hear, exactly, that told her it was him?" Phelan asked.

"I asked her the same question on the drive home. He kept repeating the same phrase, something along the lines of, 'It's good to share the things you hold most dear.' We stepped in at that point, which seemed prudent. When Caeli crashed into the woman, breaking the spell, Mrs. Shedd already had the bracelet off her wrist and was about to hand it over."

"So you got there just in time."

"We did."

"And he did a runner straight off?"

"Not quite. He was angry. You could tell by the way he'd reacted, and in his facial expression, though he didn't say a word. We'd maneuvered in so that Mrs. Shedd couldn't see him, figuring that breaking eye contact would help. Caeli leaned in close and spoke to her, forcing her to listen. That seemed to do it. But Mrs. Shedd abruptly noticed that the 'nice young man' she'd been talking with – words to that effect – was gone, and she wondered what'd happened to him. That's when we determined that he'd disappeared, for want of a better word or phrase."

The line turned into a contest, which I can only say by way of explanation that the detective sergeant started.

Phelan: "Like buggered off."

Me: "Cleared out."

Phelan: "Scarpered."

Me: "Skedaddled."

Phelan: "Bunked out."

Me: "Slipped away."

Phelan: "Turned tail."

Me: "Absconded."

Phelan: "Took a powder."

Me: "Hey, that's a strictly American phrase, boyo."

We both laughed, and I thought again how meeting Phelan had turned into a nice bit of serendipitous fortune, on many levels.

I'd chosen to relay the story of our pursuit of the suspected thief in chronological order, and I was now at the point where the surprise attack and threat came into play.

"I left the women to look for him, but he found me instead, minutes later, outside of a gift shop," I said.

That caught his attention.

"What do you mean, he found you?" he asked. "I thought you were the pursuer." But he didn't wait for a confirmation, shooting out his thoughts in staccato fashion. "I would've figured he'd bolted for good, given that you'd caught him red-handed and could identify him, if need be. Or am I missin' things entirely?"

"Just a little. He did a good job of disguising his looks, what with the ball cap and sunglasses and stubble on his face – a couple of days' worth, maybe. We never did get much of a look at him, even when we initially closed in on Mrs. Shedd. Our intent then was to shield her from the guy, figuring it would help break whatever hold he had over her. And then, of course, he vanished."

"You said he disappeared earlier. That's when I added scarpered."

"Exactly, though you mentioned buggered off first," I said. "I thought he'd head for the castle, which is where you mentioned he'd met your aunt, and maybe try for a new mark. Instead, he crashed into me outside the shop, knocking me into a wall, and followed that up with a nasty threat."

"He did that? Really?"

"Yup."

"What exactly did he say?"

"Word for word: 'I don't know what kind o' game the both of ya are playin' at, Yank, but I don't like it. Stay the fook away from me if ya know what's good for ya, boyo. I won't be after tellin' ya again.'"

He took his time before responding, digesting the words.

"That's quite specific on yer part, ya know," he eventually said. "That must be yer reporter's background kickin' in, I'd expect, though yer accent needs work."

I laughed.

"Well, there's that, I guess. But I've got an ear for threats. I've heard more than my share, and this was a good one."

" 'Twas. You've come to some conclusions then 'bout the manner of man ye were facin', I take it."

"Technically, my face was to the wall, but yeah. His accent was decidedly Irish, likely west coast Irish: maybe Limerick, but maybe someplace smaller. He was chewing breath mints – peppermint, I think. His cologne reminded me of the dusting you'd get in a barbershop, after a trim and a shave. He took me for a Yank straight off, even though I'd adopted my best Dublin accent while talking with Mrs. Shedd. And his hat was …"

"Hold on – let's reload, boyo," he said, interrupting. "You were using an accent?"

"We both were."

"Might I ask why?"

"Caeli figured we'd have better cover if something blew up, after the fact."

"And why would she be after thinkin' that?"

"The guy was scary. Plus, she was intent on putting the poor woman at ease."

"Mrs. Shedd then."

"Exactly."

He was quiet for a time, absorbing the ramifications of this wrinkle, for reasons that I couldn't immediately fathom.

"It's no biggie," I said when the connection between our two phones produced nothing but lingering silence. "For what it's worth, Caeli's accent is quite good. She speaks Irish, you know … or at least enough to impress me."

"It just caught me at ends, is all. But all right, you both used an accent. No need to jump the beam on matters that don't amount to much, I suppose," he said. "Tell me what happened next."

"After the threat? Nothing. He was gone again before I could pull my face off the planks, so I returned to the women and didn't give it much thought until Caeli and I were alone, much later. The three of us, you see, enjoyed the feast before we put Mrs. Shedd in a taxi for her next stop, the hotel at Dromoland. She was scheduled, according to Caeli, to stay the night and fly out of Shannon sometime later today, heading home."

"That taxi ride'll set her back 20 Euros, at least, plus tip," he said. "Maybe I should get into the hackney business on the side."

"We offered to give her a lift, but she was adamant – insisted she'd put us out enough for one night," I said, figuring that he was kidding about moonlighting.

"Good on ya, though it's still a cost."

"I'd say she can afford it, judging by her adornments," I said. "My understanding, again from Caeli, is that Mrs. Shedd was going to do – or is it get? – a spa treatment at Dromoland before heading out, so you'll still have time to chat her up if you want to supplement my report. It's the reason I called early. You also might get CCTV footage of the guy if you check the tape outside the pawnbroker's shop at 4:45 p.m. That should give you something to run through your database and track him down, even with the sunglasses and ball cap."

He paused, thinking it through.

"Given that I've been ordered to let it go, I'm not sure I'll be able to make the request," he eventually said. "The DCI's made it clear to stay well away from the whole business – too close to the aggrieved party and all that."

I was about to suggest hacking the security feed, thought better of it when I considered again who I was talking with, and did my best to provide instead a detailed description of the charmer: height, weight, the aviator sunglasses, the DK ball cap, and a general accounting of his clothing.

"Anything else?" he asked.

I thought about it for a long moment, picturing the guy in my mind after Caeli had first pointed him out and then as we approached, and came up with one additional item.

"He was wearing boots, highly polished – maybe military grade," I said. "Don't know why that didn't register earlier, but there it is."

We spent another few minutes talking about the guy's general appearance, with Phelan pressing me as though we were in a courtroom.

"Does Caeli agree with yer description?" he asked once I'd repeated the same information more than a few times, answering questions that varied in both phrasing and approach but that essentially covered the same ground.

"She does. We talked about it last night. You're welcome to chat with her, but I suspect she'll tell you the same."

"All right then. I might well ask anyway, but let me see how far I can get with the locals and maybe even gain access to the CCTV footage without a warrant card. That might resolve the whole business if I strike a bit of luck and keep the boss off me tail and none the wiser."

He was about to sign off when I remembered the second part of my reason for making the call – another sign of too much mead.

"Before you go, Alan: Tell me your cousins have access to plates and glasses and silverware and set-ups for the wedding. It would save us a trip into town."

"Can't see why they wouldn't. But either way, I'll make it happen with a call and let you know if there's an issue," he said. "If ya don't hear from me, it's done. Rest easy. You've enough on yer mind."

I relayed the conversation to Caeli minutes later, starting with the choice item of how we wouldn't have to go into Limerick to chase down a rental center.

I also relayed Phelan's thanks for our efforts to locate the mystery hypnotist and his reaction when hearing that we'd taken on Dublin accents during our encounter with Mrs. Shedd.

"Tell me again why you chose to go in that direction," I asked.

"It made sense at the time," she said. "I figured that Joan would expect an Irish voice. But I also didn't want to make it easy for the guy to come at us, after the fact, if the opportunity presented itself. We've dealt with enough loons – no need to add another."

Her answer surprised me, at least initially. But our investigations have certainly placed us in the cross-hairs of some bad people through the years, and I chalked up Caeli's reaction to that, plus the approaching wedding.

"Sure – makes sense," I said. "It caught Phelan off guard, though."

"He's an Irish copper," she replied. "My guess is anything we do will look odd to him."

We were in the kitchen, snacking rather than eating a true breakfast, with Caeli's list of items to accomplish that day growing longer every time she set pencil to paper – and she did a great deal of that while we spoke.

"I'm glad we don't have to make that run into town," she said at one point while scribbling away. "Still, it's too bad I won't get a chance to see Joan again, before she returns home. She's a nice lady, one I could be friends with, I think, were we neighbors."

The phone rang 10 minutes later – Phelan again. I figured that he'd run into a snag regarding plates and glasses, but he surprised me.

"Professor Blake," he said without preamble. "You should know yer Mrs. Shedd was assailed last night, late, after she checked into Dromoland."

"Assailed? In what way?" I asked, waving to get Caeli's attention.

"Bashed in the head a couple of times, apparently."

"*Che diavolo?*" I muttered – it translates to *What the hell?* in English – and activated the phone's speaker so that Caeli could hear, filling her in with a few whispered words. I let Phelan know that two of us were on the line, and he introduced himself, minus the gushing superlatives he'd dished out previously, taking into account the seriousness nature of his call.

"The poor woman's in hospital," Phelan said. "It's touch and go, from what I gather. From the little I dragged out of hotel officials, along with our people, there was no sign of a forced entry. She apparently either knew her attacker or willingly let him inside. Is she the type of woman who'd do that?"

"No," we both said in unison.

"Highly unlikely," Caeli added.

"Right. Thanks for that. I'll pass it on. And before askin', the bracelet ya mentioned isn't on the inventory list."

NINE

A RETURN VISIT

We offered to accompany DS Phelan to the hospital to visit with the doctors and determine Mrs. Shedd's condition – and of course to be there for her. But he assured us that nothing would be gained until she woke up.

"If she wakes up," he added. "The doctors are no more than mildly optimistic, I'm told. But ya know how they can be when asked to explain things in detail. It's frustrating, really. If ya can't get a medical diagnosis from a bloody physician, who are ya supposed to ask? A clerk? A footballer?"

I wondered whether he meant that it was an issue for the police or for the patient, as well as for the patient's family, but didn't bother asking. The idea of her family not knowing what had happened persisted, however, and Caeli passed along that Mrs. Shedd had an ex-husband and a couple of grown children. But we had no additional information, beyond the states she'd told us she passed through at various stages in her life.

"Her license to drive lists an address in Nampa, Idaho," he said. "But they found documents in her luggage listing an address in California as well – San Diego, I believe. They're trying to track the next of kin, but America's a big place compared to Ireland."

"Maybe we can help," I offered. "We used to live on that side of the country."

"Thanks, but I suspect they've got it well in hand," he said. "It may take 'em a bit, but they'll get to the right place in time, I suspect."

It was a disconcerting, humbling experience, and we both felt terrible about the situation, as well as the circumstances that had brought it about, culminating with Mrs. Shedd ending up unconscious in a rural hospital in County Clare.

Phelan must have sensed our discomfort.

"Ya can't be after blamin' yerselves for what's happened," he said. "It's the bastard got into her room and smashed her on the head, surely … not the two of you."

Caeli wasn't buying the platitude.

"And if we hadn't been there at all and things just took their course? Or if we'd done nothing when we first saw them together and simply let Mister Denmark take the bracelet when they were outside the pawn shop, passing the information on to you afterward? Either way, Mrs. Shedd wouldn't have been assaulted," she said.

"Mister Denmark, is it?"

"It's better than Mister Sunglasses Guy," she said.

"Or Hypno-man, sans the mister," I suggested.

Phelan stayed focused, remaining adamant that what had happened to Mrs. Shedd was an extraordinary event that was beyond our control as well as his – and apparently even hers.

"We can't know that what took place at Dromoland had anything a'tall to do with what happened earlier at the Folk Park, when the two of ya were there," he said, mustering some conviction to sell the notion. "We're still diggin', of course, but …"

"Maybe not, but it's a hell of a good place to start an investigation," I said.

"True. And yet, who can say fer sure? Maybe the poor woman was lonely and met a stranger in the lounge and invited him into the room for a nightcap," he said.

"Not a chance," Caeli said. "Think like that and you'll waste precious time."

He was quiet for a moment, either mulling Caeli's conviction or mentally tallying additional scenarios.

"We will, of course, look at what happened at the Folk Park, first and foremost," he eventually said. "I've already advised our people to go after the CCTV footage, though I didn't tell 'em how I knew to make the recommendation. We'll do everything we can, of course, to find the person responsible."

Caeli, clearly upset, muttered a few words of thanks to Phelan for his efforts.

Once he'd hung up, I could feel the headache pounding at my temples again – like Khrushchev's shoe on a United Nations podium. I wandered off in search of the Tylenol, leaving Caeli to run a quick online search. Before long, she'd called Mulqueen Florists to arrange for flowers to be delivered to Mrs. Shedd's room at Ennis Day Hospital on Gort Road, a 15-minute drive from Dromoland.

"She may not even notice them when she wakes up," Caeli said. "But I had to do something."

We spent the morning in mindless but necessary tasks: cleaning and straightening and rearranging and revamping in various areas around the house and the grounds, preparing for the arrival of our guests, getting ready for an event that we'd been primed for, by my reckoning, for years. But then, I've been told by Caeli on more than one occasion that I tend to gloss over big-ticket items that often matter most, and our wedding apparently was a prime example. I'd first proposed five years before, and we'd even set a date … one that came and went on mutual agreement after a traumatic shooting in an early case we'd worked.

"Nothing will get in the way this time," I said, talking to myself while cleaning the bannisters of the grand staircase.

I found myself thinking about Joan Shedd a dozen times or more throughout the next couple of hours and eventually went to Caeli, who was working at a feverish pace in the kitchen, taking out her frustrations on the pots and pans (all of which were new), with an offer.

"We've made good progress this morning," I said. "How about we head north for a late lunch or early dinner? We can stop at the hospital to see how Mrs. Shedd is doing."

"I'd like that. I've been thinking the same thing," she said, brushing a lock of hair that had drifted toward her eye. "I'm not sure we'll learn much, but it can't hurt to try. Maybe we should eat here."

I adopted what I hoped would pass for a neutral look, though my card-playing skills are notoriously poor for lack of a genuine poker face.

"Let's stop along the way," I said. "Bunratty, maybe?"

She eyed me with renewed interest.

"So there's method to your hunger," she said.

"Just a suggestion," I said. "If we tour the grounds, searching for a spot to eat, and happen to run into a guy in sunglasses and a DK ball cap, so much the better."

"Let's keep in mind that he slams people into walls and hits defenseless women hard enough to put them in the hospital," she said.

"All the more reason to go, though I'd feel better if we could saddle up with the Walthers instead of Swiss Army Knives."

"We've got other things going for us," she said.

"Such as?"

"He won't expect us, nor will he know how determined we can be."

"*If* we get lucky and run into him. No sure thing, of course, but it seems worth a shot."

She nodded her agreement and asked, a moment after securing a couple of the pans in the cabinet next to the range, whether we should call Phelan and give him a heads-up about our intentions.

I thought about it and could hear his voice in my head, advising us to leave the work to the on-site professionals.

"How about we give Bill Kohlmeyer a shout instead?" I suggested. "Maybe, with some sweet-talking from you, he'd be OK with helping track down Mrs. Shedd's kids. They should know what's happened."

Kohlmeyer is a long-time friend from my investigative reporter days, when I was working for a daily newspaper in Oregon and he was running the SWAT team for the capital city's police force. We've had our ups and downs through the years, but we seem to have transitioned into a place of mutual respect, now that he's Salem's top cop and Caeli and I are in Ireland. More to the point, we're no longer regular visitors at the West Salem winery that was owned until his recent death by Vinny Fierro, a man the feds called the top mob boss on the West Coast.

We showered quickly and were on our way toward the Limerick Tunnel inside of an hour, this time driving the 2017 Cadillac CTS sedan, well-equipped, that I'd ordered from a Dublin car importer when we'd first arrived in Ireland. It boasted a mere 335 horses in a 3.6L V6 engine, unlike the 556-horse-powered CTS-V model that we left behind at our home on the Crooked River Gorge in Central Oregon. But the damn thing handles like a race car and gets far better mileage. Given the price of petrol on this side of the Atlantic, it felt like a reasonable tradeoff.

And yeah, we'd packed some necessities in the trunk … just in case we ran into trouble.

Caeli dialed up Kohlmeyer's private number once we were on the road, connected to the Caddy's Bluetooth system, and said, "It's early there right now, you know," as the phone began ringing.

Great, I thought, automatically checking the digital clock and calculating backward. *Can't wait.*

"This better be good," Kohlmeyer said when he answered on the fifth jangle. He sounded gruffer than usual, likely because he'd been asleep.

Caeli attempted to cover our tracks.

"I just realized what time it is, Bill. Sorry – I'll call back in a couple of hours," she said.

"Wait," he said. "Caeli Brown? Is that you?"

"It is. Good morning . Sorry again for the early wake-up. I'll try later."

"No – don't bother. Too late now. I figure you've got a hell of a good reason for hollering at me from the other side of the world at this ungodly hour. Tell me you finally wised up and dumped that ex-reporter for good, and I can stay home and ride my horses instead of jet-setting across the Atlantic on a mobster's airplane to attend a wedding."

"Right here, Bill," I said. "As you know, our friend is dead, sadly, and his son's charitable foundation – a son who was never involved in his father's businesses, I'd add – owns the jet in question."

I paused for a beat and added, in my cheeriest voice, "And a merry good morning to you, by the way."

He grunted – or at least that's what it sounded like.

"Good morning? It was 'til I heard your voice, Blake, though it's a pleasure to hear from Caeli Brown – even this early," he said. With every word, he seemed to be waking up a bit more – and, of course, sharpening his knife for whatever verbal lashings he wanted to fire off. "What the hell time is it, anyway?"

"Irish time is just after 2 p.m.," I said.

"Yeah, well, this ain't Ireland," he said. "Then again, my wife tells me I need to develop a rosier disposition when it comes to dealing with you, Blake. This might be your lucky day."

He paused, as though expecting a reply. When neither of us bit, he tried again.

"Or not. At least you were smart enough to have your girlfriend make the call."

I jumped in then, unable to resist.

"Hey – make that my soon-to-be wife, mister," I said. "How's the packing going? We can't wait to get you over here for a little R&R."

He laughed, good-naturedly, I hoped, though you never know.

"I leave all that to Skyla. And in your case, Blake, R&R must represent something besides Rest & Recuperation, as we called it in the military, or Rest & Relaxation, as everybody else says. So let me guess: Rum and Ritalin, maybe? Or is it Reporting and Regurgitating?"

"I like rum," I said. "I would've made a good pirate."

He snorted again, and we could hear Skyla calling out a hello in the background. He'd apparently activated the speaker on his phone as well.

We passed along some pleasantries for the next minute or so before Skyla signed off, which allowed Caeli to explain in abbreviated fashion what had taken place the previous day and ask if he could help us locate Joan Shedd's children.

"I searched online, trying the usual social media outlets, but came up empty," she said. "We're hoping you can help, using your exemplary and prestigious detecting skills, so her children know what happened."

"And here I thought you called to check on our well-being," he said. "Should've known it was just another chance to ring up taxpayer dollars on your personal dime – and this from people who no longer pay taxes over here."

"You've got that wrong, buddy-boy," I said.

But he wasn't concerned about our tax obligations.

"Whatever they're pulling out of those bloated checks the two of you get from that so-called foundation you work for can't be near enough," he said. I detected another snort. Then he jumped abruptly to business, the kind of sharp turn that Kohlmeyer exceeds at – the kind that drove me nuts when I was reporting for a living. "Tell me how you got involved in this thing again. I thought you'd turned in your PI licenses."

"We did," I said. "I was helping a friend on the Limerick force, a good guy whose mother and aunt were ripped off by the guy we suspect of thumping Mrs. Shedd."

"You know," he said, "I should fly over there and thump the pair of you for getting involved, but what's the use? Caeli I could reason with, but you, Blake?"

I was ready to answer, but Caeli beat me to it.

"What we did is exactly what any good citizen would do – you included. I'm hoping you can help us out … help Joan out, really. If you can, terrific. If not, we'll try something else."

"Yeah. That's what worries me," he said. "Give me the details again. I'll see what I can come up with, though I'd think the Irish authorities would sort it out. Am I wrong?"

"It's just that we offered to help if we could," Caeli said.

"All right. I'll run it up the flagpole."

Bill left us moments later with a promise to call once he'd tracked down anything useful. When Caeli asked whether he was confident that he could find Mrs. Shedd's children, he gave us a more-than-reasonable assurance.

"Unless they're in Witness Protection, I'll find them."

"And if they're in Witness Protection?"

"I'll find 'em anyway," he said.

Gotta love Kohlmeyer.

We passed through the Limerick Tunnel for the third time in two days and pulled into the Folk Park grounds minutes later. We both were anxious about Mrs. Shedd's condition but also were surprisingly hungry and looking forward to a relaxing meal, especially after the work we'd put in that morning.

We also knew, though neither of us mentioned it, that the longer we waited before attempting to visit the hospital, the better chance we'd have of actually finding the poor woman awake, alert, and talkative.

"We could try MacNamara's again," I suggested – the same spot we'd visited for a pint the previous day. "They serve typical pub fare, if I recall."

But Caeli was interested in something more substantial and ran a fast search on her phone. She'd soon directed us to Gallacher's, which features Irish and European fare, local seafood, and gluten-free dining options, according to the Tripadvisor website.

"The ratings are exceptionally high," Caeli said. "Plus, if you write a review, the manager – he bills himself as John O – will reply to your post within 24 hours."

"Charming. You think his last name is, I don't know, somehow Irish?" I asked. "O'Neill or O'Farrell or O'Malley or …"

"I get it, Max," she said.

We sat inside, despite the lovely day and available outdoor options, and ordered in quick fashion: steamed mussels for an appetizer, with Caeli opting for the sea bass, fresh veggies, and saffron, pea, and shrimp rice, while I ordered the surf and turf special: a chargrilled fillet with tiger prawns and broccoli. We looked at the wine list but opted for ice water instead … just in case we ran into Mister Denmark and decided that a tango was in order.

The food was spectacular, and I had a hard time pulling myself up when the time came to once again wander the bucolic trappings of the park, methodically searching for a man who was, in turn, searching for unsuspecting prey.

"It's a grand day to catch a thief," Caeli said as we headed outside.

But even the grandest of Irish days can turn quickly … and irrevocably.

TEN

ROUND TWO

We strolled the busy streets of the Folk Park for more than an hour, poking into the shops, drifting this way and that, concentrating all of our energies on finding Mister Denmark ...

... *if, in fact, he can be found,* I thought more than once, and we both recognized that we were dealing with an enormous *if.*

I wondered briefly what Bill Kohlmeyer would say if he knew that we were again out and about, searching for a brutal thug with little more than our wits for protection, especially after the caution he'd just delivered. But I dismissed it because there was little else we could do but try to help, despite the risks.

In short order, we retraced our steps from the previous day, dipping into MacNamara & Son for iced teas; spending a few minutes inside the pawnbroker's shop and hearing the same spiel that its proprietor delivered a day earlier while Joan Shedd was being hoodwinked outside its front door; ducking into the School House, which had once stood in the Irish village of Belvoir and was now a central focus of the park; and wandering into and out of the post office, the potter's shop, the bakery, and ending up in J.J. Corry's for Diet Cokes with water chasers as we sat at the bar and watched the clientele come and go.

We saw lots of folks speaking more than a few languages duck inside to get a sense of what a real Irish village pub looked like, back in the day. Half of them, give or take, stayed for a drink.

We engaged the publican in a bit of banter, although asking straight-out questions about whether he'd noticed a hypnotizing hooligan among the patrons somehow never came up. We eventually left with a friendly wave and were a dozen or more steps down the street when we spotted the same constable we'd briefly visited with the previous day. Caeli tugged on my arm, and we hurried down a narrow lane that eventually returned us to the main street of shops and throngs of tourists, avoiding the costumed beat-walker.

"We're under cover now?" I asked as she maneuvered us aside.

"No sense getting on his radar, even if he's not real police," she said, angling back toward the parking lot. "Unless you work here, who'd want to visit the Folk Park on consecutive days?"

She had a point, and I was about to acknowledge her quick thinking.

But the same rules that applied to us also would apply to Mister Denmark, and it dawned on us both that we were unlikely to see him on this day – or at least not looking the same as he'd presented himself to Mrs. Shedd.

"If he is here, he'll be in disguise, far different from his appearance yesterday," Caeli said after we talked it through. "I'd guess he'd be wearing different clothing, different sunglasses, if any, and a different hat … or no hat at all."

"He'll have on the same boots, though," I said. "The more I think about it, the more I'm convinced that his boots mean something … a military background, maybe."

"Either that or he does his shopping at Moore Street Market in Dublin," she said.

For the uninitiated, the open-air market has been feeding and clothing Dubliners and visitors alike for decades. It also figured prominently in the 1916 Easter Uprising, Ireland's most famous push for independence.

"Good point, though it's a hell of a long drive from here to there," I said, thinking back to my college days, many years previous, when I'd visited Moore Street regularly for everything from bags of apples to clothing, boots included. "I wonder if there's an equivalent in Limerick."

"Good question."

We had no answer, and no reason to pursue one, and eventually made our way toward the car park, with no sighting of our mystery hypnotist and no prospects for finding him.

I also was troubled by what we'd just seen – or hadn't.

"Don't you think it's curious that even though we provided Alan Phelan with details of the threat, and even though it's likely that the bastard who hurt Mrs. Shedd is the same guy who's been trolling for tourists on these grounds, there's no police presence whatsoever outside of the phony constable?" I asked.

"Maybe they don't want to scare him off," Caeli said. "They could be here, all right, but working undercover instead of in uniform."

"Maybe," I said, though I thought it unlikely. I'm generally adept at spotting cops, even in disguise, and I hadn't had a single sniff of a detective or plainclothes officer on the grounds.

Then I had another idea.

"Given what happened yesterday, maybe the Guards don't want him to change his hunting grounds – all the better to keep an eye on him from afar, via CCTV or cameras filming from hidden locales," I said. "Maybe they're concerned that we spooked him – or, far worse, maybe he's concerned about what we saw of his encounter with Mrs. Shedd and isn't likely to return."

"Just because we caught part of his act?" Caeli said. "No. I don't think so. He can't consider us a threat. We didn't appear threatening – not yesterday."

"But we can make a good stab at identifying him," I said.

"We didn't get all that good of a look at him."

"He doesn't know that. He might consider us Public Enemy No. 1 for upsetting his MO and potentially taking away his gravy train. He wasn't happy when he made that run at me, I can tell you – and I'll wager that if he spots us again, he'll double down on the threat."

The words had just left my mouth when we spotted him, wearing the same hat and sunglasses that he'd sported the previous day – as though reading our earlier thoughts and defying us. Worse, he was leaning against the Cadillac, standing taller than I remembered – *leaner, too.* His arms were folded over his chest, his left foot was crossed over his right and hoisted up on its toe, and you could see the sheen on his boots from where we stood, which was a couple of dozen yards away.

At least his hands are empty, I recall thinking.

His expression was difficult to categorize, although *arrogant* and *confident* and *dangerous* crossed my mind in quick succession.

Caeli said much the same afterward, adding *smug* and *devious* to the list.

Don't like the looks of that, I thought.

And I sure as hell wish we had the Walthers.

"Thought I told ya to stay the fook away from me," he said as we halted our approach beside a cream-colored Ford that had seen better days.

My initial thinking was that we were too far away for him to throw a punch, even by lunging at us. True, he could throw a rock or knife. But we could use the Ford to duck behind if he tossed something … *or pulled out a gun.*

I also figured that his comment required a reply.

"Technically, you told me that – not her," I said, trying to sound off-handedly assured, or at least equally confident in my own skills.

"And technically," Caeli added, "you're crowding us."

He grinned back, though he didn't move – not so much as a twitch.

I didn't care for the smile, or for his self-control, and did my best to make him think that he was dealing with equals.

"Something else you should know," I said. "We don't like threats from punks who prey on women."

OK, so it was a calculated risk, considering the simple fact that the only means of protection we had on our person, besides our fists/feet/knees/elbows, were our Swiss Army pocket knives. Mine was at least reachable. Caeli's was tucked into a fanny pack that was strapped to her left side – not the best spot for access when time was a factor.

He pushed away from the car and took three steps toward us, showing a hint of teeth, before halting abruptly. I used the time to hit the Cadillac's key fob, which was tucked inside my left pocket, unlocking the trunk. If he heard the sound or recognized the maneuver, he didn't seem concerned.

Caeli, ever alert, noticed what I'd done and acknowledged it with a nod.

"Yer just like all the Yanks, ya know," he said, speaking more loudly than was necessary. "All mouth, with no ability to deliver the goods, like yer man Bush, back in the days of that war he started for no good reason a'tall – and now just like yer new fat tosser, who seems bent on startin' up another."

I wasn't about to engage in a political debate, but I used his examples to send out yet another warning – one that I hoped he'd take as a metaphor and perhaps give him a moment's pause.

"You may not agree with motives or tactics, but a smart man respects the arsenal at their disposal," I said.

Unfortunately, he called my bluff.

"What arsenal's in yer pocket just now, boyo?" he said, and his grin expanded. "Carryin' a gun, maybe? I'd pay a hell of a lot more attention if ya were, but I'd guess you'd 've pulled it by now."

He started slowly toward us once more, his hands held easily at his sides, his movements steady and fluid, with no wasted motion.

"A knife then, maybe – somethin' beyond the pocket variety?" he said. "Nah – nary a chance. I'd 've already seen its flash if you were totin' a blade of any length."

I'd started edging along the side of the sedan, luring him toward me, while Caeli drifted toward the Caddy, remaining as inconspicuous as possible, saying nothing and moving with short, sliding steps meant to attract little attention.

It's worth pointing out that when we were PIs, we routinely practiced this sort of maneuver – silently hoping that the day never arrived but preparing for it nonetheless because the chances were good that we'd need it, somewhere along the line.

Like today …

"So it's yer fists you've brought that'll save the day, is it now, Yank?" he said, and you could hear the arrogance ringing in his words. "Ya think yer good enough to last more than a single missed punch 'fore I put ya down with a strike of me own and stomp on yer bloody head?"

He barked out a laugh, but he wasn't done.

"Or is it the lass ya think can save yer hide, boyo? I see her slinkin' away, ready to send out a call for help. But she won't be near fast enough to save yer old sorry ass – not a chance."

He was a hell of lot younger, to be sure, and he also was muscled in the right spots. He exuded the sense that he was ex-military, or perhaps he was still in somebody's army and was spending his time at the Folk Park, preying on the rich and the weak while on leave.

Then again, he also was making assumptions – never a good idea.

Caeli wasn't running away to call for help. It's not in her nature. If the dilemma calls for a Fight, Flight, or Freeze response, she almost always fights – so long as she's not facing a machine gun or a well-trained army with bazookas and flame-throwers.

Caeli also is an expert, along with other formidable forms of self-defense, in Krav Maga, the Israeli resistance/counter-attack technique that is lightning quick and decidedly lethal. Better yet, she's a damned sight better at its use than you'd guess by looking at her – or dismissing her without much of a glance, as Mister Denmark was guilty of doing here.

I also know my way around Krav Maga techniques and can generally hold my own, even if it had been some time since either one of us had attended the classes that we once undertook with regularity, at Bill Kohlmeyer's insistence. As he'd explained it to us, Krav Maga has little to do with strength and is all about technique, relying on a single fundamental principle: The shortest movement to prevent an attack is the best movement.

I knew for fact that Mister Denmark couldn't easily put me down with a single punch, as he'd boasted, because I also knew for fact that it was unlikely for him to land the punch cleanly – especially if he were overconfident.

I also was trusting that he wasn't carrying a pistol or a knife because, using the same logic he'd determined for us, if he had one, he, too, would've no doubt produced it by now.

But the real ace I carried was that Caeli was heading directly toward the Caddy, which he'd left unattended when he started after me, making the common gender-biased mistake that he'd eliminate the most dangerous threat first – a decidedly bad call. Seconds later, she'd hoisted the trunk and grabbed the police batons that were stashed within easy reach. She released the sections of black metal to the baton in her left hand with a hard downward motion and started back toward me, weighing the second device in her opposite hand.

By the time Mister Denmark sensed movement and pulled his eyes away from me, it was too late to stop her. He realized his error with a string of curses that were a joy to hear.

"Game on, boyo," I muttered.

He must have had the same thought because he lunged at me, perhaps figuring that he could catch me off guard and do some serious damage before Caeli could get near enough to either attack with the extended baton or toss the second one to me.

He came straight at me, his arms thrusting outward, and I recognized the move instantly. He intended to grab the back of my neck and pull me forward, setting me up for a head-butt that would put me down in a single strike and allow him the time to concentrate on Caeli and her weapons.

But Krav Maga is a powerful tool. Long months of brutally difficult training also made it instinctive. I deflected his attack by using both of my arms to catch him at the elbows and force his momentum upward and to the side. He didn't expect the maneuver, apparently figuring that I'd stand still and take whatever punishment he chose to dole out. I could see the surprise register on his face.

But he was even less prepared for my counterstrike: a swift, brutal kick to the groin that doubled him over with a howl.

Caeli tossed me the second baton as she swept in, and she cracked the back of his right calf with her weapon while I was moving sharply to my right and shoving him over with my right leg.

For what it's worth, I'm unsure as to whether Caeli was aiming for the back of his knee, which was the most logical attack point, and missed, or whether she was extending a mercy to a man who was already crashing to the ground. It didn't come up in our conversations after the fact, and I haven't thought about it again until now.

Regardless, Mister Denmark was no longer the threat that he'd been seconds earlier. Or at least he wasn't until he twisted sharply and pulled a small handgun from his pocket. It backed us up in a hurry – batons vs. a loaded pistol isn't a fair fight for those wielding the batons – and we scrambled behind the Ford while he climbed slowly to his feet. He was irate, injured, unpredictable, armed – a combustible combination.

I figured that we were in for it, but voices drifted toward us as a cluster of at least eight people, maybe more, turned a corner of the car park and walked in our direction. They were the first individuals we'd seen since entering the lot, and my initial thought was that he was going to shoot us anyway and run – or perhaps even shoot at them.

Then I looked hard at the pistol that he was flashing, recognized it as a Beretta Tomcat with a 7-shot capacity, and figured that he couldn't risk it.

Too many people to shoot, I thought.

He apparently came to an identical conclusion and lowered the pistol, turning sideways, probably so that the approaching throng wouldn't get a good look at his face.

"Should'a known when neither of ya went for yer mobiles," he said, spitting out the words in anger. His face was beet-red, and his eyes had a predator's look, dark and flashing with barely contained rage.

"Why waste the minutes?" Caeli said.

"Ya haven't heard the last of it, bitch – know that. Get ready," he said and limped swiftly away from the tourists who were oblivious to the situation and paid us no mind as they passed, even as we nodded with grim smiles in their general direction while hiding the batons.

Mister Denmark was soon out of sight.

We'd caught a break – a damn lucky one at that. We could thank good timing, Bill Kohlmeyer, Caeli's police baton, and our Krav Maga training.

It's also worth noting that we'd just landed smack in the middle of a dangerous adversary's crosshairs.

At the time, however, we didn't yet recognize the severity of our situation.

We left Bunratty in a rush, maintaining a vigilant watch for anyone who might be on our tail.

We had a hundred questions and asked many of them as they occurred to us. I was driving, faster than the posted speed but not quickly enough to shake the lingering image of what had just occurred, while Caeli used her phone to direct us toward the hospital in Ennis where Joan Shedd was currently ensconced.

"Nice move getting to the batons," I said at one point, after checking the rearview for the 15th time, or maybe it was the 16th, since we'd left the lot.

"Nice work with the key fob – and the nuts-kick," she said. "That had to smart."

Then, a moment later, she said what we'd both been thinking.

"I don't like it, Max. He knew our car. He was waiting for us. How'd he know that about us?"

"Maybe he saw us drive in," I suggested.

But I didn't believe that, and Caeli didn't, either.

"Not likely," she said. "I think he followed us from the castle last night."

"He couldn't have followed both us and Mrs. Shedd."

"Maybe he's got a partner."

"Then why didn't we see him, or her, today – in the car park? Plus, we had the Range Rover last night, not the Caddy."

We stewed about it for a time, without talking. Then Caeli made one additional observation.

"That man has the eyes of a Da Vinci angel hovering over St. Peter's," she said. "But his heart was pulled from a Mount Hood glacier."

I knew in my own heart that he'd try to deliver on his promise. I'd gotten lucky during our second encounter. The bastard was overconfident and off his guard because he'd underestimated me, probably thinking that I was old and consequently weak.

But I also knew that it was a mistake he wouldn't make again – in the same way that I knew we weren't through sparring.

I had one other disturbing thought about the encounter that I didn't raise with Caeli.

Pick-pockets, flim-flam artists, everyday thieves don't pointedly mention U.S. politics when they threaten someone, I thought.

I don't know what that means, but I don't like it.

Looking back, it's something else we should've discussed.

ELEVEN

A MATTER OF LOGIC

We pulled into the Ennis Day Hospital parking lot 25 minutes later, after Caeli's cell phone prowess led us on a round-about course of dodging and ducking to shake off potential trackers – Mister Denmark especially.

"Nobody," she said as I rolled the Caddy to a halt between a battered delivery van and a mid-sized lorry. "But if he's in the mood to track us, the hospital also is a logical place to watch."

"So we sit and wait – see if he shows up," I said. "I'd hate to attract the guy here and have him go inside, either looking for us or following us, and cause more of a mess than he already has."

Caeli remained unsettled.

"I don't get what this is about," she said. "Why would he attack Joan instead of just, I don't know, putting her under his spell again, as he did at the Folk Park? And why take such a personal dislike of us just because we threw him off his mark? So what? He got what he wanted anyway when he tracked her to Dromoland and took the bracelet."

I squeezed her hand, trying to provide assurance that the situation eventually would work itself out. But it was an empty gesture because we both knew that we couldn't control the actions of the other players involved, the injured Joan Shedd as well as our mysterious adversary.

"It's got to be an ID thing," I said a moment later. "He's after us because we've seen him and can identify him – something we've already done, in fact. Not that he'd know it, but he'd at least know it's possible. My guess is he went after Mrs. Shedd because she, too, can make a positive ID. Getting the bracelet was a bonus."

"He's going to extraordinary lengths to keep his identity secret," Caeli said, as though whispering to herself – another point worth pursuing.

We were quiet for a moment, watching the passing traffic in the hospital's parking area, with Caeli glancing over her shoulder to spot-check the lane behind us while I concentrated on everything that moved along the path we'd first entered.

"Let's scout the lot," Caeli eventually suggested. "I don't like the thought of him sneaking up on us while we're parked between these two rigs and can't see him coming. He's got a gun, after all. I'd bet he knows how to use it."

"You're right about that – military or ex-military," I said. "And, just to let you know there was method to my madness, I picked this spot because the Caddy's out of sight if he happened to drive by the hospital."

"I know. It makes sense – but I still don't like it."

I executed three slow passes through the lot and then circled the hospital twice. But we saw nothing, and we visually checked every parked vehicle, every approach to the grounds, every walkway, every possible avenue of entry.

"One more thing before we go in," I said and, pulling out my phone, connected it to the Bluetooth and dialed Alan Phelan.

He seemed pleased to hear from us, right up to the moment when I told him about our encounter at the Folk Park.

"Jaysus, Professor Blake, but yer only bringin' trouble on yerself, and no need for it," he said. "I'm runnin' CCTV footage now, with help from a techie who owes me a chit. Should have an ID on yer man soon enough, with any luck a'tall. I'll slip it to mates here as fodder for a broader search. We can get the tosser in short order, and I might just get me aunt's ring back before it's all gone to scupper, which'd make her and me mum dizzyingly proud."

I was amused by Phelan's ability to slip into and out of Irish phrases and speech patterns instead of playing the hard-edged, by-the-book, man-of-few-words copper all the time and, even better, to invent colorful phrases of his own and had to force myself to concentrate on his message.

"You're telling us to leave the rest of it to the professionals," I said.

"Yeah – but only since it's for yer own good."

Had he known us better, he would've understood that we couldn't make that promise – not until we'd cleaned up the mess at our feet.

"Our visit to Bunratty pays an unexpected dividend," I said, sidestepping. "You can get him for three additional crimes beyond 4th-degree assault and attempted theft: carrying a firearm, brandishing a firearm, menacing."

We fed him the pertinent details of what had taken place, going back and forth, with Caeli adding points that I'd missed and me fleshing out a thought or item of interest from her observations.

When pressed about our intentions for returning to the Folk Park, as well as the dangers of vigilante justice, I floated the line that we'd decided to visit the hospital to see how Mrs. Shedd was doing and had simply stopped in Bunratty for a quick drink along the way.

"And you just happened to meet up with the same man you'd gone toe to toe with the previous day while he was accosting a fellow Yank. Yer expectin' me to believe that, is it?"

"More or less," I said, exchanging glances with Caeli. "He was waiting for us in the lot, as though he already knew my car. Or maybe he saw us pull in and simply waited for us. Hard to say, but there he was when we came out of the pub."

"How in the world did you keep the eejit from shootin' ya both?" he asked.

"An intervention from the heavens that would take too long to explain, and there's no need to waste your time," I said. "If there's CCTV coverage, you'll have your answer. We just wanted to give you a heads-up."

"It's hardly a waste of me time," he protested, but neither one of us felt the urge to further clarify what had happened.

"It's all right," I said. "We're at the hospital now and ready to check on Mrs. Shedd."

When he didn't answer immediately, I got the feeling that something else was at play.

"About that," he eventually said. "It's unlikely you'll get in to see her, even if she's awake. Yer not family, after all – and ya know she was badly hurt."

"We're as close to family as she has in Ireland," Caeli said. "I'm hoping she's awake and we'll get a chance to talk, if only for a minute – to let her know that friends are with her until her children are told."

"The proper authorities have been notified, I'm sure."

"Good," Caeli said. "If she's awake, we could at least confirm that her attacker and our Mister Denmark are one and the same."

He again paused, thinking the logic through.

"It's good ya called me then," he said. "We've got a man posted to her room, in case somebody tries to pay another unwelcome visit. Give us a bit 'fore ya head in and I'll clear the way, or at least do me best to try and get ya in to see the poor woman."

We thanked him and signed off, and I left the phone in the console before locking the car. We also took a few minutes to check our perimeter thoroughly before entering the hospital and stopping at the visitor's station. A receptionist looked up from a stack of paperwork and mustered a thin smile as we approached.

"We're friends of Joan Shedd, hoping she's well enough to see us," Caeli said. "She's a patient here – brought in last night. A police friend called ahead."

When the woman didn't immediately respond, looking troubled as she stared first at Caeli and then at me, it seemed logical that she required an additional explanation as to why we'd come.

Caeli tried again.

"We were with Joan at Bunratty Castle for the feast last night, before the attack at her hotel room. We saw her to a cab, which took her to Dromoland," she said. "A friend in the States is helping us find her children – to let them know what's happened."

The woman seemed to absorb this for a few seconds before she picked up the station telephone and pressed a button. She turned her head to the side, whispered a handful of words that neither of us heard clearly, and eventually replaced the receiver.

"I'm sorry to tell ya that Mrs. Shedd passed within the hour from her injuries," she said softly. "I've just now called the officer in charge. He and others from the Guards are in with her now. Please wait – they'll be after wantin' to speak to ya, I'm sure."

We were stunned at the news and couldn't muster a reply. I found Caeli's hand and squeezed it tightly while she stared ahead, her face a mask.

"I can see yer upset," the receptionist said. "I'm sorry for yer loss."

"He'll pay for this," Caeli whispered, so softly that I could barely hear her.

But the words and threat were all the more effective for the subtlety of her delivery.

Inside of a minute, a member of the *An Garda Síochána*, the national police force, met us at the front desk. He introduced himself as DCI Thomas Óg McNeill, duly recorded our names and address into his notebook, and appeared to be more than a bit suspicious of our sudden appearance.

He didn't invite us to call him Tommy, anyway.

But as I thought it through from his perspective, the approach that he took wasn't much of a surprise, considering the fact that Mrs. Shedd had just died and that the police were now looking at a murder investigation rather than one of robbery and assault – and he also didn't know a thing about us.

He insisted that we walk ahead of him and pointed us toward a room down a narrow corridor designed for what I guessed to be medical consultations with the families of patients. He beckoned us to sit at a conference table, and he settled in only after we'd both dropped into the hardwood chairs.

Waste of time, based on what he's after, I thought.

"So why don't the two of ya inform me as to what's brought ya here today," he said, leaving no doubt that this was a statement requiring a response and not a rhetorical query to ignore.

Caeli cautiously laid it out for him in much the same manner that she'd done for the hospital's receptionist moments earlier, with no mention of our encounters with the mesmerist. He took notes as she spoke, duly nodding at a reference he found interesting, acknowledging another with a solitary grunt that sounded better than the written word implies.

He then asked a dozen or more questions in rapid-fire order, boring in on potential motive and timeline while glancing at his notebook again and again, probing our "rather tenuous relationship with Mrs. Shedd," as he dismissively phrased it.

Neither one of us liked the quick turnabout. It was apparent that he was looking for more than Caeli initially provided in her overview detailing our connection with the dead woman, although that, too, was no great surprise.

In truth, we didn't want to put DS Phelan in the soup. He'd already indicated that his superiors had ordered him to stay out of the situation at Bunratty, which is why he'd bypassed the chain of command and came to me in the first place.

But it also became apparent that DCI McNeill (the DCI represents Detective Chief Inspector, which put him higher up the food chain than Phelan) was starting to like us for the crime, and that wasn't tolerable. Among other things, we had a wedding to plan for and a growing variety of tasks to accomplish to make it happen.

That's what I told myself, anyway, when I came to the conclusion after 10 minutes of back and forth that we needed to cut to the heart of things without a lot of additional dancing. I whispered Phelan's name to Caeli before indicating with a wave toward McNeill that I was reaching for my phone to make a call.

"Nuts," I said an instant later, talking to Caeli in my best inside-church voice. "I left the damn thing in the car."

"You left what in the car, exactly, Mister … Blake?" McNeill asked, glancing at his notes to ensure that he got the right name.

"My phone – my mobile," I said. "I don't like where this is going, and I'll like even less what I suspect you'll do next. You've forced my hand – and for the record, I don't want what happens from here on out to reflect poorly on anyone, least of all the person we've been doing our best to protect."

I allowed him a moment to process the setup.

He merely looked annoyed.

"Go ahead and call yer solicitor then," he said, sweeping his hand off to the side dismissively, as though I was about to ruin his day entirely. "A lot of good it'll do if ya killed her."

"Killed her? Are you crazy?" Caeli said, her anger mounting with each word.

"Hardly."

"We've no need for a lawyer," I said. "I was going to ring up a detective sergeant I know at the Limerick station and have him vouch for us before we proceed."

That got his attention, judging by the size that his eyes turned at the news.

I pressed ahead before he could interrupt.

"I'm confident my friend can explain, in short order, how we first met Mrs. Shedd and what brought us here."

He didn't like it.

Hell, I didn't, either. I didn't want to give up Phelan, any more than I wanted to spend hours in police custody, explaining away murder charges. But a woman had been murdered, a woman we knew, and we could kick-start the investigation, so long as we weren't being treated as suspects. To flip the order of things, I figured that it was necessary to call in some help, even if that blew Spud's cover.

McNeill scowled at me.

"Yer tellin' me then yer here on a directive from a copper in Limerick?"

"No. Not exactly."

"Good. Because I can't imagine what a Limerick copper would be after doin' instructin' a couple of Yanks to visit a woman who'd been viciously assaulted, the result of which ended her life."

Caeli was quicker at the necessary response than I was. I'd like to think that she also expressed our mutual concern far more eloquently than I might've managed because, truth be told, McNeill was beginning to grate on me.

Then again, it's also possible, looking back, that Caeli was helping me along in giving up Spud.

"For the record, DCI McNeill — just so we all have this straight and there are no misunderstandings whatsoever — you are saying, without really saying it at all, that we are suspects in Joan's murder," she said. "Tell me I have that right — before we take another step."

He smiled, though grimly, keeping his teeth clenched in the process, as though the effort pained him.

"I'm saying yer presence here is suspicious, Miss Brown — at least 'til it can be explained away to my satisfaction. And I've yet to hear anything approachin' that. What I've heard thus far has been rather curious, and not in a good way."

That's because we didn't want to give up Phelan – and I still don't, I thought.

It was now our turn to hit the pause button, and I actually considered requesting a solicitor before we provided additional information. But I abandoned the idea in rapid fashion because asking for a lawyer generally always makes you appear guilty of something, and the only thing we were guilty of right then was protecting Phelan. Caeli and I sure as hell didn't kill Joan Shedd. But we did have a good idea about who had, and we hadn't yet offered that up, either – again, as a cloak for Spud.

Caeli glanced at me, making it clear that it was my call to travel the final steps.

"We're happy to cooperate, sir," I said. "Rather than relying on us to call the detective sergeant, why don't you ring him instead?"

He frowned at the suggestion – clearly a man who didn't like being told what to do, even when the telling might be in everyone's best interest.

"If yer question rings true, I suppose I could tell ya that, mere seconds ago, I had no idea a'tall that I should be after talkin' with one of me own detective sergeants on yer behalf, or with anyone else that might be connected to this case," he said, and you could hear the edge that had crept into his voice.

The guy's not happy, I thought.

"Understood," I said. "But a phone call would at least allow you to cross us off your suspect list – if you've even started one. When you finish, perhaps we can abandon this waltz and discuss the man who actually killed Mrs. Shedd."

"Yer now sayin' ya know who assaulted Mrs. Shedd last night?"

"We do – or at least we have a healthy suspicion about who is responsible," Caeli said. "We'll be happy to fill in all the details you'd like, although, as Max indicated, a talk with his detective friend in Limerick will help set the stage for whatever you decide to do next with regard to us and our presence here."

His by-now perpetual look of annoyance and puzzlement deepened.

"Meanin' what, exactly?"

"Meaning we'd rather work with you as cooperating witnesses to events that may have led to last night's assault instead of being treated as suspects in your investigation, which seems to be where we are now," she said.

He scowled, wrestling with Caeli's logic, thinking it through.

We sat silently, allowing him to consider the situation.

I started counting seconds in my head after the silence grew uncomfortable and got to 28 before he spoke again.

"I'm interested enough to call this friend of yers, whoever it might be – and I have me suspicions about that, mind ya," he said at last. "I also suspect he won't be happy to get the call."

Caeli and I exchanged glances again.

"DS Alan Phelan – am I right?" he said.

"His friends call him Spud," I replied, and he shook his head slowly from side to side a couple of times, as though confirmation of bad news had just floated in from an unlikely, and most unwelcome, source.

"Why did I already know that?" he muttered.

We didn't respond, thinking this time that his question was strictly rhetorical. But I still couldn't resist placing the situation into its proper perspective.

"I'm not sure I'd want to be in Spud's shoes right now," I whispered, speaking directly to Caeli.

McNeill heard me anyway.

"Right now, I'm not sure ya want to be in yer own shoes, Mister Blake – or you, Miss Brown," he said as he fished in a pocket and eventually produced a hefty police-issued mobile phone, with more bells and whistles than we were used to seeing. "But we'll see what we shall see soon enough – that I can bloody well promise."

He stabbed at a few buttons and looked away after a moment, either marking time before someone answered or drafting a plan of verbal attack, and eventually growled with conviction.

"It's McNeill. Find DS Phelan and put him on the line. Right bloody now."

TWELVE

AN UNEXPECTED WRINKLE

To say that Spud Phelan was surprised at this turn would be, I'd guess, an understatement of monumental proportions – even now, months later.

And that wasn't a third of it.

I suspect that he figured – rightly so – that we'd thrown him under the bus to save our own skins, or at least to keep us from being tossed into the Irish judicial system. But I kept coming back to the fundamental point that, even though I'd agreed to do him a quiet, nobody-needs-to-know, off-the-books favor, Joan Shedd's unanticipated murder meant that all bets, and verbal agreements, were off – especially when Caeli and I were being treated as suspects.

Here's what happened.

DCI Thomas McNeill sat stoically in place for a minute or more before Phelan was dug up from whatever sandbox he'd been digging in and scrambled to the phone. We only heard half of the exchange, but it was mildly entertaining from the outset, despite the dire circumstances.

"Phelan," McNeill snapped when his underling answered. "Tell me why a" – he consulted his notes again – "Max Blake and Caeli Brown, Americans, are sitting in front of me, trampling the grounds in Ennis, mucking up my murder investigation."

Poor Spud. That'll take some explaining, I thought.

Whatever filled McNeill's ear continued for 70 seconds, by my reckoning, and the look on the chief inspector's face changed from impatient to decidedly angry to puzzled to angry again (less so this time) and then, finally, to somewhat temporarily mollified.

That was my reckoning, anyway. Caeli's take was that McNeill looked forbidding – *stern* was the word she returned to a couple of times – throughout Phelan's windy explanation of our involvement.

McNeill eventually leaned back and stretched his ample legs beneath the table, giving me the impression that he was getting comfortable.

Looks like we're in it for the long haul, I figured, an unappealing consideration. "So yer telling me ya sent these two Yanks on a fool's errand in an effort to find the man responsible for stealing yer aunt's heirloom – correct?" he said a moment later. "And this after you'd been advised to stay well away from the doings at Bunratty."

Phelan's response wasn't nearly as lengthy this time, and McNeill nodded at times as he listened. His expression had turned from hardened to what I'd now classify as mildly intrigued.

Caeli's take this time, whispered in my ear, was that McNeill was trying not to let anything show in front of his two main suspects and was merely tolerating a fool to put the department in the best light possible.

"By fool, are you talking about Phelan or me?" I'd asked her, also whispering so that we wouldn't interrupt the main conversation taking place across the table.

"You're a bright guy, Max – mostly," she said. "You figure it out."

At least she was smiling.

Phelan eventually finished, allowing McNeill to pounce again.

"And I should recognize the Yanks as famous private detectives?" he asked, this time incredulously, a word that both of us later agreed on. "Seriously?"

He glanced at us, as though imposters had entered the room.

"I always hate it when somebody adds a *seriously*," I whispered, though Caeli ignored me.

Phelan yapped into his master's ear once more, for 33 seconds this time, while McNeill continued to stare at us, as though seeing us for the first time.

"I'd say you've got some additional explaining to do, DS Phelan," McNeill finally said. "I want to hear it – all of it. Fortunately, you'll be after talkin' to me instead of DCI Abbot."

"Abbot must be Phelan's immediate supervisor," I muttered to Caeli, although McNeill's sensitive ears picked up the observation because he flicked his wrist, as though it were obvious.

Phelan went on for a minute or more and somehow placated McNeill, judging by what came next.

"All right then, he won't hear it from me, son," McNeill said. "But my advice is to charge into his office straightaway, long before we return, and have a chat about what you've been up to with the Yanks. We're in a murder investigation, after all – not the kind of thing that's easily swept away with a missing ring, is it now?"

The usual bobbing and weaving of signing off took place next, and McNeill cut the connection and shook his head for a brief moment while staring at the table top, as though trying to will away an ugly reality, before returning his attention to us.

"It seems ye have a history of sorts with DS Phelan, Mister Blake. Or should I call ya Professor Blake, crusading journalist, private detective, and, judging by my sergeant's gushing report, noted author?"

"Call me Max," I said.

"We'll see about that in due course, won't we?" he said. "And what of you, Miss Brown? I hear that you, too, are a former journalist, an esteemed private detective, and a famous capturer of serial killers, as well as being the niece of the late Archbishop of Armagh, god rest his weary soul. Have I left anything out?"

"Only that we're both retired, and I'm told that I'm an excellent cook," Caeli said, smiling evenly.

I wanted to interrupt with a testament to Caeli's culinary skills, but McNeill, pressing on, didn't seem to be a man who appreciated a light moment.

"We can sort that out in time, perhaps, the three of us, as there seems to be quite the story to tell. I for one want very much to hear it," he said. "But we've a pesky murder standin' between us and that time of enlightenment, I'm afraid. Don't ya agree?"

He didn't give us time to respond.

"So then, I'll ask ya both to accompany me to the Limerick station and see if we can make some sense of what young Phelan just passed along, especially as it concerns yer participation in events that may well provide the identity of a suspect in Mrs. Shedd's tragic demise," he said. "Would that be agreeable?"

"As opposed to, say, being placed under arrest?" I asked, only half-kidding.

That remark was rewarded with what I'd call another dour frown – a look that McNeill was adept at displaying.

"I don't see the need to arrest ya presently, nor even caution ya to yer right to seek a solicitor's advice," he said. "Understand, I'm extendin' a courtesy while I weigh the information DS Phelan passed along – with a need for verification, of course. Ye can do that, I take it?"

"Do what, exactly? Verify Phelan's account of whatever he told you?" Caeli asked.

"Yes. Quite."

"We'll need to know his actual comments, of course, but sure, we can do that," Caeli said pleasantly.

"I'd like to hear it fresh, without DS Phelan's gushings, but … grand. Let's be off then," he said.

He stood and waved his hand, beckoning, much as Ahab did to the crew of the Pequod while ensnared in the ropes attached to his great white whale.

"Please," he said. "I'll do me best to keep it all manageable and have an officer return ya here when we're through."

"You want us to ride with you?" I asked as we shuffled around the table and out the door, heading toward the hospital's main entrance.

"Most certainly."

"Why don't we follow you to the station house instead?" I suggested. "That'll save everyone valuable time, us included, with no need to send anyone out this way on our account. We live west of Limerick and south of the Shannon."

"I'm afraid that I …"

I figured that he was going to add the obligatory "... must insist," but he stopped for whatever reason and looked us over again.

"I can trust ya then?" he said, and he might have hidden the slightest of smiles in the question.

I had to laugh.

"I take it you never saw *The X Files*," I said.

When he looked confused, Caeli stepped in.

"You can trust us, DCI McNeill. We're happy to help – both of us are. Isn't that right, Max?"

"Of course," I said and mostly meant it.

We left the hospital in short order and walked to the Cadillac. I hit the key fob, unlocking the doors, and the car chirped in reply.

"That's yours then?"

"It is," I said. "How 'bout I race you back to Limerick?"

His look matched Caeli's this time, and I laughed at their near-identical reactions.

"Just kidding."

"I'll drive," Caeli said and angled to the correct side. She glanced at McNeil, pausing before climbing in. "I'll follow you? Max is hopeless when it comes to using the GPS."

"Outed again," I said as McNeill told us (it sounds more polite than ordered us) to wait while he retrieved his own vehicle. He appeared a moment later in an unmarked Ford sedan and waved at us before merging into traffic on the N18, moving slowly and checking his rearview mirror more than was necessary to ensure that we were there – a pattern he employed all the way to Limerick.

I can report that with certainty because Caeli felt obligated to stick close.

"Anyone following us?" she asked once we were on the road.

"At least one car, likely unmarked police," I said after a moment later. "Guess he doesn't trust us after all."

We chatted back and forth during the drive, and Caeli was clearly rattled by Joan Shedd's death. I once again apologized for placing us in the middle of things, adding that Mrs. Shedd would be alive if I'd declined Phelan's request for help. She was gracious enough to brush it aside.

"I've yet to meet your friend, you know. Hope he's worth the fuss," she said.

"Then it's Spud's lucky day because I'll bet he's present during our pending interrogation," I said. "More to the point, something tells me he'll need some luck by the time we're done."

"The same might well apply to us before we're through, Max," she said.

But sadly, I didn't pay her line a moment's heed.

We eventually parked in front of the dark brick building that housed Limerick's *Garda* operation and waited for McNeill on the steps leading inside.

"Thanks again for comin' along," he said after stashing his car.

But I suspect that he was thinking something more along the line of, *Thanks for being compliant and not forcing me to loose the hounds* – if not the dogs of war.

Still, he was welcoming as he led us down a lengthy corridor and into a room occupied by four other members of the Guards, including my friend Alan Phelan.

And yeah, I wondered whether that remained true.

But Spud stood as soon as we entered and rushed over to shake hands with Caeli, fairly gushing as he made his approach.

"Ah, it's Caeli Brown then. Jaysus, but it's good to connect a face to yer voice," he said. "Lovely to finally meet ya, though I feel as though I've known ya forever."

He dialed his voice down a couple of notches and added, "Call me Spud – I'd be pleased if ya did. But you'd best not do it here, right now – not with all the brass about."

He beamed an overly bright smile, pumped her hand up and down a couple of times too many, and eventually let her go, reluctantly, I thought, and extended a greeting in my direction, though his eyes lingered on Caeli for a moment longer.

"Professor Blake," he said next, speaking this time for the room. "So good to see ya once more. Let me introduce the two of ya then – I trust that's agreeable to all here."

The room contained a lengthy table and accompanying chairs spaced around it, with shelves along one wall, a mini-refrigerator, a bookcase filled with binders containing legal material, and a back wall featuring a picture window of dark glass that served as a mirror.

"I'll bet we're being watched," I whispered to Caeli.

"Probably filmed as well," she said, leaning in close to my ear.

In short order, we shook hands and exchanged polite hellos with DCI Declan Abbot, Phelan's direct boss; Chief Superintendent David Sheehan, who was in charge of the Limerick branch of the Guards; and District Detective Superintendent James Ryne, who apparently was Sheehan's boss.

For what it's worth, the *An Garda Síochána*, or Guardians of the Peace, serve as the country's police force. You'll hear its members called both *Garda* and *Gardi* in Irish, or simply the Guards in English. Its headquarters is in Phoenix Park in Dublin, with all of Ireland's major cities hosting a local branch.

DCI McNeill took charge once the introductions were over and brought the upper echelon up to speed on the murder case he was ramrodding. I was surprised, as was Caeli, that so many upper-level big-wigs were interested in the case – and so quickly. But I soon figured that because an American tourist was the unfortunate victim, the Dublin brass was being overly cautious in covering the necessary bases.

Then again, maybe they're concerned because they've been blowing this threat off for some time now …

Sheehan and Ryne sat quietly by during McNeill's briefing, allowing a consumate professional to lay out the fact without unnecessary meddling or questioning. Given the number of meetings I'd attended while working in the newspaper business that were taken over by bottom-line publishers who insisted on running every facet of important stories, most always to the detriment of the coverage, this was a welcome change. (The same can be said, by the way, for my time in academia, where meddlers and know-it-alls and micromanagers, as well as the snooty *I'm-smarter-than-you* types, hovered and sniped at most every gathering.)

McNeill next turned the spotlight on Phelan, asking him to bring the assembled personnel up to date "on how, exactly, our distinguished guests from the wilds of far-flung America were brought onto the case."

If you haven't figured it out, he was talking about Caeli and me – and he wasn't being kind to Spud.

He stood, fidgeting with his hands, and launched into a passionate recounting of what had happened to the family ring, and how he'd been told to leave the case to others because of his close ties to the victims of the theft, but that he couldn't let it go entirely, given the sentimental nature of the heirloom and, far worse, the devastation its loss had caused both his mother and his aunt, and how he later determined – in his own mind, at least – that if he hired someone who was not connected to the Guards in any way to do a bit of poking around, he would technically be fulfilling the directive to stay out of the way while still aiding his family.

"Go ahead and draw a breath, Spud," I whispered as encouragement, which made Caeli smile, at least.

He followed up his rambling introduction with another lengthy statement. I'm able to provide a word-for-word account because I'd activated the app on my phone that turns it into a recorder.

"But here's the bit that's likely of interest, ya see. It's only when I remembered from readin' one of his many fine books that the two of 'em was movin' into the big Fierro estate west of town that I took the chance to introduce meself and see if I might entice 'em to take a look and maybe recover the ring and the rest of it and, well, solve the bloody case. They're really quite the pair, ya see – brilliant. All ya need to do is read the professor's books."

Spud looked on expectantly, trusting that his enthusiasm might be catching and reflected back at him.

But the bosses eyed him suspiciously, or at least skeptically, and remained silent for a long enough period that he eventually sat down with a thud.

It rhymes with Spud, I thought as I connected the dots in my head and figured that we could buy him dinner and drinks when we'd finished.

And maybe even serve as a reference once he's been summarily dismissed from the force – which should be coming any time now.

"Should we offer him a job as a wedding planner?" I whispered to Caeli.

Her response was a decidedly withering glance that I pretended to ignore.

At this point, McNeill made eye contact with Abbot to determine if he wanted to say anything. When Abbot waved him off with a flick of his index finger and a scowl, I knew that Spud was in for an old-fashioned ass-chewing, after the fact, and that we were up next to explain our part in what eventually led us to where we were, which was sitting in a police station in Limerick, stared at by four expectant coppers.

"All right then," McNeill said. "How 'bout the two of ya fill in the blanks now, as appropriate, so we can determine where we concentrate our limited resources to get to the bottom of this sordid business – shall we? Professor Blake then: How 'bout we start with you?"

I stated for the record that because DS Phelan and I were guilty of the initial conspiracy – "and it's not his fault at all, mind you. That rests entirely on my shoulders because I was bored and looking for something meaningful to do" – my fiancée would do the honors.

If you think that my intro got a strange look from the assembled police brass, you should've caught the expression on Caeli's face – a condensed version of *You'll pay for that, mister,* fired squarely at me – before she provided a by-the-numbers recitation of facts, at which she excels.

Spud, at least, was happy.

Caeli's recounting took little more than a couple of minutes. She explained that we took a break from the many tasks we had to accomplish before our pending wedding (the revelation elicited perfunctory congratulatory comments) to visit Bunratty "because we hadn't been there in a while and were looking forward to the feast."

"You didn't go just to satisfy the needs of DS Phelan then?" Abbot asked while thumping a rigid finger on the table.

"If Max wanted to help a friend along the way, that was fine with me, given what was at stake for his mother and his aunt," Caeli said. "I know how wretched I'd feel if someone poached a precious heirloom. I'm sure your wife would say the same, sir."

Phelan looked as though he was about to leap across the table and hug her.

She then laid out our initial sighting of a likely suspect, our quick visit inside the pawnbroker's shop to determine whether this was in fact the right guy, the open window and eavesdropping that followed, and her collision with Mrs. Shedd as we left the shop, which led to the guy's disappearance.

At no time did she refer to him as Mister Denmark.

"We figured that it was all over – or at least our part in it," Caeli said. "We could give DS Phelan an exact location and a specific time for him to check the CCTV cameras and ID the perp, which eventually would lead to the return of his family's treasures, as well as getting a thief off the tourist circuit, making everyone happy. We spoke with Joan after the miscreant bolted and hit it off, so we invited her to attend the feast with us. We already had tickets, as did Joan, and she was alone – her husband abandoned her ahead of the trip. It seemed like the logical thing to do."

Caeli asked for some water, Phelan was quick to produce a handful of bottles from the mini-fridge behind him, which he distributed around the table, and Abbot got us started once more.

"And your visit today, Miss Brown – the one that's now landed you here?" he said. "Was that merely another opportunity to take a break from your pre-wedding tasks?"

I figured that he was playing the snark card for no good reason and wanted to fire back a shot or two. But Caeli was too quick, and far too polite.

"Exactly," she said. "We'd put in a busy morning. Max suggested that we get a bite for lunch, and then we learned from DS Phelan that Mrs. Shedd had been assaulted at her hotel, sometime after we'd packed her into the cab for Dromoland. We felt terrible – worse than you can imagine – and wanted to see how she was doing and let her know that we'd reached out to our contacts in the States to locate her children and let them know what had happened."

"We stopped at Bunratty for lunch because it's on the way," I added quickly.

Abbot picked up the more vital thread.

"Just so you know, Irish authorities are reachin' out to Mrs. Shedd's relatives as we speak. There's no need for ye to be after pokin' yer nose in business that's not yer concern a'tall," he said. "But then, it seems the pair of ya 'ave a knack for findin' yerself in all manner of … things."

He didn't offer that last observation as a compliment, and I'll admit it: The guy was starting to grind on me.

"I'm not sure how you'd know that with certainty, sir. But even if you think it's true, we also have a knack for producing results," I said. "You'll note that after a single visit to the Folk Park, we were able to provide you with a suspect, not only for the robberies – plural – that have taken place there but also for what's sadly turned into a murder."

I wasn't looking for congratulations. And yeah, Caeli hadn't even gotten to the part about running into the devious bastard in the parking lot and the confrontation that quickly followed, which would have demonstrated just how dangerous this guy was and why quickly dispatching him to a jail cell was imperative.

Instead, the four hot-shot coppers exchanged looks of concern, and I guessed again that Phelan was going to have a tough go of it once we were dismissed.

If we get dismissed ...

But I still didn't have it quite right.

DDS James Ryne, the big boss in the room who'd been silent until now, slowly stood, quite formally, and addressed the two of us as though he were the head master at the finishing school we attended and was duty-bound to tell us that we were being booted out for not properly making our beds.

"I'm afraid, Professor Blake, Miss Brown, that your rather unfortunate intrusion into this affair, even with the earnest if misguided efforts of DS Phelan to bring ya along, has had some unintended consequences regarding an ongoing investigation that we, along with other agencies, have been conducting at Bunratty, and I am not referencing Mrs. Shedd's unfortunate demise," he said. "I am loathe to inform you that, due to the nature of this inquiry, I am not at liberty to explain to you what we've been looking into exactly and why your presence and interference, for lack of a better word, however well-intended, is so damaging. It's a matter of national security, ya see, which is absolutely as much as I am authorized to say. This is also the reason why DS Phelan was told – in no uncertain terms, I might add – to stand down."

I waited for more, but there wasn't any.

Yeah, exactly. Talk about a kick in the teeth. Not only were we suddenly *persona non grata* with the Limerick Guards, but we wouldn't even be able to learn why. Caeli and I exchanged glances, and we both automatically began formulating questions that we knew would never be answered – not by Ryne, anyway.

But that's precisely the moment when Liam Gallacher, a wolf in sheep's clothing from our *Emerald Ridge* case, entered the room through a side door that I hadn't even noticed previously and sidled up next to Ryne, directing him with a simple wave to sit.

"I'll handle the briefing from here," Gallacher said. "I've worked with this pair before, ya see, and have every reason to believe that not only can we trust 'em, gentlemen, but they also can be of some use to us."

Yup. Ryne didn't see that coming. Neither did Sheehan, nor Abbot, nor McNeill. How could they?

Spud, too, was left with a decidedly curious look etched into the lines of his face.

As for Caeli and me, well, we, too, were caught flat-footed, especially when he settled in and let us all have it, straight from the top.

But things only got stranger from there.

THIRTEEN

A PIECE OF THE PIE

We'd first met the dapper Irish special branch operative more than a year earlier, during what might best be described as trying times. We were attempting to save Caeli's Uncle Jack, the former archbishop, from himself and his many sins, and Liam Gallacher (with some urging from the home front) had been kind enough to toss us a lifeline at a crucial moment.

On second thought, he'd actually tossed us more than a few lifelines.

He remained trim, fit, well-dressed in a sport coat with dark slacks (minus the tie), his graying hair neatly cut, with teeth that gleamed and shoes that were buffed to a prodigious shine – pretty much what you'd expect for an Irish spook. He beamed at us for a lingering moment, as though he'd bumped unexpectedly into long-time friends, before swinging around the length of the conference table to greet us, extending his hand, first to Caeli and then to me.

We both stood, genuine surprise evident on our faces. I know that because I was damn near bowled over at the sight of the man, and Caeli, from my vantage point, anyway, appeared to be damn near gobstruck.

"It's grand to see ya both – truly," he said, and he sounded as though he meant every word.

Caeli responded with something that I didn't catch, likely because I was still too stunned by his arrival to concentrate properly.

The best that I could manage?

"Where the hell did you come from? And what the hell are you even doing here?"

He barked out a laugh, dazzling us with another wide smile that must've been mildly reassuring to the assembled police brass who were no doubt wondering what was taking place, right along with me. They'd been grimly running the show, after all, conducting a murder investigation that had been compromised by a pair of pesky Yanks who had no good reason to be involved – and now this.

Whatever this is …

That refrain kept running through my head as we stared at Gallacher in disbelief and he grinned back at us as though he'd just returned from the shores of Loch Ness with video of its famous if elusive prehistoric occupant.

Or so they claim in Scotland.

Sheehan blinked first.

"Excuse me, sir," he said, sounding as tentative as the guy who stumbles into the wrong meeting and realizes that the boss is giving away his job. "I must confess to being more than a little …"

He struggled to find the right phrase, but the look on his face delivered his message of confusion and concern well enough.

"I understand, David," Gallacher said. "Let's let it play out … shall we?"

Sheehan appeared as though he was inclined to register a fervent protest and glanced at Ryne for confirmation of his indignation. But the big boss said nothing, and Sheehan took his cue there and let it go – at least momentarily.

I wasn't going to let it go, however. I wanted answers and explanations, and I didn't want to wait.

"Liam Gallacher? Seriously? What brings you here?" I said. "And what the hell is going on, exactly?"

He laughed again, heartily.

"At least the pair of ya aren't runnin' with mobsters from all sides of the Atlantic this time around – a decided improvement," he said.

"How do you know for certain?" Caeli asked. She has long bristled at any finger pointed toward our old benefactor, Don

Vincenzo Fierro, and she wasn't about to let Gallacher get away with an easy shot, even in fun.

I jumped in as well.

"Alleged mobsters," I said.

If Gallacher was troubled by our response, he didn't let it show. His eyes instead sparked with mischief, as though he'd been baiting us.

"I know far more than ya think, which should come as no surprise a'tall," he said.

But he offered nothing more concrete than that – not then, at least. And he must have noticed the dark, questioning expression on my face, a look that I dredged up from my reporting days … the one that demanded an immediate explanation of his presence.

"We'll get to it, all right – all in good time."

We'd first met when he was posing as the *major domo* at Castle Ballygarvan, a massive private estate near Cork that had housed Caeli and me, along with our traveling retinue of bodyguards supplied by our friend Don Vincenzo. Our patron was on his death bed at the time, not that we knew it, extending us one last line of aid. And yeah, this is the same Don Vincenzo who gave us the deed to our Limerick estate.

But it turned out that Gallacher wasn't a gofer at a luxury castle accommodating an upper-end clientele on short notice – not in the slightest. We discovered as we were leaving Ireland in a late-night rush that he was a muckety-muck at G2, the Irish Directorate of Military Intelligence, which is responsible for the safety and security of all defense forces and the island's national safekeeping as a whole.

For what it's worth, G2 is Ireland's equivalent of the FBI and Britain's MI-5 and doesn't maintain a high profile. Finding reliable information about the organization is damn near impossible.

We also were fairly certain that Gallacher wasn't his real name, though we never got confirmation, during or after the time we'd spent running around the Irish countryside in pursuit of Caeli's uncle, the one-time archbishop of Armagh, a man intent on violently overthrowing Britain's hold on Ulster while dragging Ireland into a guerrilla war with its longtime nemesis.

Yeah, I know –crazy stuff. Worse, we never got the chance to ask Don Vincenzo about how he'd arranged for G2 to keep an eye on us while we traipsed across Ireland in search of Uncle Jack and his revolutionaries. Hell, we barely had time to say goodbye once we returned to Oregon.

What Gallacher was doing here now, in Limerick, jumping into a meeting with us when we hadn't heard a word, either from him or about him, since leaving the country many months previous, was a hell of a mystery.

"That nasty wound to yer face seems to 've healed nicely, Professor Blake," he said as he waved us into our seats. "Quite the trophy scar – gives ya a man-of-the-world look."

"I'm not a fan," I said of the scar, a legacy of being struck by shrapnel kicked up by machine gun fire during the battle with Caeli's uncle's forces on Mutton Island.

"As with all things, it fades with time," Gallacher said. "I must say, again, it's lovely to see the pair of ya – you especially, Miss Brown. Ya look grand, as always."

He offered this last part as though we'd last seen one another days previous and dropped into an empty chair immediately next to Caeli.

"But things are not as they seem, and timing, I believe, is everything – especially now, in these dark days," he said. "And here the two of ye are then, findin' yer way to us in our own hour of need."

Yeah, that was Gallacher, all right – a master at lobbing verbal bombs. This one reminded me of a couple of the gems he'd unloaded the last time we crossed paths.

But he laughed when he again caught the looks of disbelief that registered on our faces, and he rubbed his hands together in anticipation of things to come and called for refreshments for the room, flashing his teeth, using his charm.

"Some biscuits, maybe – and more water, to be sure, and fizzy drinks for our American friends," he said. "Diet Cokes, as I recall – right?"

"Your memory is as good as your disguises, or at least as good as your many identities," Caeli said as DS Phelan, with a nudge from his commanding officer, reluctantly got up and ambled out the door, his eyes on Gallacher the whole time, clearly upset that he'd be missing part of the action. "I'm guessing that you are incognito now?"

She offered the line in question form, inviting him to elaborate on his presence at the table and especially to determine whether the *Garda* brass in the room knew his true affiliation, if not his true identity. But the opportunity to come clean merely made him laugh again, and I realized that we'd seen him smile more in a matter of minutes than he had during the entire time we'd been at Castle Ballygarvan and then again at the airport during our last encounter, when he'd revealed his true affiliation.

"No need. It's all good, as you Yanks put things," he said. "An' to answer yer questions, Miss Brown, two of the gentlemen here were brought up to speed before yer arrival – no need to concern yerself with tellin' tales out of school. We'd notice ye were comin' in, ya see, once DCI McNeill radioed the details of yer involvement in the unfortunate Dromoland situation. Despite the tragedy, I can't tell ya how delighted I was to hear yer names again."

"I'll bet," I muttered, though he didn't respond. Gallacher was intent on getting to the point.

"As it happens, we seem to be after the same individual, one we've had our eye on for some time," he said.

"We, being G2?" I asked, feeling that we needed to get that on the table and have him acknowledge the fact.

"Quite," he said.

But we weren't going to get the rest of it right away. He glanced toward the door, as though hopeful that Phelan would scurry in with an armful of cookies and Cokes and bottled water and assorted other delights – the kind of feast that the staff at Castle Ballygarvan routinely laid out for us during our stay.

As it turned out, much of that staff was working for G2.

"So then, how've the pair of ya been since last we spoke?" he asked, killing time. "I see you've acquired the Fierro estate on the Shannon and are – what? – living the life of the retired gentry. True?"

"You already seem to know the answer," Caeli said, which triggered another grin.

"Yes. I suppose," he said. But he caught us flat-footed when he followed that with a startling revelation.

"You know I was instrumental in the clearances ye eventually obtained from the republic to live here – moving into a reputed mobster's manor house and all? It was touch and go for a time, you'll recall, with yer own State Department involved and a great many questions asked and few answers attached, for obvious reasons, seeing as … well, we all mostly know what happened back then."

"I don't," DCI McNeill protested.

"Nor do I," DCI Abbot said. "And I'd like to hear it."

But Gallacher merely grinned, sweeping his hand across the table as though removing specks of dust.

"Tales for another day, gentlemen," he said, directing the line to the two inspectors before again returning his attention to us. "Just think of my involvement in yer moving adventures as a little gift for the help ya provided, however unwittingly, during the episode with Miss Brown's troublesome uncle."

I recalled the red tape that we'd run into ahead of our move to Ireland, which included a number of insistent visits from representatives of both nations once we'd declared our intention to live in the estate that had been built a decade earlier for Vincenzo Fierro. Things were on the bubble until the Irish government eventually acquiesced, for reasons we'd never understood … until now, anyway.

"That was you?" Caeli asked.

He nodded.

"How were we to know that?"

"Ya weren't," he said. "I'm telling ya now because, well, it's the first I've seen ya in … how long's it been, exactly? Seems like forever – or yesterday. My, but the time does indeed scurry past us."

I wasn't buying it.

"My guess is you're telling us now because you want something," I said. "Any comment to that?"

Gallacher smiled but didn't reply, determining how much he wanted to admit to, perhaps. Then Phelan tapped on the door and came in with an armful of bottled water. Another officer followed, carrying a tray containing a half-dozen Cokes and a selection of cookies and some paper napkins.

"No pastries then – nor cheese?" Gallacher asked, though he received no reply.

"Thanks very much, the two of ya," Ryne said as the tray and water bottles were deposited. "That'll be all for now, lads."

Phelan was ready to protest, but it was clear that Ryne wasn't a man to be argued with. Spud glanced in my direction with a look that said, essentially, *You must tell me everything,* and reluctantly followed the second copper out the door.

"All right then. It's not me place, exactly, but help yerself to a bit of freshen-up," Gallacher said. "Then we can get straight to it in earnest."

He grabbed a couple of cookies, along with a water bottle, and appeared content.

"What do you think?" Caeli whispered as she leaned in close.

"I have no idea," I said. "But I can't wait to find out what he's up to."

The break didn't last long, likely because Ryne was impatient to determine what Gallacher was up to – especially as it concerned his department and its relationship with the two Yanks who'd just been recruited to assist with a murder investigation.

If body language was any indication, he wasn't pleased.

"I trust ye can put a good light on this business," Ryne said once the goodies were distributed. He'd tried to keep the edge from his voice, I thought, and mostly succeeded. Still, you could detect his concern when he followed up with another icy line, before Gallacher responded to his first entreaty.

"I must say, for the life of me, I'm not seein' the benefits – not as they apply to my outfit, especially after what's taken place at Dromoland and Bunratty. Tell me I'm wrong."

"All right, but only because ya asked: Yer wrong, my friend," Gallacher said. "But not nearly so much as ya think."

Ryne looked on blankly.

"I'm not sure I follow …"

"I'm not surprised a'tall," Gallacher replied, enjoying himself. "So I'll lay it out as I see things. Then we can parse the lot of it from there. Satisfactory?"

Sheehan, McNeill, and Abbot each mumbled their assent, with deferential glances toward the larger police presence in the room. But Ryne was troubled.

"Are ya really certain it's all right to proceed with these two in the room?" he said, waving his hand toward us. "We're talkin' highly sensitive information here."

Gallacher, grinning, was happy to give him some line, just to see how far he'd tug it.

Ryne cracked open a Coke and poured the contents into a glass, dragging it out, either for dramatic effect or to determine exactly what he wanted to say next. He got there a moment later, after a high-octane gulp.

"I must say I'm uncomfortable with this," he said. "We're entertaining civilians here – Yanks at that, at least until a couple of months ago."

Gallacher frowned, his facade of easy-go-lucky charm at an end, apparently. I'm not even sure why he'd adopted it when he arrived. Maybe he was trying to sell Caeli and me to the assembled coppers in the best possible light, and he figured that his embrace of our presence would do that. Then again, maybe he was playing a long game that none of us understood. Or maybe he just had a wild hair that needed shaving on this day, and he was fresh out of sharp blades.

"It's all right, boyo," he said. "It 'tis."

When Ryne looked as though he wanted to jump in again, Gallacher cut him off.

"Right then," he said. "I'll cover the necessary details as though no one knows any of this – and in the case of our American friends, that's mostly the case. One other thing: What's recounted in this room stays here and isn't mentioned again to anyone … including DS Phelan, who'll no doubt press Professor Blake for the full story as soon as we're done."

He gulped some water and got to it.

"G2's tracked a terror cell for weeks now – a segment of which is operatin' close by," he said. "We believe it's run by a Frenchman, with a code name of Frog One. To date, he's recruited a gaggle of mercenaries, well-trained and like-minded, active on multiple fronts, which has required our working with a variety of other agencies, from the Continent and Britain as well as across the pond."

He took a deep breath and frowned noticeably, as though what he was about to offer next was exasperating.

"I'd like to think our partners are fully open with us – providing us with details we're in need of to act accordingly and stop this madness," he said. "But I have my doubts, and it concerns me."

He paused again, giving us time to process.

"Even so, we know that a handful of the recruits Frog One has pulled together for whatever he's planning are Irish – including, we believe, the sorry excuse for an ex- soldier who's been operatin' out of Bunratty these past weeks, stealin' from tourists. Why he's doing that, exactly, we've no idea – at least not yet."

A soldier ... military boots ...

"Maybe it's to help fund whatever operation Frog One has in mind," Ryne said, interrupting Gallacher's recitation of facts – a move that caught the spook by surprise. I got the distinct impression that he didn't appreciate the interruption.

He was doubly surprised when a second member of the Guards chimed in.

"Ah, good on ya, sir – that'd make sense," Abbot said. "We're talkin' big-ticket items here, gems and the like that are worth a bit."

Gallacher smiled thinly as Sheehan also offered his opinion.

"Maybe he's simply tryin' to line his own pockets, which makes as much sense," he said.

Ryne and Abbot muttered their disagreement, and the three men seemed ready to take over the discussion entirely.

"Anybody else?" Gallacher asked. "Other thoughts before I go on?"

"Yes sir," McNeill said. "Do you mean to indicate you've an ID on a suspect in the murder of the American woman? And further, can I gather you could've taken this bastard off the board well ahead of the business at Dromoland?"

"We'll get to that, DCI McNeill – every bit of it, though maybe not to yer likin'," Gallacher said.

McNeill scowled, apparently ready to disagree, but a single glance from Ryne stopped him.

Caeli also shifted uncomfortably at the admission, but she didn't respond. I figured that would come later as well.

Instead of forging ahead, Gallacher belted down more water, looking grim in one moment and pleased in the next. I wondered again what game he was playing, and why, and what it had to do with us.

On his next pass, he addressed the *Garda* officers exclusively, ignoring our presence. He even turned his back to us.

"I could spend the next hour explainin' why I believe our American friends are right for the job I have in mind," he said. "But I know yer all professionals, so it won't be necessary – and I don't have the time anyway. Still, yer cooperation's required. I very much ask – nay, demand – that ye treat 'em as equals and not as bloody foreigners. I was thrilled when I heard their names in DS McNeill's radio report, for reasons that'll soon become apparent. But I'll mention, for starters, this much: They think unconventionally and produce results in unexpected ways. I've seen it firsthand."

He glanced our way for an instant.

"I'll waste no more words or time, gentlemen, as both are in limited supply. Let me offer this instead. Some of those now involved in Frog One's operation were, until a short time ago, associates of the Very Rev. Sean O'Lennox, late of Armagh, the one-time archbishop of the cathedral there, and as you've already heard, Miss Brown's uncle – on her mother's side, I believe."

He glanced toward Caeli for an acknowledgement, which she provided with a nod.

"What ye may not know, contrary to what ya read or heard at the time about the archbishop's heroic death, is that he is, in fact, very much alive, livin' in Rome under the protection of the church and out of the reach of mere mortals."

The reaction was immediate.

"Yer joking, surely," Sheehan said, speaking for all the brass.

"Not a'tall," Gallacher replied. "Perhaps Miss Brown can confirm?"

Caeli glanced at Gallacher, and then at me for just an instant, before she turned her attention to the rapt members of Ireland's national police force.

"It's true," she said. "You can get the details in Max's most recent book … just published."

"For the love o' Christ," Abbot muttered.

Gallacher smiled.

"I'm not sure anybody's love has much to do with it, but I can tell ya this: We've every intention of breakin' this cell, and we could use the archbishop's help in makin' that happen. We've had no way of gettin' to him, of course … until now. My proposal is for the Yanks to help us knock down the Vatican's doors."

Yup. Pretty much what I thought, too.

I had a strange dream that night.

I was with my cousin Tim, my mother's older sister's eldest son, and we were driving in his car along Oregon's Hwy. 101, which follows the coastline. I'd been staring out the window, relishing the passing scene, and was suddenly struck by the fact that the stunning views I was enjoying weren't available from the road. When I looked more carefully, we were swooping above the waves like a seagull, darting toward rocky cliffs in one moment and then back out across the great expanse of ocean, rising with a lurch that made me gasp.

"What do you think of the flying car?" Tim said when he heard my startled cry. "It cost a million and change, but the damn thing sure soars. You should get one."

I wondered later whether the dream had something to do with the fact that Tim was the best man at my first wedding, years before, a union that lasted mere months, and the date that Caeli and I would exchange vows was fast approaching.

My uneasiness awoke Caeli, and she asked if I was all right. I didn't tell her about the dream, but she sensed a disturbance in the gears of time and space. She took my arm and pulled herself close and whispered in my ear.

"I wasn't exactly on board with this whole thing, not in the beginning – not with the wedding so close. But after what's happened to Joan, I'm in – all the way. We need to get her killer, regardless of this other business."

This much I know: Give Caeli a cause and you'll find a wonderful ally. Mess with someone she cares about and you won't find a more tenacious enemy.

FOURTEEN

SOME ADDITIONAL PLOTTING

The man we knew as Liam Gallacher was knocking on the front door to our home early the next morning. And by early, I'm talking about damn early … well before 5 a.m.

We didn't realize that it was the G2 operative straight away. That took moments of stumbling and grumbling on my part. We also didn't realize that his arrival would usher in the start of the longest day we'd put in since … well, since Ronald Reagan was shot when we'd both worked as reporters, back in the day when people actually read a newspaper to get the latest news.

"What the hell is that?" I mumbled when the racket initially began. I'd managed to open an eye and check the alarm clock, groaning after staring at the digital readout, ensuring that what I was seeing was actually what I was seeing.

"*Who* is more likely," Caeli muttered and turned away from me, pulling the covers with her.

"Huh?" was all I could manage.

"You said what … '*What* the hell is that?' It's evident that someone's at the door. So '*Who* the hell is that?' makes more sense … don't you think?"

She purred the words.

Then again, my addled brain made me wonder whether I was listening to Koko, who often sleeps beside her.

I checked the time again as another round of door-pounding invaded the splendid silence of what promised be an otherwise glorious morning. The clatter was instantly followed by an aggressive attack on the doorbell, which our unwelcome visitor must have just now discovered.

"Will I ever be delivered?" I sputtered and rolled out of bed, steadying myself before stumbling to the closet to grab a robe.

"Doubtful," Caeli replied, though softly, and I had the feeling that she was already falling asleep.

"Don't worry, dear," I said, tightly cinching the robe. "I'll find out who it is, not what … take care of it … send 'em packing … whatever."

I heard some additional sounds that may have been Caeli's voice, or perhaps it was just the rustling covers as she and Koko again shifted positions. Either way, I trekked down the stairs, cursing as another barrage of door-banging and bell-ringing began in earnest.

I thought seriously about sticking it to the bastard, whoever it was, and heading straight back to bed.

He'll let it go eventually … figure we're not at home … just go away …

I also thought, albeit briefly, about turning about to get one of the police batons that we keep in the bedroom. In the old days, I would have automatically grabbed a Walther P99 before answering such incessant banging at such an ungodly hour. But we weren't granted that amenity in Ireland, and Caeli's duly registered shotgun was secured in a gun safe in the study.

"Might have to fix that – move the safe," I muttered.

I groaned when I eventually glared through the security lens and spotted a man resembling Liam Gallacher staring back at me, rolling his wrist over in a *Hurry-it-up* motion.

"For god's sake, man," he called, loudly enough to be heard through the door. "An' here I thought you'd be long since up."

"Are you completely mental?" I asked as I disarmed the security system, threw open the door, and started back for the stairs.

"I've been told that," he said as he rumbled inside. "More than once. I need the jacks – thought I was going to lose it out there. Too much coffee this morning. Where's yer nearest?"

"Down the hall, on your left," I said without interest and trudged toward the stairs. "Let yourself out. Lock up before you leave."

I could hear him racing down the hall, his boots thumping on the marble floor as he scurried along. But I didn't care about Gallacher's unexpected visit, or his current plight, and made it back to the bedroom in short order, crawling into the still-toasty sheets and doing my best to regain a share of the covers without disturbing either Caeli or Koko.

I wasn't successful.

"Who was at the door?" Caeli asked.

"Liam Gallacher."

"What did he want?"

"The bathroom."

A lengthy silence ensued, and I was about to doze off – or perhaps I'd already drifted into sleep – when Caeli nudged me.

"He came out here to use the bathroom?"

"Yes."

She was quiet for another moment before she spoke again.

"Where is he now?"

"Probably gone. I told him to let himself out."

"You what?"

"Don't worry," I said. "I also told him to lock the door."

She fully shifted positions, disturbing the cat in the process, turning to face me. Koko, annoyed, walked over my head and jumped down from the bed with a feathery flight, sashaying away, her pads softly skimming the hardwood floor. I could see her tail flashing this way and that, a clear sign that she wasn't happy.

"Max – don't you think he may want something, once he's finished?"

"He didn't say he wanted anything – just that he needed the jacks."

"Even so, there must be more to it – especially after yesterday," she persisted.

"Then he should come at a decent hour … call ahead, make an appointment. It's what civilized people do."

I'd buried my head beneath the covers and was muttering instead of talking forcefully. I wonder in retrospect whether Caeli could hear me.

But she followed after Koko a moment later, gently rolling out of bed, and I didn't wake for another 20 minutes, when the smell of fresh coffee hit me like a gut-punch. I'm not a coffee drinker, mind you – can't stand the taste. But it smells wonderful, a splendid celebration of the senses, and it rousted me out of the sack and down the stairs.

"There you are, Max – right on time," Caeli said, too kindly, and she looked radiant, as always.

I kissed her cheek and spotted Gallacher leaning against the kitchen island, coffee mug in hand, a smirk covering his face. Koko, the heinous little traitor, was winding herself around his feet, purring contentedly.

"Always thought I'd retire one day," he said when I mumbled a greeting. "But after seein' ya this morning, twice now, I'm rethinkin' that strategy entirely. Might stay on 'til they haul me off in a box."

"Funny," I said, though I meant the opposite. "It's clear you lost your way this morning to end up here. Forget your watch, too, along with a GPS signal?"

"Hey, don't start at me," he said, bending to reward Koko with an ear-scratch. "I've been at it all night, long after we sent ya off from Henry Street. After our little chat, I figured you'd be up early, concoctin' a dozen plans to connect with Caeli's uncle, or to end the scourge of terrorism, or at least determine a way to rescue the family jewels that seem to so obsess poor DS Phelan."

I scowled at him.

"It's all easily done. Arrest the bastard who killed Mrs. Shedd and stole the ring. You'll be doubly served – triply, considering the tourists who won't be accosted – and make a dent in the terrorist ring to boot. You'd also get a decent night's sleep, as would we. Everyone's a winner."

"Easier mentioned than accomplished," he said.

When I filled a tea cup and placed it in the microwave, he shook his head in mock disgust.

"That's another thing," he said. "I looked about for a kettle, before yer charmin' intended was kind enough to come to me rescue, offering hot drink and smiles. Couldn't find a bloody thing. I was shocked to enter a proper Irish manor and not locate a tea kettle anywhere about. It'll go in my report."

Caeli was engaged in what I'd come to think of as the jotting process, pensively adding to her list of items that required prompt attention ahead of the wedding. But she answered without glancing up.

"A kettle seems like a lot of bother – one more thing to clean," she said. "Plus, it takes far longer to boil a pot than it does to nuke a single cup."

He frumped audibly.

"Tea isn't tea without a proper kettle," he said.

"Why concern yourself?" I said. "You seem perfectly happy with coffee. And if you're happy, well, I don't care."

"Hey, I was bloody-well coffeed out by the time I got here – along with the notion that I could make sense of yer automatic device there " – he swept his arm toward the Ninja Coffee Bar on the counter, hand-picked by Caeli because of its versatility – "once ya let me inside and then abandoned me."

"When all else fails, read the instructions," I said and secured a teabag.

"You've hidden them, apparently. I know. I looked."

"That's what a cell phone's for these days … instructions online," I said, stifling a yawn. "So what's on your mind anyway?"

Caeli glanced up from her note-jotting.

"Yes, Liam. Do tell. Either that or I put you both to work."

I'd been puzzled by his early reluctance to reveal his reason for the pre-dawn visit … but then he started talking.

"Here's the truth of it – something I couldn't mention yesterday when we were with the Guards," he said. "There's a mole inside the operation, and I'm hopin' the two of ya can help us learn who it 'tis and end the damage."

"This is the same operation we discussed on Henry Street?" I asked.

"Yes and no," he said. "I'll tell ya what I can, which'll at least allow ya to see the scope o' things. As ya know, we're involved in a massive bloody venture, agencies and commissions alike, along with an Irish politician of limited significance. You'll note the usual suspects: Interpol, MI-6, the CIA and NSA from yer own country …"

Gallacher opened the refrigerator, looking for something to eat, and spotted a packet of sliced cheese. He didn't bother asking, not that it mattered.

"It was all fun and games yesterday, in front of Jimmy Ryne and his lads," he said. "I sold 'em the notion that we're old pals, that I trust ya fully, that I was bringing ya in 'cause of yer ability to think clearly in a crisis, plus ya get things done. That's all true, of course. So was the part about Caeli's uncle and the remnants of his crowd who we believe are connected to the terror cell. I expect ye can help there, too."

That didn't sit well with Caeli.

"There's something you should know, Liam," she said. "Even if we do help, and I'm not saying we can, I'm not a bargaining chip to ensure my uncle's involvement. By mutual agreement, with Jack and also with the church, we're to keep our distance for a period to be determined. I'm not to make contact, nor is he."

Gallacher shook his head in frustration.

"Surely, given the gravity of things, arrangements can be made," he said.

"I don't care to find out," Caeli said. "For now, anyway, I'm done with Jack and everything he did: in Armagh, in Cork, on Mutton Island, even what he's been up to since. I won't – I can't – get dragged back in. It's not negotiable. If you need his help, ask the Pope directly."

Gallacher appeared stunned, and hurt, and moderately angry. I got the sense that he wanted to argue – to convince Caeli that she was being shortsighted or that she was unaware of the big picture and would relent once he delivered the rest of it.

But Caeli is no easy mark. As their eyes locked and you could sense the test of wills between them, pushing and shoving back and forth with the seconds slowly ticking by, the Irish spy reluctantly figured it out: This was a fight he wouldn't win.

He soon decided on a different approach.

"Ya wouldn't have some bread, maybe – somethin' I can use to make a proper sandwich?"

"Sure. Grilled cheese, perhaps?" Caeli said.

"Ah, Jaysus, that'd be grand. Yer willingness to take in a stray is admirable, even if yer choice of relatives is not."

He waited patiently while she produced a loaf of Italian bread, a frying pan, some butter, and started the process.

"So where was I – before I touched a sore point?"

A sore spot? I recall thinking. *That was a minefield.*

"The mole," I said. "You have suspects?"

He shrugged.

"One of your own?"

He waved that aside, so I tried again.

"Someone in the Guards, perhaps?"

This time his face contorted into a grimace that was easy to read.

"Maybe," he said. "Politics, ya see, plus manpower limits, dictates that we can't run an operation without help from the locals. But again, we've many people from many backgrounds, organizations, agencies, political interests – all workin' toward the same end, save one. Somebody's feedin' information to the enemy, and we don't have a clue who the bastard is, nor his affiliation nor country of origin."

"He's male?" Caeli asked.

"Unknown. It's likely, of course, but ... who can say? Some women are included in the operation – in addition to you, Miss Brown."

"I've not agreed to anything."

"Yes. So you've said."

He scowled again.

I changed directions, hoping to bypass another uncomfortable confrontation.

"So yesterday, in Limerick, Ryne really didn't know you were going to spring us on him?"

"He did not."

"Sheehan and the rest were out of the loop as well?"

"Correct," he said. "Believe it or not, you two were on my list to recruit, well before I left Dublin to oversee the operation. We've people on our payroll across all of Ireland, of course, listenin', watchin', reportin' in when they see or hear items of interest – in pubs, flophouses, grand hotels, tourist spots like Bunratty. When I heard yer names come through from DCI McNeill, it just seemed too good an opportunity to pass by. It'll work to yer favor, ya know – add to yer credibility at Henry Street."

"We're not interested in padding our résumés. We're retired," Caeli said as she finished with his sandwich, sliding it onto a plate.

"Fine. But we still need ya," he said. "And this looks lovely – thanks, indeed."

"You're welcome. And you don't need us," Caeli said. "You've plenty of people to sniff out your mole."

He took a bite and smiled, chewed, took another.

"We don't have anyone who can do it as quickly and effectively as you," he said. "You aren't connected to the team, and you don't know the players – a plus. I've seen ya work, you'll recall. This is the sort of thing ye can do in a day or two, tops, then return to yer wedding."

Caeli wasn't mollified.

"The wedding is days away, and there's much to do between now and then," she said.

"I understand, even sympathize. But it can't be helped," he said. "There's more."

FIFTEEN

A SIMPLE DOSE OF REALITY

We spent another hour talking logistics, which is a strange conversation to have with a man charged with keeping the secrets of state.

And after a great deal of wrangling, we eventually agreed to help as best we could because, hell, it seemed like the right thing to do. We were living in Ireland, after all, and individual contributions to the greater good were expected.

Of course, Caeli's instant connection to Joan Shedd was the clincher.

Still, despite his hints at other issues, Liam Gallacher was reluctant to provide us with specifics regarding the actual threat, and he brushed off most of our attempts to force some answers with pointed questions, the kind that former investigative reporters ask, regarding how the taskforce worked and the role he saw for us. He reminded me of a prize fighter, dancing and weaving to avoid a knockout punch. The difference here was that he finished his sandwich and snacked on cheese and fruit and revived himself with sips of coffee before the bell rang for each successive round.

"Jaysus, but ye ask a lot of bloody questions," he said after another interruption, minutes into his recitation. "Trust me on this: It's all grand."

"Until it's not," Caeli said.

Even that was shoved aside with a chomp, a nibble, a slurp, and a wicked grin.

I asked at one point whether his operation was sanctioned by the elected officials to whom his agency reported. He snorted out a laugh that held little mirth.

"Let's just say we give 'em a view of the overall, the big picture," he said. "But to trust that lot with the truth?" He kicked out a one-note snort, waving his hand in disgust. "Jaysus, but a man'd have to be daft. They'd lock me up in Portlaoise Prison, E Block, to be sure. And they'd hand the key over to the captain of the boat that sails 'tween Dun Laoghaire and Holyhead and order him to toss it in, halfway 'cross the Irish Sea."

"I take it that's a no," I said.

"Ya catch on quick, lad. No wonder I've enlisted the pair of ya," he said.

"I don't like the sound of that," Caeli said.

"Call it what ya will, darlin', but yer adopted country appreciates yer willingness to help."

From what we could gather, Gallacher was running the show out of a warehouse near the Crossagalla Business Park, southeast of Limerick's heart. The M7 motorway is close by, allowing access to anywhere you might want to get to in and around the city. It's a 20-minute drive, give or take, from our home, a revelation the spymaster somehow believed made up at least partially for the fact that we were being inconvenienced, as he put it, so close to our wedding.

When Caeli countered that the location of his base was precious little reason for us to sing his praises, he again reminded us that were it not for his considerable influence, we might still be rooted in Oregon – an idea that wasn't pleasing, given all the work we'd done since moving into the estate on the River Shannon and the amenable nature of the Irish as a whole.

Gallacher hit yet another note.

"I can't imagine what it's like there now, back across the pond – after that last backwater election," he said, barely concealing a smirk. "Things seem to be in a bit of an uproar still, even now, long months later."

I found it odd that he'd pick this occasion to talk about international politics, although we determined later, when Caeli and I discussed his visit, that he was simply deflecting from whatever picture he refused to paint for us.

Still, this wasn't the first time we'd been confronted with scorn because of the presidential election, with the curious demanding to know "just what in the name of the bloody saints were the lot of ya thinkin' over there?"

I was surprised at the vehemence the first time it happened. But after a number of similar outbursts from unlikely sources in succeeding weeks – clerks at the supermarket, servers at restaurants, whiskey-slingers in pubs, the occasional worker around the estate – we soon determined that answering the apparent outrage with a flippant response was akin to pouring gasoline on a spark.

"It's one of many reasons we moved," I'd taken to replying – a line that usually mollified the accuser.

Gallacher seemed to require a response to his political observation as well, though I chose to answer him in the form of a question.

"How do the American spooks on your payroll react when you bring that up?"

His sneer disappeared.

"First off, they aren't on my payroll," he said. "Taskforce, true, but payroll? Not a chance. More to the point, you'd have to be a total nutter to think I'd mention that bit to those lads. They take themselves far too seriously for the likes of me to have a bit of a go at 'em. Then again, I'm afraid of what some of 'em'd tell me."

But he placed things in perspective with his next comment.

"Besides, it's a deadly game of cat and mouse we're after chasin' here – no time a'tall for a bit of cheek – not after what we've seen in Paris, Amsterdam, multiple times in London, and in Berlin, Brussels, Barcelona," he said. "Careless talk, plus yer man's steady barrage of insane tweets, are likely to start more attacks than to stop 'em."

His eyes grew distant as he considered the lives wasted and the senseless carnage that fresh terrorist assaults had inflicted on the innocent.

"I'll be damned if we'll allow it here," he said, seconds later, and I got the sense that we were getting a true picture of the Irish spy's soul and a considerable dose of what was driving him. And yeah, it's difficult to argue with someone fighting terrorism on a global scale. A wedding date didn't seem to amount to much in the overall scheme of things.

He soon provided a thin accounting – given names and ranks and affiliations – of a few of the key players operating in his taskforce.

"I don't expect ya to remember it all – not yet," he said. "But you'll want to know who's who when the time comes."

"Which is when, exactly?" Caeli asked.

"Right now, if yer up to it – if ye can afford the time."

What the hell, I thought. *It beats pulling weeds and dusting furniture.*

I didn't say that aloud.

Caeli had another question.

"How will you explain our presence?" she asked.

"Yer my consultants, of course – experts who helped end yer uncle's madness," he said. "Yer *bona fides* are legitimate, of course. As soon as I mention yer names, every agent in the place'll be after lookin' the two of ya up on whatever database they've got at their disposal – not just those we use for common linkage but the ones exclusive to 'em and whatever outfit they're with. Think of the stuff the NSA crowd can do with a few keystrokes. I trust ya don't have all that many skeletons in yer closets."

He laughed, enjoying himself.

Caeli wasn't swayed.

"I'm unsure what you think we can learn by hanging around," she said. "It seems like a waste of everyone's time."

"Not a'tall. You'll get at the truth, my dear," he said. "We've been compromised on two occasions, at least. Both times, what we'd taken days to set up was derailed in little more than a minute. I've been at this a long time and know when a bloody rat's in the kitchen, stinkin' up the place. Right now we've a fat one, feedin' what we say, what we do, what we plan, directly to the other side. It's damn well gonna stop. So I'm takin' a leap of faith, trustin' the two of ya to find the thing I haven't yet seen."

It was flattering, sure. But it also seemed disingenuous somehow.

"Come on, Liam," I said. "I don't think you're being serious here. We met some of your people in Cork, and again on Mutton

Island when last our paths crossed. You run with a top-notch crew. I'm not buying your ..."

"No, you're wrong," he said, cutting me off. "They're great, sure – all of 'em. But that's the bloody point. They're the best 'cause they've been trained in tradecraft their entire careers. They know how to keep secrets, make things disappear, leave no trail. Like me, they're spies dealin' with spies, and we know how to deal with each other. But you two aren't spies. Yer the farthest thing from spies – and I say that in the best way possible. I want ya at the table – for whatever time ye can spare, whatever time it takes – 'cause I think you'll see what the rest of us can't."

Well, nuts, I thought.

But I didn't say that aloud, either.

We were on the road 30 minutes later after tidying up. Caeli was driving her beefed-up Range Rover and closely following Gallacher's Mercedes-Benz S-Class government-issued black sedan, which featured armor plating, tinted bulletproof windows, a turbo-charged engine, and his very own driver, Danny O'Herlihy, a no-nonsense G2 operative.

"I wonder why he didn't invite the guy inside," I said after watching Gallacher's bodyguard/chauffeur hold the door for the boss. "The poor bastard sat in that car for damn near two hours while we enjoyed the comforts of home."

"Maybe the discussion was for our ears only," Caeli suggested.

"Possibly," I said. "But if a man can't trust his driver, it's time for a new driver."

"Good point. Maybe he didn't want to impose on us."

"You mean any more than he did by showing up unannounced before 5 a.m.?"

"It was 5:03 when I found him," she said. "Maybe the driver was keeping an eye on things while we were inside. Gallacher's a spy, after all. Spies don't trust anyone."

"We'll need to keep that in mind."

We didn't address the underlying point that our house might be under surveillance – by Gallacher's people, or perhaps, after our Bunratty encounters, by the very thugs he was chasing. But it hung heavy in the air, a cloud that wouldn't easily lift, and I thought about it as the SUV chewed up the kilometers.

This could get ugly – far worse than being roused from a warm bed, I thought.

Hell, it was bad enough getting pulled into an investigation that had far more serious implications than we'd initially thought, when Alan Phelan first showed up. God only knows what we'd see … *or what we might turn up*. And that bothered me.

I fished inside the glove box and came out with a Mozart CD that we used to play while enjoying the hot tub at Raptor's Ridge, our home overlooking the Crooked River in Central Oregon.

"Nice choice," Caeli said when the opening strains of Symphony No. 25 in G minor rattled the speakers and I dialed down the volume to a more reasonable level.

"You must've been listening to Country & Western the last time you went into town," I said – a joke of sorts, as neither of us are fans.

"More like *Céilí* & Western," she said, referencing Ireland's traditional up-tempo dance music.

We were another mile down the M7, driving in the slow lane behind Gallacher, when Caeli realized that something was off. And yeah, keep in mind that everything takes place on the opposite side of the road in Ireland, just as it does in Britain.

"Check out the sedan coming up behind us," she said. "It's flying."

"Kilometers or miles per?" I asked, and it came out more flippantly than I'd intended. But even as I swiveled to take a look, the car roared by, giving every indication that its driver was in one hell of a hurry.

"What's so important that he can't …"

But I got no farther than that when a side window powered down as the sedan drew even with Gallacher's Mercedes and braked to the same approximate speed. A short-barreled sub-machine gun – likely an Uzi, though it was difficult to be specific, given our speed and the general excitement that followed – poked through the opening and began burping a line of lead at the spymaster and his chauffeur.

I muttered a curse and grabbed for the *Oh, Jesus* handle above the door as Caeli goosed the engine and swerved us into the speed lane, immediately behind the shooter.

For what it's worth, I wasn't greatly surprised that she was taking us into the hazard zone. Caeli is hard-wired to fight when danger comes at her or when someone she cares about is placed in harm's way.

The occupants of the sedan, an S-class Volvo, determined at this stage that the target car was armor-plated, and the shooter now aimed for the tires.

Instead of swerving away from the line of fire, as most people would, Gallacher's driver jerked the wheel hard, forcing the Mercedes to veer toward the attacker. As the Volvo instinctively jerked aside, its driver tugged on the wheel more sharply than was either necessary or expedient, overcorrecting, which opened him up for a direct side-swipe.

The subsequent screech of metal on metal sent the Volvo out of the speed lane and onto the M7's shoulder. It also forced the shooter to momentarily pull the machine gun inside the open window, which in turn provided Caeli with the opportunity she'd been waiting for. She kicked the Range Rover hard, and it responded as though it had been hit in the flanks with spurs, shooting us directly into the Volvo's bumper.

I should add here that the Range Rover had been specially fortified by Fierro Enterprises International, with a number of extras you won't find in the stock list price. Like Gallacher's car, it's armor plated, with an engine upgrade, and it also has a custom steel grill guard that wraps the entire front end in a protective cage.

In this case, that cage melded nicely with the Volvo, as though the parts were made to fit like a jigsaw puzzle. Caeli hit the accelerator once more, turning slightly to the right, which in turn forced the Volvo to the left.

Cops and race-car drivers call it a PIT maneuver, for Precision Immobilization Technique. You can probably find the formula in a college physics book, but the result was predictable regardless. When the Volvo's front left tire, cocked as it was, hit the soft earth away from the paved shoulder, it dug in, which sent the car flipping over from side to side.

Caeli braked just as suddenly as she'd accelerated, and we watched in mild fascination as the Volvo rolled again and again before finally turtling, spinning to a stop in the dirt and grass between the roadway and a wire fence that separated the M7 from a farmer's field.

Gallacher's Mercedes, which had shot ahead of us while Caeli was dusting off her considerable driving skills, screeched to a halt on the shoulder, and both of the spies were out of their vehicle as Caeli pulled in a short distance behind the Mercedes, giving us a prime view of what was to follow.

"We're not armed," I said when she automatically reached for the door handle. "Let them clear the scene before we even think about getting out."

I thought for a moment that she'd ignore me and join Gallacher and his driver. But she held up when I reached across the console and gently tapped her arm.

"Caeli dear," I said, drawing her attention with the whispered words. "Nice driving. You made that look easy."

She laughed then, as the tension slowly dissipated and our heartbeats, or at least mine, returned to something approaching normal. It's hard to say with Caeli, though. She's generally cool in a tight situation, and this one could've turned ugly – for us and for Gallacher – in a flashing second.

"Seems like we've done this before," she said. "Never a dull moment."

We monitored the action as Gallacher and his driver, with their sidearms pointed toward the now-smoking Volvo, slowly approached the upended vehicle. A few passing drivers slowed to get a better look, but they roared on after spotting the pistols.

"You think they made it?" Caeli asked a moment later, referring to the occupants of the Volvo, who hadn't stirred so far as we could tell.

"I hope so. Because whoever they are, or were, or whatever, they can provide some answers – and last I looked, dead men and pirates tell no tales."

"You think we should call 9-9-9" – Ireland's equivalent of 9-1-1 – "and request an ambulance?" she asked.

"No. Let's let Gallacher decide."

"All right. But it won't be his decision, either. I'll bet a dozen motorists already phoned it in."

After some shouted commands that we could hear from our vantage point, which was perhaps 25 yards away, Gallacher's driver dropped to his knees to check on the occupants inside the Volvo, peering through the shattered rear window. He was soon on his belly, yelling directives that we couldn't fully hear, and he stayed there for a time: 15 to 20 seconds. He eventually stood again, though he kept his weapon drawn as he spoke to his boss.

Gallacher lowered his pistol, a Beretta 92FS 9mm, and began walking toward us. We powered down our windows as he approached.

"Thanks for the assist," he said, leaning in next to Caeli. He was all business, though he didn't appear rattled. "Is yer vehicle right enough to drive?"

"Absolutely," she said.

"Good. We'll have people on the scene" – he glanced at his watch – "inside of 3 minutes. We head to the warehouse for a debrief. Got it?"

"Sure," we said in unison.

He paused, watching momentarily while his driver barked into a phone, before looking us over with renewed interest as another thought struck him.

"Given yer history, I'd 've thought you'd come chargin' out of yer rig, lendin' a hand," he said.

"We aren't allowed to carry firearms," Caeli said.

"That didn't stop ya the last time you were here."

"We were representing Interpol then," I said, thinking back to the IDs that had been supplied by our bodyguards. "Plus, we weren't living in Ireland."

"Interpol – right. Sure ya were. But given this, along with what Danny" – he motioned toward his driver – "saw outside yer house while we were havin' our chat this morning, all that needs to change."

He walked away in clipped strides that brought to mind his military background. His pistol was held in his right hand, tucked in close to his side.

"So what the hell did Danny see?" I called after him.

But he kept walking, forcing us to wait for an answer.

SIXTEEN

ORIGINS

[What follows was assembled from security footage in the Sainte-Geneviève Library on the *Place du Panthéon* in Paris, along with G2 and Interpol interviews with the participants.]

The internet was amazing.

There was no telling what you could find, on any given day …

He fiddled with the mouse, maneuvering it into the correct position on the monitor, added the name of the search engine in the header, and sat back as the computer hummed to life and produced a fresh burst of color and a website that promised to unleash the riches of the known universe, if only he could type fast enough.

It didn't take long to find what he'd been searching for, exactly as the podcast he'd listened to earlier in the day described it in gory detail: the Bath School disaster, the first act of domestic terrorism in the United States, years ahead of the Oklahoma City bombing – "the deadliest act of mass murder in a school in U.S. history."

It was all there, period photographs included.

Location: Bath Township, Michigan

Date: May 18, 1927

Attack: Shooting, explosives, suicide bombing, fire

Weapons: Rifle, pyrotol, dynamite, club

Deaths: 45

Injured: 58

Perpetrator: Andrew P. Kehoe

"Jackpot," he muttered aloud, using the English word as though it held a special meaning.

Kehoe, a handyman who performed regular maintenance at the Bath Consolidated School, was upset by a property tax that had been levied to fund the construction of a new building. He blamed the tax for a foreclosure proceeding against his farm, even though his wife's persistent tuberculosis caused her to frequent the local hospital and run up staggering medical bills far beyond his limited means.

For reasons that defied logic and were known only to Kehoe, he planted both dynamite and hundreds of pounds of pyrotol in the school building during the months when he was performing his handyman duties.

"Pyrotol," the website lurker said aloud.

He wrote the word on a notepad and continued reading.

On May 18, Kehoe killed his wife, bludgeoning her with a blunt object, before setting his farm buildings on fire after securing his livestock inside.

The drama quickly escalated. When firefighters arrived at his home, an explosion devastated the north wing of the nearby school building, killing many of the second- to sixth-graders who were there that day. As the horrified rescuers raced to the site, Kehoe drove to the building and detonated another bomb that he'd planted inside his shrapnel-laden car, killing himself and the school superintendent and injuring several others, including an 8-year-old boy.

During the subsequent rescue efforts, searchers discovered an additional 500 pounds of unexploded dynamite and pyrotol, a World War I munition, that Kehoe had planted under the school's south wing.

"Good god," he muttered, again in English. "The man was a genius."

He returned to the computer's search engine, looking for another site that would provide additional details, jotting notes on what he'd learned and items that needed additional investigation.

When a librarian approached, asking whether he needed assistance (*"Puis-je vous aider, monsieur?"*), he replied cryptically, once more in English.

"What a great time to be alive."

SEVENTEEN

SHUFFLING THE CARDS

We arrived at the nondescript warehouse housing Liam Gallacher's terrorist-hunting taskforce following a steady-paced drive from the crash site.

Given what had just taken place, and the closeness of our wedding, it was difficult not to think, if just for an instant, about racing toward the safety of our home. But we'd spotted at least three trailing cars in our procession on the M7 and through the narrow back streets that spilled us into the industrial area. They included a couple of big SUVs with tinted windows and ample room for firepower inside, and we guessed that a handful of additional friendly vehicles also were lurking nearby – just in case somebody wanted to take another run at G2 branch.

We didn't talk much on the drive, certainly not about the attack. What was the point? There was still too much we didn't understand. Guessing at the issues, as well as the identities and affiliations of the participants, was a waste of time.

"We'll know when we know and not a second before," Caeli had said.

The most meaningful item that we delved into came up minutes after we'd left the scene. It turned out to be something that would haunt our thinking, and our actions, for days to come. It began innocently enough … with an observation.

"It's a good thing the boys in the Volvo didn't know we were trailing Gallacher," I said after pointing out one of our escorts, three vehicles behind and traveling in the fast lane, effectively blocking traffic.

"But they'll know us the next time," Caeli said. "My guess? The attack was monitored, maybe even filmed, either by a tailing car or drones. I didn't see any, but that doesn't mean they weren't there."

An unshakable logic permeated her theory.

"Lovely," I muttered. "Just lovely."

Yeah. It was that kind of day.

A number of Gallacher's people swept in once we'd passed through a chain-link fence with an automatic gate and pulled inside the building, asking after his well-being as he exited the scraped-up Mercedes. He deflected the attention, taking a moment to confer with his driver. We couldn't hear what they discussed, but I got the idea that business as usual no longer applied.

We recognized at least two G2 agents from our time at Castle Ballygarvan and again on Mutton Island, when we were chasing after Caeli's uncle. I also remembered them from the visit that Gallacher paid to us on the airport tarmac as we were leaving Ireland in one of Don Vincenzo's private jets, stationed closed to the boss, their eyes searching the grounds suspiciously as they awaited orders.

Interestingly, if they recalled us, they gave no outward indication, although they remained aggressively alert as the trailing members of our convoy rolled in. The main door into the building was monitored both by armed security and video stations that were set up nearby. You could view the screens showing areas of the surrounding grounds in four-piece sections on the oversized monitors.

Our presence was closely scrutinized by two additional agents who stood in the shadows, each holding a full-auto rifle, barrel pointed downward, their eyes locked on our every move. We exchanged glances, acknowledging the surveillance, ensuring that they knew that we knew.

The place was a hub of activity, with perhaps 25 agents and/ or law enforcement personnel of one stripe or another huddled at tables, pouring over documents, or glued to computers, laptops and towers alike, searching and researching with a frantic madness. I guessed that more than a few were involved in determining who was responsible for the attack on Gallacher's Mercedes.

"Remind me again how we got roped into this," I muttered.

Caeli's frown required no words.

Wary of the focused security detail, I held my hands well away from my side and walked to the front of her SUV, checking the grill guard after the nifty PIT maneuver.

"Nary a scratch," I whispered to Caeli, who'd trailed me out of curiosity, I suppose, to see what I was up to.

"Gotta love it," she said, patting the uppermost section of the thick bars. "Didn't you do something similar the last time we were here – also to a Volvo, when you were driving from Dublin to Armagh?"

I was about to answer in the affirmative, wondering if we were seeing a pattern, but Gallacher finished discussions with his driver and stuck a couple of fingers in his mouth, producing a shrill whistle that caught the attention of everyone in the structure. He delivered a couple of hand gestures before pointing toward a corner of the building that seemed to be unoccupied.

He walked at a fast pace, with his driver and the two aides we'd previously seen now glued to his side. But he halted and called to us after turning to determine our status, which was stationary.

"Come along, you two," he said. "There's much to be done – especially now."

He started off once more, forging ahead with determined strides, and I shrugged off my lingering guilt at getting Caeli involved and offered my arm.

"Looks like we've been summoned," I said, stating the obvious.

"Let's hope it's not to our execution."

The guards who'd apparently been assigned as our personal security detail, not necessarily to keep us safe but rather to keep an eye on us, trailed along without a word.

We were ushered into an area that was walled off from the rest of the structure and shooed through a heavy metal door into a conference room that featured three easels with thick pads of fold-over paper, lined with details and dates; two corkboards with an explosion of data pinned to the surface; a whiteboard with a couple of erasers and the appropriate marking pens, also filled with scribbled writing featuring names and timelines; and a pull-down projection screen designed for PowerPoint and video reports.

I spotted a mug shot tacked to the cork board that featured the unsmiling face of the man we'd met outside of the pawnbroker's shop at the Bunratty Folk Park, the one we suspected of killing Joan Shedd, and pointed to it, nudging Caeli.

No name was attached to the photo, and nothing else on the walls looked familiar.

Caeli stared momentarily, then leaned in close.

"Why are we even here?" she whispered. "They know this guy. All bets are off."

And yeah, I should have listened to her right then.

What served as a central work space was comprised of three heavy-duty fold-up tables that were pushed together, with a dozen or more metal folding chairs stationed on either side.

"Have a seat, one and all," Gallacher said.

Six men and two women, plus the two of us and Gallacher and his driver, were now assembled inside, along with additional security. Our own detail was stationed outside the room, though we could see them through the glass walls. It was clear that they hadn't taken their eyes off us from the time we'd first entered the warehouse.

I reached inside my pocket and activated the app on my phone that turns it into a recording device, thinking it was odd that our mobiles hadn't been confiscated when we'd entered the building.

Gallacher waited for everyone to sit before he dropped into a chair in the center of the action, directly across from us, his back to the white board.

"Allow me to introduce everyone so we can connect names and affiliations with … whatever," he said. "You all know the drill. Outside of these two" – we got a hand-wave – "it's given names only. Positively nothing leaves the room."

He stared at us momentarily.

"I offer that last bit for yer benefit exclusively," he said. "That's especially true if yer inclined to write one of yer books about this venture, Professor Blake."

"Depends on what happens next. But we'll talk," I said.

"No. We won't," he replied.

I was about to argue when Caeli poked my arm, and I'll admit something here. I'd go toe to toe with an Irish spy and his bodyguards if the circumstances were right, but I wouldn't dare do the same with my fiancée.

He started with Caeli, leading with the fact that she was a noted private detective with sterling credentials, formerly from the USA and now living in what he described as "the late mobster Vincenzo Fierro's country manor west of town." Apparently our new home was well-known, as its mention generated nods of acknowledgement.

"In addition to being a one-time reporting scribe, back in the days when our friends in America had functioning newspapers and presidents who actually knew how to read, Miss Brown is the niece of the Rev. Sean 'Jack' O'Lennox, late of St. Pat's in Ulster. The former archbishop is Miss Brown's mother's brother."

Gallacher smiled at Caeli momentarily, pleased with himself.

"She's engaged to be married in short days to our second guest, one Maxwell Blake, seated to her left," he said, more theatrically than was necessary.

I was described as "a one-time investigative journalist who worked at the same newspaper as Miss Brown; a former college professor; an obscure novelist working in the tell-all genre, though you won't find him in the local book seller's; and a working private detective."

"Retired," I said. "We're both retired."

"Not anymore," Gallacher replied and quickly made his way around the room with a pointed finger, listing in order Danny, his driver, a member of G2; Brendacht, also with G2; Mary Elizabeth from the *An Garda Síochána*; Sir Dennis, who represented MI-6; Fritz, described as "an intelligence agent from the other side of the pond"; Angharad, also from G2; and Eamon, "who represents the government."

Gallacher drew a breath and mustered a fleeting smile.

He didn't look rattled after what had happened on the road — not to my eye, anyway. But he did look tired, as though he'd been up all night.

Which he was …

"The two lads in the corner are Mickey and Sean, from my division," he said. "They don't often speak, even when addressed directly. Their duties are to keep watch on things. As for me, the newcomers know me as Liam. I'm not about to disabuse them of that notion, though it could get confusing if the rest of ya hear them say the name aloud and look to me. Most all here, or at least the ones from my division, call me Boss or Chief. Let's leave it at that."

So Liam Gallacher isn't really Liam Gallacher, I thought, exchanging a brief glance with Caeli. We'd both suspected that we hadn't been given his true identity when we'd first met him in Cork. But it didn't matter – not after we'd learned what he and his team were after and what had just happened on the M7. (For the record, he's called Liam Gallacher throughout this narration.)

When he didn't offer particulars regarding the two men who sat opposite his security detail, I prodded him with a question, waving in their direction as I spoke.

"Ah, well, ya see, we don't say anything a'tall about these two, at their request – not even an acknowledgement that they're in the room," he said.

"Which tells us everything we need to know," I said, a line that produced a smattering of chuckles. I wasn't trying to be a smart-ass, mind you, but Caeli would tell you that I can't help myself, especially when a softball begs to be swatted.

The two agency types weren't amused, which only increased the likelihood in my mind that they were CIA or NSA … *or maybe one of each.*

Gallacher mustered a thin smile, though he kept his focus on me.

"You'll want to keep that in mind the next time, Professor Blake," he said.

I thought about asking the obvious question – "Keep what in mind, exactly?" – but let it go when Caeli again nudged me.

Gallacher was ready to begin in earnest anyway.

"All right then, first things first. Let's discuss the incident on the road before we get on to the rest of it," he said. "What do we know?"

"We're pretty sure they're Frog One's men," Brendan, one of the G2 agents, said. "We're running a search now on fingerprints and facial recognition software. We should have something back within the hour."

"Why not ask 'em?" Eamon, the government representative, asked. "If they don't cooperate, we should force 'em, given what's at stake."

"Sorry to report they're both dead," Gallacher said.

Caeli and I exchanged glances because we both were thinking the same thing.

Damn – he's going to blame us, if he hasn't already ...

Then I had another thought.

"No seat belts?" I asked, reasoning that the crash, bad as it was, shouldn't have left the car's occupants dead, especially with the Volvo's impressive safety ratings.

"Safety restraints won't protect you from self-administered poison," he said.

"Say that again," the government official sputtered, shaken at the news.

"Cyanide. We've seen it before – just like the two back at Castle Ballygarvan, more than a year ago," he said, addressing Caeli and me. "We thought at the time it was another war entirely. It's but one of the reasons I wanted the two of ya here, lookin' at this business with fresh eyes. This pair survived the crash well enough but didn't take the chance of givin' up a thing. Their mouths were already foamin' when Danny checked."

"You could smell it," Danny said, without emotion.

"Lovely," I whispered.

Gallacher waited for the murmurs around the room to settle.

"We should again examine the link between the former archbishop's cadre of self-described freedom fighters and the current tossers we seem to be up against," he said. "Are they a splinter group? Are they one and the same? Or are we graspin' at straws?"

"So you think they're related," Caeli said.

"I do," Gallacher replied. "What else would explain such extremism? You don't kill yourself when the wolves gather 'round unless you're a fanatic protecting a cause. And I must say, my dear, that your uncle was the last of those to be after roamin' about the country."

He looked at Caeli directly, staring deep into her eyes for longer than was necessary, making his point to the rest of spies and support staff.

"How 'bout it, Miss Brown?" he said. "What can ya give up about yer Uncle Jack that we don't already know?"

"I can't help you there," she said.

"And I assure ya, darlin', the circumstances 've changed – or haven't ya noticed?"

Two hours passed and we were no closer to solving the dilemma of whether the leftovers from Caeli's uncle's army, the ones who'd blindly followed his ill-advised foray into revolution and lived to tell the tale, were integral to Frog One's plans, whatever those plans might ultimately be.

Two of the agents in the room proposed that a connection with Jack and whatever was on Frog One's plate was little more than coincidence, albeit a gigantic one.

"Keep in mind these bastards are bloody mercenaries, sellin' out to the highest bidder," Brendacht, a G2 man, said. "A year ago the archbishop was large and in charge. Today Frog One's payin' the freight. But tomorrow – who knows? It could be somebody else entirely with cash in hand."

"Them that's in it just fer the money don't poison themselves when caught," Angharad countered.

I mentioned that I didn't believe in coincidence, or happenstance, or even the serendipitous alignment of stars. Surprisingly, only Caeli and Gallacher agreed.

But something interesting took place along the way that changed the complexion of the discussion. Sir Dennis, the Brit from MI-6, muttered a crude remark about the Irish in general, "excluding the ones in this room, of course," which set eyeballs rolling. He followed it up with a crack about Yanks, zeroing in on the recent presidential election, and then took a specific shot at Caeli and me, which I found odd because we didn't know the guy and likely wouldn't want to spend time with him anyway.

There's no reason to repeat his comments here. I'd heard worse and easily could have overlooked it as the product of too much tension and time spent fighting a mostly invisible enemy, in addition to the recent carnage that London had seen from all manner of terrorist lunatics. But Dennis wouldn't let it go, leveraging the comment with asides about Caeli's uncle in an attempt, I'd guess, to open a division in the ranks over the ages-old conflict between the Irish and the British.

What he didn't realize was that he was risking Caeli's ire by poking into family loyalties that run deep and aren't easily dismissed. Then again, I'm not sure it would've stopped him had he understood the size of the hornet's nest he was kicking.

"If the old bastard's really alive, as you maintain, you can bet whatever you hold dear that he's up to his eyeballs in this mess," Sir Dennis said, his disdain evident. "I never did hold with all that desperate clutch at religion and, I must say, after hearing this rubbish, I am even less impressed. If only I'd been there a year ago …"

Predictably, the observation came after a lengthy and often vigorous discussion regarding the former archbishop's activities during the past couple of years and what the upshot might have meant for the British government had he succeeded.

Caeli wasn't pleased.

"You are wholly misguided, sir," she said. "You have absolutely no idea …"

"No. I'd say you're the one without a bloody clue," he snapped.

I figured that Gallacher would put an end to it in short order, but Caeli didn't give him the chance.

"Your belief is not only erroneous but also is contradicted by irrefutable fact, if only you'd get over yourself to look," she said in measured tones, speaking slowly so that he could gauge each word. "Before allowing your overstuffed ego to outpace your malnourished brain, I can assure you, sir, that, unlike you, I *was* there."

"See here, poppet," he said as his face colored. "You are wading into waters that are well above your pay grade and hardly concern the likes of …"

"No. You see here, Sir Nonsense," she said, somehow remaining calm. "You weren't in the field or on the front lines when any of this transpired. Were you sitting behind a desk at Vauxhall Cross, looking out at the Thames, filling your head with your own importance? Or maybe you were drinking at the local pub, trying to convince your mates, or the pretty girl at the next table, how smart you are with cutting remarks that miss the truth entirely – about Ireland, about a history you apparently don't understand, about my uncle's political and religious beliefs, about all of it. I've seen your type before, many times over, and I remain unimpressed."

Sir Dennis glared at Caeli, his eyes pinched and hateful. He was ready to step in again when Gallacher cut it off.

"I suggest we take a few minutes to use the jacks, perhaps grab a water or coffee, bad as it is," he said. "And Dennis … a word, if ya please."

The MI-6 agent continued to stare at Caeli before Gallacher's request fully registered. He stood abruptly, shoving his chair with enough force to tip it backward, and started for the door.

"I'm in need of the loo," he said.

"It can wait," Gallacher said more forcefully. "I require a word."

We were escorted from the room, though we would have preferred to stick around, hoping that the fur would fly in earnest. Gallacher waited until we were gone before he engaged the Brit in conversation.

"I'd like to be a fly on the wall for that," I whispered as we found a box-lined lane that led to the restrooms.

Caeli was again a step ahead.

"If a good reaming is about to begin, I'd like to be the one doing it," she said.

"Do you think he's Gallacher's mole?"

She shook her head.

"If you were a mole, would you draw that kind of attention to yourself?" she said.

"Maybe. Poking the bear is damned unexpected."

"I don't think so. I'd classify him as ignorant, boorish – not conniving."

We reconvened minutes later, after freshening up and grabbing water bottles. As interesting as the discussion had been, I figured that we were wasting our time, that everything we knew about Caeli's uncle was out of date and could be passed along easily enough to Gallacher from Vatican sources, that we didn't need to sit through endless discussions in folding metal chairs, that we'd had enough.

Besides, Mitty is hungry and on the prowl for his momma.

The thought made me laugh, and I almost missed Gallacher's subtle prompt to the British spy. Sir Dennis, looking uncomfortable, twice cleared his throat unnecessarily and formally apologized "to all present who were forced to listen to me blather on," as he put it.

"I've been enlightened on myriad details regarding the one-time archbishop's circumstances, both currently and at the time of his supposed death some months ago, at least some of which slipped my mind and caused me to … well, to babble on, as it were," he said.

I sincerely doubted that anything slipped the old bastard's mind, but Caeli was gracious and also apologized, needlessly, I thought, for her own sharp words.

The speculative conversation began anew and was interrupted, 30 minutes in, when one of Gallacher's minions knocked on the glass, got the hi-sign, and entered, leaving the door open as he scurried toward the boss.

"Jaysus, boyo. Were ye raised by bloody wolves?" Gallacher said, firing for effect, though we only knew that because he winked in our direction.

The aide blanched and retreated toward the door. I was sitting near enough to it that I waved him on and kicked it shut. The two men then engaged in a whispered conversation that took perhaps 15 seconds.

Gallacher turned the aide loose and looked the rest of us over as though debating how much, if anything, he wanted to report.

"It appears as though real wolves are at the actual door," he said. "How that's happened, exactly, I don't have the foggiest beyond wild speculation. But I suggest we take our assigned stations until we determine the extent of the breach. Miss Brown, Professor Blake … follow me, please."

And with that, everyone hurried out into the heart of the warehouse.

"What the hell?" I said as Gallacher held the door.

"That's exactly what I intend to find out," he said.

EIGHTEEN

A VIEW FROM THE INSIDE

We hurried to keep up, jogging after Gallacher as he raced through the cavernous warehouse, straight toward the techies who were monitoring the exterior cameras that kept track of all activity surrounding the structure.

Or so we thought.

As it turned out, it wasn't that simple – or that easy.

"Now what?" I said to Caeli as we ran in stride.

"Let's hope we live to find out," she replied.

Yeah. I didn't find that particularly encouraging, either.

On the opposite wall from the conference room, to the right of the main door we'd used earlier to gain access to the warehouse, a conclave of computers and monitors and harried support staff were huddled in a grouping of portable partitions often seen in open-concept offices; a call center springs to mind. Gallacher and Danny O'Herlihy halted near a bank of oversized screens and began talking with the technician stationed behind the display.

As we approached, a full contingent of armed agents formed a tight circle around the computers. The same two gun-toting security guards who'd been monitoring our every movement since we'd first arrived eyed us suspiciously, their index fingers hovering dangerously close to the triggers of their rifles.

It wasn't a good feeling, made worse an instant later when one of the agency types who'd been in the conference room with us, silent and unintroduced, tapped me on the shoulder.

"We know who you are, Professor Blake. We know all about you and Miss Brown – just so there's no mistake," he whispered in a snake's hiss.

"Terrific," I said, turning to face him. "You must be proud of your Gestapo ancestors."

He smiled thinly before walking away, and I couldn't help but think of scenes from a half-dozen WWII movies – the ones filmed in black and white that featured chiseled heroes and Nazis who looked the part.

Caeli, who'd been focused on Gallacher and his people when the bozo snuck up behind me, missed the agent's opening shot, though she heard my response.

"What was that about?"

"Nothing important. Brave new world, I guess."

She took me at my word and let it go, which was good because we didn't need the distraction.

We weren't close enough to overhear the initial discussion between Gallacher and what must have been the operation's head technician, a guy in his 20s who sported a prematurely balding head, a thin ginger mustache, clothing that was rumpled and coffee-stained (Caeli insisted that the spots on his sleeves were beer stains), and dark, horn-rimmed glasses that gave him a nerdish appearance. The best we could do from our vantage point was watch him point out various features on the monitors that were unclear to us, punctuated by mouse-clicks that occasionally altered the viewpoint or the camera selection of the building's exterior, which in turn produced additional chatter.

Gallacher's phone crackled to life. He pulled it from his belt, spoke briefly, listened for slightly longer, and snapped it off without comment. He watched the monitor for another minute or so before half-turning, seeking us out from the crowd of interested parties who also were milling about, wondering what had generated the alarm.

"Miss Brown, Professor Blake – over here, if you would."

Duly summoned, we pushed past the security guards and joined the spy master. The desk monitors he was watching provided varying angles covering the perimeter of the warehouse. Most were fixed-position, although two were focused solely on a single target. A lone panel truck was moving slowly around the cyclone fencing that surrounded the building, as though its occupant was searching for something … *or someone.*

"There's no good reason for anyone to be out there, lookin' for all the bloody world like they know we're here," Gallacher said. "So I'll ask ya both: Anything look familiar here – from the road this morning, maybe? Or at Bunratty when you were after nosin' about?"

We edged closer.

"Must be hundreds of these vans in Ireland," I said. "Can you zoom in for a better look inside?"

The techie answered in a thick accent that reminded me more of Belfast than it did of Limerick.

"Tried it, mate. The windows are tinted, overlaid with a sort of skin on the inside, we think," he said. "They look normal 'til ya move in close. I doubt it's legal."

He demonstrated, changing the point of view on the screen, which didn't help.

"What about license plates?" Caeli asked.

Gallacher took over, pointing at the screen.

"The plates are missing or obscured," he said. "Yer sure ya haven't noticed this one since ya started in with this business?"

We shook our heads, though it was difficult to pull away from the van's slow-motion crawl. I thought of OJ Simpson's infamous white Bronco chase and was about to mention it. But the techie swiveled his chair for a better view of us and was suddenly enamored with Caeli.

"Charmed," he said, grinning like a grade-schooler. "Name's Aedan – with an *e*. I'm with the Shades."

"Easy, boyo," Gallacher said, placing a hand on the kid's shoulder to calm him. "The less mentioned regardin' affiliations, the better."

If Aedan was stung by the rebuke, he gave no outward sign, and Gallacher didn't seem overly concerned about the apparent break in protocol anyway. It occurred to me that our ever-suspicious host may have believed that we wouldn't recognize the Irish slang term for members of the *Garda*, whose street uniforms are two shades of blue.

A handful of technicians also were busy at their stations, talking back and forth while zooming in and out on the target from varying perspectives. I stared at the van for a long moment and mentioned aloud that it could be used by painters or plumbers or any number workers in the construction trades … along with terrorists with gun-wielding fanatics inside or, and far worse, a bomb designed to take out a city block, warehouse included, which is what we all were thinking anyway.

"Nobody knows we're here," Gallacher said after another minute slid by. "If nobody knows we're here, how did this bloody fool suddenly show up on our doorstep, right after the attack on my car?"

"You think they followed us in?" I asked.

"It's possible, along with a dozen another scenarios, including the ones sayin' this is just some poor eejit knockin' at the wrong bloody address."

"But you don't believe that," Caeli said.

"No. Not for a second. It's unlikely we were followed – not after the precautions we took following the attack. Still, I'm forced to adjust me thinkin' – somethin' scrabbly here … that or I'm losin' the plot entirely."

Gallacher cursed softly.

"My guess is if we weren't followed, we were tracked," he said. "Don't know how, but it makes sense."

"Drones?" Caeli asked, harkening back to her earlier observation.

"Maybe. Still, the minute I run out to yer place, I'm attacked on the highway and this tosser arrives for a creep-around. That's a remarkable set of coincidences."

"We're the scent that attracts the flies," I said.

"Must be," he muttered softly, keeping his eyes on the monitor.

The van continued its slow roll around the warehouse, as though its driver had nothing else to accomplish.

"Why not tap on the window and ask what he's up to?" I said.

"In time," Gallacher said. "We've a team ready, out of the picture, waitin' for him … in case he bolts, either inside the fence or away from the grounds entirely."

"Maybe someone planted a tracker on the Range Rover," I said. "We drove it out to Bunratty on the day we met Mrs. Shedd and her killer. It's unlikely, but maybe he figured out what we were driving, while we were inside at the feast or when we put her in the taxi."

Gallacher nodded.

"We've thought of that, of course. We're checking yer rig now."

Caeli disagreed.

"He had no way of knowing anything that first day," she said. "The next day, when he was waiting for us in the parking lot, he knew exactly who we were and what we were driving. But we had the Cadillac then, not the Range Rover. He was standing next to it when we approached – leaning against it, in fact."

"So we'll need to check that as well," Gallacher said.

"But you're guessing that we're the issue," I said as the ugly thought played out in my head. "You either think our vehicles were compromised – or, far worse …"

"… that Max and I have been compromised," Caeli said, finishing the thought.

"If I believed that, you'd be in lock-up, not here," Gallacher said. "I may be alone among those in the room, but I know yer the good guys."

Then Caeli came up with a scorcher.

"What if somebody paired our phones?" she suggested.

"Paired yer phones?" Gallacher asked. "How do ya mean?"

"It's simple enough," the techie said, jumping in. "Ye can gain access to another mobile, usin' a bit of trickery that allows yer own device to twin up with the original. The technique's been 'round forever, it seems – the Yanks'd call it old school – a clever ploy on the unsuspectin'. But it's difficult to pull off, takin' specialized equipment and a good break that the mobiles are compatible. It also requires proximity at the outset."

"Which he got when we tangled with him on two occasions at the Folk Park," I said.

Gallacher didn't look convinced, and I can't blame him. It was an off-the-wall idea. Then again, that's the kind of thinking he'd asked of us.

Caeli underscored her point.

"We used it when we tracked Michael Corbin from Cork to Mutton Island," she said, referencing one of Uncle Jack's henchmen during the *Emerald Ridge* affair. "Once in, we knew his every move because he never once turned off his phone. We even saw a couple of texts between Corbin and my uncle in real time."

Gallacher remained skeptical, but he wasn't going to take chances.

"One way to find out, I suppose," he said. "Give us yer phones so our lads here can take a quick look." He poked Aedan as an afterthought. "Ye can find it if it's in there – right?"

"We can try, though I'm not the expert – not on that," Aedan said. "Let's have 'em and we'll let Mi…" But he halted in midsentence, before he could finish enunciating Michael's or Michaleen's or Macaulay's name, and shot a look at Gallacher. "Sorry. So we can have a look."

We handed off our phones, and he yelled to another tech, waiving him over, and muttered a few words of instruction before sending him off.

"I'm surprised the Yanks, knowin' the possibility, didn't protect themselves," he said, talking to no one in particular.

"Who in the world would suspect we had our phones paired?" I said.

"We should have, apparently," Caeli said.

"Nothing to be done now," Gallacher said. "But I think it's time we paid a visit to our curious friend."

He pulled his mobile, pounded out a few quick numbers, and offered a single word when the call was answered.

"Go."

"I want cameras on the chase vehicles and the van," Gallacher said, but Aedan already had the appropriate screen-grabs on the monitors.

We followed the van as it continued its steady crawl along the perimeter fence, from time to time slowing its already glacial pace, ostensibly so that whoever was inside could better observe some portion of the warehouse.

The chase car was more difficult to follow because it was moving at a high rate of speed and racing from camera position to camera position, requiring the techies to adjust the coverage areas to keep up.

"Under 15 seconds, give or take," Aedan said.

"Unless something changes," Gallacher replied softly.

I was puzzled by the van's infrequent stops and began thinking about what might prompt its driver to halt at irregular intervals, sometimes for a few seconds, sometimes drifting to a stop before moving off.

"Maybe he's looking for soft spots to breach," I muttered, half-aloud.

Caeli heard me.

"I've been thinking the same thing. Either that or it's a distraction and something else is going on – something we haven't yet seen," she said.

That observation got Gallacher's attention.

"To what end, Miss Brown?" he asked.

"To get inside? To gather intelligence? To plant bombs or listening devices or cameras? Who can say?"

You could see the gears turning in Gallacher's head as he gave Caeli's speculative idea some consideration. Then she hit him a second time.

"Do you have full camera coverage of the exterior?" she asked.

"Mostly, I guess," he said quickly, though turning to Aedan for confirmation.

"Not entirely," the tech admitted. "Never really thought we'd find ourselves under scrutiny here, ya know. I mean, who spies on the spies?"

Gallacher shook his head in frustration and was instantly on his phone again. He didn't look happy, nor did he sound it.

"Bring 'em in," he said. "No screwin' 'round – whatever it takes, though alive. Understood?"

He didn't wait for a reply, instantly cutting the connection. He spun around, calling out names, and jogged toward the spot where we'd first entered the building, barking commands as he scurried along. I didn't catch all of it – not enough to provide exact quotes. But I heard enough to know that he was sending a second team outside to determine whether the van was nothing more than what Caeli had suggested: a distraction that would allow something more drastic to take shape.

"What do you think?" I asked her a moment later.

"We've got a lot to do before the wedding."

"I've been thinking the same thing."

Then I had another thought.

"Maybe we should elope – if people even do that anymore," I said. "Then, when our friends arrive, we can throw a big party instead of a wedding and won't have to worry about flowers and cakes and …"

But I saw the look on her face and let it go and was instantly distracted anyway as Gallacher reappeared and began snapping fresh orders at Aedan and his fellow techies.

"Keep 'em in yer sights at all times," he said. "I don't care if ya have to send somebody outside, camera in hand."

Aedan began rearranging the images on the monitor in front of him, searching for the search team.

"They've pulled the van over, sir," another tech yelled, and we all swiveled our heads to find a screen that provided the appropriate coverage.

"Good," Gallacher muttered as his chase team, four men with rifles in hand, surrounded the van and within seconds extricated a single occupant: male, mid-40s, wearing what looked to be plumber's overalls. The picture was clear enough that I spotted a logo on the ball cap he wore.

I pointed it out, Aedan obliged by focusing on the image, and you could actually read the script.

"Tommy McNevin Heating & Plumbing," I said. "Wonder if it's real or a decoy."

"Talk to me," Gallacher yelled.

"It's real, sir," a female voice hollered seconds later. "A website lists the address as *Radharc Na Coille*, Corbally, in Clarina. We're seein' the same image online as the one on yer man's hat."

By this time, the chase team had the driver tucked away and the van secured. One of Gallacher's men jumped inside the intruder's rig, and both vehicles looped around and headed out of the frame we were watching, a maneuver that I guessed would lead them back inside the warehouse.

"Where's my second team, dammit?" Gallacher snapped, nudging Aedan as he spoke.

"Lookin' for 'em now, chief," the tech said.

But the various monitors remained static except for blank exterior shots of the warehouse and the surrounding perimeter fencing, and Gallacher cursed softly and barked another demand at the techies – all of them this time.

"Find 'em, lads. Now," he yelled.

That's when the feed shut down entirely, as though someone had pulled the plug connected to every monitor inside the warehouse.

"That's not good," I whispered.

Caeli automatically reached for the reassuring feel of her Walther P99, the one that was secured in the gun safe at our home in Central Oregon, and of course came up empty, sending me a look that I recognized all too well.

"No. It's not," she said.

The words that Liam Gallacher shouted at his team serve no illuminating purpose here.

NINETEEN

UNEXPECTED GUESTS

It dawned on me as we stood in the semi-darkness of an industrial warehouse near a bank of dead computers, listening to Liam Gallacher issuing multiple if colorful terse directives, that Caeli's assessment, before the lights went out and the screens went dark, was exactly the reason why he'd invited us in – insisted on our presence, in fact.

He recognized that we offered something the rest of them did not: We saw the world from a perspective that didn't rely on police or military training or a spycraft background.

I wasn't sure whether to be gratified or terrified.

I only knew with certainty that I wasn't appreciative of the invitation – not at that moment, anyway. Everyone in the warehouse expected to end up in the middle of a full-blown firefight. We certainly did. And the last time I checked, no one looks forward to that – not if your head is screwed on straight.

Still, you're going to get punched if you step into the ring. And like it or not, I'd agreed to the fight when Alan Phelan first knocked on our door.

I know. What the hell was I thinking, bringing in Caeli, too? We were supposed to be retired, on easy street, living the good life.

I was struck by the thought that, despite all of the resources Gallacher had at his command to dismantle a global terrorist ring operating on Irish soil, he may well have been outgunned in this instance, if not outmaneuvered.

It wasn't a pleasant consideration. It made me wish, just as Caeli had seconds earlier, that I was carrying some form of protection when the doors finally imploded and the Huns stormed through.

And yeah, I was expecting exactly that and kept glancing toward the roll-ups that allowed vehicles to enter the warehouse. A couple of three-man teams had the area covered, with AR-15 rifles and sub-machine guns pulled to their shoulders, ready to engage at the first instance of pending trouble. But it wasn't enough to make me feel secure.

The tech team, at least, went about its business as though nothing had changed. I viewed them as professionals who'd simply adjusted to the power hiccup and carried on, although it was equally apparent that an unmistakable tension had leaked into the room. It wasn't enough to throw them off their game, so far as I could tell. But it was there, a rancid odor on the wind.

"Can't reach 'em, sir," one of the techies said, addressing Gallacher. "My guess is someone's jammin' the mobile signal – that or it collapsed on its own."

"Yeah, right," another tech grumbled. "Like that'd happen."

Gallacher, a good hunting dog, remained on point. He checked his watch for the third time that I'd noticed, using a button on its rim to illuminate the digital face in a bluish tint.

"Wait for it," he said. "The auxiliary generator should start up in 12 seconds … and counting."

And sure enough, the lights kicked on a dozen beats later, seconds I'd counted off along with everyone else in the place, no doubt. The monitors flickered and fluttered as the power drives buzzed and recharged or rebooted or whatever happens when the plug is pulled and then is shoved back into its socket again.

"Good," Gallacher said, without apparent emotion. "I want a full assessment – right away."

"I'm on it, sir," Aedan said as his fingers flew across the keyboard.

Gallacher collared Danny O'Herlihy, his hovering bodyguard, whispering in his ear. Whatever was said didn't mesh well, and Danny began to protest with choice words and a few hand gestures expressing his dissent. But a second firm order set the unhappy aide in motion, and he soon nabbed two agents for a vigorous discussion. I lost track of them when Gallacher called to us.

"Stick close in case this turns serious," he said.

By this time, however, I had my doubt about a pending attack, figuring that if a breach of the building was on someone's list of critical disruptions to Gallacher and his team, it would've taken place as soon as the power was cut.

The timing seemed right to bring up another point.

"You mentioned guns earlier," I said. "Now would be good."

"Right now?" he asked.

"It's hard to think of a better time," Caeli said.

His eyes roamed the vast warehouse, flitting this way and that toward distant walls that remained dark and forbidding.

"Yeah," he eventually said, though half-heartedly – or perhaps he was distracted by the multiple balls he had in the air. "What is it the two of ya prefer again? I remember many things, but yer taste in firearms is not among 'em."

"Walther P99s," Caeli said. "The full-sized model, though the compact version is adequate."

Gallacher pulled out his chirping phone to check a text message, but he did his best to stick with the conversation, even as he replied to the note.

"Sorry," he said. "Fresh out. If it's important, I suppose we can work on it for the duration of yer conscription. How about a 9mm Beretta 92FS instead?"

"Conscription?" Caeli asked, ignoring the question. "Who said anything about conscription? I don't like the sound of that."

We exchanged glances, and the looks that we shot each other were not what you'd call hopeful.

Gallacher returned his phone to his belt and refocused.

"Nor do I," he said. "But we play the cards we're dealt, my dear, and right now, you've been sent my way, slidin' 'cross the table to join with the rest of what's in me hand."

He grinned.

I didn't want to fight with him, not with everything else that was going on – not with a dozen other sets of ears perked up and listening – and I jumped back to the salient point before Caeli could press her protest.

"We can argue it later. Right now, a Beretta beats nothing at all. Where do we sign up?"

Before he could reply, one of the rolling doors began folding up. A half-dozen agents wearing combat vests and carrying assault rifles swooped in on either side to guard the entrance, joining the security team that was already in place. The chase car's tires squealed loudly as its driver cranked the wheel sharply, making room for the trailing white panel van. The door thundered down before either vehicle pulled to a stop.

Gallacher was already half-trotting toward the activity, with orders for us to stay put.

"Did ya check it for bombs?" he shouted, pointing at the van as he pushed ahead to confer with his men.

"Double-checked, sir," an agent replied.

They huddled for a time, their voices too low to hear, which prompted us to view the monitors in front of Aedan, the smitten techie, who tried to sneak furtive looks at Caeli as he manipulated keyboard and mouse, searching for the missing recon team that Gallacher had sent out earlier.

"Still nothing?" I asked.

"Feed's jammed," he said. "All I get's a stationary picture, meant to keep us from seein' what's really takin' place out there."

"Sounds like a gaping hole in the security installation," I whispered to Caeli, and we turned away from the monitors to talk privately.

"A great deal seems wrong here," she said. "But we don't have to fix it or take part in any way. You know that, right?"

"Yeah. I do," I said, and I even meant it … for that instant, anyway.

Caeli saw through me, though.

"You're the original leopard who can't change his spots, Max Blake," she said. "I don't know why that makes me love you more, but it does – just as it doesn't make me love you less, which it should."

I wanted to parse the line to make sure that it meant what I thought it meant, but one of Aedan's helpers appeared with our phones in hand.

"Ye were right 'bout being 'snarfed," he said as he handed them over. "I've disabled the connection an' made it damn near impossible for someone to get inside again – unless they're bloody clever. But I'd suggest ye take precautions, given the stakes."

We'd just offered our thanks when another of Gallacher's high-pitched whistles caught our attention. He was standing near Caeli's Range Rover, waving us over. As was typical for him on that day, he continued moving, this time back toward the conference room at the rear of the building. We jogged to catch up.

"Tracking device," he said as we joined him. He extended his hand, displaying the evidence, a metal disc the size of a Euro coin with an adhesive backing. "Stuck up under the wheel well and disguised with a dollop of mud to make it disappear. Elementary stuff but clever nonetheless."

"Our phones also were hacked – all of it done when we were in Bunratty, no doubt," I said.

"These lads don't play around," he said. "Yer lucky he didn't take ya out, ya know – just like Mrs. Shedd."

I thought back on the encounter in the parking lot and wondered at the assailant's true intent and whether our training was the main reason why we remained alive or whether he was merely toying with us … or even testing us for later opportunities.

Maybe this time we're the minnows, meant to help catch the larger fish, I thought. *Maybe it's all ass-backwards …*

But Gallacher grabbed at his chirping phone, read a text message, and offered a couple of additional facts that made our current situation all the more real.

"Search team's finished clearin' the grounds," he said. "The building's exterior was compromised. They took advantage of a weak link in video coverage we hadn't noticed. How they found it – well, it's damn perplexing."

"Your instincts about inside help seem correct," Caeli whispered.

Gallacher nodded, though grimly.

"It's the one thing makes sense, which means everyone's now officially under the microscope, you included," he said. "I don't think yer the culprits, of course. The dirty work was done well 'fore ye signed on. But everyone on the team'll ask the question if ye aren't scrutinized with the lot, and that's going to take some time – time we can't afford. I trust ya understand."

"Hang on, Liam," Caeli said. "We'll help you catch Joan's killer, sure, but …"

Gallacher held up his hand.

"I understand yer reluctance with the changes comin' yer way," he said. "Let's take it a day at a time, shall we?"

"I don't think that's wise, either," Caeli said. "It's no coincidence your operation was compromised at the same time you asked us in. We're already known to the bad guys because of our inadvertent interference at Bunratty. That alone puts your team and your entire initiative in jeopardy. Cutting us loose is your best option – and ours."

"If only it were that easy," he said.

"But it is," Caeli said.

"No. Much as I'd like to agree, Miss Brown, I don't," he said. "I can't cut ya loose – not just yet, anyway."

Before she could register a more encompassing argument, and before I could jump in to help, we arrived at the conference room and he changed the topic.

"Thought you'd like to sit in as we question the van operator," he said. "All I ask is that ya remain quiet 'less spoken to."

He didn't wait for a reply and pushed the door open, holding it for Caeli, waving her through. Inside were four armed agents, the government representative we'd met earlier, a woman seated behind a laptop computer in the far corner, and another operative I didn't recognize. Caeli and I dropped into a couple of chairs that lined the wall facing a man in plumber's garb who gave every impression that he was angry and, more to the point, ready to have at whoever was responsible for sticking him in his current jackpot.

"He didn't do it – whatever it is," I whispered to Caeli, as discreetly as I could manage, figuring that the guy in the hot seat didn't demonstrate signs of either arrogance or nervousness.

"I know," she whispered.

Gallacher was oblivious to our snap assessment and wouldn't have believed us anyway – not without first asking some choice questions.

"Let's begin, shall we?" he said.

Tommy McNevin was a member of the plumber's union. You could find his name and photograph, albeit one that was taken years earlier, on the group's website, duly registered with the trade organization.

He also had a nebulous social media presence through his wife's steady efforts on Facebook. Photos of his family, three kids and a dog, were projected on the wall behind the poor bastard, who was seething as he sat at the center of the table, looking for all the world like a common crook. His hands were cuffed with plastic ties in front of him, and his face was screwed up into a nasty sneer that didn't easily tolerate fools, especially the officious types. I sensed that the woman working the laptop in the corner was digging into his background, displaying insights whenever she stumbled onto something revealing.

But there wasn't much to find.

"All right then, Tommy boy, you've been apprised as to why yer here," Gallacher said as he dropped into a chair facing the plumber.

"I've no bloody idea why I'm here, sure as hell not like this" – he raised his secured wrists in protest – "an' after bein' treated like a fookin' criminal," McNevin said. "What's this about then? I was sent to check the bloody heatin' unit."

"Sure ya were," Gallacher said. "A few questions first, if ya don't mind. Let's start with an easy one: What were ya doing outside this building, prowling about?"

"Listen, boyo, I do bloody mind. Check the work order," McNevin snapped. "It's right there an' plain enough on the form, if the lot of ya can read. I was hired for the job, with specific instructions to remain patient while drivin' the fence line 'til I found the proper gap givin' me access inside, as it was hard to spot. At that point, I was to ring a bloody buzzer and be let inside."

"What was the job?"

"Are ye deaf? Again, check the bloody work order," McNevin said, his frustration rapidly mounting. "The heatin' system's a mess, I was told, needed mendin', and the job was gonna take up to a week – maybe more. This was a look-see first-time visit I was here for, gettin' the lay of the place to see what manner of things I'd need fer the fix."

"Who hired ya?"

"It's on the fookin' work order, fer the love o' Jaysus – all of it," he said, waving his hands wildly. "Take a bloody look. I don't recall the name off hand, but it's all there. Who the hell are ye people? What in the name o' Christ's going on in here? What is it yer after doin' that's got me in bloody chains?"

"To be precise, you're in plastic ties, not chains," Gallacher said calmly. "If we wanted you in chains, you'd be in chains. What's happened to the name of yer firm then, the one you'd expect to see on the side of a van such as yers?"

"Ah, Jaysus. That's it then – shoulda known. The rig's on loan as of this mornin' from me brother-in-law," he said. "Had a run on business of late – hard-pressed to keep up. Expandin' the operation's no easy call, ya see, and this seemed like a good bet. I've three other lads out on jobs this day, and the wife was usin' the car to see her mum up in Truagh."

"No license tags?"

"Yeah, well, ya see, me brother-in-law's a bit of a wanker when it comes to that sort of thing. I'm not sayin' he doesn't believe in the need an' nature of government, mind ya, but it's not the first thing jumps into his fool head. Hell, it's not even the second fookin' thing."

"And on this day of all days, ya take yer brother-in-law's van out – for the first time ever? Ye expect me to believe that?"

"Believe what ya like, boyo – and it's not the first time I've used it, either. Jaysus, man. Frank dropped it off last night, after I rang him up to ask for the loaner. Simple as that. I didn't give the tags a bloody thought. I just needed it fer the day, with the promise of a decent payoff. Told him I'd fill the fookin' thing up with petrol and give him some work if the job played out."

Gallacher stared at McNevin for a long moment, assessing the man and his story, searching for truth in his words. McNevin, for his part, stared back at his inquisitor with angry impatience – a man who recognized that time was passing and that he was being deprived of a good day's pay by pencil-pushing fools. It was easy enough to see if you weren't emotionally invested, and Caeli and I were the only ones in the room who fit that category.

Gallacher eventually made a hand-signal – a quick flick of the wrist and then a scribbling motion with his fingers – to Eamon, the government man. A sheet of paper, folded in half, slid across the table, and Gallacher scooped it up and studied it for a time, reading it over and then scrutinizing the details a second time and perhaps even a third.

"Where do we find yer brother-in-law?" he asked a long moment later.

McNevin delivered an address and demanded the return of his phone.

"His number's in the mobile – on quick-dial," he said. "Ye can check to see we talked last night, about the loan of the van. Shades of shite, man, but had I known it was gonna cause this much fuss, I'd 've damn well rented one in short order – even bloody walked."

Gallacher shook his head in disgust and stood abruptly, giving Danny first and then Caeli and me a sign that we were leaving.

"Hey. Wait a bloody minute, boyo," McNevin called out. "What the hell's going on here? Who are ye people? What are ya up to? What gives ye the right to treat an honest workin' man like meself as a fookin' gangster? Let's have it then."

The door hadn't quite closed when the sounds of gunfire demanded everyone's immediate attention – even Tommy McNevin's.

TWENTY

A SPY IN THE OINTMENT

Liam Gallacher broke into a flat-out run, heading directly toward the oversized folding doors and the steady burp of what sounded suspiciously like automatic weapons fire. He was carrying a pistol loosely at his side.

We'd started well behind after watching the grilling of Tommy McNevin, and gaining ground on a younger man isn't as easy as it once was – or at least that was true for me. Caeli seemed to be doing just fine, jogging in a steady rhythm with a distance runner's form.

Danny O'Herlihy produced a handgun from his shoulder holster and took the lead, cutting in front of his boss, ensuring that if the building was breached, he'd be in line to either take or return the first bullet.

I hope to hell he's wearing a vest, I thought.

But more to the point, I also was hoping that nothing uninvited ran through the door because we weren't wearing protective vests. Hell, we weren't even armed, and the realization was neither warm nor fuzzy.

Gallacher, to his credit, allowed Danny the right of way. Much as I hate to say it, a bodyguard can be replaced far more quickly than a spy master whose sole job is to stop a terrorist plot.

Or so we'd been told. But I still wasn't convinced that I truly understood what was going on just then. Too many questions lingered.

Gallacher called to us then, over his shoulder, and it was difficult to interpret what he'd yelled.

"What was that?" I shouted to Caeli.

"Not sure – maybe stay back or stay away," she said, slowing a bit so that I could better understand her.

"We're not armed," I yelled – stating the obvious. "We can't help anyway."

As if to accentuate the point, Gallacher slowed his run and half-turned so that we could better hear him.

"Stay out of this. That's an order," he yelled, stabbing a finger at us, before taking off again.

The line made me laugh, an odd occurrence considering the circumstances.

"We don't work for him," I said. "He can't order us around."

"But he has a point," Caeli said, and she reached out and grabbed my arm and slowed me down, tugging forcefully to follow the new pace she set, which was little more than an easy jog. "I want you in one piece for the wedding."

She pulled us up beside the Range Rover, which was parked perhaps 50 feet from the mechanized door that seemed to be the focal point for assorted warehouse mayhem, and we took a moment to assess what Gallacher and his people were up to. Initially, all we could determine was that at least a dozen personnel had the door surrounded, with the spy boss directing traffic and his bodyguard hovering close by.

The steady gunfire that we'd heard earlier was now little more than an occasional distant burp.

"Hate to disagree because it never gets me anywhere but the doghouse," I said, following up on Caeli's last observation while gulping air. "But you want me in one piece to finish whatever work needs doing around the house. That's the truth of it."

She glanced at me as though I'd lost my mind entirely, a true *Seriously, Max?* moment, and the absurdity of the line struck us both. We were embracing trouble without adequate protective gear and no weapons whatsoever, outside of our hands and feet, and I was making jokes.

Her response?

"You know me too well."

"I also know this: The next time you mention retirement, I'll listen."

"Sure you will, Max. Let me write that down. You can sign and date it. I'll frame it and hang it on the wall."

At least she was smiling, but I got the point – even if I'd meant what I said.

"And you know me all too well, which brings us full circle," I said.

By this time, the gunfire had died out entirely.

"Wonder what's going out there," I said.

As it turned out, we were able to make some educated guesses. Gallacher began barking into a hand-held walkie-talkie, and a variety of crackling voices soon cut through the static, providing him with enough information to open the side door and send out a second contingent.

"Sniper," I said after a few seconds passed. "It's the only thing that makes sense."

"Agreed, set up in a car or van for a quick getaway. Gallacher's men were firing at ghosts, most likely, with the shooter long gone."

"Let's hope so for their sake," I said, nodding toward the departing agents.

We watched with interest as agents and law enforcement personnel scrambled near the door, trying to determine what to do next.

"We've no business getting involved in this," I eventually said. "We should pull the plug, regardless of what Gallacher says about conscription. What do you think?"

Caeli smiled, though grimly.

"That's the best news I've heard all day – from anyone," she said. "The trick will be getting Gallacher to agree."

"Nobody says we have to ask."

"He won't be happy."

"He won't have a choice," I insisted. "What's he going to do – arrest us? That would look good in the newspapers. We just need to find the right time. As always, timing is everything."

We soon climbed into the Range Rover and settled into the leather seats, which seemed to be a reasonable way to wait out the situation. Caeli grabbed her phone so that she could access our home security system to get an online snapshot of the various camera positions.

"You're checking on the cats," I said. "Fess up."

"Caught again," she said, and we both laughed.

I closed my eyes, attempting to allow the events of the day to wash away, figuring that she'd update me if she spotted anything. Gallacher tapped on the window maybe 20 minutes later, waking me up.

"Jaysus, man," he said. "You can fall asleep in the middle of a firefight?"

Caeli beat me to it.

"He can fall asleep anywhere. Nothing surprises me anymore," she said.

He gave us a quick rundown on what had transpired.

"Likely a sniper," he said, confirming our assessment. "Thank god nobody was hurt."

"Did they see him?" I asked.

"No – not a hint," he said, and you could tell that it bothered him to admit it.

"So what were they shooting at, exactly?" Caeli asked.

"Aye. Exactly, Miss Brown. That was me very own question."

I pointed out another potential issue.

"Gunfire, especially sustained gunfire, isn't easily explained away," I said. "Good luck with that."

"Ah, but that's the thing now," he said, and this time he offered a smile that was genuine if fleeting. "We chose this place carefully – no real neighbors to speak of. And if folks come prowlin' about, our friends in the Guards'll explain it away as kids abusin' fireworks."

I shook my head in disbelief.

"You really think anyone who heard that racket will write it off to firecrackers?"

"If sold properly," he said. "The Guards have a nice selection of spent husks to pull from the bag should anyone press the matter." He laughed dismissively. "No – neighbor scrutiny's the least of our worries."

"You're right," Caeli said. "Your location is compromised."

"I agree, Miss Brown," he said. "We've already begun the movin' process and will be gone in" – he glanced at his wristwatch, calculating numbers in his head – "two hours, give or take."

He checked his watch once more, distracted as he pulled away with his bodyguard close to his side.

"What about us?" I asked. "This conscription business isn't sitting well."

"Asked and answered," he called.

"Not good enough," I said.

He halted in mid-stride, steadied himself, and turned halfway about, looking over his shoulder.

"Yer right enough about one thing," he said. "Looks like you'll be needin' that bit of firepower we discussed. I'll take care of it now."

Caeli asked the obvious question.

"You don't think it's over then?"

"Over? No, Miss Brown. Not by a long shot, I'm afraid."

We were shut out of the activity for the next 45 minutes or so as every man and woman working for Gallacher raced about in a madhouse frenzy, packing up this and moving that and making a case for the universal civil servant's daily complaint of being overworked and underpaid.

This time, I thought, they'd have a point.

Aedan, the chief techie, was a whirlwind of motion as he directed his team to break down what must have been miles of wires and cables, box up monitors, pack and store laptop and desktop computer platforms – dozens in all – and to take special care of each and every mouse and mousepad belonging to each and every computer.

"Nothin' works without a bloody mouse," I heard him mutter as he wrapped and re-wrapped and then wound and tied and sealed and packed away item after item.

His minions, a dozen in all, were mimicking his actions in varying rates of speed and fastidiousness.

We spotted three agents inside the conference room, snapping digital photos of everything that was on the corkboards, blackboards, whiteboards, and walls before removing each item and packing it in corrugated boxes that miraculously appeared from … somewhere.

I wondered for a moment what had happened to Tommy McNevin, the errant plumber who'd been plucked from his wanderings outside the warehouse.

Maybe they've boxed him up as well, I thought.

We continued to look for opportunities to drive away from the madness, but the unknowns far outweighed the veil of protection, uncertain though it was, that being with Gallacher and his people currently afforded.

Besides, we wanted the pistols that Gallacher had promised. With everything that was swirling around us, it seemed prudent.

A number of agents were buzzing about an area that appeared to be the size of an average three-car garage, close to the conference room. We couldn't tell what they were doing inside the box-like structure, but we did notice their comings and goings from time to time and the constant use of a swipe card and keypad for entry.

"What do you think – armory?" I asked Caeli.

"Most likely," she said. "It's the only secured area we've seen. But who knows what's under the floorboards?"

In this case, the floorboards were poured concrete, but I understood. There was much we didn't know about the operation, and even less that we wanted to know.

"I wonder if they have a couple of nice Berettas in there with our names on them," I said.

"They'd better figure it out quickly. The place'll soon be empty."

"Let's hope they don't decide to leave us behind – us and Tommy McNevin."

Yeah, I know: a bit of gallows humor. But the fact that we were essentially stuck inside the warehouse, and had been for hours, was beginning to chafe on us. Combined with Gallacher's comment that we'd been unwillingly drafted into his army, it made us wonder what was ahead – and what, exactly, we'd do if things kept spiraling sideways.

We continued wandering, trying not to get under foot, offering to help when the need was apparent. But we were either ignored, which was OK, or looked at suspiciously, which was disconcerting, though we understood the logic behind it. The place had operated for weeks without a hiccup, after all – right up to the moment when the boss brought in the two Yanks and the lid was peeled off in a hail of gunfire.

We eventually returned to the SUV, absorbing the situation as best we could. We said little about our predicament because we saw little reason to speculate.

"We'll wing it once Gallacher hands over the hardware – right?" I recall mentioning at one point.

I also remember Caeli's response, word for word:

"You're damn right we will."

I poked around for some music and was about to pop in the Limerick band the Cranberries, a recent passion, when Gallacher's bodyguard tapped on the window before opening the door on the driver's side, where Caeli sat.

"Two Berettas, and two sets of paperwork," he said – the first words he'd spoken to us. "Ye both need to sign, and I'm to determine ya know how to use 'em. The boss says yer good to go, but … regulations an' all."

Caeli grabbed one of the pistols, racked the slide once and released it, then did it again before removing the magazine and slide, checking the barrel to ensure that it was clear, reattached the slide and inserted the magazine into the heel seconds later, racking and releasing the slide one more time, and handing it back to Danny so that she could take the necessary paperwork, which was attached to a clipboard.

"Whoever cleaned it last did a poor job. What about ammo?" she said as she signed her name in three highlighted areas, initialed two others, and handed the clipboard and its accompanying pen to me, pointing out that my paperwork was under hers.

Danny reached into his left-side jacket pocket and produced five boxes of Federal HST 9mm rounds, 20 rounds to a box, along with four additional magazines from the other pocket, all of which were loaded.

"This should hold ya a spell," he said. "Don't get into trouble. The paperwork's a killer – far worse 'n this bit."

I thought that we were done, but he leaned in and handed me a second pistol after I'd completed the paper shuffling and returned the clipboard.

"Let's see what ye can do, boyo," he said. "Impress me."

Caeli snickered.

"I've been telling him the same thing for years," she said.

Danny seemed to appreciate the line, and I went through a nearly identical drill to the one that Caeli had just performed, racking and re-racking and removing the slide before reassembling it.

"Feels solid enough, though it's no Walther," I said. "Barrel's clean anyway."

"Must be the one I did then," Danny said without a hint of humor and handed over one final item. "Here's a side holster for you, professor – attaches to yer belt. The lady can use her purse, I suppose. Best we can do on short notice."

Gallacher arrived as we finished the exchange.

"Ah, good – yer covered then," he said. "I likely don't have to offer it, but I'll tell ya anyway. Be damn certain ya need to save yer life or somebody else's before ya pull those things and have a go. If we weren't in such desperate times, I'd never think, not fer a minute, of handin' over a firearm to … well, just be damn careful."

"Right," I said.

"So what's next?" Caeli asked, all business. "Hate to say it, Liam, but my cat is hungry and we have a thousand things to do at home."

"Our convoy awaits, so I suggest ye buckle up, get ready for …"

"No – you don't understand," Caeli persisted. "We need to go. We've …"

"I'm sorry, Miss Brown – sorry for the both of ya. But it's not safe – not any more. It's not safe here, as you've seen, and it won't be safe at yer home, either. The pistols yer armed with are little more than a stopgap for when the wolves and other buggers gather. I'm sad to report the only marriage yer like to see anytime soon is the one between the two of ya and me. I wish things were different – I truly do. But they're not, and they won't be 'til we clear this mess."

"We can take care of ourselves," Caeli said.

"I know that. But ya don't know who yer up against, exactly – or the numbers yer up against. And that should frighten ya both – greatly. Come now. Time to leave."

I wanted to jump in with hard logic and cold facts, but I had neither one at my disposal. Gallacher was correct: We didn't know the strength and depth of the forces that we were tangling with, and it's tough to strike at an enemy that knows who you are and where you live and that has the resources to get to you … but you can't see them at all.

"Where to, exactly?" I asked.

"Ah, but that would spoil the fun – would it not?" he said, and he chuckled as he walked away.

"We're not done," Caeli called after him.

But Gallacher didn't acknowledge her, and all I could do was take her hand and assure her that we'd figure something out.

TWENTY-ONE

MUSICAL CHAIRS

We left the warehouse an hour later, with a full contingent of *Garda* vehicles accompanying as many as 15 rigs belonging to various intelligence and law enforcement agencies, not counting Caeli's SUV.

It was a hell of a parade given our vantage point, which was smack in the middle of things.

It's worth noting that our SUV was better equipped for the task than many of the vehicles in the procession, and we felt far safer in it than we had at any time inside the warehouse. Frankly, the warehouse gave us the creeps, especially after Liam Gallacher's remark about conscription, though the loss of power and a sniper attack didn't help.

Accompanying us were the same two agents who'd viewed us so suspiciously when Gallacher first brought us to his supposedly secret compound, hours earlier – and yeah, it felt like days instead of hours. We weren't happy with the company. Worse, they insisted on relegating us to the back seat ("What's a Yank know 'bout motorin' on the correct side of the road, anyway?" one of them muttered), and they wouldn't accept our repeated insistence that Caeli was the most qualified driver in Limerick, if not all of Ireland, with me a distant second.

"Is that a fact?" one of the pair asked. "A regular Mario Andretti, is it?"

"Or that smokin' hot Danica Patrick, maybe?" the second agent said, whacking his partner's arm as though he'd fired off a good one.

"She's far better on all counts," I said, though I didn't bother launching into a dissertation regarding Caeli's training and myriad qualifications behind the wheel. "Much better."

They laughed but remained unbending, and the only reason we didn't press the point was that both were armed with AR-15s, along with pistols in tactical holsters strapped to their thighs, and looked as though they'd had plenty of practice. That was fine in a firefight, sure, but it had no appeal as we stood outside the SUV, intent on making our point while keeping the atmosphere tolerable.

"When this is over, I'll wager a thousand Euros that Caeli can outdrive you in the Range Rover or even in the car you own," I said to the driver as he started the engine.

"You'd be throwin' money away, Yank," he said.

"So it's a bet?"

Caeli poked me in the arm, and he didn't respond for a few seconds while he familiarized himself with the layout of the dashboard.

"When this is over, boyo, we'll talk," he said.

We were soon threading our way through the back streets of Limerick's industrial area, heading north toward the city center.

"Where are we going, exactly?" Caeli asked moments later.

"We're after followin' the car ahead of us, which in turn is followin' after the one ahead of it," the driver said. "When we get to wherever it is we're finally goin' to, I'll be after lettin' ya know we've arrived. Fair enough?"

Not exactly what we're looking for ...

"Just be careful with the Rover," Caeli said. "You'll need more than good insurance if you wrap it around a pole."

The guy riding shotgun started to respond, but he let it go when the driver muttered something in Irish that I couldn't interpret and that Caeli apparently didn't catch.

We could hear the cackle of their intercoms reporting locations and "all clear" remarks at times, and it became apparent that scouting teams were clearing the path we were taking, which made sense.

What happened next was the stuff of being overly tired, or perhaps being slightly off my game, or … well, judge for yourself.

I spotted a couple of gunmen on top of an industrial building, the barrels of their rifles gleaming in the sun, and just about came out of my shoes, reaching across the seat for Caeli's arm in an attempt to pull her down, out of the line of fire.

"Snipers at your 3 o'clock," I shouted.

The boys in the front seat laughed merrily, as though I'd told the best joke they'd heard in years. Caeli stared at me incredulously, her face providing a textbook rendition of *I can't believe you just hollered that*.

But that's not what she said.

"You're just now noticing?" she asked, so calmly that I wondered whether I'd issued the correct warning – one that would resonate immediately and cause our personal security force to take evasive action. "That's the third sniper team I've seen since we left the warehouse."

"Fourth, actually," the driver called after another round of guffaws.

"All right, so what'd I miss?" I eventually asked.

"They're with the Guards, stationed along the route," shotgun said. "They've also got a couple of drones up, I'm told, keepin' an eye on t'ings. Bloody unwieldly beasts, but useful. It's quite the sophisticated operation, ya know. You'd think somebody important was bein' maneuvered about."

He barked out another laugh, with his partner joining in – a couple of lads having a grand time.

"Of course, the pair of us know bloody well better 'n that with the cargo on board this crate," he added a moment later.

"What about Liam Gallacher?" Caeli asked. I suspect that she'd taken pity on me and was attempting to get the two terriers to let go of my ankle.

"Liam Gallacher?" the driver asked, and you could tell from the tone of his voice that he wasn't kidding. "Who the bloody hell is that?"

"The top dog," Caeli said. "The guy calling the shots."

"Ah. James Bond, ya mean – Agent 007 himself then," the driver said. "Sure, it 'tis. He likely qualifies as somebody important enough to warrant a motorcade with scouts and snipers on the rooftops mindin' the works, I suppose."

"And drones," his partner added. "Don't forget the bloody drones."

I stepped in it again when I pressed the issue.

"So what's his real name if it's not Gallacher? It's sure as hell not James Bond."

"Yer bright for a Yank, I'm told," the driver said. "Haven't seen any signs of it meself, but then … it's early in the day. In yer Oregon, anyways."

"It's pronounced Ore-ah-gun," I said.

"Right – sure it 'tis. You Yanks and yer bloody guns."

That elicited another round of laughter, and I shook my head in frustration and let the matter drop – something I should've done when Gallacher roused me from a deep sleep hours earlier.

The trip from the warehouse to the City Centre Car Park on Anne Street, our eventual destination, took a little more than 20 minutes. After that last exchange, Caeli and I sat silently, viewing the passing scene. If additional sniper teams were secured along our route, I didn't detect them – and I can't say whether that was a good thing or a bad thing.

The logistics of getting everyone inside the parking garage became a routine that most likely had been rehearsed during some long-ago drill that law enforcement types adopt and prepare for with gusto, itching for the day when the savage hordes come calling. As some of the cars in our parade turned into the structure, others continued down the street and circled the block before veering in, heeding the sweeping-armed gestures of two *Garda* officers who were energetically directing traffic.

Within 15 minutes, give or take, all of us were deposited on the second floor of the massive structure, which apparently had been secured by another team of coppers before our arrival. The cars and SUVs we took from the warehouse were then duly abandoned in nearby parking spots, the Range Rover included. Other sedans and SUVs materialized from the shadows, and we piled into the fresh vehicles and were told to wait our turn.

"It's like a scene from a Western, where the teamsters change horses at a relay station out in the desert," I said.

"If the idea's to throw off pursuit, I can't see how this helps," Caeli replied. "Why would anyone in their right mind want to try and hit this many …"

But she let the line drift into space when she saw it through and determined the logic of initiating an attack on a grouping of vehicles carrying most of the country's anti-terrorism squad, with the two of us along for the ride. We'd all learned a great deal from watching footage of IED attacks on convoys of armored vehicles during the Gulf wars.

"Never mind," she said.

As best I could tell, the fresh cars and their occupants left at intervals that ranged from 2 minutes to 4 minutes, depending on … well, whatever was going on out on the street that determined where they went. We had no way of knowing, and no one was anxious to give up any details, least of all Gallacher, who was MIA as far as we could tell. Caeli and I were now in a Ford Explorer that had seen better days and again were teamed with the same two irreverent guards.

Based on my count, it appeared as though we were the 9th rig scheduled to leave the structure, for parts still unknown.

"Where to now?" I asked once we were secured in the back and the four of us settled in for the wait.

"It's best ya don't know, Yank – not yet, anyways," the driver said.

"Do you know?" I pressed.

"Well now, as to that, if I didn't know where we was after gettin' to exactly, how could I get us there, eh? Tell us that now."

"Easy enough," I said. "You could take us anywhere at all, a park or a restaurant, which would be nice, or to King John's Castle or St. Mary's Cathedral, or even to the Hunt Museum, and we'd have no way of knowing if that's the spot we were supposed to get to. You could take us to your mother's, or to your partner's mother's, for that matter. We'd figure out eventually that you were shining us on, but hey – you'd have your fun."

He glanced in the rearview at me and shook his head a couple of times, as though taking pity on me.

"Ya think too much, Yank. Anybody ever tell ya that?" he asked.

"All the time," I said. "It's a badge of honor – far better than thinking too little, which is what this exercise amounts to."

But he let it go, and we waited.

Caeli broke the silence a moment later.

"What about my car?" she asked.

"It'll be moved," the driver said. "The plan's to get it back to yer house, I t'ink, but you'll need to check with the boss."

"The boss being James Bond?" I asked, figuring *What the hell*.

"Better him than that arch-villain Ernst Stavro Blofeld," he said.

His partner, who'd been as stoic as a mannequin after we'd changed vehicles, couldn't lay off this fresh opportunity.

"Or Emilio Largo," he said, and the pair of them went back and forth like eager participants in a 007 marathon ping-pong match.

"Or Rosa Klebb and her pointy shoe."

"Or Scaramanga, the man with the golden bloody gun."

"Or Auric Goldfinger, the golf-cheatin' bastard."

"Or Karl Stromberg, the fool with the fake ocean hideaway."

"Or Hugo Drax, the eejit with a bunch of bloody space ships."

"Or Jaws, the big ugly bloke with the metal mouth."

"Or that evil little wanker with the accent and the bowler hat … what the hell was his name again?"

"Nick Nack," the rest of us replied in unison.

The driver laughed.

"Well now, it's good to know we're all of us up on our Bond movies," he said. "If the worst comes, we'll take that much to our graves, so long as we haven't left anyone truly important off the list."

His partner cranked his head sideways.

"List? What list?" he asked.

"The list of Bond villains, boyo. For god's sake, man, get a grip."

We were waiting patiently if reluctantly minutes later when a distinct report that sounded like a car backfiring caught everyone's attention.

"What the hell was that then?" the driver asked.

"Don't know, boyo, but I don't much like it," shotgun replied.

They exchanged glances, as did Caeli and I, and powered down their windows. I tried to lower mine as well, but the damn thing was either broken or set on child lock and wouldn't open.

"What's it about then?" the driver called, addressing the question to a handful of officers who were milling about a couple of vehicles ahead of us.

We couldn't hear the response, but our guards simultaneously grabbed their respective door handles and bolted from the rig to join the nearby gathering.

The driver took a few steps forward before spinning around, pointing a finger.

"Stay put – just in case," he yelled.

I offered a wave and half-smile in reply.

Caeli, meanwhile, was diligently working her phone, swiping and flicking and stabbing at its face, working up what I trusted was some sort of magic to either determine what was just happening (*Fat Chance she'll find that online*, I thought) or, better yet, to extricate us from the parking garage, minus our escorts.

Yeah, you read that correctly. We'd both had enough of Gallacher and his crew at this stage. We just needed to find an easy way out. My hope was that the distraction that had momentarily pulled the guards away would give us the opening we needed to slip our protectors – once Caeli was done with her phone work, of course.

"This could be our best chance," I said a moment later. "Then again, maybe we heard gunshots outside."

"Hard to say," she said. "Let me finish this – then we'll figure it out."

I wasn't sure what she was working on, but I trusted her and passed the time by watching the spies and coppers who'd gathered nearby, trying to gauge how interested they were in the situation. Perhaps 20 seconds later, our driver and one other agent broke off from the group and headed down the length of the parking structure on an apparent scouting mission.

I relayed the news to Caeli.

"Good. What about our second guy?" she asked without looking up.

"Shotgun is stationary for now, along with 8 – no, make that 9 – others. What are you looking for, exactly?" I asked.

"A way to leave here without being seen. We can't exactly drive the Rover out the way we came in. A lot of somebodies will notice."

"Why not walk? Must be stairs somewhere, heading to level ground."

"How will we get home?"

"We can call a cab."

"I'd rather not leave the Rover," she said. "I'd like to be done with this bunch for good, our escorts especially."

Good point, I thought.

The intercoms of the gathered police officers began crackling. One of the Guards, a burly man with a frumpish demeanor and ginger hair that clashed with his uniform, keyed his microphone and attempted to converse with someone at the other end.

My guess was that the transmission was spotty because of the layers of concrete and rebar reinforcing the floors. While we couldn't determine exactly what was being said, it was clear that the discussion was one-sided. Ginger grew tired of the futility and eventually pointed to a couple of his fellow Guards, issuing a directive that had them scooting down the length of the structure in search of the men who'd left earlier, our driver among them.

Shotgun, our second escort, momentarily noted that we remained in our designated places inside the Ford and then took off in pursuit of the departing Guards, calling something over his shoulder after he was a dozen yards down the line.

"Now's our chance," I said. "How about we slip out, grab something to eat, and come back and rescue the Range Rover."

"Good idea. But I don't have the key, and we'll need it for later."

"Maybe they left it in the ignition," I suggested. "That'd make sense if they plan on shuffling the rigs in and out with multiple drivers involved."

"Sure. I'll check – see if I can snare it without attracting attention."

"Think we can make it past the Guards?"

"They do seem preoccupied. Let's get out on my side," she said. "It's closer to the Rover."

"Right. Hang on a second."

I popped the plastic cover on the Explorer's ceiling light and removed the bulb without incident, keeping an eye on the remaining Guards. Not wanting to be accused of theft of government property, I left the bulb on the console in plain sight, along with its cover.

Caeli eased her door open, slipped out of the vehicle, and waited while I slid across the seat and joined her, gently shutting the door. I started for the Range Rover, but Caeli was too quick and, staying low to the ground, scrambled a couple of vehicles down and peeked inside, using the rig's bulk for cover. She gave me a thumbs-up sign, leaned in silently through the open window, removed the keys, and waved me over.

"Nothing to it – almost too easy," I whispered.

"They've got bigger fish to worry about than us, and our minders are out of sight anyway. Let's work our way down to the stairs," she said, pointing away from the spot where the Guards were stationed. "Plenty enough restaurants around, but I don't want to take long. Mitts will be hungry – and I don't like the idea of somebody casing our place."

"Agreed. I've been thinking about that since Gallacher's hint at … whatever his driver saw outside our house this morning."

I should explain that Mitts, Caeli's Maine Coon cat, must be hand-fed because Koko loves to eat Mitty's food but quickly barfs it up. Interestingly, Mitts pays no attention to Koko's food whatsoever, which is good for Koko, I suppose, but not so good for the always-hungry Mitts. I have some sympathy for the big guy, but he's in no danger of slipping away if he doesn't eat every hour on the hour – much as he'd like to.

Caeli led the way, I followed, keeping an eye on the gathered Guards, and we soon reached the stairwell and hurried to the first floor without incident.

"All right," Caeli said as we approached the door. "Let's look like we belong, act normal, and move quickly down the street to our left. I found a couple of eateries online that are two blocks away. We can pick one and hide out."

"Good – high time we left this zoo," I said. "Plus, a good meal sounds great."

We didn't make it half a block when we heard what might have been gunfire coming from the parking structure.

Terrific, I thought.

But we never considered turning around, which might've been the smartest thing we'd done that day.

TWENTY-TWO

ON THE ROAD AGAIN

It's a safe bet that Liam Gallacher wasn't pleased with us.

Then again, Caeli and I don't do well being drafted, conscripted, or otherwise sucked into a numbing vortex of someone else's making.

Oddly, we weren't all that worried about Gallacher's reaction to our unscheduled departure, nor even about the sharp reports that had sounded like gunfire as we slipped away from our security detail and hustled down Anne Street. Both of us were close to exhaustion and damn hungry on top of it.

We'd headed northeast after leaving the parking structure, bypassing a place called Eats of Eden to put some additional distance between us and G2. We turned left on Thomas Street, which afforded two options: the Cornstore Restaurant, advertised as a stylish steak and seafood operation, and Bella Italia, which provided a decent view of approaching activity on the street – or so we thought.

"Italian it is – unless you disagree," I said.

"Only because the geography works better," Caeli said as we hurried toward the entrance, anxious to get off the street and away from prying eyes. "I hope they have an expanded menu. I don't need the carbs."

Given all that was happening, I had to laugh.

"Carbs and pasta? What will they think of next?"

But Caeli is serious about what she eats, and she favored me with a serious look, which I chalked up to the circumstances.

"I was thinking of a Caesar with salmon, or a chicken breast, maybe," she said.

"Much as I hate to admit it, pasta sounds good to me," I said.

When Caeli shot me another look, as though she had concerns that I wouldn't fit into a tux, I surrendered quickly.

"I'll ask for the low-fat, no-carbs version first, or for whole wheat or white wheat pasta. If they don't offer it, then yeah, I can manage with a Greek salad and a nice piece of salmon or halibut or even shrimp."

"You can't go to an Italian restaurant and order a Greek salad, Max," Caeli said. "It's un-American, if not un-Irish."

"Ah, but is it un-Italian?" I asked. "That's the bigger question."

We entered the restaurant then, only to discover that it was a bistro designed for take-away traffic.

"Nuts," I said as we shrugged it off and, given no other nearby choice, started across the street for the steak and seafood place. "I was excited about the chance to dust off my *abilità di lingua Italiana*. It's been awhile."

"Sure you were," she said.

We maintained a careful watch on passing traffic and the comings and goings of pedestrians of all shapes and sizes as we crossed Thomas Street.

"What the hell kind of name is Cornstore for a restaurant anyway?" I asked as we studied the brick façade and black French doors with impressive leaded windows. Caeli had no answer, and we slipped inside and discreetly asked for a booth that would allow us to keep our backs to the wall, provide a view of the restaurant's entrance, and was far enough away from dining room windows to prevent passing foot soldiers from spotting us, should they happen by while on the lookout for two escaped Yanks.

Retired escaped Yanks, I reminded myself.

"So what do we tell Gallacher when he catches up? — because he's going to catch up at some point," I said as we browsed the menu.

"We tell him the truth," Caeli said as she scanned the selections. "He won't want to hear it, but it's what we have."

We bypassed the wine list because we already were overly tired and needed to stay sharp if we were to eventually retrieve the Range Rover without being discovered. Menus, water, and a bread dish followed in short order, and after a rapid scan of the impressive fare, Caeli ordered the salmon starter and chicken breast entrée with a salad, while I bypassed the appetizer entirely and went with a steak (medium) and tiger prawns. We both ordered seasonal veggies.

The staff was friendly and efficient, the service was excellent, and the food was sensational. As my grandfather used to say, the dining experience made me wish that I had a neck as long as a telephone pole. Truth be told, I was never quite sure what he meant, exactly, but the line somehow conveyed a sense of hunger.

"Should we feel bad about bolting from Gallacher and his plans for us, whatever they were?" Caeli asked at one point.

"No. You already helped save his ass this morning. He should pin a medal on you and eliminate our need to pay taxes over here for the next five years."

"Yeah, right. What about not going back to help when the gunfire started?"

"The muffler noises, you mean?" I countered. "That's all I heard. A few cars, backfiring at the same time."

"So you tell yourself."

"That's exactly what I tell myself. Somebody keeps reminding me that we're retired, off the clock, easing into our golden years," I said. "But I'm the one who got us into this mess in the first place, and I feel terrible about that, given the timing. I promise to do everything possible to get us out and keep us out."

"As if that'll happen," Caeli said.

"Hey, it's already happened. Trust me."

She laughed, softly.

"The last time a man told me that …"

She didn't finish, so I tugged her along.

"Pray tell, do let me hear it," I said. "Every rich detail, no stone unturned …"

"The last man who told me that was you, Max. Sorry to disappoint," she said. "It's the reason we're stuck in the middle of this madness ahead of the wedding."

"Hey. I already suggested eloping. You wouldn't hear it."

"Good point. Is it too late to reconsider?"

"Hell no. Let's finish here and find the nearest preacher."

We laughed and finished our meals and ordered tea and were coerced by a waiter with a wicked brogue to at least consider one of the choices on the dessert menu to split between us. He'd just handed us the day's listings when Liam Gallacher sauntered in as though he owned the place and, glancing about, spotted us and strolled across the floor sporting a toothy grin as he pulled up a chair.

Behind him, standing resolutely near the door, were four of his crew: Danny O'Herlihy with another man I didn't recognize, and our own contingent of guards, the pair we'd left behind.

They didn't look happy.

For his part, Gallacher dropped into a vacant chair and smiled politely.

I did my best to ensure that his smile would remain in place.

"Ah, Liam, you're just in time," I said. "We're about to order dessert. Go ahead and choose – it's on us."

Despite the half-grin that he maintained, I was expecting a well-aimed insult, a dress-down, a harangue, a vociferous series of complaints, even a mini-tirade. What I wasn't expecting, nor was Caeli, apparently, judging by her own reaction, was his automatic response.

"Give us the menu then," he said, stretching out a hand. "Might as well have a look."

"What about your entourage?" Caeli asked, nodding in the direction of the all-too conspicuous bodyguards.

"They're on duty, the lot of 'em, and can fend for themselves," he said.

I figured that we were in the clear, but he surprised me, something he does with regularity.

"Then again, there's little need for 'em to hear the scoldin' I'm about to deliver," he said, speaking softly, though his eyes remained on the menu. "Of all the cockamamie, ill-considered, bolloxed-up notions to take in the midst of a bloody crisis. I'm bound to ask: Whatever were ya thinkin', if a'tall?"

Caeli took exception.

"You don't have the right to pound sand on our table, Liam," she said, speaking calmly and quietly, as though discussing flights of birds on the River Shannon. "We're in the middle of wedding plans, and nothing gets in the way. Not even you and your war on … whatever, along with your plans for us. Whatever's going on is your problem, not ours – not until after the wedding. If you haven't solved it by then, we might be convinced to help – if you still want an outsider's perspective, as you claim. Then again, maybe not. We've our honeymoon to consider."

She leaned in close and took his arm at the elbow and stared into his eyes, which had widened as she spoke.

"Nod if you understand," she said.

Gotta love Caeli – and I do. Every single day.

I figured that his anger would get the better of him. You could see it, lingering just below the surface of the calm façade he worked so hard to present. But he surprised me again. Hell, he was making a habit of it.

"Fine," he said. He even nodded, a single time, just as she'd asked. "We'll take it slow then, for now. But when trouble calls, and it will, all bets are off. Agreed?"

"We'll see," Caeli said.

"I wish you'd call yer bloody uncle – give us an inroad to talk," he said.

"Ask the Pope," Caeli said. "I can't help you."

"Tell me you'll think about it."

"Not a chance."

He glared.

Caeli ignored him.

"Just one thing – before we move it along," he eventually said.

We acknowledged him with curt nods.

"The Berettas you were assigned, back at the warehouse. You have 'em – yes?"

Here we go, I thought. *Don't play ball and you get your hand slapped.*

Caeli must have thought the same thing because she glanced at me, an indication that we both knew what was coming and that there was nothing we could do about it.

We acknowledged his question without speaking.

"Good. Keep 'em close 'cause somethin' tells me – and it's not intuition – yer gonna need 'em, well before yer wedding. Promise me."

This guy is full of surprises, I thought.

"Sure," I said.

But he wasn't finished.

"I can't tell ya what to do. But I can offer advice as a friend. I wouldn't be after headin' home – not anytime soon," he said, as matter-of-factly as he could deliver the line. "They know who ya are, and they bloody well know where ya live. Yer gonna have to deal with it – like it or not. It's why I brought ya in, placin' ya under the protection of G2. Yer not safe – not after Bunratty. Ya have to understand that."

If his intention was to scare us into submission, he'd apparently underestimated our independence, and that's OK. He wouldn't be the first to do so.

Then again, it occurred to me that maybe he was merely covering his ass by offering token assistance to the Yanks who'd inadvertently stumbled into his agency's fight. If the home office asked, after the fact, whether he'd made every effort to keep us safe, he could check the box and maintain that he'd done exactly that with a straight face.

"Explain how you know this with certainty," Caeli said. "Is it what your driver saw this morning, while you were in our home?"

"That's part of it, sure," he said.

"So what did he see? What did he tell you?" she asked.

Gallacher shrugged subtly, perhaps wondering how much he might offer, if anything.

Caeli pressed.

"Well?"

"He saw the same vehicle, a dark sedan, pass by the gate three times," he finally said.

"Maybe somebody was lost," I said. "It happens."

"Not when we've tracked the same car in and out of Bunratty for a fortnight now," he said. "Ya have yer admirers – beyond the ones in my office, it seems."

This wasn't the type of news we'd wanted to hear, but we took it in stride.

"We know the risks," Caeli said, and she was as matter-of-fact in her reply as he'd been. "But I'll say it again, Liam: Nothing gets in the way of our wedding, and that include your operation and the people you work with, including those four" – she waved a hand toward the door – "and even the murderer we tangled with at Bunratty."

"Yer sure ya want to play things that way?"

"As sure as we're here."

He threw his hands to the side as though he'd done all he could, and he actually managed a grin.

"All right then. Yer decision, of course – far be it from me an' all. So I'm after thinkin' the flourless chocolate cake with fresh cream. How 'bout you?"

We nibbled in relative peace. Gallacher was pensive, to a fault. He didn't make a single observation without being invited to do so, and the answers that he provided to questions asked were cryptic and of the one-note variety. In a few cases, grunts and/or body language – a nod, a shrug, a raised eyebrow – sufficed.

He's reverting to spy mode, I thought.

He was more animated when I asked about the sounds we'd heard as we left the parking structure.

"Car muffler – or something else?" I asked.

"At first, a pure backfire on the level above," he said. "Then a few of the *Garda* – newcomers to the detail – took it upon themselves to investigate for potential terrorists and de Valera's ghost and who only knows what else? One of the lot fired at a shadow, which prompted a couple more to pull their guns and join the fun. Before wiser lads interrupted, they'd managed to kill a bloody Volkswagen. God knows how we'll explain it to the owner, let alone an anxious public already on alert 'cause we'd commandeered the garage."

He mumbled something under his breath that sounded suspiciously like "dolts and bleedin' eejits" and favored Caeli with a slight smile when she suggested that the car likely needed killing.

Moments later, once the dessert was polished off and the bill was presented and I produced the required plastic and sent the waiter away happy, Gallacher turned solemn.

"I lost a good man last night," he said. "His name was Rory O'Rourke, with a pretty wife and two lovely kids left behind – all because of this madness. Right now, there's not a bloody thing I can do about it – not for her and sure as hell not for the wee ones. I don't even know what to say, how to explain it."

In no hurry to leave, he eventually waived at the waiter and asked for more coffee, signaling another round of discussions.

"Tell me, Miss Brown," he said a moment later. "In yer old life, before ya chased after archbishops with revolutionary tendencies, did ya live a normal existence? Or was it filled with moments of madness?"

Caeli smiled wistfully.

"I met Max, which should tell you everything you need to know," she said.

He shook his head thoughtfully, as though her response contained the wisdom of the ages.

"And what about you, professor?" he asked. "Was yer life ever free and easy – no crazed killers on yer doorstep? Was there ever a time ye were forced to meet a woman with two little ones wrapped around her legs to say, 'Yer husband's dead, and for no good reason'? Tell me that then, eh?"

You could almost feel the man's pain leaking into the room. The waiter returned with fresh cups of tea and a pot of coffee, and we thanked him and I pulled a handful of Euros and placed them on the table because he'd already rung up my credit card. He waved them off, but Gallacher muttered something in Irish that made Caeli smile, and the waiter nodded graciously and picked up the bills and moved away.

The spy returned to his musings.

"I could use a good laugh," he said. "Failing that, tell me what to say to the young'uns who'll never see their father again."

"Tell them you're about to arrest his killer," Caeli said. "Then go out and get the bastard – along with the guy who murdered Joan Shedd. You know who he is, at least – and I'll bet you know exactly who killed your man last night."

"If only things worked that way," he said.

"Maybe they should," Caeli suggested. "No reason they can't."

But Gallacher shook his head, and we had nothing more to offer and passed a few minutes in silence, sipping our drinks, contemplating the vile nature of the world in which we now lived.

TWENTY-THREE

SEEKING OLD FRIENDS

Before we left the restaurant, with the conversation spinning in circular fashion around moral certainty and the greater good and leaving minnows behind so that sharks could be reeled in, Liam Gallacher changed from annoyed spy master to misty-eyed bearer of bad news to nostalgia seeker to the *paterfamilias* of unwanted advice.

To my way of thinking, only the first role suited the man well. But I admired his persistence.

"I know ya won't listen to reason," he said. "I even understand the why of it to some small measure. I wish I could change yer minds on returnin' to the fold, or at least in contactin' the archbishop. Tell me you'll do that now."

But we both shook our heads, subtly but effectively, and he seemed resigned to our decision to press on without his presence, although he had one more go at it.

"I don't want ya headin' straight back to the manor house," he said. "I don't have the authority to forbid ya from doing so" – he paused for an instant and muttered, "Well, I may have it, but I won't push it given the way ya both feel" – before continuing. "I'm strongly suggestin' ya seek another path. Take a vacation: Shetland, Norway, Oregon, for god's sake. But stay away from yer place and, better yet, stay out of Limerick and Bunratty entirely – at least 'til I send the all-clear."

He looked tired – ready to give up rather than fight on, against even the most docile of enemies. But in retrospect, I suspect that he was thinking ahead to a pending conversation with a Dublin-area widow and her two small children.

"Promise me. I insist on it, to the point where I'll make things uncomfortable if ya don't agree," he said. "That much, at least, I can do."

I rolled my wrists over, a signal that we understood his concerns and would at least attempt to comply. Hell, playing it safe is a good thing.

Caeli returned his hard stare with one of her own, and I thought for a moment that she might resist or even tell him to bugger off, though in more polite terms. But she nodded her head up and down, a single time, and offered a single word in reply.

"Fine."

Still, things were anything but fine, and we recognized it well enough.

Gallacher required one more item.

"Any thoughts on what ya saw at the operation earlier – in the warehouse?" he asked. "Anyone stand out – look to be on a path of subterfuge?"

"The plumber' guilty of stupidity for asking his scofflaw brother-in-law for the loan of his van, though I'd check where he found that job," I said.

He acknowledged me with a wave.

Caeli fished in deeper waters.

"Watch your tech crew," she said. "They do things no one else understands … work magic the rest of us take for granted. If I was worried about a mole, I'd start there."

He smiled, *a true Cheshire cat's grin*, I thought, and nodded thoughtfully. Then he waved to Danny, and the bodyguard hustled across the restaurant floor, oblivious to the concerned looks of patrons who recognized an interruption of the status quo.

In short order, Danny produced a couple of burner phones, pre-programmed.

"Use these mobiles to stay in touch," Gallacher said. "I'm programmed in the first slot. The *Garda* station in Limerick's next, ringin' straight on to yer man DCI McNeill, who seems to respect ya well enough. Yer own numbers are programmed next, with Miss Brown's set for Professor Blake's third slot and vice versa. Use 'em to the exclusion of everything else 'til this is done."

We glanced at the phones, at Gallacher, at each other, and shrugged – or at least I did. What the hell was there to say?

He had one additional piece of advice.

"Back in Cork, when we first met, when Miss Brown was chasin' after her elusive uncle and I was posin' as yer chief cook and bottle washer at Castle Ballygarvan, the pair of ya had yer very own bodyguards," he said. "As I recall, ya had two Yanks on yer flank and, for insurance, the two Italians arranged by your mob friend, plus another contingent at the ready. Whether ye knew it or not, ya gave the impression that nothin' could touch ya, even though plenty enough nonsense was knockin' at yer door, the archbishop and his horde included."

He paused, as though stuck in a bad dream he couldn't shake.

"My advice is to return to those days of caution and precaution," he finally said. "Let me give ya the loan of Gavin and Ian, the boys who brought ya from the warehouse to the parking garage. They're right here and …"

"Not a chance," Caeli said, without hesitation.

I muttered some subtle reinforcement – "Hell no" – but he focused on Caeli.

"Why not, exactly?" he asked.

"Because you have to trust the people you work with, and I don't trust them," she said with a conviction that was unmistakable.

"You think they're the moles?"

"I think they're loyal to you, not to us."

He nodded.

"You agree, Professor Blake?" he asked.

"Absolutely. Hell, they didn't even trust Caeli to drive her own rig. What do they know?"

"I strongly suggest you reconsider …"

"Forget it," Caeli said. "We'll be fine."

"I believe you're underestimating the nature of …"

"And we have places to go and things to see and do," she said. "I'm certain that you and your men will be cautious in whatever comes next. Rest assured, Max and I will be equally cautious."

"What would it hurt to …"

"You've more need for numbers than we do, given the situation you face: the run on your car, the attack on the warehouse, a mole in the ranks, whatever else has been escalating," she said. "Given all that, the farther we stay away, the better off we'll be."

He shook his head in frustration, or perhaps it was disgust, and he scowled and whispered a directive that sent Danny scurrying out the door, taking the remaining bodyguards with him.

When he looked at us again, his eyes were cold and unpleasant.

"Yer after bein' incredibly shortsighted – foolish, even bull-headed," he said. "Ya remind me of yer uncle in many ways, Miss Brown. Still, I've done me best … for now. Stay in touch. Call straight away if ya see anything suspicious. While that may seem a burden at present, somethin' ya might spot – even the smallest item – could be just what we need to rid Ireland of this threat."

He seemed to require a response, so I gave him one.

"Sure," I said. "You'll be the first guy we call."

"Can I take ya back to the garage?"

"No," Caeli said. "We'll walk – thanks just the same."

He nodded once, stood, and strode resolutely toward the door. Every patron in the place stared at him for the entire time that it took him to leave, and they watched the door for a long moment after he'd pushed through.

"Think he'll keep his men away?" I asked.

"No," Caeli said. "My guess is two teams, working in shifts. They'll be outside, in a car of some sort, unmarked and undistinguished, and then again in the parking garage, close to the Rover."

"Yeah. That's the way I'd play it. Should we slip out the back? Hail a cab? Make a run for it?"

She thought about it, playing out scenarios.

"No point," she eventually said. "It'd only make them more determined. But he was right about one thing."

"The need for some help we can trust," I said.

"Exactly."

She picked up the burner phone that Gallacher had just given her and examined it suspiciously, eventually peeling off the back and checking the compartment holding the battery and sim card.

"You think he bugged it?" I asked.

"Of course he bugged it. Wouldn't you bug it if you were him?"

It made sense. Gallacher was playing for keeps, and he'd use every available tool, including the two of us, to track and then eliminate the terrorist threat that swirled around him like wisps of smoke.

"It'll be software then, not a physical device," I said. When she glanced up, I felt compelled to add a single word: "Probably."

"You're right," she said and set it down. She reached into her purse, pulled her own phone, and considered using it instead.

"We'd better not chance it," she said after a moment's hesitation. "When they checked our phones at the warehouse, you can bet they added trackers – god knows what else. We either get these swept by someone we trust, or we pick up burners of our own."

"Or both, although lugging three phones around seems like overkill."

"OK, so let's be sure ours are clean. If we were in Oregon, I'd know who to call. Over here? Not so much – not yet anyway."

She glanced at me, trusting that I'd have an idea.

"Anything?" she asked after I looked on blankly for a few seconds too long.

I eventually produced the answer.

"Spud Phelan," I suggested. "He's got his fingers in enough pies around town to at least give us a lead. Hell, one of his relatives can probably do it."

"Good. Let's go see him, in person. Then we call Fredo and make the request."

"Elmore and Leonard," I said, confirming what we'd both been thinking.

"Much as I hate to say it – though for their sake, not ours."

"Maybe they'll be pleased to know we're thinking of them."

"Not likely," she said. "But I'll talk to Freddy anyway."

I took it as a good sign – a corner turned, a step back from the brink.

The distance from the Cornstore Restaurant on Thomas Street to *Garda* District Headquarters on Henry Street can be walked in little more than 9 minutes.

We took a bit longer.

We quickly spotted the driver of a gray sedan who did his best to remain out of sight yet stood out as though his car featured flashing lights and wailing sirens, loudly and nonstop.

"Think he knows we've made him?" I asked after we'd been walking for a couple of minutes.

"Let's find out," Caeli said.

She smiled at the driver and waved. His face reddened as he offered an apologetic grin in return.

"He'll have to call it in. Someone won't be happy," I said.

"He should work harder at disappearing," Caeli said. "We've done him a favor."

I held her hand, and we peered into store windows and spent a moment reading the menu in the window of the Texas Steakout restaurant on O'Connell Street – and yeah, I, too, wondered what a Texas steak joint was doing in Ireland.

Our supposedly covert overseer continued behind us, shadowing our progress while puttering along, stacking up traffic. He was soon forced to wave on the annoyed drivers behind him, encouraging them to pass or change direction. I was tempted to go into the street and direct traffic when the horn-blaring and insult-hurling through open car windows became a distraction, and I actually took some pity on the guy.

Then again, how often do you get to see that sort of entertainment staged entirely for your benefit?

A minute later, when a dust-up with an aggressive lorry driver threatened to take the sedan out of commission entirely, Caeli couldn't stand it any longer. She signaled the driver, and he looked as though he'd again been caught with his fingers in a place they didn't belong.

"We're going to the *Garda* station on Henry Street to talk with DS Alan Phelan," she called. "Why not just meet us there?"

He nodded his head vigorously, looking relieved.

"I'll tell him yer on the way," he yelled before powering up his window and damn near flooring it in his haste to leave.

"There," she said as we watched him race away. "We've done our civic duty, helping alleviate traffic congestion."

"So long as he doesn't run anyone over between here and the station," I said.

The backed-up vehicles began streaming past us, and I took a moment to point out the other entertainment on the street – in case Caeli hadn't noticed.

"At least the clowns on our 6 won't cause a traffic jam," I said.

She turned discreetly and spotted the pair. I'd seen them moments earlier, when the traffic was getting dangerously long, and wondered whether Gallacher might have assigned more than two teams to watch us.

These guys at least look like spies, I thought, noting the rumpled suits and scuffed shoes that were well-suited for the chase. One of them even wore a fedora, though not as stylishly as me.

"Gallacher apparently has too many men at his disposal," Caeli said.

We ignored the pair and reached *Garda* headquarters minutes later.

"Think Spud knows we're here?" I said.

"Depends on the sedan driver's nerve," Caeli said. "Let's ask the two behind us to go in and find him. Then everyone's base is covered."

I laughed and waved at the pair.

"Hey, you guys want to help us get a message to one of the coppers inside?" I called. "I tip generously."

The glares we received were not favorable, and Caeli soon pointed out the sedan that carried our initial minder, which was parked nearby. Apparently unhappy with being recognized again, the driver slunk down in the seat, covering his face with a hand.

"It's the amateur hour," I said.

"I wonder how they'd do if we actually needed help."

"Let's hope we don't need to find out."

With no other options available, we walked inside, approached the front desk, waited in a queue of five people, and eventually asked the harried clerk if we could visit with Phelan.

"Are ye expected?" he asked.

"No, but he'll be pleased to see us," Caeli said.

"And who should I tell 'im is come a'callin'?"

But we didn't get that far. Phelan rounded a corner in a rush with his boss, DCI Declan Abbot, snapping at his heels and then at us. The sedan-driver apparently had passed along our message after all.

"Do ye have any idea a'tall of the trouble yer after causin'?" Abbot griped as he approached, fairly hissing the words. "Me mobile hasn't stopped ringin' since the pair of ya left the bloody restaurant."

Yup – not the greeting we were expecting, and it pushed all the wrong buttons for Caeli.

"I had no idea Irish manners have slipped so badly in Limerick," she said.

She turned toward me, before a surprised Abbot could respond.

"Perhaps a letter to the editor of the *Limerick Leader* is in order," she said.

I was happy to play along because, what the hell, it had already been a long and ugly day.

"We can copy DCI Abbot's boss's boss. His name is Ryne, if I recall."

Abbot, furious, was ready to snap back, but Caeli cut him short.

"Or get Chief Superintendent Sheehan involved."

Phelan, his eyes wide, took a step back and attempted to cover his mouth before sniggering. He failed miserably, and I hoped that we wouldn't get him into trouble again, though I also had a hunch that it was too late.

Abbot was unamused.

"Go ahead and have yer fun," he said. "Send a copy to me wife, for all the good it'll do ya. You'd be after missin' the point."

I couldn't tell if he was truly angry or just putting on a show for Phelan and the desk clerk, not that it mattered. We'd already pegged him as a sanctimonious blowhard, and besides, we'd come to see Phelan, not Abbot.

"What is it ye even want here?" he barked. "I've better things to do with me time than look after yer lot."

Caeli's frustration leaked through her normally placid facade.

"This may come as a surprise, but we're not here to see you," she said. "We're here to see DS Phelan on a matter of some urgency."

Abbot seemed stunned to learn that our presence didn't revolve around him.

"What in the bloody hell do ya want with Phelan?" he demanded, puffing out his chest.

I'd had enough and turned to the clerk, who was having a difficult time deciding whether he should call for reinforcements or enjoy the growing storm.

"Would you please ring up Chief Superintendent Sheehan and ask him to come out here for a moment?" I said. "I trust he's in."

"Then you can call James Ryne," Caeli said, addressing the clerk though her eyes remained on Abbot. "He was helpful the last time we met. I'm sure he'd be happy to hear us out."

"Or G2 branch," I said. "They'll want to know that certain individuals here are less than helpful."

"Forget it – all of it," Abbot shouted. He waved off the desk clerk, scowled at us, and shot a lingering look of disgust toward his sergeant.

"Take care of this quickly, Phelan," he said. "See me when yer done."

He turned smartly and all but ran down the hall.

"He'll be awhile," Caeli called, and this time Phelan couldn't hide his concern.

"God's teeth, but you'll be after gettin' me sacked," he said solemnly.

"Not a chance," Caeli said. "We'll say nice things about you."

"At your disciplinary hearing," I added.

His eyes widened even more, and I thought it best to change the subject.

"What the hell was that about, anyway?" I asked.

But Phelan retained his horror-stricken expression, and we couldn't immediately determine whether it was because of the exchange we'd had with his boss or whether something else was at play. He pulled us down the hall with him, grabbing our arms as he slipped between us and urged us ahead with lengthy strides. He eventually located an empty office and tugged us inside.

"Professor Blake, Miss Brown – I've been more'n concerned, ya see," he said. "Ya haven't returned the dozen or more messages I left on yer mobile."

"Sorry. Our phones have been compromised, according to G2," I said, and I'll confess that I wasn't picking up the overriding anxiety that Phelan was pushing. "What's gotten into Abbot, anyway?"

He frowned again, pushed off track by the question.

"Abbot's an eejit on his best day, and this isn't it – not by a bunch. He's bloody-well nervous. The whole place is," Phelan said. "We got word about the warehouse, ya see, and Sheehan sent out a dozen more men. With the ones already there, it's a bunch of us all told. He and Abbot disagreed about staffin' there and throughout the city, and the two of 'em are makin' a fine row of it."

"And that concerns us because …?"

"Well, the two of ya seem to be at the head of it," he said. "Abbot's of a mind, after Bunratty, that both of ya should be locked up. He's been makin' a case for it with the Dublin brass. When the phones rang in with yer walk from the restaurant to here and the exchanges ye had with our lads along the way, well, he blew a cork and is threatenin' all manner of mayhem."

"Let him blow," Caeli said. "We've no intention of staying involved anyway."

But Phelan now looked apologetic as well as harried.

"Too late for that, Miss Brown," he said. "Me cousin was out to yer home, ya see, no more than an hour ago, gettin' an idea of the size of the place and the layout so he can make the proper arrangements – for the wedding."

He paused, ensuring that we were following along, and I waved him on.

"There's activity out yer way, it 'tis – eyes that don't belong," he said.

"It's likely G2, ordered by Gallacher," I said. "Either that or it's your men."

"No," he said. "I checked. It's something else altogether – something connected to what's happened out to Bunratty."

Well, crap, I thought. *That's not good.*

TWENTY-FOUR

THE NEWS IN BRIEF

The story in the *Irish Times* was buried on an inside page and was easy to miss, even if you were looking for it.

Tucked under a header that read, simply, **Suspicious death**, the prose was stark and devoid of solid information, or at least anything meaningful:

A body found floating in the Liffey this past Tuesday has been identified, according to local police.

Rory O'Rourke of Dublin 6, Rathmines, a general handyman and day-labourer by trade, was reported missing by his wife after he failed to return from his night job the previous Saturday.

He was last seen during his shift at James Toner on Baggot Street Lower near St. Stephen's Green, where he also worked as a part-time publican.

Sources said the death was suspicious in nature but provided no details.

Police are asking anyone with information on O'Rourke's movements during the last few days to make contact for a possible reward.

TWENTY-FIVE

CALLING IN THE CAVALRY

We reacted outwardly to the news that our home was being scrutinized by unsavory forces with a practiced indifference that would fool you if you didn't know us well or weren't paying careful attention.

It's true that we've had experience with this sort of thing, but that wasn't the point. You always do what you can to mitigate the fallout when others are watching – and Alan Phelan was eyeing us closely now.

I cursed silently and exchanged a glance with Caeli, who remained stoic despite the complication. Then I damn near laughed out loud when it occurred to me that she was probably more concerned about the potential for disrupting plans for the wedding, or maybe for the safety of her cats, than she was about terrorists and hypnotists and killers and any other manner of cretin inclined to make our lives difficult.

Still, it was clear that we needed to put Plan A into place.

And yeah, we didn't exactly have a Plan B.

"Do you have access to a secure line?" Caeli asked Phelan, who seemed confused by our lack of emotion. He stood motionless, his mouth slightly agape, one eyebrow significantly raised, and appeared as though he didn't understand the question.

She tried again.

"A line we can use that can't be traced or tracked – something you'd use in emergencies, maybe, or to contact national headquarters?" she said.

That got him moving.

"No, not really. We'd make the call on a normal line. What bloody fool would tap the Guards?" he said. "But there's a record, of course, if yer concerned about such things. Why not just use yer mobiles?"

I cursed under my breath at that last part, recognizing that we'd have to go in a different direction.

"We can't. They've been compromised, Spud," I said, a gentle reminder.

"Yeah, right – I remember. How 'bout ya use my mobile instead then? It's not on anyone's radar, so far as I know, Abbot's included," he said, reaching into a pocket to locate his phone.

"It's a call to the States," Caeli said.

"No worries. This'll handle it nicely." He'd fished it out by this time and offered it to Caeli.

She declined, however – a decision that I fully understood.

"It's a gracious offer, Alan," she said. "But I don't want anything coming back on you, or costing you money or eating up your minutes, or for your superiors to find out you were helping us – that last part especially."

What she didn't want – what neither of us wanted – was to take the chance that Spud's phone also had been compromised, which would place him in potential jeopardy.

He remained committed to help.

"Too late for that last one, ya know," he said, easing out a mirthless laugh.

"OK, so how about this?" I said. "Is there a place somewhere nearby that sells burner phones?"

"Burner phones?"

"The pay-and-toss kind," I said.

"Ah, a pre-paid. Sure," he said. "CeX on Cruise's Street sells 'em, I believe. It's close, actually."

"Within walking distance?"

"Depends on how long ya got. Why don't I give ya a lift?"

That prompted another confession.

"Again, Spud, we don't want attention directed at you," I said. "G2 is concerned and has at least two teams on our tail, one on foot and the other in a gray sedan that's parked out front. We'd just as soon they didn't …"

But he already knew of our plight.

"Yeah, so I've heard," Phelan said. "It's partly what's got Abbot's knickers in a knot. Me car's docked out back, and no reason for anyone on G2's payroll to know what I drive. So long as ya keep yer heads down as we motor into traffic, we'll be fine."

"You're sure?"

"Hey, it'll keep me out of Abbot's sights a bit longer, which is lovely."

"Perfect," Caeli said. "If you're up for it, so are we."

He steered us down a long corridor and, after a couple of detours to avoid passing coppers, eventually out a side door to a paved area where employees parked personal vehicles.

"This way," Phelan said, calling over his shoulder as he hustled toward his car, the aging Mini Cooper he'd driven to the estate when we'd first met.

We managed to tuck ourselves as discreetly as possible into the back seat, which was just large enough to accommodate us in an upright position. But we'd have to lie down, keeping our heads out of sight, if we were to slip past the watchers who lurked in front of *Garda* headquarters.

"Do yer best to stay low, despite the close quarters," Phelan said once we'd settled in. "I'll shout when the time comes, and then again when it's clear."

We squirmed and shuffled to contort our bodies onto the rear bench seat with little success and finally decided to sit normally and lean forward, as though we were in an airplane that was about to crash.

"Good thing we ate light today," I muttered.

"Avoided pasta, you mean," Caeli said. "You can thank me later."

"I'll thank you now: *molto grazie di tutto*," I whispered as Phelan chugged out of the lot and around the building, pausing for passing traffic on Henry Street, waiting for an opening.

"Jaysus. I know those blokes on the street – used to be with us," he said seconds later. "So they've been recruited by G2, the lucky tossers. Wonder how they managed that plum."

It's not much of a plum when you're getting your ass shot off, or tying up traffic and flipped off for your troubles, or chasing after a couple of Yanks who'd rather be somewhere else – anywhere else, I thought.

But I didn't say any of that to Spud Phelan.

"Hey," I offered instead. "They're stuck on the pavement with no prospects for improving their lot. You, on the other hand, have the pleasure of our company."

"Yer right," he said as he eased into the lane. "I should be honored."

"You mean you're not?"

"Oh, I'm bloody well honored," he said. "And I mostly mean it. We're clear, by the way. Yer free to sit up, relax, enjoy the ride … whatever ya like."

Phelan dropped us in front of the all-things-digital CeX store a moment later, apologizing that no immediate parking space was available.

"I'll circle 'round 'til ya come out," he said.

We secured two phones inside of 10 minutes, paying cash and getting a quick lesson on the setup from the kid behind the counter who, after hearing us talk, pestered us with a dozen questions about life in the States. When we explained that we'd just moved to Ireland and were delighted to be out of the American rat race, he seemed disappointed.

"Ya mean ye left the excitement of New York and Boston and the like, places I'd give me left bollox to get to?" he said incredulously. "Are ye daft then, the pair of ya?"

I explained that New York and Boston seldom applied because we'd lived on the left coast.

"Better yet then, boyo," he said. "LA, 'Frisco, Seattle – cities with grit. And Hollywood – bloody Tinseltown itself. Jaysus, man, it's every Irishman's fantasy."

We smiled at his enthusiasm, encouraged him to save his money, and asked before he got wound up again if a private setting was available somewhere in the store for us to make a phone call without prying ears and eyes listening and watching. He thought it over, looking this way and that, giving no indication that he found the request to be out of the ordinary.

"Well now, ye can always try the jacks, I suppose, an' hope for the best."

But the restroom didn't seem like a good bet, so we trudged outside and waved Phelan around the block and took a booth inside a nearby McDonald's, which at least got us off the street. Caeli had Fredo Fierro on the line a moment later, asking him to ignore the bustle of on-the-go diners and shout-outs for completed order numbers. Under normal circumstances, or better ones, anyway, she would've keyed the phone's speaker so that both of us could hear. But given our current location, the best I could do was sit close and pick up a sense of what Freddy had to offer.

For reasons that I can't adequately explain here, reaching Fredo was like grabbing a lifeline an instant before you were about to be swept over Multnomah Falls. I'd been concerned that he might ignore it when the call came in, seeing as the number was unfamiliar. But he apparently recognized the international code as coming from Ireland and picked up after a handful of rings.

Of course, it helped that Caeli called his personal line. Damn few people have that number – certainly no one in Ireland beyond the two of us, now that Don Vincenzo was gone and his Celtic operation was being slowly dismantled.

Fredo was willing to help, though he didn't refrain from giving us the needle.

"You sure know how to step in it," he said. "What happened to being retired?"

"I've been asking myself the same question," Caeli said. "Best I can say is it's a lesson learned … until the next time, anyway."

I could hear Freddy's laughter at the other end, and it was both comforting and reassuring to recognize that he was supportive.

"He's far too good to us," she said once she'd signed off.

"He reminds me of his father."

"Absolutely," she replied. "I had my doubts, you know, when Vinny first passed and Freddy had to step in. But he's been great. I sometimes feel that we've learned more from him than he has from us."

Her thoughts echoed my own, though I was more interested in the details.

"I didn't catch everything. He's agreed to send Elmore and Leonard?" I asked.

She took a moment to fill me in. Freddy determined early in the discussion that we were in need of his two prized bodyguards and offered them up without indicating that he'd ask them first as to whether they'd be OK with the assignment.

"He figured it'll take four hours to make arrangements to secure the crew for one of the jets, file a flight plan, and get under way," she said. "That puts them at Shannon in 17 hours unless they run into a snag. If that happens, he'll let us know."

"I hope to hell Leonard is OK with this," I said after thinking it through.

"Leave Leonard to me," Caeli said.

But there was no telling what Leonard might do once he arrived on our doorstep, and I remained wary, even as we exited MickeyD's and moments later hailed Spud Phelan, pressing him for an update on our G2 minders.

Nothing is easy.

I've said that previously, though it bears repeating.

Case in point: In yet another extremist terrorist attack in the heart of London, the good people of that stoic nation were forced to fight with bottles, pint glasses, and chairs when three knife-wielding fanatics entered pubs and restaurants, slashing and stabbing random victims after running down a number of pedestrians with work vans – hardly a fair fight.

I was certain that the viciousness of this latest attack influenced Gallacher and his team. It may well have been the reason why he consented to provide us with the Berettas.

But that decision also influenced the way that we dealt with DS Phelan.

We'd entered into a circuitous discussion when we asked him to drop us a block or so away from Caeli's SUV so that he wouldn't be viewed as willingly helping us by lingering G2 or *Garda* personnel assigned to watch us – or, and far worse, get caught up in some ill-advised gunfight with crazed lunatics bent on creating a new world order.

We were now armed, after all, and Irish police officers, as a rule, are not. Not that our pistols would provide much protection against sub-machine guns or AK-47s or other assault weapons capable of firing multiple rounds in mere seconds. But they were better than nothing at all, and certainly better than anything Phelan might have on his person.

I didn't mention any of that, but I didn't have to. Phelan knew the score.

Besides, he had other thoughts.

"I don't mind attention from the spies," he said. "That's not a concern, given the detail I'm stuck on. But I don't want to see ya turned out on the street shy of gettin' yer rig – not with scoundrels about."

I decided to change the subject.

"You have contacts all over Limerick, Spud – correct?"

"Ya know I do," he said.

"How about someone equipped to look at our phones and clean out any bugs that may have been slipped inside?"

Of course, I failed to offer that we were concerned about Gallacher's people as well as the hacking that had likely taken place in Bunratty. Why muddy already murky waters?

"Ah, a vermin infestation, which is why ya needed the pre-paids then," he said, connecting the dots. "Sure. A cousin on me mother's side knows a bloke who lives near somebody who specializes in such things. He does fine work – highly recommended, I'm told."

"Perfect," Caeli said. "How about we give you our phones and you can turn them over? We'll pay up front."

"No need. I'm happy to help."

"That's great," I said. "We'll leave you to it. You can drop us off here, by the way."

He wheeled the car down a side street until he found a free parking spot and brought us to a lurching halt.

"Still happy to take ya in," he said. "I'd rather see ya safely inside the garage than leave ya on the street."

"Kind of you, Spud," I said. "But if the bad guys are about, we'd rather you weren't involved."

I produced out my wallet and secured a €100 note that I keep tucked away for emergencies.

"Here, in case something comes up," I said as we gave him our phones. "I'll contact you in a couple of days."

"Again, it's not …"

"It's OK," Caeli said. "We want you safe, Alan, and free of this mess."

"But I'm the one who pulled ya in," he protested. "If not for me, you'd be at home now with yer cats and no spies runnin' after ya."

"It's fine," Caeli said. "Be sure to keep Abbot entertained."

"He's a nasty one, all right," he said. "Yer sure I can't …"

"I'm sure," Caeli said, and that was that. We left Spud behind, two city blocks from Caeli's Range Rover.

TWENTY-SIX

THE WAITING GAME

We walked cautiously toward the parking garage, our situational awareness on high alert because of the day's events – and I also couldn't shake the feeling that a hell of lot more bad stuff was coming our way.

I was fairly certain that we'd be stopped before we got to Caeli's SUV, though I put the odds at 90-10 that we'd find Gallacher's minions lingering about, waiting for us with subtle threats and demands that we come in from the cold. Caeli was equally certain that the man we'd run into at Bunratty Folk Park would show up with help a'plenty and guns a'blazing – more than we could handle with a pair of pistols we'd been discouraged from using.

How bad can it get? – that's the real question, I thought and, a moment later, said as much to Caeli.

"It's a hell of a mess we're in, you know."

"True," she replied.

"I don't expect it to get any better anytime soon, either."

"Agreed."

Not exactly the reassurance that I was looking for, but it was pointless to get into it in detail as we arrived at the garage and took the stairs to the second level to collect the Range Rover.

I was tempted to again apologize for getting us into this windfall of bad tidings but figured that we were well beyond that

point. I determined, however, that I'd get Caeli something special
for the wedding, a gift she wouldn't expect.

*A trip to the Greek Isles, maybe ... Rhodes and Milos and
Crete*, I thought. *Maybe we can spend a couple of months.*

It was easy to get carried away, and I did my best to store the
idea and keep my mind on more pressing matters.

We maintained a critical eye on the vehicles we passed,
searching for signs of furtive activity or evidence that someone
was lying in wait. But the garage was largely deserted. We saw
neither spies nor coppers and only one other person, a woman in
her mid-60s who was dragging a shopping cart on wheels, wearily
tugging it behind her, on the first floor as we first entered.

"I'm surprised," I said as we slipped inside the Range Rover.
"I was expecting a greeting committee, telling us to play ball or
return to the fold or … something."

"Maybe Gallacher's slipping," Caeli said as we climbed
inside.

"He was sharp enough to keep two teams on us when we left
the restaurant," I said. "Not much gets by him."

"Maybe. Then again, maybe he's no longer interested," she
suggested.

I studied her for a moment, trying to read her thoughts. But
Caeli's poker face is absolute, which forced me to ask the obvious
question.

"Do you really believe he'd let us just walk away?"

She laughed, though without humor, and I thought that she
looked tired, as though the long day's events had crashed down
on her all at once.

"Hell no," she said. "Gallacher's eyes and ears will be on us
until this is settled, which only makes me hope it ends soon."

She stared through the windshield for a few seconds before
starting the engine, looking pensive.

"Too bad it's out of our hands," she said. "The best we can
do is wait it out, stay safe – and prepare for the wedding. Can't
forget that."

That last part came with a smile, and I leaned across the
console and pulled her close and kissed her on the cheek and did
my best to reassure her, for just an instant, that everything would
be all right so long as we worked together.

Then she asked the inevitable question, the one we'd both been dreading.

"So what do we do now? We can't go back to the house – not if you believe G2," she said. "At this stage, much as I hate to admit it, we need to buy into Gallacher's logic. We don't have many options – none that are good anyway."

"I agree. So rather than going home, how about we head to Bunratty and wait there?"

Caeli looked at me as though I'd grown a second nose.

"Are you …?"

But then the logic of it hit her, and she smiled.

"No, you're right. It's a good call," she said as she put the SUV into gear. "We speed up the process and stay out of the line of fire at the same time."

"It works to our advantage if we play our cards carefully and stay safe until the cavalry arrives" – I pointed toward the digital clock on the dashboard – "which should be somewhere around 16 hours from now, give or take."

"And while we're at it, we poke around for Joan's killer," she said.

"How else will this mess end if we don't personally do something stellar?"

She laughed again. This time I heard merriment.

"Gallacher will find out and arrest us and lock us away for a hundred years."

"Maybe more," I said.

"He'll surely want his pistols back."

"And attempt to beat us about the head and shoulders."

"But I love it – despite the risk," she said. "We'll be doing something."

"Which is why it makes sense, regardless of the added exposure. Gallacher as much as said he won't arrest this guy until bigger fish are on the line."

Caeli took my arm, gripping tightly.

"I don't care about the rest of it – not right now," she said. "Joan deserves better. We didn't know her long, or well, but I liked her."

Then she spotted a snag.

"Wait – the cats," she said. "We can't leave them alone. Mitts needs food."

"I'm on it," I said, and I was. "We drive to the house and get them – a pit-stop. It's doubtful that anyone will take a run at us in daylight."

"Gallacher's people are probably watching the estate anyway."

"Right. So we nab the cats, run around Limerick's one-way-streets to throw off potential chasers, find a pet-friendly hotel, and do some surreptitious hunting. Mitts will be thrilled, and Elmore and Leonard will be here before we know it."

Caeli nudged us forward, heading toward the exit sign that would take us to street level, when I spotted the older shopper I'd seen earlier, dragging the wheeled cart.

Why is she still wandering around? I wondered. *Is she lost?*

"She should be long gone by now," I muttered, more to myself than to Caeli.

That's precisely when the woman dropped the handle on her cart and pulled a silenced pistol from the right pocket of her coat, taking direct aim at the Range Rover.

Caeli is an expert driver – certainly the best I've seen, known, and happily been on the road with. What we'd told the two G2 spies who'd commandeered the Range Rover when we left the warehouse earlier that day was accurate, despite their insistence that we get into the back seat. We both were trained by professionals, although Caeli is better at it than me – good enough, in fact, that one of her instructors, a former agency spook with scary credentials, told her that she could find work as a wheelman for bank robbers, security firms ferrying VIPs about, or even for the government.

High praise, indeed.

In this case, her skill behind the wheel, combined with her natural instincts and quick reflexes, kept the subsequent damage from the sudden intrusion to a minimum.

Then again, we caught a couple of breaks.

For starters, the shooter didn't realize that the Range Rover is armored, equipped with an outer shell designed to withstand a bullet and bomb blast, along with glass that's also bulletproof, or at least sufficient to keep us from harm when someone pulls out a silencer-equipped handgun and tosses rounds our way.

The length of the parking garage also gave Caeli room to maneuver, which again worked in our favor.

"Dammit. The old bag's shooting at us," I said, incredulous.

Yeah, I know. It wasn't eloquent, polite, or age sensitive, but it was accurate.

The first three shots, aimed directly at Caeli, were deflected as neatly as an NHL goalie's kick-save.

They also pissed us off.

Caeli swerved the Rover slightly, an instinctive reaction, and gunned the engine, which snapped us back in the seat as the turbocharger kicked in.

I was tempted to grab the Beretta, lower the passenger's side window, and get the shooter's attention. But Gallacher's words of warning about using our borrowed pistols only in the direst of emergencies rang in my head, and the shooter's snap decision to try another tactic made the issue moot.

Recognizing that the windshield, at least, was bulletproof, the woman thumped a couple of bullets into the driver's side door as we shot past. The slugs were turned away by the SUV's thick hide, although an examination later revealed that they left dents in the metal the size of an old Irish half-crown piece and would require professional eradication.

Try explaining that to your insurance company.

The shooter's next move was to attempt to take out the rear tires. She stepped into the lane behind us and fired off five shots in methodical fashion, as though initiating the countdown to a rocket's launch. I know this for certain because I was watching and mentally totaled them up.

Caeli wasn't happy about any of this. She slammed on the brakes, which brought us to a screeching halt, and pushed the gearshift lever upward two slots into Reverse before flooring it. She didn't say a word, nor did she turn her head to look behind her, navigating instead via the mirrors.

The maneuver reminded me of a grand master's command of all of the pieces on a chess board. It was unexpected – hell, it was damn frightening, and I was inside the protected SUV – and, best of all, it was effective. The shooter, no doubt expecting us to continue racing away, scrambled to flee as the Rover's tires smoked and screeched again and launched us in a path that would either brush the woman aside or mow her over. Moving with a dexterity that belied her years, she ducked between a BMW and a Volvo, both of which were parked along the interior aisle of the garage.

I lost sight of her for the next several seconds as Caeli again slammed on the brakes, rocking us to a halt in the approximate position where we'd last seen the shooter.

"Do you have her, Max?" Caeli asked as she pulled the Beretta from her purse and grabbed the door handle. Her voice was calm and cool – soothing somehow.

"No – and that concerns me," I said.

"Yeah – me, too. Let's go find her."

I was prepared to argue the point, or at least discuss it, but Caeli was committed.

When she began pushing the door open, however, another burst of gunfire slammed into the driver's-side door – five consecutive shots, followed by a brief halt, and then six more. Caeli pulled the door shut, and I did the only thing that I could think, which was unconventional at best. I opened the glove box, found the gunfire CD that I'd tucked away for emergencies, never thinking that it would ever be played – *Not in a million years*, I recall thinking – slammed it into the Range Rover's stereo player, cranked up the sound, and opened my door.

Caeli looked on as though I'd lost my mind, but damned if it didn't work. The stereo cranked out the sounds of a Walther P99's sustained double- and triple-taps, one after another, echoing throughout the cavernous parking garage, as though both of us were launching an all-out assault on our adversary.

I clicked the stereo off momentarily, then hit the play button once more and opened my door even wider. I let the sounds rumble and burp on for 20 seconds this time before shutting it down.

Silence.

Glorious silence, in fact.

"You've got to be kidding me," Caeli muttered.

"Maybe I should take out a patent," I said.

But we didn't take time for high-fives.

Caeli pushed the door open just wide enough to slink through, and I followed her lead and exited the SUV on the opposite side, slipping around the rear to obtain a line of sight on the area between the Beamer and the Volvo. Caeli had already sidled up behind the Volvo, crouching near the trunk, peeking around the sedan's right side, pistol in hand. I checked its opposite side before shifting my position slightly to get a look at what was beyond the BMW. But all I could see in the gloom was another aisle of vehicles and the shooter's abandoned shopping cart.

Caeli started forward, duck-waddling between the Volvo and a panel van that was parked nearby. I didn't like our position, or circumstance, or whatever potentially was lying in wait, and I called out to her in an exaggerated stage whisper.

"Hey – hold up," I said. "There's too much we don't know. Let's call it in instead of kicking the hornet's nest."

"She'll get away," Caeli replied, speaking just loudly enough for me to hear.

"She already has," I countered. "Maybe we'll get lucky and find some fingerprints on the shopping cart. But I've got a decent description because I also saw her when we first came in. We can give that to Gallacher – let him deal with it."

Truth is, the attack made me nervous, and I found myself not only wishing that we hadn't been hamstrung by Gallacher's caution about the guns he'd given us but also that we weren't carrying our Walthers, reliable pistols we were comfortable with.

With no good options available, I pulled out the phone that Gallacher's driver had given to me and hit the first speed dial button.

"I don't like it, Max," Caeli said, and it was plain that she wanted to pursue the shooter with the same determination that she uses for – well, for most everything she does. "I don't like being shot at."

"I don't, either, but we can't risk a pursuit," I said. "We don't know who's out there – and we're not supposed to use these damn pistols unless we're forced to."

"You don't think this qualifies as a genuine emergency?"

But I didn't bother answering because Gallacher picked up with a terse grunt that might have been a "What?" or a "Yeah" or an Irish phrase I didn't recognize.

"We were just attacked at the parking garage," I said. "Older woman, mid-60s, disguised as a shopper, pulling a cart with packages tucked inside. She was carrying a Glock or a SIG P226

– hard to tell which, exactly, because of the silencer. She fired at least 21 rounds."

"Jaysus," he muttered.

I didn't give him the chance to start asking questions.

"She was wearing a frumpy hat, a cold-weather coat that was dark in color – deep gray or black – and dark gloves. Her weight was between 115 to 125 pounds as we measure it. You'll have to convert to stones," I said, referencing the unit that the Irish use to determine a person's heft. "She had what I'd call a fair complexion, though ruddy from the weather. Her hair was turning from a light ash to gray from what I could see. Then again, it might have been a wig – hard to tell with the hat."

I stopped here, thinking about the woman, trying to pull items of value from memory.

"Where are you now?" Gallacher barked.

"In the garage," I said. "She was alone and didn't get a chance to police her brass, so that should help. She also left the cart behind once Caeli took a run at her with the SUV."

"She did what?"

"Caeli scared her off," I said. "What's your pleasure? Should we stay and keep the scene clear of shoppers, or would you rather we skedaddled?"

"Are you safe for the moment – certain the shooter's gone?"

"Yeah – so far as I can tell. There's no sign of her or anyone else. The place seems deserted, likely because you'd commandeered it earlier."

He paused, either thinking the situation through or coming up with 20 ways to pin us down once his team arrived.

"All right – don't leave the site 'til I get somebody there," he said seconds later. "Shouldn't take longer than two minutes. That rig of yers is armored, right?"

"Yeah."

"Good. Get inside, if you're not already, lock the bloody doors, and don't move 'til you get the all-clear sign from my people. Meantime, don't let anybody near the spent casings, the shopping cart, anything of value."

"Got it."

"If she shows up again, hit the bloody pedal and bolt. Do not engage. Got it?"

"Yeah," I said, wondering how Caeli would take that order. But Gallacher sealed it with his next question.

"Did either of ya you shoot the Berettas?"

"No."

"Good. Don't – not unless there's no other option. Drive away if she returns. Tell me you understand."

"Sure. We get it," I said.

I wasn't sure whether he was done or not, but I was. I severed the connection and shrugged as Caeli looked on.

"Gallacher wants us to stay in the rig and secure the scene 'til the cavalry arrives," I said.

"If we do one, how can we do the other?" she asked, still steaming because of the attack and the shooter's ability to slip the net.

"I didn't ask."

"I think we should track her," she said. "We don't take orders from Gallacher."

But the situation concerned me, and I laid it out for her. The last thing we needed was an all-out assault from the old woman and a raft of her compatriots, all of whom I could envision waiting for the right moment to strike – and this seemed to be the right moment. Hell, to my way of thinking, we'd been saved from further attack because of a CD … a gimmick at best.

Caeli was still grumbling when I had another thought.

"Maybe this was a trap to lure Gallacher and his people back here," I said.

"Maybe. Unlikely, though," she said. "This seemed personal."

I thought about calling him with my suspicions anyway, but 5 seconds turned to 10 and then 10 more, and Caeli eventually returned to the Range Rover and joined me in the waiting game.

"Any thoughts?" she asked once we'd climbed inside and locked the doors, still holding the borrowed pistols.

"Yeah – an overriding one," I said. "When Gallacher's people show up, let's point out the obvious and get the hell out of here, before they either object to our departure or force us to come in for a contrived debriefing."

"I'm with you there," she said, and that became our central focus as we impatiently waited for the good guys.

TWENTY-SEVEN

A RESCUE OF SORTS

They showed up minutes later in five rigs, three Ford sedans and two black GM SUVs with tinted windows and souped-up engines, all unmarked, swarming into the garage as though they owned the place.

Then again, maybe they did.

Surprisingly, Liam Gallacher was not among them. But the two agents who'd been assigned to us earlier that morning, when we'd first arrived at the warehouse to view the massive anti-terrorism operation, stepped out of one of the sedans and favored us with nasty frowns that conveyed much about their state of mind.

We secured the Berettas and stepped out to greet them.

"It's Gavin and Ian, right?" I said as they approached, hoping to blunt the pending invective. We ignored the other nine agents who fanned out to search for the shooter.

"Actually, it's Ian and Gavin," Ian said. "Best not forget it."

I ignored the remark, recalling that he had insisted on driving Caeli's SUV, and I used that as a reference point to keep the pair straight in my head. They glanced at one another, their eyes dark and their manner frosty, with a dollop of *We know better than you* spread across their faces, determining which one would rip into us first, no doubt.

I was mentally preparing to ward off the blows, but Caeli struck first.

"Did you find her?" she asked.

The question startled Gavin.

Ian, at least, was ready to answer.

"Not yet, but we've teams combing the area, inside and out," he said. "If she's out there, or in here, we'll get her. So let's just back up and ..."

Caeli didn't allow him to finish.

"Your chances of finding her will improve if you actually look for her instead of fake babysitting us," she said.

Yeah. She wasn't happy. I chalked it up to her continued displeasure with being shot at by the old women and not as a personal grudge against our two minders.

Ian seemed equally annoyed.

"And we'll do just that – soon enough, surely. But we need to get the details out of the way," he said.

I figured that she'd start in again, giving as good as she got. But she paused, glancing at me after a lingering stare-down with Ian produced no quarter on either side, and favored me with her best *Let's see their cards* look. I took that as a positive sign, and we leaned against the Range Rover's flank, close to the spot where the old woman's bullets bounced aside, and watched two forensics specialists work the scene, recognizing that no amount of tough talk would forestall the inevitable grilling.

Ian folded his arms across his chest and scowled.

"So tell us, if ya would, what bloody well happened here."

"I gave a report to Gallacher," I said. "It was rich in detail."

"Yeah. He radioed us," Gavin said, his accent as thick as Guinness as he snarled the words. "Why don't ya start at the beginnin' and give us the sequence so we have it straight and can move on from there."

From there? Where, exactly, is there? I thought.

Caeli was more direct.

"Would you like to try that again?" she asked.

Gavin shook his head in frustration.

"No," he said. "Tell us what ya saw – what ya know."

I got the sense that they were more interested in taking charge, flexing their muscles and demonstrating that they had some measure of control over what they'd allow us to do from that point forward, than they were in actually hearing another accounting of the attack. I might have been wrong, of course. But

Caeli and I discussed the meeting in detail afterward, and we both saw evidence of the let's-pull-it-out-and-measure behavior that you often get from males in law enforcement, regardless of what country you're in.

We also concluded that our cooperation, or at least a hint of it, would be the only way we'd shake free anytime soon.

"We entered the parking level on the first floor on foot, and I spotted the woman

as we moved past her, from a distance," I said. "She looked to be nothing more than a typical elderly shopper, returning from a trip to some nearby store, pulling a cart. She even had a couple of packages in the damned thing."

I pointed to the spot where the cart had been abandoned, close to the Volvo that Caeli had used for cover.

"I didn't give her a second thought until I spotted her a second time, as we were attempting to leave. She was …"

"Leave? Leave where?" Gavin asked.

"Leave here – the parking garage, driving off this level."

"All right … got it. Proceed."

I wondered about his mental capacity but chalked it up to the idea that he wanted to be thorough.

"She appeared from the shadows, pulled a pistol, and aimed at the windshield once Caeli started forward," I said next. "She fired three shots at Caeli, figuring the bullets would penetrate the glass."

"And you know that how, exactly?" Ian said. "Yanks can read minds, is it?"

"We can read bullet patterns on glass well enough. She was trying to kill me," Caeli said, brushing her hand toward the front of her rig. "Try to keep up."

"Quite," Gavin said, glancing for an instant toward his partner before leaning in close to locate evidence of the shots. "So yer vehicle's armored, with special glass then."

I refrained from muttering any number of smart-assed comments that sprang to mind and merely nodded.

"Why?" he asked.

"That's classified," Caeli said.

He looked on blankly. Hell, they both did.

"What does that mean, exactly?" Gavin finally asked.

"It means you're wasting time on items that have no relevance to what happened," Caeli said. "You should be out there" – she waved toward the great beyond – "trying to find her instead of interrogating us. You both know what happened."

They glanced at one another, pausing momentarily, switching tactics.

"I'm sorry, Miss Brown, but you'd be best served by cooperatin'," Gavin said. "I know this must be upsettin' for ya, bein' shot at and all. But believe me, worse things by far could be in store if only you'd …"

"That's just it," Caeli said. "I've been shot at before – we both have. I'd be upset if she'd hit me. You should find the shooter instead of wasting my time."

Gavin flashed a hint of anger, and perhaps some shame and even amusement, I thought, and was about to press on when Ian took over.

"All right, boyos, what say we end the snipin' and get through it as quick as we can manage, eh?"

He smiled, thinly, ready to proceed, but Caeli was again too quick.

"See the brass lying there?" she said, pointing toward the nearby spent casings that littered the pavement.

Both men instinctively glanced toward the empty shells and nodded.

"Check your database for fingerprints," she said. "You might get lucky. If not, ask Interpol for help, or the FBI. Then check the CCTV footage. Max already provided a detailed description of the shooter. Given that, you can match a face to a name on file."

I jumped in with a thought.

"So long as she doesn't change her appearance," I said. "Because if they haven't found her by now, she's likely long gone and this means nothing."

"Unless she decided to jump inside a truck or a van and wait for the commotion to settle," Caeli said, talking again to the agents. "That's the way I'd play it, given your response time. You should check everything parked in the garage right now, big or small, boots and back seats as well as fronts, just in case she's still here."

I offered her a smile.

"That's good thinking – a line of inquiry worth pursuing."

But it was too soon for a quick getaway to see if we could solve the puzzle on our own and get on with our lives. Gallacher's men weren't appreciative of the suggestions, and they weren't done with us, either.

"All that aside, let's get back to the shootin' then," Ian said. "I'm still fuzzy on a couple o' points. What say ye start from the top and tell us what took place after the initial shots?"

Caeli was losing patience, and she doesn't suffer either fools or persnickety time-wasters well. But I also suspected that much of her ire resulted from the length of time we'd been away from our home, and she was worried about the cats.

"Listen carefully. We tried to leave the parking garage," Caeli said. "The old woman appeared from over there" – she waved toward the line of cars that stretched out before us – "and opened up with some sort of pistol."

"A silenced Glock or SIG," I said.

"Ya know yer guns then, professor," Ian said.

"Yeah. I do."

Caeli picked up the story again.

"She fired three times at the windshield. As I sped by, she fired at the side door" – she pointed again after shifting her position – "right here."

The spooks stared at the SUV for several seconds without reacting.

"We were now past her. I hit the brakes when she started shooting at the rear tires, five rounds this time," Caeli said. "I reversed and took a run at her, forcing her to jump aside right here" – she pointed toward the Beamer and the Volvo. "You can see the tire marks up ahead there" – yet another pointed finger – "both from where I gunned it to get by her and then again where I stopped and reversed."

Ian and Gavin took another look up the line, registering Caeli's observations.

"The shooter then disappeared between the cars and fired another volley, Max called your boss, and you arrived when you arrived. Here we are. End of story unless you find her," she said.

Ian wanted to pursue other avenues.

"You didn't provoke her in any way?" he asked.

"No," we answered in unison.

"Yer sure?" he pressed.

"Yes," both of us said, though I added, "What the hell difference would it make if we had? You're wasting time again."

I got a scowl for that, and he jumped back in.

"Did either of you fire your weapon?"

"No," we again answered in unison.

"Ye can prove it then?"

"Do you want to see them?" I asked.

"Yeah. Straight away."

I didn't think we'd gain much by arguing or getting anyone unnecessarily excited and nodded instead toward the Range Rover.

"The Berettas are secured inside," I said. "Caeli's is in her purse. Mine's in the center console. Check the mags, smell the barrels – whatever trips your trigger."

Sure, a dicey choice of words – but I, too, was growing weary of the nonsense.

Gavin opened the driver's-side door to check the pistols while Ian, glowering fiercely, continued his debriefing.

"Do ye have any idea a'tall as to why this woman would see fit to attack the pair of ya?" he asked.

Really? Are you serious? I thought. But I went in another direction instead.

"You mean, did we fail to hold the door for her or call her a *Culchie* or something worse?" I said. "Is that what you're asking? Because if it is, you can ..."

"What's a Yank know about *Culchies*?" he said.

"I attended UCD," I said, referencing the University/College in Dublin. "I know about *Jackeens*, too – not that I'd easily bandy either term about."

"It's a damn good thing ya don't, Yank," he said without a trace of humor.

For the uninitiated, a *Jackeen* is a derogatory term used by those who live outside of the Irish capitol and its immediate satellite communities to describe a person from Dublin. A *Culchie* is an equally derogatory term used by *Jackeens* to describe someone from rural Ireland – anywhere that isn't Dublin. You'll sometimes hear the terms tossed back and forth during football matches. For what it's worth, *Culchie* may be derived from the Irish phrase *cúl an tí,* which translates to "back of the house," a reference to the common rustic practice of entering someone's home through the back door to avoid tracking mud into the living area. *Jackeen* is thought to derive from the Union Jack, the British flag, affixed with the Irish diminutive suffix *-een* (or little), because British occupiers once believed that Dubliners were the most English of the Irish – a true slam.

I was surprised that I'd brought it up. Nether term is safe on the lips of outsiders, Yanks under scrutiny in the aftermath of a parking garage shooting especially.

Ian decided to switch gears – not for the better.

"The boss wants us to bring ya in," he said. "Yer welcome to follow …"

"Are we under arrest?" Caeli asked.

"No – of course not," he said quickly. "It's just to keep ya safe, and to …"

"In that case, we're leaving," Caeli said. "He knows how to reach us."

Gavin pulled his head out of the Range Rover, and Caeli slipped past him and slid behind the wheel without another word, or even a glance to determine Ian's state of mind. I looked the pair of them over, trying to determine whether they'd press the issue. When neither man made a move or responded, I climbed into the passenger's seat.

Caeli started the engine, engaged the transmission, and rolled us forward. Ian and Gavin stared as we passed, saying nothing and offering no protest, and I got the sense that they'd anticipated the move.

"See if he took the pistols," Caeli said.

A quick check of her purse, which rested on the console between us, along with the inside of the console itself, confirmed that the Berettas were still in play.

"They left the guns, but I'll bet they also left a tracker," I said. "Take your time while I look around."

She allowed the SUV to idle its way toward the exit, reporting three teams of uniformed coppers, methodically searching the many rows of parked vehicles, along the way.

"I don't see anything obvious in here," I said after poking around the console, the glovebox, and under the dashboard and front seats. "Maybe he didn't leave a present after all."

"You can almost bet he did," Caeli said. "Check my purse."

"How would I know if I saw anything suspicious?" I said automatically, before I could bite back the words. I was rewarded with a decent frown, but damn if she wasn't correct: I located an electronic tracking device a moment later, tucked inside a zippered portion of her handbag, where she keeps her lipstick and a compact folding mirror.

"Take a look at that," I said, holding it up for scrutiny.

I was about to toss it out the car window, but Caeli had another thought. We'd just left the garage, passing the Guards who now had the exit covered, and were on Shannon Street, a one-way thoroughfare heading in a northwesterly direction toward the river. Caeli brought us to a halt and pointed toward a car that was about to exit a nearby parking spot.

"Quick – ask for directions," she said.

"Where do we want to go to?" I asked, not yet catching on. "We can just …"

"We don't care about directions. Drop the bug inside when he rolls down the window," she said. "Hurry or he'll be gone."

Caeli, at least, was right on it.

We arrived at Bunratty two long hours later after a quick stop at our home on the River Shannon to grab our emergency-ready pre-packed overnight bags and secure the cats, along with their food, a filled litter box, and a few toys. Poor Mitts, upset that we'd been gone for so long, remained at his food bowl for a good 10 minutes, doing his best imitation of Captain Crunch once he'd chastised Caeli for abandoning him.

Koko, for her part, strolled into the kitchen, sat for a moment, aloofly watching us, and then strolled out again without showing any interest in Mitty's plight and precious little regarding our arrival. But I got her attention when I brought the carriers in from the garage. Koko isn't a happy traveler.

We had no luck in booking a room in the Bunratty Castle Hotel, our preferred choice, but were fortunate to stumble into a late cancellation at the nearby Bunratty Heights Guesthouse, which is little more than a mile from the Folk Park, according to GPS, and not only is pet-friendly but also features free parking, WiFi, and a full Irish breakfast – a hell of a deal.

Before heading for the tunnel, we hightailed it around Limerick's one-way streets and alleyways and even spent a few moments in a lot at Griffith College on O'Connell Avenue, just to see if anyone was tailing us.

Curiously, we hadn't run into any surprises once we'd left the parking garage, along with the G2 tracking device, behind and returned home. The security alarm was on, the house was free of terrorists and/or thugs, and Caeli's list of items to accomplish before the wedding remained on the counter, exactly where she'd left it.

A car belonging either to the *Garda* or G2 was parked a quarter-mile down the road – an eventuality we'd anticipated. We spotted two men inside, both of whom tried to make it appear as though they were resting.

We waved as we passed.

Caeli scrounged through the kitchen before we left for Bunratty, and we stopped this time and offered Ginger Nuts biscuits (Yanks call them cookies) and bottled water. They looked chagrined before declining, but I left the goodies on the top of the car before we motored off.

"The least we can do," Caeli said.

I had another thought, pulled out the burner phone, and ran a quick online search of pizza delivery businesses.

"I'd rather have pizza on a stakeout than cookies, especially Ginger Nuts," I said.

Caeli's reaction surprised even me.

"Yum. We haven't had pizza since we were in Florence, at the *Piazza Santa Croce*," she said. "Sounds heavenly."

I laughed.

"What about that no-pasta business you gave me not more than … how long ago was it?"

"You don't know how much temptation I would've faced had we stayed," she said.

I eventually gave her the address for the closest pizza place I could find, no more than 10 minutes out of our way.

"I'll pay in cash in case Gallacher is tracking credit cards," I said.

We both went into the shop on St. Nessian's Road just south of Dooradoyle so that Caeli could satisfy her pizza craving without having to eat a bite.

"The aroma alone is enough to last me for a few days," she said.

I only wish that I had her discipline.

I gave the store manager instructions on how to find the unmarked car that was parked near our house, wrote a note for its two occupants, paid for a large classic crust with Italian sausage, pepperoni, and green peppers, along with bottles of soda and some wings on the side, topped off with plastic cups and plates and plenty of serviettes, and tipped the driver and manager generously.

"Are you hungry?" I asked Caeli before we left, hoping that she'd break down and consent to a pie for the road.

She suggested instead a nice dining experience once we'd settled in at Bunratty.

"I was thinking fish," she said.

"As opposed to anchovies?"

"Exactly."

The drive once we crisscrossed the city was uneventful, with steady traffic and another pass through the Limerick Tunnel before we found the guesthouse. The cats were grateful to be out of their carriers and doing what cats do best, which is pretty much nothing except with a great deal of poking around involved. Mitts again ate like the beast that he is, while Koko merely sniffed at her can of Friskies, which Caeli spooned into a plastic dish, and decided to check out the closet before lounging on the queen bed, watching Mitty's assault on his food bowl with disdain.

Caeli began scrolling through a number of online dining menus using the burner phone, taking her time, offering observations or asking questions along the way.

I was smart enough to defer to her in all cases.

"How about a seafood restaurant on Old Bunratty Road," she eventually said, definitely a statement. "It's close by, the offerings are locally caught, according to the website, and the prawns, mussels, trout, and chowder all sound wonderful."

"Better than pizza, you think?" I said.

"Absolutely. I'm glad we didn't cave in, although the smell was tempting."

I asked about our after-dinner plans on the way out the door.

"Simple," she said. "We roam the castle grounds and Folk Park and try to find our guy. If we spot him, great. If not, we collect Elmore and Leonard when they arrive and start kicking ass and taking names, just like the old days."

TWENTY-EIGHT

OLD-HOME WEEK

Our bodyguards arrived on a Fierro Enterprises corporate jet two hours late from the estimated time they'd texted as they left Oregon. Refueling during a stop in Boston apparently dragged on longer than expected.

They were tired from the flight and understandably cranky, although predictably, Leonard was far grouchier than was Elmore, who is forever the optimist.

Caeli got a hug, I got a fist-bump, followed by a hug, and Leonard watched it all unfold with a look of disgust, or something close to disgust. With Leonard, it's difficult to gauge the degrees to which he can express his dissatisfaction through a simple facial expression. On this day he was Picasso, painting a surreal if enigmatic masterpiece – not that it bothered anyone. We're all used to Leonard's antics.

Elmore spoke first.

"My friends – I'm so happy to be here ahead of the big day," he gushed, though you could tell if you listened closely that 13 hours in transit had taken a toll.

He smiled to stifle a yawn, covering his mouth with a massive hand, and added, "You look great. And we've missed you, back home. Things haven't been the same."

Touching, I thought, with reason. What you see, what you hear, is exactly what you get from Elmore. He's been a good friend to us through the years that we've known him, even when he's not looking after us, which was why we'd requested his presence in Ireland once more. His instincts are impeccable, along with his ability to pull his charges out of tight situations – valued traits, indeed.

"Are you speaking for both of you?" I asked, nudging his elbow.

Elmore laughed, and Caeli joined in, and Leonard scowled ferociously, and it was old-home week for the four of us.

I'd first met the pair when they burst into our detective agency in Oregon's capitol city years earlier, guns flashing, indicating with no room for debate that they were taking me to meet with their boss, Don Vincenzo Fierro. He just happened to be the *capo di tutti capi* of the West Coast, according to the federal agencies that monitored his activities.

In brief, I wasn't thrilled with their unannounced arrival, words were exchanged, and additional hardware was produced that soon sent them packing.

But Don Vincenzo persisted, and uncomfortable meetings eventually produced lasting friendships, and our respect for the don turned into admiration of the people who kept him safe, our two current visitors especially.

Their names really aren't Elmore and Leonard. Those are my own appellations, selected because of the way they first entered my office, which was something directly out of an Elmore Leonard novel. Elmore, at least, loves the moniker and even refers to himself with that designation in written notes, emails, and telephone messages that he leaves with us. Leonard is never happy about much of anything, it seems, although he does take a perverse delight in spitting out a terse "That's not my name, dammit," when I use it.

As a general admission here, assigned to the whatever-it's-worth department, Caeli and I also weren't operating on all cylinders when our friends rolled into town, given the odd occurrences and length of the previous day's activities, an unsettled night in a cramped hotel, restless cats that prohibited meaningful sleep for long stretches, an early morning jog/stroll through Bunratty Folk Park on the thin chance that we might spot the mesmerist/terrorist we suspected of killing Joan Shedd, and a fast trip home to return Mitts and Koko to familiar surroundings before racing to the airport.

That side trip proved interesting. Our G2-ordered protective detail had changed during the time we'd been away, and we introduced ourselves on the way in and invited the two officers to join us at the house for tea or coffee, along with something to eat and a bathroom break during the time we'd be there.

Caeli took it a step further.

"You're welcome to stay inside and have the run of the place," she said. "We're off to Shannon in a couple of hours, but you'll be better served indoors than out."

They declined the long-term offer but did join us and insisted on checking the house and grounds before waving us inside.

Now, hours later, it was easy to value Elmore's presence and good cheer, just as we could appreciate Leonard's steadfast role as the man apart, the crotchety outsider who was superb at what he did but who took no joy in doing it – or at least he didn't with us.

Why do we tolerate Leonard's intractability and constantly glum nature and miserable disposition?

I've been asked that question more than once, and it's worth addressing here. We were in need at that moment of a professional problem-solver, and Leonard is exactly that. Despite all of his personal shortcomings, he's a gifted protector with sufficient credentials and knowhow to work for the Secret Service.

Yeah. He's that good.

But he'll never be the life of the party, the first guy picked for the class popularity contest, or your No. 1 choice for that long road trip you've been contemplating – unless, of course, bad guys are on your tail. If that's the case, Leonard would be the go-to guy. He's saved our hides more than once, without hesitation. I'd also venture that, despite his ornery temperament, he'd do it again if necessary. We remain in his debt.

"How's it going, Leonard?" I said, nodding in his direction. "It's good to see you – thanks for coming on short notice."

But he said nothing, which surprised me. I was expecting his automatic response ("Don't call me Leonard"), followed by a biting, derisively delivered, "As if I had a choice, Blake" – the kind of retorts we've come to expect. The fact that he ignored me entirely was an indication, I suppose, that he was resigned to his fate but wasn't happy about it.

Either that or he's asleep on his feet …

Even Caeli's quick words of welcome, delivered warmly and appreciatively, went untended, and Caeli is better at handling Leonard's persnickety nature than anyone I know … other than Don Fredo, of course, now that Don Vincenzo is gone.

"He'll be OK," Elmore whispered, doing his best to cover for his partner, who'd moved well away from us, staring off into the distance as though seeking divine intervention or righteous salvation from unexpected quarters. "You both know how much he hates Ireland."

"Not as much as he hates me," I muttered.

Elmore laughed.

"Well – true enough, but I didn't want to say that."

He checked to see if I'd been offended, his face wide open, and Caeli assured him that it was all right, that we both understood Leonard's penchant for wallowing in misery of his own making.

I also wondered, for just a moment, what he'd been told by Don Fredo ahead of stepping onto the corporate jet and whether he'd argued about being ordered to ride to our rescue once more.

I'm sure that Freddy phrased it diplomatically, I recall thinking. *But he wasn't going to give them a choice – and Leonard won't be happy about that. Hell, he won't be happy about any of it.*

"You've been well, Elmore?" I asked. "Everything good back home?"

I was hoping in a roundabout way for some insight into life at the winery that might reveal Freddy's current state of mind, which in turn might even explain Leonard's current funk. But Elmore, as is typical, I suppose, went in another direction entirely.

"I've been studying up on computers, Professor B," he said. "The ins and outs and in-betweens of finding stuff people don't want you to see. It's the future, you know."

"So you're becoming a Grade A hacker?" I asked.

"Something like that. I'm getting good at it, too."

"Perfect. It's nice to see you branching out," Caeli said. "That skill would be a big advantage in your line of work."

As we began escorting our guests/bodyguards to the Range Rover and the mandatory date with waiting customs officials, an SUV with a Fierro Enterprises Ltd. parking sticker on the windshield drove onto the tarmac and screeched to a halt close to Leonard. Its driver was an older man with a ruddy complexion and hair the color of mined salt. He hopped out with the dexterity of a teen-ager and stood by the door, allowing Leonard to approach him, even as he maintained a wary eye on Caeli and me. They exchanged a few words before Leonard rejoined us and the old guy climbed into his rig and pulled away without so much as a wave or an acknowledgement that the rest of us existed.

"Delivery," Leonard said – the first word he'd spoken. He pointed vaguely off in the distance, well beyond the airport's boundaries, and Elmore nodded, as though he understood.

I figured that Leonard was talking about the necessary tools of the trade that our bodyguards required while we resolved our kerfuffle: pistols, extra magazines, boxes of ammunition, holsters to accommodate the handguns, bulletproof vests (four would be nice), communications devices, and god only knows what else. But I didn't ask, and Leonard didn't volunteer an explanation.

They spent time with customs officials moments later, after Caeli drove from the tarmac to a hanger situated in the expansive area reserved for private aircraft. We watched from a distance, ready to lend support if need be. But the questions that were asked and answered came with rapid-fire precision and were over inside of a couple of minutes.

"Nothing to it," Elmore said once they'd returned and stowed their carry-on bags.

"We need to get our stuff," Leonard said moodily.

"It truly is good to see you, Leonard," Caeli said, smiling.

"Yeah, well, wish I could say the same," he muttered, so softly that it was difficult to pick up his words. I only heard them because I was close by.

When Caeli didn't reply, he spoke again in a normal voice.

"I'll tell you where to go, though you already know where you can go, Blake."

One glance was proof that he meant it, but I didn't bite.

He directed Caeli with a series of arm-waves and grunts to the Radisson Park Inn's reserved lot for overnight guests at the airport's southern end, within walking distance of Barley Harbour, where we met the Fierro Enterprises SUV driver for a quick hand-off. Leonard hopped out, handed over a wad of Euros, and returned with two duffle bags that he dumped on top of the luggage.

"Get us out of here," he said to Caeli. "Someplace out of the way where we can suit up."

"How much did you give him?" Elmore asked.

"Gas money and a tip. Enough to take him to and from Dublin and grab a meal."

"Maybe Fierro Enterprises should set up shop in Limerick," I suggested.

"We already have," Leonard said. "In case you haven't figured it out, Blake, you're it. Get with the program."

"That's more like the Leonard I know and love," I said.

"Up yours – sideways," he countered.

Caeli, at least, smiled at the exchange, and it made sense once I'd thought it through. Our estate on the River Shannon, built by Don Vincenzo as a waystation for his Western Ireland operations, came our way in the old man's overly generous will. Who knows what treasures once passed through its doors?

"Are the two of you packing?" Elmore asked us as we pulled out of the parking lot.

"Yes," I said. "We've each got a Beretta 92."

"What happened to the Walthers?"

"It's a long story, Elmore."

"Seems like we've got some time," he said. "Why not spill it, along with details of whatever's going on that's caused the boss to put us on a plane before we had time to properly pack a bag."

"Sure," I said. "Sounds like a plan."

I could hear Leonard's voice, grumbling a line that sounded suspiciously like "Not much of one," which made me think that he was perking up. Caeli pulled to a stop behind a closed petrol station, Elmore and Leonard hopped out to strap on their handguns and bulletproof vests beneath their suit jackets, and we were back on the N18, heading toward our estate, with nothing but sufficient time to bring them up to speed.

By the time we neared our home, we'd filled them in on the relevant minutiae of our dilemma. Among the details we discussed:
-DS Alan Phelan's initial visit to enlist our aid;

-Our subsequent Bunratty trips and both encounters with the hypnotist/terrorist;

-Joan Shedd's murder;

-Liam Gallacher's early-morning visit the previous day – and yeah, they expressed surprise that the man we'd first met at Cork's Castle Ballygarvan was once again involved in our affairs;

-Our trip to the G2-run anti-terrorism warehouse/command center, including the attempt on Gallacher's car;

-The subsequent attacks on the warehouse;

-The loan of the two Berettas, along with the dire cautions regarding their use;

-The pains that we took to slip away from Gallacher's care;

-The near-calamitous shooting at the parking garage; and

-The eventual call to Don Fredo, which produced our visitors.

"I guess that pretty much covers it," I said when we'd finished.

"Just another day at the office," Elmore said.

"I've got questions," Leonard said. "Let's start with the woman."

"What woman?" I asked. "The shooter, or …"

"Joan Shedd," both Caeli and Leonard said at much the same instant.

"All right," I said. "What do you want to know?"

"You're telling us Gallacher knows who killed her – correct?"

"Yeah. I don't know what evidence he has that would stand up in court, but we're both sure he killed Mrs. Shedd."

"So why not arrest him?" Leonard asked. "If a killer's running around, you put him behind bars. What's so hard about that?"

It was a question that Caeli and I had pondered more than once in the days since Mrs. Shedd's murder.

"Best we can tell is Gallacher's trying to spear larger fish, so he's keeping this one in the pond."

"Huh."

Leonard folded his arms across his chest and frowned, thinking it through.

"Something else is going on," he said. "Not sure what, but it seems damned easy to put this to bed, or at least the part that's got you tangled up in horseshit, which was pretty stupid of you to get involved, by the way. Arrest this guy and get a killer off the streets, the cop gets his family crap back, and you're off the hook while Gallacher concentrates on the rest. What can be easier than that?"

We were nearing the security detail parked outside our home, and Caeli powered down the window. The two officers followed suit.

"Two friends will be staying with us for a few days," she said.

"Hours," Leonard shouted from the back.

Caeli smiled and tried again.

"Our friends will be with us for an unspecified time, which should make your spy boss happy," she said. "You might call – tell him that Elmore and Leonard have joined us."

The youngish officer behind the wheel seemed confused.

"This Elmore and Leonard – do they have last names then?" he asked.

That got me laughing, which in turn set Elmore off, which in turn produced a smile from Caeli.

"He knows who they are," she said, referencing Gallacher.

"All right then," the copper said. "I'll send the information along. But I suggest ya also send it in yerself. Surely he'd rather hear it from you direct."

Caeli smiled politely, assured him that she, too, would notify Gallacher, and was about to drive off when the copper hollered.

"If ya don't mind me askin', ma'am, how do we know the two blokes in the back aren't holdin' a gun on the pair of ya and are after taking ya off to, I don't know, kill ya, maybe … or somethin' worse?"

"Good question," I muttered, trying to keep a straight face but generally failing to refrain from laughing.

Caeli was about to answer, and I could tell that she was doing her best to treat the query as legitimate and the officer with the respect he deserved. Hell, he was looking out for us. But Leonard beat her to it by powering down his window and looking the copper over with as much disdain as he could muster.

"Only one of 'em's worth killing," he said. "If I wanted him dead, he'd be dead. So would you. Got it?"

The copper blanched, a cartoon-worthy moment.

"Yes sir," he managed to sputter as he glanced at his partner for support.

Our bodyguard wasn't done.

"I'm Leonard," he growled. "The other one's Elmore. Don't forget it."

So how do you top that?

Gallacher returned our call later that day, after Elmore and Leonard stretched out for a few hours of badly needed sleep. Our hope was that the break would freshen Elmore and take some of the edge off his partner, but that last part was wishful thinking.

Gallacher asked Caeli to activate the speaker so that we both could listen in. He seemed grim, worn down, even resigned to his fate – whatever that might be – as the events played out in real time. Under other circumstances, I might have offered verbal support. But he didn't want to be sidetracked.

He confirmed for a second time and then a third that Elmore and Leonard were, in fact, on the job but didn't seem to require additional information, nor did he initially volunteer anything. Thinking it strange that he didn't have more pressing matters, we automatically fired off a couple of questions that had come up since last we saw him.

But he cut us off without seeming to notice.

"We found her – yer shooter, I mean," he said, which ground everything else to a halt. "Thought it best to tell ya."

"Good. One less thing to worry about," I said, wondering why he'd buried the lead (and yeah, the phrase finds it origins in journalism).

"No. You misunderstand, Professor Blake," he said quickly. "We found her, as in we located her on CCTV footage and were able to ID her. We don't have her in custody at present. That's why I confirmed yer bodyguard arrangements. This is a dangerous woman we're dealing with. I'm afraid the Limerick force is outclassed. I'm thinkin' of pullin' the detail outside yer home entirely. I don't want to see anyone needlessly killed."

That got our attention.

It also caused me to move the blinds aside in an effort to catch a glimpse of the *Garda* car that was parked down the road.

"What happened at the parking garage – after we left?" Caeli asked after an awkward moment of silence.

"She abandoned the place three hours after the attack," Gallacher said. "She must've been hidin' inside a vehicle and simply waited for police activity to die down before walkin' away."

"Nobody challenged her?" Caeli asked, incredulous.

Gallacher took his time before answering, as though tamping down his outrage before he could find his voice.

"Even if we'd still had people there, which we did not, it's unlikely anyone would've challenged her," he said. "She looked far different from the woman described, ya see. What the two of ya gave us was the disguise she wore: wig, frumpy clothing, a hat you'd see an elderly woman wear in church. The woman on video hours later was in her early 30s, hair tied in a ponytail, wearin' designer slacks and a stylish jacket and one of those floppy beach hats ya see models wear. Sunglasses, too, of course, and she carried a bag from Brown Thomas Limerick – the big store on O'Connell Street."

He paused momentarily, allowing the image to sink in.

"Tell me, both of ya – were her eyes the most vibrant green you've ever looked at?" he eventually asked.

We glanced at one another and shrugged.

"I don't recall her eyes at all," I said.

"She wore contact lenses then because, had ya seen her eyes, you'd surely 've remembered. Her eyes are as green as Ireland itself."

"So she disguised herself and hid out after she went after us," Caeli said.

"Yes … just as ye suggested to my agents, Miss Brown," Gallacher said. "They told me you'd gloat when you heard this."

"You'll get no gloating here."

"Doesn't matter. It's a blessing our people abandoned the garage before she left," he said. "Had they stayed, it's a good bet some of 'em, maybe all, would be dead right now and I'd be with their widows instead of having this chat."

"You know her then," I said. "Your paths have crossed."

"We know of her, and her resume, which is as long as the River Shannon and as deep as the bloody Irish Sea."

"Does this green-eyed demon have a name?" Caeli asked.

"Aye. Kathleen MacAmhlaoibh," he said. "The English equivalent is McAuliffe. She's dangerous – incredibly so."

"I've heard that name," Caeli said, almost as though she were talking to herself.

"I'm not surprised," Gallacher said. "She was one of yer uncle's former confidants. It may be yer own paths meshed. At one time, when the archbishop was still rooted in place, she hung 'round the cathedral in Armagh for a time."

Caeli shook her head.

"No – I don't think so," Caeli said. "Outside of a short visit with Max more than two years ago, and then again when we looked for him last year – both of which you know about – I didn't spend any time in Armagh. Uncle Jack's housekeeper is the only woman I recall. Still, my uncle must have mentioned her at some point because the name is familiar."

Gallacher waited, thinking his words through carefully, before cautioning us to pay close attention to what he offered next "because I feel responsible for ya, for reasons that don't make much sense, even to me."

When Caeli assured him that he needn't worry, he was quick to object.

"Let's hope yer good fortune holds, Miss Brown, and ya never have occasion to run into our Kathleen," he said. "She's a cold, ruthless killer, and she has yer scent, I'm afraid. Damned fortunate, ya were, to come out of the car park intact. Amazing, in fact – as though you had an Army at yer back instead of two pistols ya didn't even fire. Right now, I'd only caution ya to remain alert – that and keep yer men close. If tradition holds, if what we know about her remains true, you'll need more than a little luck to remain upright. God help us all if she decides to take another run."

His line about having an Army at our back made me think again of the gunfire CD, though it wasn't something I shared.

Caeli was insistent on pressing her key point anyway.

"Then do something about it," she said. "You know who she is, just like you know who killed Joan Shedd. It's time you took them off the board."

"It's not that easy," he said.

"But it is," Caeli insisted. "Suppose we told the Irish press what was going on – TV and newspapers alike. What do you think they'd say about killers running loose while certain agencies fiddled the day away."

"That's hardly fair – nary the case," he said, and you could tell that she'd struck a nerve.

"Depends on how you spin it, and who gets the story first," Caeli said.

"You wouldn't."

"It's something to keep in mind," she said.

Gallacher wasn't happy, firing off choice remarks that bordered on threats and aren't worth repeating in full. Caeli didn't reply – neither of us did – because the point was made, the groundwork laid, and we figured that Gallacher would chew on the idea that we could rat him out without hesitation, buying us time in the process.

For now, at least, incidental questions that would only produce incidental answers could wait.

A few minutes after the call, I went outside to look for the police car that had been assigned to guard our home, but the damn thing was long gone.

TWENTY-NINE

COUNTING DOWN

Bill Kohlmeyer called that night, reaching us on our landline. He was halfway around the world and sounded as though he were sitting at the kitchen counter.

"This mission you've got me on, the business of finding your murdered friend's children, is a fool's errand," he said once he'd passed minor pleasantries with Caeli and she switched the phone to its speaker setting.

Caeli lifted a single eyebrow in surprise.

"It seemed like a straightforward request at the time," she said, her tone indicating that Mrs. Shedd had been on her mind.

"That's what I thought, too. Hell, it's why I agreed to take a look," Kohlmeyer said. "But when I finally carved out some time, I asked around and got in touch with a contact who helped me reach out to the State Department. Here's the deal: Something isn't right, and I can't tell whether it's at your end or mine."

"What the hell does that mean?" I asked.

The sound of my voice apparently surprised him.

"Blake," he said. "Good to know you're still with us, I guess. I figured, with the wedding drawing close, you might've caught a plane to some faraway place – China, maybe, or the Arctic Circle."

"That would make you happy?" I asked.

"You bet. It'd save me a long plane ride," he said, "though, in fairness, Skyla is looking forward to visiting Ireland. And I guess I wouldn't mind seeing Caeli Brown in a wedding dress."

He chuckled, and Caeli and I exchanged glances and waited for him to explain his "something isn't right" observation.

"What's that, Blake? Nothing to say?" he finally offered.

But Caeli responded, another indication that she remained troubled by Mrs. Shedd's death and wasn't in the mood for sidebars.

"You were saying, Bill, that you weren't sure whether the problem was at your end or ours," she said. "What exactly is going on?"

Kohlmeyer flicked the appropriate switch.

"Generally when a U.S. citizen dies overseas, the locals notify the American Embassy, which in turn notifies the State Department. The families are then contacted through information supplied during the passport application, and arrangements are made to bring the body home. But in this case, nobody's notified anybody about anything, so far as I can tell – and I've been poking around this thing for some time. The only word that's come through regarding Mrs. Shedd's death is from you."

"Wait. Are you saying Irish authorities failed to notify the State Department?" Caeli asked.

"That's just it. I can't tell," Kohlmeyer replied. "You probably don't know this, seeing as how you left us behind, but since the last election, things have gone sideways in any number of areas, including hiring at key federal positions. Countless people were fired as part of the switch from one administration to the next. It happens. But many of those jobs have gone unfilled, which is unsettling to the people I talked with about your Mrs. Shedd. They say it's likely, even probable, that Irish authorities notified the U.S. Embassy in Dublin about her death, which in turn prompted a bureaucrat on your side to reach out to a still-on-the-payroll bureaucrat on my side. In fact, they can't imagine a case where the Irish would fail to reach out. It's protocol – common practice. But nobody on this side knows a thing about it, which means your friend is in a morgue somewhere, unclaimed, with her kids none the wiser about what's happened, though likely worried by now about what's happened to mom."

We remained quiet for a long moment, trying to absorb the news.

"Yeah. That's what I thought," he said when we didn't automatically respond. "It's a hell of a mess – a hell of a puzzler, too."

Caeli was clearly troubled.

"Just to be clear, Irish authorities most likely notified the State Department. But there aren't enough people on duty over there, and nobody's looked into it or passed word to her children. Is that correct?"

"It's a good bet," Kohlmeyer said. "The other possibility is that nobody in Ireland, for whatever reason, bothered to alert anyone over here. My money, after wading through it, is on the chaos in D.C. right now, which is staggering – like nothing you've seen. Without getting into the politics, the sheer incompetence is overwhelming. It's a wonder we don't see riots in the streets, and I'll tell you something else. My department, along with a bunch of others around the country, is preparing for the day when just that happens if this nonsense continues."

He drew a breath, reeling himself in while Caeli and I again exchanged puzzled glances.

"Sorry," he said. "You'd understand better if you were here and watching it take place. It's on TV, in the news, all the time, every damn day. It's nuts. But the bottom line is your friend's dead, her kids don't know and are probably wondering where their mother gone off to, and nobody seems inclined to fill them in because of ineptitude on either my side or yours."

"Maybe it's something else entirely," I said. "Maybe the fault does lie over here, but incompetence has nothing to do with it."

It was Kohlmeyer's turn to blink.

"Wait a minute, Blake. You think this goes deeper than a robbery gone wrong?" he asked.

Caeli got there first.

"In a word, yes. It's possible," she said.

"So what haven't you told me?" he pressed.

But we weren't anxious to jump into that box, not right then and not with Bill Kohlmeyer, a man we greatly respected but one who couldn't do much to help us. Besides, Gallacher had demanded caution on our part when the terrorism mess came up, even with insiders such as DS Phelan. You didn't need to read minds to know he'd insist that we keep a U.S. police chief off the clued-in list.

"Let's just say that when this ends, Max will probably write a book," Caeli said.

"God help us," Kohlmeyer said quickly before snorting out what might've been a half-laugh. "I'm at least three of the damned things behind, and the only reason I read 'em at all is to count the times Blake mentions me."

"You should be flattered," I said.

"You should be so lucky. I'll tell you who does read them, though, besides Skyla: my lawyer – that's who. We're counting on a big payday."

"Wait. Who's we, exactly? You and your lawyer, or you and Skyla?"

"The lawyer, Blake. Skyla likes 'em, for whatever reason," Kohlmeyer grumbled. "She thinks it's cool to see my name in print in something besides what's left of the local newspaper, which is damned little and nothing any good."

I figured that the conversation had taken a beneficial turn, seeing as how he'd lost the scent, at least momentarily. But Kohlmeyer is a top cop for a reason, and he's not easily deterred by distractions over minutiae.

"All right, so I get it," he said. "You guys told me you were moving to Ireland to retire to the good life, but now you can't leave the old life behind. Nothing wrong with that, I guess – unless it gets you killed. This new life of yours isn't gonna get you killed, is it?"

"We certainly hope not, Bill," Caeli said.

"You'll be the first person I call if it happens," I added.

"Good luck with that," he said. "Just don't tell me, somewhere down the line, I didn't warn you."

Leonard strolled into the kitchen during this last line and apparently recognized Kohlmeyer's voice. He made a face that was laughable, turned abruptly, and ambled out of the room.

Time to get serious, I figured.

Just in time, too.

Caeli put in another call to Liam Gallacher that night. His direct line was picked up by an aide, who asked whether she was reporting either an emergency or a significant tip that would help break the case. When she said that the call was more of a complaint, he told her that he'd pass on the message to his boss and hung up.

Early the following morning, while Elmore and Leonard were still asleep, Caeli paid a visit to the *Limerick Leader* at 54 O'Connell Street and asked to see an advertising representative. I tagged along because bad guys were about, she refused to rouse our bodyguards, and I was curious about what she was up to, exactly, more so because she wouldn't tell me when I'd tried to wheedle it out of her ahead of time.

"I don't think you'd approve," she'd cryptically said.

"Since when has that ever stopped you from doing anything?"

I got a look signaling that I was in the danger zone, so I fleshed things out with the hope that I could better explain myself.

"Stopped you from doing anything you thought was right or needed doing," I added. "That's what I meant."

"Sure you did, Max," she said. "Nice try, though."

"So … no dinner for me tonight?"

"Only if you fix it yourself."

I trusted that she was kidding but didn't want to take any chances.

"How 'bout I take us all out instead? – anywhere you'd like."

"Now you're trying to wriggle off the hook."

"True. I wouldn't want to miss dinner. Or is it supper over here?"

"In Ireland, the last meal of the day is usually called tea. The Brits call it supper. Dinner in the UK is generally served at noon, the meal we'd call lunch."

"OK, got it," I said. "Thanks for that."

"You're welcome. I'll think about a nice place to eat … somewhere Elmore and Leonard would enjoy. But only if you behave."

I started to reply but got the look again and let it go.

We were at the newspaper office 30 minutes later.

"Once the ad guy shows up, no questions or comments," she said. "Let me do the talking. Did you bring any money?"

"Cash or card?"

"Cash."

"Sure. How much are we talking?"

"A couple of hundred Euros should cover it."

"I've got my emergency stash. Maybe I should run across the street," I said, waving in the general direction of the nearby Ulster Bank.

"We'll see in a minute," she said.

The ad rep, Brian something or other, was a hipster in his late 20s, nicely attired in a suit that he'd most likely had custom-tailored and shoes that appeared to be Italian-made and considerably expensive.

Maybe it's not all doom and gloom in the newspaper biz after all, I thought.

Over here, anyway.

"And how can I help today?" he asked, glancing back and forth between the two of us.

Caeli nodded curtly.

"I'd like to purchase a display advert, 3 columns by 10 inches deep or so. I can convert to millimeters, if you like," she said, reaching into her purse. "I've sketched out an idea of what I'd like. Let me show you."

She withdrew a sheet of computer paper and pushed it across the counter, along with a photograph of Mister Denmark, one that had been surreptitiously supplied by DS Alan Phelan. How he got it, she didn't ask – and I wasn't about to.

A headline was sketched across the top:

Do you know this man?

She'd drawn a square beneath it representing the photograph. Beneath that was a simple message:

If so, do not approach or engage him in any way. He is a thief and a liar and is armed and extremely dangerous. Contact Garda headquarters in Limerick …

She included the street address and telephone number in the same font.

"Yes, I see," Brian said as he scrutinized the display. "Well now, the likes of that doesn't cross this desk every day. I'm not even sure it's authorized … legal, as it were."

Caeli was prepared for that. She produced in short order her Interpol credentials, which we'd both received from Elmore when we made the trip to Rome to find her Uncle Jack. Elmore had insisted at the time that the authorizations were real – legitimate, he'd called them. I had my doubts, then and now, but Brian took a careful look, nodded his head sagely after a moment's appreciative study, and returned the credentials with care and a far greater respect in his eye.

"Right then," he said. "I guess we can do this without difficulty. The photo is no trouble a'tall. What are ye thinkin' for the actual letters then?"

"Exactly what it says on the sheet," Caeli replied.

"No, the style of letterin', for want of a better word."

"The font, you mean."

"Ah, so yer a woman knows her type fonts, is it? That's grand. Which one are ya thinkin', exactly?"

"I'd like to achieve the look of a Wanted poster from the Old West," she said. "So Rio Oro, Ol' Cowboy, Helldorado, Rustler – all represent the style I'm after. If those aren't available, Playbill or Cooper Black will suffice."

"Yes … I see. I'm sure we can find somethin' suitable. How long would ya like the advert to run, exactly."

"Daily for a week, for starters," she said. "I'll call if we need to renew."

He jabbed at a pocket calculator for a moment, determined a price, wrote it on an order form that he attached to her sketch, and she prodded me to produce the cash.

"Are ye Interpol too then?" Brian asked as I slid the bills across the counter.

I mustered up a scowl that I imagined Leonard would appreciate and said nothing.

"Sorry," Brian said. "No need to say a thing on my account."

The entire transaction took no more than 10 minutes.

"Thanks for holding your tongue," she said as we left.

"That's what good boys do – even if they think you're making a tactical error," I said. "Nobody's going to like this: not Liam Gallacher; not the gang back on Henry Street, DCI Abbot in particular. They'll all hate it, along with the guy who's face is plastered on your Wanted poster for all of Ireland to see."

"Good. I hope he hates it – enough to make the mistake of showing his face long enough for somebody to catch him."

"You're thinking us, of course."

"Who else?" she said. "It's plain enough Gallacher and his taskforce won't bring him in. The Guards won't do anything to rock that boat, either, which means …"

"Yeah. It's up to us. That's what I thought."

"Come on," she said, tugging on my arm. "We need to go to the bank."

"And we need do that … why, exactly? I was able to cover the cost of the ad."

"Because now I want to stop by the *Limerick Post* and a couple of the TV affiliates."

"You want to buy ad space on the telly?"

"I don't think they'll run a PSA for me," she said – shorthand for a Public Service Announcement.

"But you're an Interpol agent," I said. "It says so, right on your credentials."

"You're right," she said. "It won't hurt to ask first."

I was surprised by this move and, it's safe to say, concerned as well. I figured that Mister Denmark would quickly determine who was responsible and come for us at some point – not a pleasant thought.

But part of me also was delighted because Caeli made the commitment to attack the problem head-on – despite our retirement, despite our pending wedding. And while the adverts set off significant alarm bells, I did as ordered and kept my mouth shut, even when Elmore, who was munching on some thickly buttered toast when we returned, asked us where we'd been.

THIRTY

A SIDE VENTURE

We started out for Bunratty Castle and Folk Park a little more than two tension-filled hours later, with Caeli behind the wheel of the Range Rover and Leonard riding shotgun at his insistence.

I didn't see the point in arguing the seating arrangement, any more than bickering about our dash into Limerick, which our bodyguards railed at when we'd returned home and found them up and about and furious, anxious to learn where we'd been and why we hadn't bothered to let them know.

"Pull that stunt again and I'm outta here – and I don't care what Fredo says," Leonard snapped.

Elmore was more conciliatory.

"You brought us here for a reason," he said. "But it won't mean a thing if you don't let us do our jobs."

We tried not to further antagonize them, Leonard especially, with apologies and promises to behave, which is why I merely smiled when Elmore tugged my sleeve and pulled me with him toward the back seat, whispering that his partner wouldn't have it any other way.

I've learned one thing since meeting the pair: A happy Leonard might well be an impossibility, but a disgruntled Leonard is … impossible.

Elmore was his typical talkative self during the first few miles, asking a dozen questions in short order, hardly pausing to absorb the answers. He was curious about our new home, our new life, whether we'd made meaningful friends, the wildlife we'd seen on the river and around the estate, the quality of life in Ireland as compared with home, our favorite local restaurants, American cuisine vs. typical Irish fare, the price of petrol and even the cost of a pint of stout … you get the idea.

Leonard, who'd remained busy by stabbing at the screen of his cell phone while this was taking place, eventually cut him off.

"Hey – just leave it," he growled. "Let's figure out what's going on and fix it and get back home – never mind life on the farm. Got it?"

He swiveled his body position to better face Caeli.

"Tell me about the guy that killed the woman and everything you know about the shooter in the car park," he said. "Let's start there."

I wanted to tell him that proper English called for a *who* instead of a *that – the guy who killed the woman –* but he was too quick and glanced over his shoulder at Elmore.

"Pay attention. Take notes," he said. "I wanna wrap this up and be on the plane in two days or less."

Elmore, though bothered by Leonard's tone, judging by his frown, said nothing.

I'd seen this side of Leonard previously – an all-business, let's-get-it-done, full-assault strategy designed to spend as little time as possible with us. And I can't say that it wasn't welcome, given the situation. Sure, I'd miss tossing insults back and forth, but that was a small price to pay for a quick resolution.

Caeli spent a few minutes on the basics regarding our adversaries, with me adding incidentals as we picked up the N69 near Mungret Woods and Leonard asking occasional questions. Elmore remained quiet, but you could tell that he was concentrating on what was being said – just in case Leonard quizzed him.

"So Gallacher thinks the car park shooter is the more serious threat?" Leonard asked at one point.

"It's hard to tell what Gallacher thinks," Caeli said. "He hasn't answered most of our questions. Even so, we've had up-close experiences with both and have seen the hypnotist in action twice. He's not a nice guy. I'd like a third go-round."

She paused as Leonard silently absorbed her observations, although I could hear Elmore's muttered aside – "Careful what you wish for, Caeli" – because I was seated next to him.

Leonard eventually motioned for her to continue.

"The woman impressed Gallacher from the minute they ID'd her," she said. "He's got an extensive file on her. But whether she's the bigger threat is like picking between Dillinger or Capone. Both spell trouble."

"Back to the woman for a second," Leonard said. "She ran with your crazy uncle at one time, right?"

"According to Gallacher, at least, though I do recall hearing her name somewhere along the line," she replied.

Leonard bored in.

"If she ran with your uncle, it's a good bet she knows about you, which might explain the attack," he said. "Maybe Gallacher isn't the only one keeping files."

"I don't like the sound of that," I said.

"If it makes you feel any better, I don't, either," Elmore said.

Caeli didn't exactly shrug it off, but she was quiet as the suggestion registered.

Leonard took a moment to consider the information he'd heard.

"So you've seen the guy and can ID him straight off – right?" he eventually said.

Caeli and I both answered in the affirmative.

"But the woman knows disguises, and you don't know what she really looks like – correct?"

"Correct," Caeli said.

"All we know for certain," I added, "is Gallacher says she has the most incredible emerald eyes. If we spot someone matching her general age and bearing, with green eyes to match, we might be on to something."

"Or not," Leonard said. "We can't grab every green-eyed woman running around Ireland. Hell, the country's full of 'em. Besides, if she's smart, she'll be wearing contacts or sunglasses and won't give us a good look at her face."

"Doesn't matter about the face," Elmore said. "The two of us don't know what she looks like anyway."

"Yeah, but she doesn't know that," Leonard said.

He shook his head from side to side and shifted positions so that we all could see him.

"She's holding all the cards. You get that, right? She knows what Caeli looks like, she knows what Blake looks like, and we don't know what she looks like. We should rethink strategy – unless you're OK playing sitting ducks at a turkey shoot."

I was about to point out that ducks and turkey shoots didn't quite mesh, but Caeli jumped in first.

"Granted, the circumstances aren't ideal," she said. "But we've got some things going for us that they won't see coming."

"Such as?" Leonard asked.

"You two, for starters," she said. "They don't know you're here, which works in our favor."

"Maybe – maybe not," Leonard said. "For all we know, they tailed you from the estate to the airport when you picked us up. Maybe they got pictures. Hell, they might be on our tail right now."

I fought the urge to turn around, but Elmore did a quick about-face to review the traffic behind us. I'll also admit that I hadn't considered Leonard's scenario and didn't like hearing it. But he was correct, a fact that didn't surprise me. Leonard is good at what he does. That's why we'd called him in.

"Unlikely but possible," Caeli said after thinking it through, shaking her head enough to rustle her hair. "We took precautions."

"So has Gallacher. But he's still playing catch-up, which is why we're here," Leonard countered. "What else have you got?"

She wasn't quite as quick with her response this time.

"They won't expect us to take the game to them," she said. "If we do this right, we can get the jump on them – force them into mistakes."

She waited for Leonard to poke additional holes.

He took his time, thinking it through, before he finally squared up in the seat once more and stared straight ahead as we approached the tunnel.

"I don't know," he finally said. "There's plenty of risk involved, and your hides are hanging out. Why not just hide out for a month and leave it to Gallacher? He's better at playing this game than you are."

"We're getting married in a couple of weeks," Caeli said. "We can't just take off for a month and hide."

"So postpone it – or call it off. Blake already did that once. Why not again?"

I figured that getting us back on point was in order.

"Look, Leonard, we're not running away. And Gallacher is playing the long game," I said. "He'll get there, but he's only interested in the terrorism angle – nothing else. In the meantime, I get the sense that he's shut down the murder investigation entirely, fearing it'll muck up his operation."

"And that doesn't work for me because it doesn't take Joan's killer off the chess board," Caeli added. "Nor does it eliminate the threat to Max and me, now that we're involved in this … whatever it is. I don't even know what to call it. A mess? A fiasco? A disaster?"

"How about a situation?" Elmore said cheerfully. "Sounds better than a disaster."

"It does," Caeli said. "Thank you."

Leonard dug in again as Caeli braked the Range Rover, paid the tunnel fare with two bills that I handed her, and flipped on the lights as we rolled inside.

"Whatever you call it, we'd damn well better cover our bases, along with your asses, or we'll lose the little advantage we have. 'Cause I'll tell you – it ain't much," he said.

"We've got one other edge," Caeli said. "They don't have a clue about our resolve to end this. By the time they figure it out, it'll be too late."

"Still seems thin," Leonard said. "We don't have many cards, and the ones we do hold are crap. I don't like it. Running around in this guy's hunting ground seems stupid."

"Got anything good to say?" I asked.

"Sure, Blake. It's a good thing I don't see you near as much as I used to."

"Good one, partner," Elmore muttered, though he looked embarrassed when I glanced at him.

Even Caeli smiled at the line.

But it wouldn't last for long.

THIRTY-ONE

ANOTHER DAY AT
THE OFFICE

We entered the Folk Park minutes later, looking for two wolves among the sheep that milled about the grounds.

But as is often the case when you desperately seek answers, the minutes dragged on and soon turned into hours as day rolled to night and still we wandered, forcing the issue, taking our time because we had plenty of it, bored to weariness once the reality set in but never abandoning hope that we'd spot something – anything at all – that might lead us to our prey.

We at least had comfortable weather: mostly clear skies and a gentle breeze that lasted into the evening. This part of Ireland isn't always so accommodating.

During the times that we grew foot-weary from endlessly walking the grounds, we visited the pubs and local shops, took seats on the various benches spread throughout the park, and carefully eyed the passing traffic with feigned indifference, splitting up to cover more ground.

Caeli teamed with Leonard at his insistence.

We had a late lunch at Durty Nelly's pub and tea at the Cornbarn in the Folk Park, which featured traditional Irish music. We also snacked during the afternoon on the biscuit cake at Lily Mai's Café. In each case, Elmore was instrumental in deciding where we would eat and even when it was time to move our hunt indoors.

Caeli told me later that Leonard remained mostly sullen and silent throughout their vigil together, initiating almost no conversation and answering her questions about life in Oregon with monosyllabic replies when he was feeling generous or, and more often, shrugs, grunts, and gestures. It was typical of what we'd come to expect, and it didn't seem to bother Caeli.

In contrast, Elmore was his usual cheery self, offering all manner of observations about the shops, sights, amenable weather, and people he saw – especially those who looked hinkey, which amounted to dozens of candidates as the hours slipped away.

"Check it out, Professor B – 3 o'clock," he said early on, representative of similar conversations we had throughout the day. "That could be our guy."

"Nope. Not even close," I said, and that, too, became a familiar refrain.

"You sure?"

"Yup. He looks like a stockbroker from New Jersey, on vacation and wondering when it'll all be over so he can get back to work."

"So where's the rest of his family?"

"Two shops ahead: wife and two teens, sizing up how much junk they can stuff in their suitcases."

Elmore was particularly adept at spotting women of varying shapes and ages, speculating about whether they could be our garage shooter in yet another disguise.

"Hey – take a look, wearing sunglasses, which aren't needed right now," he said after subtly alerting me to the presence of a woman in her mid-50s who was window- shopping. "She could be up to something – what do you think?"

"She's up for a spending spree," I said. "I don't think it's her."

After each such exchange, he would cheerily acknowledge me in some small way – a nod, an indistinguishable murmur, a mild utterance, a softly spoken word – and cast about for the next likely candidate, male or female, that struck his fancy.

We returned to the Range Rover in the later afternoon and drove around the parking lots, the streets and roads and narrow lanes surrounding the castle and Folk Park, and into Bunratty itself, closely watching every car, van, lorry, motorcycle and scooter and bicycle, and every pedestrian we saw. The venture proved to be particularly difficult for our bodyguards because, despite our detailed description, we had no photograph of the woman and no way to obtain one.

I'd even called Spud Phelan and asked if he had access to a decent photo of our garage shooter. He whispered a hushed response that he was under watch by DCI Abbot and couldn't talk before adding in breathless whispers, "As to gettin' a bloody photo, good luck with that, boyo. The whole business is under wraps. You'd think no one was dead, no one was robbed, and nothing a'tall occurred."

I relayed the gist of the conversation once we'd finished, and Caeli again seethed at the apparent indifference of Irish authorities.

"I wonder how they'll react when we get this guy," she said.

It sounded like a rhetorical comment, but Leonard took the bait.

"You're guessing that anyone'll find out," he said.

"We know how to work the press, Leonard," she said. "Good reporters will be plenty interested."

"Maybe," he said. "Then again, maybe Gallacher'll swoop in and throw up a media blockade or whatever the hell you call it when the suits protect their asses."

Caeli was undeterred.

"No. They won't know what hit them," she said. "Not 'til it's too late."

But it was Elmore who got the last meaningful line.

"We need to find 'em before we can fix 'em," he said. "And we're a long way from that."

It was a sobering thought – a good reminder that we'd come up empty after a long day of doing little more than trying to remain unobtrusive while seeking out two seasoned killers/terrorists, traveling alone or together, only one of whom we could positively identify, and then only if he, too, hadn't decided to take on a disguise, which was entirely possible. I know that I would've been incognito had I still been hanging around.

Hell, in similar circumstances, I wouldn't be hanging around Bunratty at all, in disguise or not. I'd be long gone to some Mediterranean hideaway featuring secluded beaches, gorgeous vistas, and the best table wines on the planet.

But that, too, was a pipe dream.

The futility of the pursuit struck all of us late in the evening. We'd just finished our meals, eyeballing every person who entered the room, server and patron, mentally IDing plenty of tourists from a variety of countries and plenty more locals who were out for an evening's entertainment after a hearty meal. The band was on stage and warming up before its first set, and we all were drag-ass tired from the long day's low-key non-events and our inability to find anything helpful in and around the park and the castle. I was beat. Elmore and Leonard looked as though they'd just made a transatlantic journey on too little sleep. And though I hate to say it, Caeli also looked worn down from the day and the stress of making good on her vow to find Joan Shedd's killer, to the exclusion of everything we weren't doing for the approaching wedding.

Leonard didn't help by pointing out the reality of our circumstances.

"It's like looking for a fish in the damn ocean," he grumbled. "Plenty enough of 'em around, but finding the right one? Not gonna happen. Only you two know what we're looking for, despite that picture Caeli put in the paper. The woman could be anybody. She could be in this room right now, for all we know."

"Maybe I should call Gallacher again, demand to talk with him this time, and get a mug shot," Caeli said. "If we had a clear photo, we'd triple our odds of finding her."

"Do that and Gallacher will shut us down," I said. "Hell, I'm surprised we haven't run into his people, ordering us to cease and desist. You can bet he's got a detail out here somewhere, keeping watch."

"I don't know what else to do, Max," she said. "I tried an online search and came up with nothing – or at least nothing under the name Gallacher gave us."

"It's not like she'd advertise on Fakebook," Leonard grumbled.

"I think you mean Facebook, partner," Elmore said.

"Not to me it ain't."

"Maybe we should ask Kohlmeyer to dig her out," I said, grasping at straws. "With his long arm, he could …"

"No," Caeli said, without emotion. "He'd be forced to reach out to the FBI. Even if they wanted to help, which is doubtful, they'd go to the CIA, which would ask G2 and MI-6. Then

Gallacher would be alerted, and someone in there – his mole, or a player who doesn't think we should poke around – would alert some bureaucrat who'd feel obligated to protect the country's spy agency and might be inclined to boot us for good."

She shook her head back and forth, slowly and deliberately, and made eye contact with each one of us.

"No," she said again. "We're on our own – without a photo."

"So we improvise," I said.

"We have been. It's gotten us nowhere," she said. "Elmore's right."

"It's only been a day. We'll come back tomorrow, try again."

We could've gone back and forth on the same track for hours, I suppose, but Leonard forced the issue.

"No. We change the game," he said.

"How?" Caeli asked.

"I'm supposed to know?" he said sharply. "I've been over here how many hours now, and I'm the expert?"

He snorted, tossing his hands sideways, a gesture of frustration – or hell, maybe it was indifference that I saw in his eyes. I couldn't tell exactly because Leonard is a master at misdirection, even when he's trying, as was the case here, to get from Point A to Point B in a straight line.

"So we try another approach entirely," Elmore said when the silence persisted.

"What are you thinking?" Caeli asked.

"Let's see," he said, warming to the notion that Caeli was taking him seriously. "You suggested, early on, they were watching your house – right?"

"Yes," Caeli said. "Gallacher's people saw them."

"Seems simple enough then," Elmore said. "Instead of trolling for bad guys out here, we do the same thing closer to home."

"You think they're still watching the place, looking for us," I said.

"That's what I do," Leonard said, pointing toward Elmore. "He's right, especially when they see that you've called for some help from us. We've just gotta draw 'em out."

Caeli spotted a flaw.

"They won't come at the house to get us, not unless they bring an army," she said. "It's too big – too much security, too defensible."

"I wasn't thinking about luring them to the house," Elmore said. "We troll for them on the roads instead – take the fight straight at 'em."

I could count up a dozen holes and a hundred different dangerous scenarios playing out if we tried to engage in a rolling pursuit, but Elmore and Leonard, along with Caeli, were excited. And yeah, you can argue that I didn't have a problem with a pursuit inside the confines of Bunratty, which in retrospect seems shortsighted somehow. The bottom line was that we all wanted to put an end to a volatile situation – before things blew up entirely.

"We'll need another rig, with armor," Leonard said. "I'll call Dublin – see what they've got."

"I thought they were phasing out over here," I said, wondering whether the Fierro mother ship could actually come through.

"They are," Leonard said. "But a few guys are around who can help, or at least access what we need."

"Good," Caeli said. "When can we start?"

Leonard produced his phone.

I considered dampening the bonfire that was starting to kindle with some straight-forward logic. But the look that I saw in Caeli's eyes – one of hope and optimism and even of excitement – forced me to hold it in.

Yeah, I know.

We were back at the estate two hours later, after sticking around to hear some authentic Irish music while keeping an eye on the comings and goings of the crowd … just in case.

The cats – particularly Mitts, once again ravenous – were happy to see Caeli.

We'd maintained a careful watch on the road, the traffic around us, vehicles that passed us by and vehicles that lingered, and especially the pedestrians we passed as we exited the parking lot and left Bunratty behind. I can't say for certain because I was again in the back seat with Elmore, but I suspect that Leonard had his pistol drawn in case fast action was required.

But as was the case during our earlier activities, we were both disappointed that nothing unusual had presented itself and relieved at the same time.

Leonard trudged off to his assigned room after a quick update about the phone call he'd placed to Dublin.

"They've got something and will drive it across," he said. "I told 'em to call when they're close and we'll meet in the city. No sense showing our hand."

Elmore tossed out a recommendation, but Leonard waved it off and left without another word.

"It'll be OK," Elmore said a moment later. "We just need some luck, and this is the place to find it."

I was tempted to ask about his belief in Leprechauns and shamrocks and four-leaf clovers and whatever other tokens he'd mentally conjured up to share that piece of optimism. But Caeli, who has a soft place in her heart for Elmore, got there first.

"You're right, Elmore," she said. "This is the place for magic and miracles."

She may have even believed it – right then, anyway.

But the events of the next 24 hours would alter that perception.

Liam Gallacher called within hours of the publication of the Wanted poster, reaching me on the phone he'd supplied.

"I take it yer responsible?" he said without preamble.

"For what, exactly?" I asked.

"That damned advert makin' the rounds in the newspapers and, worse yet, on the telly. What else?"

"Hang on a minute," I said, waving to get Caeli's attention. "I'm putting you on speaker."

"So what it is then, eh? Have ye lost the little sense ye were born with?" he fairly shouted.

Caeli, who'd expected the call, was ready.

"I've got one for you, Liam – and thanks for calling back so quickly. The U.S. State Department has no record of anyone from Ireland, in any capacity, providing information about Joan Shedd's death. Would you like to explain that to me – or better yet to her children?" she said.

"That's not us then," he said quickly. "You'd best be lookin' closer to home."

"I don't believe you," Caeli countered.

The silence dragged on for close to 30 seconds.

We both decided, through little more than a passing glance, to wait him out.

"The two of ya are playing a dangerous game," he eventually said.

"As are you," Caeli replied. "The next time we speak, you'd better have details about the arrangements to return Joan's body to her children. Got it?"

She made a slashing sign with her hand, and I cut the connection.

Our security alarm system was activated that night, blowing its top at 1:17 a.m.

I grabbed the shotgun from the safe, met Elmore and Leonard in the hallway, and the three of us snuck outside and prowled the grounds for a good 35 minutes but found nothing amiss – and we checked thoroughly.

Caeli stood guard inside the house at my insistence, armed with both Berettas and a police baton, after dealing with the alarm company and the police.

When it did the same thing an hour later, roaring to life like a tea kettle on high alert, we again roamed around the estate, guns in hand, while Caeli this time spoke with company technicians about mandatory repairs.

Yeah. We didn't get a lot of sleep, though we did hear some choice invective from an angry Leonard.

"Another reason I hate Ireland," he said.

THIRTY-TWO

THE EARLY BIRD

Leonard roused me from a sound sleep at 4:35 a.m., pushing at my arm, which had slipped outside the down comforter, until my eyes flew open in shocked surprise. I tried to bolt upright, but he forced me down, leaning heavily on my shoulder.

At the time, I didn't realize that it was Leonard.

My first thought, a fuzzy one, was that the killers/terrorists had somehow forced their way into the house, defeating the dysfunctional alarm system and catching us all unawares.

What the hell? I wondered as my mind clawed its way toward full consciousness.

Maybe I even muttered the words. It was difficult to tell as the reality of the situation, along with its potential gravity, began to take hold.

Our bodyguard's growl, lightly whispered, was unmistakable though equally unsettling.

"Come on, Blake," he hissed, leaning close to my ear while casting a glance toward Caeli, who was snuggled deep in the covers. "We've got a run to make."

A run? What's he talking about? And what time is it? I wondered.

Not that it mattered. I was awake at this point.

"What's wrong with Elmore?" I muttered, speaking softly because I didn't want to wake Caeli, so much so that I wasn't even sure he'd hear me.

But he must have anticipated the question because he came back with an immediate answer.

"Sleeping," he said.

"So was I."

"Not any more. Let's go."

He left the room so quietly that his disappearance made me wonder whether I'd dreamed the entire exchange.But I also didn't want to make the mistake of ignoring him and falling back to sleep, which would've been easy to do. The last thing I needed was to find him at our bedside moments later, wondering where the hell I was and raising a ruckus to determine why I'd become such an underachiever.

I wandered into the kitchen minutes later after assuring a sleepy Caeli that things were under control and found Leonard examining the inner workings of his pistol, his fingers relentlessly caressing the frame with a lover's touch. He glanced up, his impatience showing, anxious to move. I was unsure what was driving such an early morning venture, but it had seemed useful to slip my own Beretta-on-loan into its holster and fasten a couple of extra fully loaded magazines to my belt before leaving the bedroom to determine what had tripped Leonard's considerable trigger.

God knows it can't be good, I figured.

"You know where the Limerick Greyhound Stadium is?" he asked.

"Where the hell is Elmore again?" I pressed.

"I told you. Asleep. Answer the question."

He reassembled the Beretta and slipped it into a shoulder holster.

When I didn't immediately respond, he tried again.

"Blake. The Greyhound Stadium. Do you know where it is?"

"Not off hand, but I'm sure I can find it," I said, stifling a yawn. "Why? Bit early for dog races. You want coffee – something to eat?"

"No. I want to get the rig from Dublin," he said. "We're meeting in" – he checked his watch – "45 minutes. Text said it's on the west side, close to Greenpark Race Course off Dock Road. You know where that is?"

It came roaring back to me then. Leonard had called Fierro Enterprises Ltd. in Dublin the night before and asked for an armored vehicle so that we could better hunt our elusive quarry of tourist murderers and committed terrorists.

"OK, sure. Dock Road is the N69 as you drive into Limerick," I said. "Piece of cake – 30 minutes tops, even less at this hour. We've got time for coffee, or tea, maybe, or something to munch on. Toast, or some …"

"Forget it," he said. "The faster we get this done, the faster …"

"Yeah, I know," I said, cutting him off. "I've heard this part before – more than once. The sooner we get this done, the sooner you can board the corporate jet and head home, leaving Ireland – and me especially – far behind."

"Close enough," he said. "You need to look up where we're going?"

"No. I've got the general idea. Bring your phone. You can give me directions from the GPS when we get close."

"Not a chance," he growled and started for the door leading into the garage where Caeli's rig was parked. "I'm not getting in a car with you driving."

"The Ranger Rover's an SUV, and I'm a fine driver – the second-best wheelman in the house."

"Sure you are. Give me the keys, Blake," he said, calling over his shoulder. "Let's get this done."

We were on the road minutes later, carefully checking our surroundings as we pulled away from the estate, looking for vehicles or furtive personnel that didn't belong, which would be anybody who was out and about at this ridiculous hour. The security system malfunction weighed heavily on both of us.

And yeah, I'd tossed him the keys, as instructed. You want to pick your fights carefully, and this one didn't matter.

Using the burner phone, I spot-checked the location of the Greyhound Stadium, committing the route to memory, and issued a series of brief directions – "hang a right"; "merge here"; "stay on the left side of the road – the other left, dammit" – as we traveled toward Clarina and the N69, a major thoroughfare that becomes Dock Road once you cross the N18, the same thoroughfare that takes you to Bunratty.

"What's up with Elmore?" I asked at one point. "It's not like him to miss a road trip."

"Why bother Marcus when I can mess with you?" he said. "Besides, someone needs to stay if something happens."

It took a moment to connect Elmore with his true name – an indication, I guess, that I wasn't yet operating on a fully charged battery.

"All right, I get it," I replied, and I did. Leonard was just being Leonard, and you can't fault the guy for being himself. He was doing us a favor, after all – a big one.

No. He's doing us another favor in a long line of them, I recall thinking.

"So why drop off the rig at some dog park and not the estate?" I asked minutes later. "Would've saved us a lot of sleep."

"Why let the bad guys know what the good guys are up to, Blake – or what they're driving?" he said. "I want you to drive straight back and do whatever you want – go to bed or take a hike or plant a tree for all I care. I'll tail you, just in case, and hang loose, keep out of sight. Give it a few hours and then dangle some bait. Sound off about running into town – call Gallacher and your cop friend, let 'em know. Just keep me in the loop before you leave. I'll follow from a distance – keep an eye on things."

"Should I bring Elmore?"

"No. You're on your own. He can stay with Caeli – see if anybody gets close to the house. If they do, we swoop back in. Play it however you want, so long as you clue me in first."

"Caeli will insist on going – driving, even," I said. "God forbid I'd tell her to stay behind, or even suggest it. That wouldn't end well for me."

"In that case, be sure and tell her to stay home," he said.

"Thanks for looking out for me, Leonard," I said.

"It's why I was sent," he said. "And stop calling me Leonard."

"Sure I will."

We traveled in silence for another mile or so when he poked me in the arm – hard, I'd add – and reached for his pistol, latching on to the steering wheel with his left hand.

"Car's coming up like a storm outta hell," he said. "Get ready – just in case."

Nuts, I thought.

But I didn't say that word aloud, nor any other. I pulled down the visor and opened the vanity mirror, which allowed me to see the vehicle that was screaming up on our position.

"Pull your gun," Leonard said. "Looks like the real deal."

"I'm not supposed to shoot it unless there's an emergency," I muttered.

He glanced at me as though I'd lost it entirely, conveying in that fraction of a second what he no doubt thought about whenever my name came up.

"Seriously? He's gonna show up on your side. Get ready — don't screw it up."

I powered down the window and pulled the Beretta, momentarily thinking about all the paperwork I'd be forced to complete to satisfy Gallacher and his overseers if I fired a shot but getting ready to do exactly that anyway.

The approaching vehicle was within 50 yards now and would be even with us in less time than it takes for you to read this sentence. But just as the car was about to pull alongside, Leonard yelled at me ("Hang on") and slammed on the brakes.

As the tires grabbed the pavement, a black Mercedes shot past us in a rush. For reasons that I can't explain, I recognized it as an S-class with sleek lines and an engine pushing far less weight and every bit the equal of the Range Rover's horsepower.

He can outrun us — outmaneuver us, I recall thinking.

I leveled the Beretta outside the open window, pointing it toward the now evil-looking Mercedes. But I also noted that nothing was pointed at us — no machine guns or extended pistols or sawed-off shotguns — as the sedan flew past. The glass also was tinted, and I couldn't tell whether its occupant was some poor bastard running late for an early-morning tee-time or a terrorist preparing to fire a howitzer.

Leonard apparently believed in the latter. He swerved into the same lane as the Mercedes and stomped on the accelerator, shooting us forward.

"Are you nuts?" I yelled, truly alarmed.

"That's your department, Blake," he said, glancing at me for just a flash, letting me know that he meant it.

This may sound like fun and games when you're reading about it. But it's far from that when you're in the middle of it.

Trust me. My heart was racing, my pulse was up, and it struck me that I could die – we both could die – and Caeli would never know the full story of what had happened out here on a lonely stretch of Irish highway without another vehicle in sight to provide witness.

Screw that, I thought.

Leonard was thinking about other things.

"Why didn't you shoot?"

"His window's up. No gun, no threat – nothing but the bastard zooming past. And he didn't brake."

"He's slowing down now," Leonard said, pointing ahead with his Beretta.

Terrific, I thought. *Just what we need.*

What happened next played out in slow motion in my head, a *SportsCenter* moment like the ones involving some arcane quasi-competition: lawn bowling, maybe, or mumbley-peg.

The Mercedes carried two occupants. I figured that out when a hand appeared on the passenger's side (*He's got the window down*, I recall thinking, demonstrating a firm grasp of the obvious), and an exploding device of one sort or another arced high in the air, rapidly approaching the Range Rover's windshield.

"Bomb," I shouted.

But Leonard had been intently watching the action as well. Instead of hitting the brakes, a natural defensive maneuver when someone tosses a bomb at your car, he buried his foot in the gas pedal, nudging the wheel gently to the right so that he didn't roll us in the process. The bomb seemed to float in the air for long seconds before it began its descent and eventually exploded on the empty road surface after we'd passed by.

The maneuver no doubt saved our asses, though we had little to cheer about. We continued rocketing ahead, the Mercedes driver unexpectedly hit the brakes, causing another smoking squeal of tires desperately grasping at the roadway, and both vehicles were now on a collision course, with four lives at risk, two of which I cared about.

"Hang on," Leonard muttered, the second time he'd issued that directive.

In truth, I wasn't overly concerned about a crash. Caeli's SUV is thoroughly armored and overbuilt. But I was concerned, greatly so, about another bomb dropping from the sky, and damned if I didn't see the mystery hand pop out of the Mercedes and flick another missile our way.

"I see it," Leonard said before I could holler a warning. This time he abandoned the road entirely and steered us toward the empty field that lines the shoulder. I got a better look at the device this time as it sailed by – "definitely a pipe bomb," I whispered – and watched as it left my viewpoint and exploded behind us seconds later.

"Good thing nobody's on the road," I said.

"Screw that. And screw this," Leonard growled. "Shoot the bastard, Blake. Let him know we're here."

This time I didn't hesitate, nor did I consider Liam Gallacher's copious warnings. I hoisted the pistol, stuck it out the open window, and was about to touch off a couple of rounds at the sedan's tires when the Range Rover hit a soft patch of grass and lurched us sideways. The wheels dug into the uneven turf, bucking us about.

"Dammit," Leonard mumbled as he fought for control. The tires spun furiously, and he turned hard to the right to get out of the track that we were digging, which in turn effectively eliminated my line of sight to the Mercedes.

The SUV continued to thrash about, the Mercedes seemed to slow down – *Maybe the bastard wants to try it all over again*, I thought – and a big lorry whizzed past, which frightened the hell out of me because it happened so unexpectedly.

The truck also apparently caught the attention of the bomb-thrower and his driver buddy. The Mercedes pulled abruptly to the shoulder, rapidly slowing down, and I figured that the guy was trying to make the lorry driver believe that he was coming to our rescue.

I couldn't tell whether the ruse actually worked because the pursuit was cut short when Leonard negotiated a fortuitous junction that appeared from nowhere and took us off the main thoroughfare in a single jerk of the wheel, spilling us onto a narrow exit lane that eventually turned into …

… a housing development with no outlet, a dead end, I thought, just as a road sign appeared to confirm what I already knew.

"Dammit," Leonard growled once more, though with additional enthusiasm.

"Maybe they don't know it doesn't go anywhere," I said. "Go to the end and turn around. If they come at us, we'll be ready."

"And if they don't?"

"Then we count ourselves damn lucky and get the hell out of here."

"No – screw it," he said and slammed on the brakes, bringing us to a quick halt. "I wanna get these bastards."

"We're outgunned," I said. "We've got pistols. They've got pipe bombs."

"Maybe not." He was looping around, executing a hard right, followed by a harder left in reverse, and roaring out once more in a squeal of burning rubber, heading back to the roadway, anxious to confront the Mercedes and battle it out – the last engine running.

"They've got the advantage," I said.

"I wanna get 'em."

"Me, too, but with the odds in our favor – and they're not in our favor now. Just the opposite."

He hit the brakes again, hard, and pulled us short of the entrance to the roadway we'd just left.

"Dammit," he said a third time.

He paused, and I waited for mysterious cosmic powers to align and the complex gears of the universe to click into place, forcing him to admit that he was wrong.

Right. Fat chance – I would've had to wait for a hell of a long time for that. He slammed the heel of his hand into the steering wheel and cursed softly under his breath.

"OK," he said after 30 seconds or more slipped by and nothing else came at us: no Mercedes, no pipe bombs, no gunshots from off in the distance, no sneak-attacks from crazed terrorists roaring up from the weeds. "So how do we get outta here? They're up there somewhere. How do we slip the net?"

He kept his eyes focused on the intersection, anticipating threats as much as he was waiting for me to respond.

"Right," I eventually said. "We can go back to the estate. We can pretend nothing happened and head directly to the Greyhound Stadium as planned. Or we can take the first exit, which is Mungret. It leads to Mungret Woods, a village off the R859. There's a bunch of residential streets along the way – plenty of places to shake followers and get to the dog park that way. Any of that strike your fancy?"

"You actually spend time out here?" he asked, shooting me a curious look.

"It pays to know the neighborhood."

"Yeah. I guess. So we'll try that last one, see what happens," he said. "Take my phone" – he pulled it from his jacket pocket and handed it across the console – "and hit speed dial 3. Tell him we've been delayed and will get there when we get there."

"This is the guy dropping off the SUV?"

"It ain't George Bush."

"You're hopelessly out of date, Leonard," I shot back. "He was either three or five presidents ago, depending on which Bush you mean."

Leonard ignored the civics lesson.

"Never mind, Blake. Make the call. Then call Marcus and let him know what's happened," he said. "I don't think we've seen the last of these guys."

He was right about that as well, though not in the way you might think.

THIRTY-THREE

THE MILLS OF GOD

He waited three days before his request to meet with the Holy Father was granted.

He wasn't happy with the delay, especially when he required so little time – *especially when the need was so great*. But there was nothing he could do to speed the layers of papal bureaucracy along.

"What is it, my son?" the Pope asked once his visitor entered the modest office and kissed the *Annulus Piscatoris*, or Ring of the Fisherman, symbolizing a pontiff's fidelity to the Roman Catholic Church.

"I'm after askin' permission to leave Rome on an urgent mission, Yer Holiness," he said. "It's a matter of great importance."

"So is the work you do here each day."

"I understand, Yer Excellency. I do. But I believe in me heart that I must make the request. Lives are at stake, ya see. At least one of 'em is someone we both care about."

The Pope absorbed the message thoughtfully.

"If I asked, would you tell me everything I need to know?" he eventually said.

The priest didn't hesitate. His face was as open as an oft-read Bible, his eyes as expressive as a Michelangelo painting.

"Of course, yer holiness. The long days of darkness are behind me."

The Pope smiled, nodding his head sagely. He'd also heard the whispered rumors, and he wasn't surprised by the request.

"Then I'd best not ask," he said. "You have my permission to gather whatever, or whomever, you need, my son."

He blessed the man who humbly stood before him.

"Go with God," he said softly, then repeated the phrase in Spanish and a final time in Latin.

[The following conversation was assembled from Interpol surveillance recordings.]

"Why are ya callin' me?" she asked. "I thought we'd agreed to …"

"Never mind. It's unraveling – all of it," he whispered, his accent masking the urgency in his voice.

"What is? What's wrong?"

"They just raided the Tokyo operation," he said, so softly that she had to strain to hear his words. "They're jittery in New York, afraid the authorities are closing in there, too. Jittery. I think that is the word – like coffee, yes? *Nerveux*. And the operation here is … well, unraveling. It's only a matter of time."

The pause on the other end of the line lasted 15 seconds.

"A leak?" she asked.

"No – I don't think so."

"Then yer people are bloody sloppy."

"Does it matter?"

"Of course it matters," she said. "If they were committed to the cause instead of motivated by greed, ya wouldn't be after makin' this call."

"I am calling to warn you," he said. "Get out while you can. We can try again, perhaps."

"No. We'll never get another chance. Besides, I've unfinished business – a task reachin' far beyond yer operation."

"He's not worth it," the Frenchman said.

"He is to me. Both of them."

"I fear for you, *mon chéri*. Get out. Listen to me. You can …"

The line went dead.

THIRTY-FOUR

MUSICAL MOBILES

We took the Mungret cutoff with no sign of the Mercedes. Even so, Leonard began weaving through side streets that showcased modest homes in modest residential neighborhoods catering to commuters.

The idea was to buy time.

Leonard's contact from Fierro Enterprises grunted when I provided an update and, after a slight pause, grumbled something under his breath that sounded suspiciously like an amiable expletive, followed closely by a slur against Yanks in general, followed by an Irish expletive that wasn't nearly as polite.

I ignored it all, told him we'd be in touch, and hung up before he could hit me with additional insults.

"That's the guy we saw at the airport, the one who dropped off the …"

"Yeah," Leonard interrupted. "Should've gotten a rig then."

"Next time," I said while punching Elmore's number.

"Ain't gonna be no next time, Blake."

"Hey, if all goes well, we'll clean this up today and you'll have a couple of weeks before coming back for the wedding."

He didn't say anything, but the look that he fired my way was a doozy.

Elmore's sleepy voice sounded on the fourth ring.

"Yeah," he muttered, figuring that he was talking with Leonard because I was using his partner's phone. "Whatcha need? What time is it?"

"Elmore, it's Max," I said.

"Professor B?" he said, and some clarity rang in his voice this time. "What's wrong? Where's Leonard?"

"Next to me, driving. He's fine. We're both fine. But we've run into a snag on the way to pick up the SUV, and he told me to call and …"

"Wait. What are you doing there? I'm supposed to make that run," he said.

"It's all right. He wanted you get some sleep."

Leonard interrupted the back-and-forth by smacking me in the arm.

"Put it on speaker, Blake. I wanna talk to him."

I fiddled with the phone for a few seconds, trying to unmask its complexities, while Leonard jabbered angrily and Elmore's voice drifted in from the ether, one issuing directives, the other asking innumerable questions. When I finally found the right button, connecting the dots and the two bodyguards, they were going full force at one another, without giving ground, even though neither man could make sense of what the other was saying.

Hell, I couldn't follow the barking adequately, and I was an impartial observer who could hear both sides.

"All right, you two love birds," I said, getting their attention. "No time for small talk – plenty to do."

Leonard continued to bluster, but I cut it short.

"Just shut up and drive," I said. "Better yet, pull over before you run us up a pole."

Ignoring his glare, I told Elmore about the passing Mercedes and its attempts to take us out with two pipe bombs, followed by our fortuitous escape and current location. Leonard continued to drift randomly through side streets, and I'll give him credit: He was careful, and cautious, and he spent as much time watching for activity in the rearview mirror as he did looking at what appeared though the windshield.

Elmore, unsurprised at the attack, continued fuming that Leonard didn't take him along on the SUV procurement run.

"What the hell?" he said. "All you had to do was knock on the door. It wasn't like I needed more sleep than you did."

Leonard waved him off, though his partner couldn't see the gesture.

"Look, forget that crap. I wanted you with Caeli in case they came at the house," he said. "We've got real problems now, not what-ifs. Let's deal with them first. Then you can bitch all you want."

Elmore took the high road.

"Forget it. What do you need?" he said, and they were right back to business.

"Let Caeli know what's going on," Leonard said. "Then get the security system fixed. Check the credentials of the techs they send – no mistakes. Be ready for anything. Blake'll alert Gallacher" – he gestured with another hurry-up motion – "and get him to send out reinforcements."

"I'm on it," Elmore said. "I'll find Caeli and check on the alarm."

I'd already pulled out my burner phone, setting Leonard's mobile on the console, and activated the speed dial menu to call the spy boss.

Leonard continued to yammer on about protecting Caeli and the estate until the cavalry showed up, and Elmore assured him that it was under control, and I was trying to recall whether Gallacher's speed dial was the first, second, or third in line on the menu display.

It wasn't exactly bedlam, but it was close.

That's precisely when Caeli entered the conversation, running into Elmore in the upstairs hallway.

We could hear her call out, reacting when she spotted him.

"He's on the line right now – Mister Denmark, the bastard who killed Joan," she said, not realizing that Elmore already had a phone line open with the speaker activated. "He wants to meet Max, and I can't raise him. Do you know where they went?"

"Whoa," Elmore damn near shouted, which of course drowned out my own yell of surprise and one from Leonard as well. "I've got Max on speaker right now."

"You do?"

"I'm right here, Caeli," I shouted.

"Max – where are you?"

She called out the words to ensure that I could hear her, although the connection was sound enough to make me believe that we were standing next to one another.

"With Leonard," I said. "What's this about Mrs. Shedd's killer?"

"He's on the landline right now, on hold, and will only talk with you," she said. "How he got the number, I don't know and didn't ask. I told him to hang on while I tried to find you. He wants a meeting. What should I tell him?"

A half-dozen different scenarios ran through my head, none of them appealing. I abandoned each one in rapid-fire fashion and started in fresh, thinking the problem through, when Caeli spoke again.

"Max? Are you still there?"

Nuts. No time ...

"Yeah. Tell him you can't reach me – I'm running errands and my phone's dead," I said. "He can negotiate with you. Keep him on the line as long as possible. Don't agree to anything easily. Argue if you have to for a neutral spot, someplace with plenty of people. Hell, argue with him even if he proposes someplace good. You need to keep him talking."

"You aren't going to meet with him," she said, stating a fact rather than asking my intentions.

I avoided the issue.

"I'll leave this line open and use my burner to call Gallacher – see if I can get him to trace your call. That's why you need to keep him talking."

"I get it," she said.

"OK, I'm calling Gallacher now. Be sure to string him along."

I did my best to concentrate on the burner phone, ignoring the ongoing back-and-forth on Leonard's line about whether I should keep a meeting date with a killer, with Elmore jabbering away and Leonard weighing in after once more smacking my arm and Caeli listening to their chatter. I stabbed at the first speed dial number, hoping that it would produce the spy chief and not the busy signal I'd get from calling Caeli's line instead and wasting valuable seconds, and then activated the speaker.

Gallacher picked up on the second ring.

"Professor Blake," he said. "It's really not a good time …"

"Shut up and listen," I said while giving Leonard a slash-across-the-throat sign to knock it off.

But it also occurred to me that everybody else could hear the conversation as well – except, of course, for the terrorist thug who remained on hold.

"Joan Shedd's killer is on our landline," I said. "He wants to set up a meeting. Can you track the call – find out where he is, give us an edge?"

He muttered an under-the-breath curse.

"Yeah. I've got the number in question here – from yer file. Hang on. It'll take a minute to reach the techs."

"We don't have a minute – not if we …"

But the line went silent, and I shouted toward Leonard's cell, which was still open and riding smartly on the console.

"Did you hear that?"

"Yes," Caeli said. "I'll get back to him now. How soon before you're back here?"

"Inside of an hour, I'd guess. You all right 'til then?"

"Sure," she said.

"We're fine," Elmore shouted.

"OK. Keep him talking, Caeli."

I was repeating myself, but it didn't matter.

Elmore bounced in with a question for Leonard about the SUV that we were collecting, and Leonard's response was a muttered growl, and I was having difficulty keeping up. But it occurred to me that Caeli could talk with the killer while the rest of us listened in, if only we allowed it to happen.

"Hey. Knock it off," I said, ignoring another Leonard glare. "Caeli? Can you hear me?" I more or less whispered the words this time, leaning in so that I was close to Leonard's open connection, hoping that she could detect my voice while keeping the killer in the dark. But Elmore checked in instead.

"No. She's gone, Professor B – down the hall to grab that phone. It's too confusing otherwise," he said. "Even I can't hear what she's saying."

Gallacher abruptly popped up on my phone.

"Professor Blake?"

"Yeah. What've ya got?"

"We're tracking the call now. Tell her to keep him talking. It takes time to zero in on the signal," he said.

"She knows that. She's talking with him now."

"You can see her?"

"No. I'm in Mungret. You need to hurry."

"Patience. She must keep him talking."

"She knows," I repeated. "Hang on."

I leaned in toward Leonard's phone and hollered.

"Elmore. Is she still talking?"

"Yeah," he called back. "Still going at it. I can see her – down the hall."

"So that's good," I said, holding my own cell phone close enough that Gallacher could hear me along with Elmore and Leonard, who was listening in as he negotiated additional residential streets.

"Right then," Gallacher said more than a minute later. "We've got a location."

"Hang on – I'll let Caeli know," I said into one phone before switching gears to the other. "Did you get that, Elmore?"

"Yeah. I'm on it," he said.

Gallacher chimed in seconds later.

"What say we gather before ya do anything else, Professor Blake – especially meeting our terrorist? It's not wise to …"

"Go get him, Liam," I said, interrupting. "Take him out or we go to the press. I'll tell them everything, especially the part about G2 leaving a killer on the street."

"We've been over this," he said. "You need to consider the bigger …"

"What's that?" I called before scratching the phone's casing against my shirt, generating a sound that I figured would pass for a failing connection. "Liam … can you … me?" I called, though softly this time. "Are … still …"

That's when I clicked off the connection, stranding him in cell phone purgatory.

Leonard stared at me for a long time – longer than I was comfortable with, seeing as how he was driving.

"What the hell was that, Blake?" he finally said.

"That was me cutting Gallacher out of the picture."

"Yeah. I got that much. Why?"

"It should be obvious. All he's going to do is shut us down, keep us away from a meet. Screw that. If we want to end this, we need control – not hand it over to G2."

"So why get him involved at all, for god's sake?"

But Caeli was back before I could answer.

"Did they get a location?" she asked.

"Gallacher says yes."

"Good. Think he'll act?"

"He'll have to. I threatened press exposure."

Leonard flashed a sign of recognition.

"Because if Gallacher gets to him first, ahead of the meet …"

"… which he's now forced to do," I added.

"… then they could get into it and this guy could get himself killed," he said.

"Which would be one down and one to go without us having to do a thing," Caeli said.

"Everyone's a winner," Elmore added.

It at least made sense at the time.

THIRTY-FIVE

A CHANGE OF DIRECTION

For reasons that I couldn't fathom at the time, we eluded the bomb-tossers who'd met us on the road that morning. Whether they lost interest or were picked up for littering or simply ran out of bombs or were called off by unseen, unknown forces, we had no way of knowing and could only guess at.

Lord knows they didn't stick around long enough to ask.

Still, we maintained a careful watch and continued preventative maneuvers down residential streets and into a shopworn strip mall in what passed for tiny Mungret's business district before returning to the main road.

The pistols that we carried remained unholstered and within easy reach. Leonard's sat in his lap as he drove. I kept mine in my left hand so that I could monitor and manipulate if necessary the SUV's GPS system – and I wasn't about to adhere to Liam Gallacher's words of caution should the need suddenly arise to shoot the damn thing.

Not any longer.

The encounter and the tension of its aftermath were exhausting, made worse by the early hour and the letdown that generally accompanies a big adrenalin rush – and yeah, flying pipe-bombs more than qualified.

I figured that the violence directed at us minutes earlier was little more than a distraction and suggested to Leonard, once we'd finished our multiple-player phone marathon, that we should return to the estate, ensuring that Caeli and Elmore had adequate support. But he resisted with sound logic.

"If we leave this now, we'll just have to come back. That'll give 'em a chance to re-arm, or pull together a bigger team," he said. "Marcus can protect Caeli – not that she needs much protection. Not like you do."

"Thanks for the vote of confidence in my bride-to-be, and your partner," I said.

"It's called truth. It's what I do, though it's not easy over here – another reason I hate Ireland," he said.

He also insisted in pointing out not only my shortcomings but also the reasons why Caeli and I found ourselves in this mess, necessitating the call to Don Fredo – which in turn brought him in.

"You just can't leave it alone," he said as we neared the greyhound stadium. "For some reason I don't get, you keep sticking your nose in places it don't belong. Look where the hell that gets you – every damn time."

"Seemed simple enough when the doorbell rang. A friend asked for help," I said, offering a weak if logical defense.

"Some friend," Leonard said, pouncing. "Besides, this guy wasn't a friend when he first showed up – not from what you told me. You didn't even know the bastard. So why invite him in? Why not just kick him to the curb? That's what you do when a stray shows up, Blake. You don't pet him or feed him or take him in. You send him packing and go right back to whatever you were doing before the doorbell rang, which in your case probably wasn't much."

"I wouldn't have sent you packing, Leonard. I'd 've been happy to invite you in – even now."

"Horseshit. That's not true and you know it," he snapped, low and menacing this time. Then he glanced over as we neared a major intersection. "Left or right?"

"Right."

He grunted an acknowledgement,

"Look, you know this as well as me," he said. "The first time I showed up at your door, back in Salem when you were running that phoney detective agency, you pulled a gun and forced me out of your office. I had respect for you then. I didn't like what you did – don't get me wrong. But I respected you for it. You know something, though? That was a hell of a long time ago. What happened to you, Blake? Why'd you go soft?"

He was at least partially correct about our first encounter, although he left out a few convenient truths: He was threatening me with a pistol when he showed up, and he wasn't alone when the hardware came out. But I didn't bother arguing. You engage Leonard at your own peril.

"That wasn't a phoney agency," I said instead. "That was a good operation, with a solid track record. Hell, it brought you to my door."

"I kicked in your door 'cause the boss ordered it, not 'cause you were some hotshot private eye – something you still ain't."

I considered a number of snappy responses but settled on one that I knew would get his mind off the rant he was honing.

"You know, Leonard," I said, "I liked it better when your biggest complaint was my persistence in calling you Leonard."

I thought that he might appreciate my efforts at doubling up on his moniker, but he rewarded me instead with a nasty scowl and pulled alongside two SUVs that were parked beside one another in a lot adjacent to the sprawling Greyhound Stadium. The same guy we'd seen at Shannon when Elmore and Leonard first arrived – the one who'd supplied them with pistols and bulletproof vests – nimbly climbed out of a black GMC Yukon XL and waited for Leonard to exit the Range Rover.

"Yer late, boyo."

Leonard was admiring the armored Yukon and didn't bite at the taunt, which only prompted an additional jab.

"I'll tell ya somethin' else, Yank. Ya could've saved us both a lot o' time had ya asked for this straight out," he said, tossing the keys when Leonard finally glanced up.

I'd left the Range Rover's passenger seat and was swinging around to the driver's side, preparing for the drive back to the estate, which provided me with a decent view of the exchange.

"Thought you liked getting your ass out of the office, Michael," Leonard said, and you could tell if you listened closely that he either didn't like the guy or that he enjoyed sticking it to him. Knowing Leonard, it was likely a bit of both.

Michael shrugged his slight shoulders and affected what I took to be a distant relative to a grin.

"True enough. But that's reserved fer quick trips to me favorite pub, or maybe out to Leopardstown or Portmarnock when I get a decent tip and the ponies are after runnin'," he said. "All-night drives to bloody fookin' Limerick to see the likes of ye and yer man here" – he stabbed a bony finger in my direction – "aren't at the top of me list now, are they? Not even on a slow day."

"Good thing it's not a slow day," Leonard said. "You'd best keep an eye peeled."

He then described the trouble we'd had, providing a thorough description of the vehicle that had attempted to take us out. Michael appeared mildly interested, shaking his head a few times, either to confirm that he understood Leonard's narrative or that he was nodding off – take your pick.

"Do ya want me to file a report with the coppers then?" he asked once Leonard finished. But he didn't wait for a response. "You'd be after doin' yer part to help take these boyos off the road, ya know. But it'd be better comin' from me than you."

"Don't bother," Leonard said. "I won't."

"Yer sure now?"

"Yeah, I'm sure."

Michael shook his head, registering what I took for a disingenuous grin.

"Anything else now, beyond this little beauty?" he asked, nodding toward the Yukon.

"Hell no," Leonard said without hesitation.

"Whatever ya say, Yank. We're off then. If ya think of somethin' ya need, don't fookin' ask me for it."

"Wouldn't think of it."

"Knickers," Michael muttered and headed toward the second SUV. He barked out a laugh and climbed into the passenger's seat without a backward glance.

"Smart-assed bastard," Leonard grumbled.

"Something else you hate about Ireland, I take it," I said.

"Up yours, Blake," he muttered.

Then he abruptly shifted gears.

"I'll follow you – near enough to jump in if things go sideways," he said. "Keep the gun handy."

But I saw nothing on the drive home, Leonard included.

I did call Caeli as soon as I climbed back into the Range Rover, hoping to get a quick rundown on the conversation she had with the man we suspected of killing Joan Shedd.

As it turned out, I didn't get much of anything.

"I'll tell you all about it when you get here," she said when I asked for an update.

"Come on – tell me now," I pleaded. "I'm itching to know."

"Itching? You're itching? Really?"

I couldn't tell if she was changing the subject to have some fun – *Unlikely, though a possibility* – or whether she was merely surprised by my choice of words. I decided to offer other options.

"Would you prefer hankering?"

"No. Too Elvis," she said. "I'll tell you when …"

"How about yearning? Or longing, maybe? Or …?

"Max," she said, interrupting – and the fun was over. "I'll tell you when you get here. I don't want you driving off the road. You wouldn't look good in your tux if you crashed."

"It's that bad?" I pressed, mentally conjuring up likely scenarios she didn't want to share just then.

"Be safe. Watch for lunatics. See you soon," she said and ended the call, just like that.

What the hell, I thought.

She was waiting as I pulled into the garage long minutes later and seemed pleased enough to see me. But then I noticed that her attention was focused on the Range Rover, which meant that I somehow missed entirely the twinkle that must have been firmly fixed in her eye.

"It doesn't look any the worse for wear," she said as she moved slowly around the chassis, running her finger across the hood before making the turn along the length of the passenger's side.

"Seriously?"

"Elmore told me they were tossing pipe-bombs. I'm checking for damage."

"They were tossing bombs at me – not at the SUV."

"I'm sure it was one and the same to them," she said as she made her way around the back and gradually approached the spot where I was standing by the driver's side door. She continued studying specs and dings and the bullet indentations from our parking garage attacker before halting her examination.

"Are you keeping that door open because you're hiding something?" she asked.

"Caeli – you've cut me to the quick," I said.

But I spotted the glint this time, and the emergence of a lovely smile, and she pulled me close and rewarded me with a kiss that was worth the nonsense of the morning.

"You're OK?" she said.

"I'm am now."

"Good. You look all right – as does the Range Rover."

"Leonard was driving," I said.

"Where is he?"

I waved a hand out toward the road.

"He doesn't want to show up in the new rig, in case someone's either watching or looking for us."

"Or waiting for us. What did he get?"

"A Yukon, one of the big ones – fully armored with a souped-up engine."

"Black, I suppose."

"I didn't know they came in other colors."

We laughed, and I gave her a hug.

"Where's Elmore?"

"Playing with the security system," she said. "That wasn't a glitch last night. It was hacked. He's trying to debug it."

"He can do that?"

"He's become quite the nerd," she said. "He's likes the upgrades we added. The new monitors are keeping him busy."

"All 15 of them. Anything to be seen out there?"

"Not so far."

"Good, especially after the nonsense on the road. I figured they'd show up at the house at the same time."

"They wouldn't have gotten far – not unless they came at us with a tank," she said.

Or a bunch of pipe bombs, I thought but didn't say it aloud. I appreciated her attempt to maintain the illusion that all was well, but we both knew that our optimism was a fiction. Bad things were coming. We could feel it, even if we didn't see the need to talk about it just then.

We had other issues to concern ourselves with.

"So what happened on the phone?" I asked. "Did you settle on a meeting spot?"

"No," she said. "He wants to talk with you first, and I'll say it again, Max. If Gallacher doesn't get to him before …"

"… which he probably won't, despite the threat …"

"… I don't think you should agree to anything. This guy's more than dangerous. He's crazy."

That stopped me. I already knew that Caeli wasn't a fan of playing ball with a terrorist, with good reason. We were certain that he'd killed Joan Shedd, and we'd seen him up close on two occasions, neither of which were pleasant experiences. I had no doubt that he was capable of additional mayhem and was willing to direct it our way. And yeah, all of that needed a careful look.

But I concentrated on the initial portion of her comment instead, avoiding a protracted discussion about safety. At that moment, anyway, I was more interested in a meeting than I was in ensuring that I'd have ample back-up. That may sound ill-advised to you, even as it does to me now as I write this, months later. But right then? It made perfect sense, which influenced the remainder of our discussion.

"He wants to talk first?" I said. "Why? What about?"

"He wants to establish some rules," she said. "And he insisted that only you could agree to them, despite my arguments."

I wasn't surprised that he'd dismissed Caeli. Many men routinely do that with women, even ones they know well. Sadly, it's a general failing of the species, made more grievous when someone formidable comes along to upset their teetering view of the world. But her reply reminded me of a scene from *Butch Cassidy and the Sundance Kid*, the Paul Newman/Robert Redford Western, and I started there.

" 'Rules? In a knife fight?' " I said, borrowing the line that Harvey Logan sputters at the Sundance Kid.

Caeli, to her credit, let it go.

"Apparently so. But we need to talk about the other part — before you call."

"The other part?"

"Yes, the part about meeting him one-on-one, without any help."

"Did I really suggest I wanted to meet him without backup?"

"I think that's exactly what you said."

"But only to lure him in – to get him to agree to meet at all," I said. "I'd be a fool to walk into a meeting with this guy with nothing more than a lousy Beretta for comfort. A Walther, maybe, but sure as hell not a Beretta."

I added that last bit to keep it light, but Caeli wasn't biting.

"I don't like it. I don't like any of it," she said.

"He left his number, right?"

"You aren't paying attention to the big picture, Max."

"One thing at a time," I said.

"Agreed. That one thing is settling on ground rules with me, well before you do the same with this murdering lunatic."

"You're right."

But my words didn't register.

"I mean it, Max. I won't settle for a brush-off," she said.

Apparently, I have to work harder …

"I know you do, Caeli," I said. "I agree. We need to hash it out, with Elmore and Leonard, too, before I make that call. But it's vital that we pull this off. We can end the whole mess, without worrying about Gallacher."

"I know. But you can't do it alone."

"Agreed. No foolish chances."

"Good," she said.

The discussion felt like three steps forward and five steps back, but I still took it as progress. We needed to assess our enemy's strengths, after all, and to do that, well, taking chances was a necessity.

THIRTY-SIX

A WARNING TOO LATE

Bill Kohlmeyer called us on our landline minutes later. I had no idea what time it was in faraway Oregon, but I didn't think that the call was a social one.

Kohlmeyer doesn't ring you up to shoot the breeze.

"Blake," he said. "What the hell are you two doing over there?"

Yeah – my thought exactly.

Open-ended questions are a journalist's staple. I used them to good effect when I was reporting for a living. But they don't play well, at either end of the line, if you're seeking an immediate reply to a specific query that instigated an overseas call in the first place. I wasn't about to point that out to Kohlmeyer, however. The last thing he'd want from me is a recommendation on discerning facts.

I waved at Caeli, who was rummaging through the refrigerator in search of likely breakfast ingredients, and whispered that Salem's top cop was with us before activating the speaker.

"And a cheery good morning, Bill – or evening, as the case may be," I said. "Because you asked, I'll tell you what we're up to, which is breakfast options: scrambled eggs and toast, maybe, with sausage – patties rather than links – and tea, of course. Earl Grey for me. As for Caeli, I'm not sure what she's thinking. Pancakes, maybe, with fresh fruit – berries, most likely. Thoughts?"

He'd tried to interrupt a couple of times, but I talked though his protests before ending up with a question that wasn't a question.

Kohlmeyer didn't give a damn what we ate for breakfast, but that wasn't the point.

"Blake – for god's sake. Forget all that," he said when I finished and let him in again, and his voice dropped a full octave, a sign that he wasn't happy. "I'll ask again: What the hell are you up to, along with those two clowns who're somehow licensed to carry guns? What the hell would prompt you to call in Mutt and Jeff? What's going on?"

He was talking about Elmore and Leonard, of course. But how he knew that they were on Irish soil, I couldn't fathom – and it struck me that he was again steps ahead of the game without even being invited to suit up.

"What are we up to? What's that supposed to mean? How do you even know …"

"Never mind," he said, this time shutting me down. "I got a call from a friend of a friend – a guy from one of those agencies you despise unless you need something. Until an hour ago, this was a guy I only knew about in passing. But he knows where I am and what I do. That means he knows all about you and your intended, Blake. And he knows about your dead friend, the fake winery owner, and the people he kept on his payroll, including your so-called bodyguard pals. That's what brings the bastard right back to me, which is why he called – and none of that makes me happy."

He paused, maybe to allow me to digest his diatribe, or maybe to calm down after successfully working himself into full-on harangue mode.

I'd heard him well enough, though. I also understood his anger. I'd often heard him express similar thoughts about our relationship with the late Don Vincenzo Fierro. I just wasn't sure what he wanted from me this time around – or why he was winding his crank so tightly while trying to let me know.

"I'm not following," I said, buying time while mentally assembling the puzzle pieces he'd set in motion. "If you've got something to say, or ask, go ahead and skip to it, minus the indignation. But you're going to have to do better than rail at me and my choice of friends. I'm happy to help or hear you out – either way. But I'm hungry, and I have my limits."

Caeli's left eyebrow lifted at that last line.

I could only guess at Kohlmeyer's facial contortions as the silence hung in the air for an extra beat, and then for another, before he started up again.

"Sure you do," he said, though I don't think he meant it. "This stuff makes me mad, you know. The only reason I get these calls, get caught up in this horsehockey, is the dead mobster who lived in my jurisdiction, along with your connection to him, Blake. It was bad enough when he was alive and the agency kooks pounded on my door, asking for coffee and donuts while they played at being a spy. That crap I could understand. I didn't like it, but I understood it. But now – all this time later? It just ticks me off."

Bill's anger at the perceived slights of federal agency blundering and interference directed his way because a reputed world-class mobster once lived in his back yard was a familiar refrain, and I did my best to ward off a meltdown.

"Right about now, Bill," I said, trying to sound reasonable, "I should ask you the same question you started on with me: What the hell's going on over there? Again, I'm happy to help, but you've got to give me something."

The line must have taken hold.

"All right, so here's the deal," he said, forcing his way back on point. "I know you're up to something questionable because certain people are taking notice. Agency activity's focused your way – again. And somebody out there seems to think I'm the go-to guy when your world's about to blow up."

I ignored the speculation and concentrated instead on the good stuff.

"Agency activity? What kind of 'agency' are we talking about, exactly?" I asked, using my index fingers to make air quotes as I spoke the word, waving the receiver up and down in the process.

Kohlmeyer couldn't see the effort, but Caeli could, and she telegraphed her concern, moving in closer after placing a few of the breakfast items she'd selected onto the counter.

Concern is the correct word here, by the way. One of the reasons we'd decided to move to Ireland was the steady attention we seemed to get from the surveillance agencies routinely monitoring Don Vincenzo's winery operation when he was alive. Trust me: No one needs that sort of scrutiny, especially when your only connection to the primary target was one of friendship and not as a participant in whatever nefarious deeds the collective law enforcement network seemed intent on finding.

Apparently, it was still going on – *not a good sign ... something we'll have to tell Fredo about.*

"Does it matter?" Kohlmeyer asked.

His grumpiness continued, and he obviously felt the need to protect his source, which is probably why he refused to blurt out a recognizable acronym.

I thought about the question, taking a moment, and eventually figured that yeah, it did matter. The FBI chews on different bones than the CIA enjoys, after all. And the NSA and Homeland Security folks are often delving into far different cuts of meat entirely.

But I also figured that I was parsing verbs, splitting tresses, and mentally counting the number of angels that could dance on the head of a 16-penny nail.

Doesn't take a genius, I thought as the CIA jumped into my head. We'd had dealings with the agency previously, during our search for Caeli's uncle at the Vatican, months before. It would make sense that the overseas spy gang might be casting glances in our direction, seeing as how we were currently mixed up with G2 operatives in their efforts to foil a terrorist plot on Irish soil – an enterprise the agency knew all about.

"You're right – doesn't matter," I finally said, for lack of something more coherent. "But here's a question for you: So what?"

"So what?" he repeated, his tone incredulous. "Did you really just say that? Haven't you heard anything I've said?"

"Sure. But you aren't making sense," I countered. "What's going on at your end that prompts this call, Bill? Vinny Fierro is dead, I'm sad to report. His son runs a charitable organization that does nothing but good around the world, as you've been advised – more than once. And we don't even live in the States, which is a fact known by everyone you've just mentioned. What are you trying to tell me, exactly, that I should care about?"

I got nothing but silence for that, which was likely a good thing. I've heard Bill get wound up a number of times, and you don't want to be on the receiving end. Still, I was about to prod him again when at least one cooler head pulled the phone from my hand and took over.

Just in time, from the sounds of things.

"**B**ill, it's Caeli. Good morning. You'll have to forgive Max," she said, giving me a look that conveyed, in a nutshell, *This is no time to poke the bear*. "He was chased by nutters on the way into Limerick, not more than an hour ago. They were tossing pipe bombs at him – and at my SUV."

That got Kohlmeyer's attention.

"What the hell," he said. "I thought you two were done with that crap. Can't leave well enough alone, can you? – which explains, at least, the call I just got."

"So tell us what you heard, exactly, and we'll tell you what we have from this end," Caeli said. "Maybe we can make some sense of it all."

"Geez," I whispered. "You don't have to be so diplomatic."

Caeli ignored me.

Kohlmeyer went first.

"Here's what I know. I got a call from a guy who knows a guy I know – deeply connected, you understand. He gave me a heads-up – told me to pass it along or not, my call, depending on how much I like you two," he said. "His agency is monitoring a global situation that's blowing up. One of the places it touches, apparently, is Ireland. And it comes as no surprise to me that you seem to be smack in the middle of whatever's going on over there."

"That's exactly why we'd called you earlier," Caeli said, speaking calmly, as though this was nothing more than a routine conversation – arranging a trip to the store or an appointment to get her nails done. "We stumbled into something when Max told a friend we'd help him out after a jewelry theft at Bunratty, the tourist spot up the road from us. That's how we got involved with Joan Shedd."

"This is a whole lot bigger than a jewel theft, and it's also bigger than a tourist's death – tragic as that might be," Kohlmeyer said.

"We know that now," Caeli said. "But we didn't realize it until we were already involved – before it was too late."

"Right. With Blake leading the charge, I'm sure that's true," he said.

Caeli let it go.

"What do we need to know beyond agency interest?" she asked.

"Beats me, though it sounds like you aren't the least bit surprised they're knocking on your door again."

"Technically, we were knocking on their door – inadvertently," she said. "But again, we weren't looking for a cause. We stumbled into one."

"You guys have a knack for that," he said.

They went on for another few minutes in similar fashion before Caeli changed the subject with talk of the wedding and how excited we were to have Bill and Skyla make the trip. That got a snort from Kohlmeyer, a bigger one from me, and promises to see each other soon – the kind of stuff you say when you run out of quality suggestions or comments, though only after he told us to "knock off the spy crap and poking around in business that doesn't concern you."

When Caeli eventually signed off, I was working on a couple of omelets, with toast and fruit on the side, wondering whether I should call Elmore to the table or let him fend for himself. I'll confess that I enjoyed the fact that Elmore was enamored with our security system and was monitoring the grounds while we were otherwise occupied.

"I don't like the sound of this," Caeli said once she'd hung up. "Can't be a good thing to have the spies poking around in our affairs again."

"CIA, I'd bet – not that it matters. One's as bad as the next."

"What do you think it means?"

"It's means we'd better watch our asses – but not before we eat."

That's when Elmore appeared from nowhere, something akin to a magician's trick. I figured at first that he'd been attracted by the smell of food and wanted to join us. But the concerned look that was stitched onto his boyish face was a hint that something was up ... *something unpleasant.*

"We've got company – coming up the drive now," he said.

I figured that he didn't mean the friendly kind when I noticed his Beretta in his right hand, with his index finger holding steady along the length of the trigger guard.

I also recall feeling surprised that he hadn't shouted at us, giving us a heads-up while he continued to monitor the security cameras and make a determination as to who exactly climbed out of whatever conveyance they were using, which in turn would give us an idea about what they wanted.

"Any ideas?" Caeli asked. She already was heading toward the security system, which serves as a safe room in the event of an assault on the estate. We can lock it down, it contains a week's supply of food and water, and it has a tunnel system that leads away from the main house – all part of the design when Don Vincenzo had the place built.

"I couldn't tell," Elmore said, and he fell in line behind her.

"We'd best get ready then," Caeli said, calling over her shoulder. "Max – grab the shotgun."

"On it," I yelled and headed for the stairs.

"Who knows what sort of firepower they'll bring at us?" I muttered, talking strictly to myself. "And where the hell is Leonard?"

I rejoined Caeli and Elmore moments later. Both were stationed at the expansive desk that contains a half-dozen monitors, with the others mounted on the wall overhead. As we stared at the screens, which were focused on the three vehicles that had pulled up to the front entrance, Liam Gallacher stepped out of the first rig, a hefty black SUV, with Danny O'Herlihy, his driver/bodyguard exiting from the opposite side. Ian and Gavin, our previous minders, hauled their carcasses out of a second vehicle and hurried along, doing their best to catch up.

No one stirred from the third rig.

"What the hell is this," I muttered – definitely not a question.

Caeli, as always, was on it, regardless of punctuation and inflection.

"Guess we'll find out," she said.

THIRTY-SEVEN

A DETOUR OF SORTS

They swarmed through the front door and into our lives once more with Gallacher in the lead, as imperious as a lord from the ancient days of wealth and power, dripping with self-righteousness and arrogance and the divine notion that a thousand wrongs could be made right again with the single sweep of a hand.

"It's bloody well time we sat down for a little chat," he said, addressing the room at large. "Past time, actually."

I detected the fleetest of smiles register for a millisecond in his eyes when he added that grammatically incorrect coda. But it was gone as quickly as it had appeared – if, in fact, it appeared at all – and he brushed past me, adroitly sidestepped Caeli, and headed toward the parlor with an assumed authority that reminded me of some of the more arrogant publishers I'd worked for in my newspaper days, along with the entirety of corporate jackasses who would sweep into town filled with malicious bluster and petty vendettas and weren't satisfied until they'd registered a few more notches in their belts.

Ask me sometime to name names.

Mercifully, he'd ignored Elmore entirely.

"Do ya remember Tommy McNevin, that plumber we pulled in back at the warehouse operation when he was amblin' 'round the place in his brother-in-law's panel van?" he said.

We shook our heads. It was easy to recall the man's outrage when he was brought in for questioning.

"He was found early this morning in that very same van, although this time it had its tags," Gallacher said. "The coroner's rulin' is a heart attack. I'm not buyin' it."

"You think your terrorists are cleaning house?" I asked.

"That's exactly what I think."

"But your plumber was no terrorist," Caeli said. "He was a patsy at best."

"Yeah, well, his brother-in-law was found dead last night – another heart attack, I'm told – so make of it what ya will. Do ya have any coffee on the boil?"

I exchanged glances with Caeli, who seemed to be as surprised as I was to hear about two suspicious deaths and Gallacher's sudden shift in direction.

What the hell is he up to? I wondered.

But before we could provide an answer to his inquiry – and that included a shrug of indifference, let alone a solitary word of acknowledgment – he placed his order as though he'd entered a café and we were little more than hired help.

"Either way, I'll have one," he said, waving a hand toward the kitchen. "Black as a hangman's heart – or is it yer new president's, eh? – and extra strong, if ya please. God knows I bloody well need it."

The performance didn't play well with Caeli, who has a low tolerance for affectation, especially when it comes from those who should know better, most especially when it comes from someone we know well, or at least from someone we thought we knew.

This was a far different side of Liam Gallacher than we'd seen before.

It also was far from pleasant, a fact that Caeli addressed.

"If you want coffee, or anything else, I suggest you get up and make it yourself," she said. "Be careful with the machine. It's temperamental."

I figured that we were in for it now – *An entire order of fresh hell*, I recall thinking – because we'd seen a livid Gallacher on more than one occasion, and he was a handful when riled, no question. He'd told us, days earlier, that only his intercession had convinced his government to relent and clear the way for our moving to Ireland, and I could picture him now, pulling the plug on us entirely with a single regal wave – just like one of the old lords, holding court over his opulent castle and impoverished subjects, issuing a fresh thumbs-down signal with relish.

But the man is forever full of surprises, and he didn't disappoint this time, either.

He barked out a laugh that was loud and raucous and entirely out of proportion for the situation, bizarre though it was. We could only guess at why he'd barged into our day, security detail in tow, or what he wanted now from us, or even why he'd purposefully provoked us with a demand for coffee.

I also found myself infuriated that he wasn't leading the charge to swarm Mister Denmark's lair and bring the bastard in and damn near said so. Hell, I'd threatened to out him and his organization if he didn't do exactly that.

But the laughter was unsettling, and I figured that he was losing it. Nothing else explained his behavior, and I wondered again where Leonard was and whether we could call him in from the wilderness.

Even poor Elmore, who remains as placid as morning waters in the headiest of times, appeared puzzled.

Worse yet, Gallacher's men seemed mystified. Their uneasy glances around the room and at each other indicated that we weren't alone in our befuddlement.

The spymaster didn't seem fazed by any of it. He laughed long and hard, to the point where he eventually was forced to wipe tears from the corners of his eyes. I began to fear for his sanity and wondered whether his men would protest if we suggested that a trip to the Dean Clinic in Galway, which provides psychiatric services to those in need in the west of Ireland, might be in order.

Danny O'Herlihy was especially uneasy at the outburst. His glances toward his boss, us, Elmore, and his fellow G2 operatives conveyed his anxiety as clearly as if he'd called out, his voice straining with rage, "For the love o' god, man, get a bloody grip."

Ian and Gavin appeared to be more perplexed than distraught. Gallacher's current comportment wasn't something they encountered every day, apparently, and they didn't quite know what to make of it. It seemed to me that they were squirming, reminding me of altar boys when the service is overly long and the church is overly hot.

"What the hell's wrong with him?" I whispered to Caeli.

"I'm beginning to worry," she whispered in return.

Maybe he saw our expressions of concern.

Maybe he detected the obvious discomfort of his men.

Maybe he just ran out of steam. I don't know the answer because I didn't bother asking.

Then again, he didn't give me a chance.

"Well then," he abruptly said, and you could tell that he was trying his best to pull himself together. "It's not every day a man at the top of his game gets sacked from his own investigation by the likes of a brain-addled bureaucrat who listens far too closely to the noxious meddlings of the bloody CIA. How in the hell that happened, I could spend a day tryin' to ascertain, if only I'd bother. But it's happened nonetheless, hard as it is to believe. Whaddya say to that then?"

The question was hypothetical, to be sure, but he waited for an answer.

I thought that Caeli might take a stab at it. But she continued to stare at him, as though he'd grown an eye on the tip of his nose, and remained silent.

Me? His mention of the CIA brought to mind the conversation we'd just had with Bill Kohlmeyer – a conversation, you'll recall, indicating that Caeli and I were again on an unnamed federal agency's all-encompassing radar.

Can't be a coincidence, I thought.

Still, given Gallacher's precarious mental state, I decided to ease into it.

"Everything all right there, Liam? You seem a bit, I don't know, rattled, which is understandable considering what's happened to you and your team," I said and pushed on before he could respond. "Sorry to hear you were fired. That had to come as a shock."

"You don't know the half of it."

Caeli jumped in.

"I'm sure that's true. But if you can bear it, Liam, we'd like to hear about the CIA's involvement."

That set him off on a new course of bellowing laughter – the kind of thing you'd expect from someone watching the campfire scene in *Blazing Saddles* for the first time.

Caeli did her best to contain the situation before it spun entirely out of control.

"You've come for a reason, I trust, and I doubt it was to tell us you were taken off the investigation," she said, speaking calmly, rationally, as though our uninvited guest was fully lucid at the moment – a state he didn't seem capable of pulling off just then. "So what happened – especially the part about the CIA? We just had an interesting overseas conversation about that very agency."

Gallacher instantly brightened at the news, as though someone had plugged in a computer that was hardwired to his brain.

"Did ya now?" he said. "So much the better – knew I'd come to the right place to find a work-around to this mess."

He favored us with a big smile, teeth bared and white and glistening in the sunlight that streamed through the windows. But the grin abruptly deserted him, and he paused for a few seconds, as though he was at a crossroads and didn't know where to turn – or why he should make the turn at all.

"Didn't I begin by advisin' how we had much to discuss?" he eventually said. "It seems I was correct for once. How bloody thoughtful of me. What is it you Yanks like to say? 'I'll show you mine if you show me yours' – do I have that right?"

"I've never said that," Caeli replied. "I've never once heard Max mention it, either. But I would like to know why you're here today, Liam, and in such a mood, and the CIA's involvement in whatever's going on."

"Right then," Gallacher said. "Time we got to it. Still, I was serious enough 'bout the coffee."

"So was I," Caeli said without hesitation.

Gallacher laughed again, though his efforts were more subdued this time.

"Ian – go inside then and fetch us up a big pot, steamin' hot and very black," he said, gesturing toward the man and then sweeping his hand out in the general direction of the kitchen. "I've a feelin' we're all gonna need it 'fore the day's done."

Ian frowned.

"What do I know about makin' a bloody pot of coffee?" he muttered. "I don't even drink the stuff."

"High time ya learned, boyo," Gallacher said. "I've seen the device in question and have every confidence ye can handle things without making too much of a bollox of it. Get on now – off ya go. We've not a lot of time."

Ignoring Ian's muttered grumblings as he set off with Elmore, who'd volunteered to help, Gallacher plopped down on the nearby couch, settled into the deep cushions, and stretched his arms upward.

"Nice to see ya both," he said. "Let's have a bit of a go at it and see what we can do about the state of the bloody world we find ourselves in. What say ya to that?"

What followed was a jumble of information, tied together by fits and starts of conversations and whispered asides and mutterings of agreements and protests and the most incredible, gasp-inducing astonishment and several resulting denunciations, along with some good old-fashioned hornswoggling of both the Irish and American varieties.

We argued, we pressed forward, we retreated, we threatened, we cajoled, we compromised. We were everything that American democracy used to be, before petty partisan gibberish permanently got in the way of common sense or the good of the nation and its people.

Whether we actually agreed to anything substantive is anyone's guess and a matter of interpretation, even now, months later, as I pull out my notes and listen once more to the tape recordings that click into place and convert seamlessly onto a hard drive whenever a detectable sound is discerned at our estate.

And yeah, as Caeli has reminded me, more than once, I'd better learn how to at least temporarily disable the damn thing, somewhere along the line.

It's worth noting that the discussion went sideways early on with an exchange that continues to tick me off.

"I want to hear about the CIA's meddling and how that got you sacked," I said.

"Before we get to that bit, tell me about yer drive into Limerick this morning," he said, holding his hand up like a traffic cop to slow me down.

I should've known that something was up when he asked the question, but I pressed ahead without a second thought, or much of a first.

"Sure," I said. "Leonard and I were damn near killed when …"

"Wait – don't tell me," he shouted with far too much energy. "You were attacked by a Mercedes that was after tossin' what appeared to be pipe-bombs out the passenger's side window, if I have me facts correct."

He grinned, exuding a better than fair impression of the all-knowing guru at work.

I stared back at him (perhaps *glared* is a better description) and asked the obvious question.

"How in hell do you know that?"

"You won't like the answer, boyo."

"Try me."

"All right then – but don't say I didn't warn ya," he said before glancing at Caeli, shrugging his shoulders slightly, as though apologizing in advance for transgressions yet to be announced.

"I sent 'em yer way," he said.

I hesitated because I wasn't sure that I'd heard him correctly.

Caeli got it well enough, however, and she kicked things into high gear, though in retrospect she managed to sound extraordinarily composed – to my ear, anyway.

"You did what, exactly?" she asked.

Gallacher, still grinning, remained steady.

"I sent the chase car after yer man and the other bodyguard, the big one who was out in the weeds, lurkin' as we drove in just now – after hidin' the rig he picked up from the company boys in Dublin. I've men out to put him to task on ..."

"Jaysus, man," I said, finding my voice, along with my anger. "You could've killed us."

"Hardly, Professor Blake," he said. "The bombs were all smoke and mirrors – just for show, ya see."

"Just for show? Are you kidding? They went off well enough."

"Yes, 'tis true – just as designed. But did ya see 'em do any damage then? Yer vehicle was perfectly intact, was it not? Even the roadway was unharmed at the spot where the bloody things set down. That's why the lorry ya saw seconds later was able to roar by as ye were after scurryin' away. Let me tell ya 'bout that lumbering beast then. It's the reason we took the actions we did."

I shook my head, as angry as I'd been in years, and began tallying up the ways in which Gallacher's stunt (and I still can't determine a better word for what he'd done) could've turned on a dime and ended up in disaster.

"I had my pistol out," I said, before he could provide us with his insights about the passing truck. "I was ready to shoot the bastards – and I'd do it right now given the chance."

Gallacher sniffed at the thought.

"And I gave ya clear warnin' not to use that bloody thing 'less yer life was in danger," he said.

"I thought my life *was* in danger, you damn fool," I said. "How could I think otherwise? They were tossing bombs at us, for god's sake. Of all the stupid, ill-advised, cockamamie, lame-brained schemes to concoct … it's no wonder you got sacked."

"Ouch," he said. "That hurts."

"Good," Caeli and I said together, in perfect stereo.

"Hear me out," he said. "There's a logical explanation, if only you'd give me a chance to … ah, here we are then."

He glanced up as Ian entered the room with a steaming mug of coffee.

"All set then, boss," he said while extending his hand, careful not to spill its contents. "Piece of cake."

"A beautiful thing, that," Gallacher said, and he appeared to be completely absorbed in the transfer, as though nothing else mattered. "Comes to that, a piece of cake or even a biscuit would be lovely. Anything about?"

"Forget the damn coffee," I said, close to shouting the words. I was incensed at his cavalier attitude and seeming indifference. "You'd best send your man to the kitchen for a bag of ice because I'm about to pop you one, smack in the nose – and I'll be happy to take on your boys, one at a time or together, 'cause I've got a feeling you're gonna need them."

Gavin bristled at the threat.

Ian took a step toward me after he'd made the transfer, uncertain but willing to jump in if needed.

Elmore, god bless him, was instantly at my side.

Gallacher, for what it's worth, was calm and steady, a ship's captain confident that he could lead us safely ashore despite the thrashings of the great storm that raged around us.

"I know yer upset, Professor Blake," he said. "And I know you've a t'ousand questions or more to push me way. Why not hold 'em a spell an' let me tell ya what's happened here – what's at stake."

"I'd rather punch you."

He barked out a brief laugh.

"I'm sure ya would, boyo – not that it'd do either of us any good."

THIRTY-EIGHT

MOVING CHESS PIECES

I snarled a handful of insults for the next few minutes while Caeli ignored me and Liam Gallacher remained stiffly steadfast in his belief that he'd made, as he put it, a grand call.

In hindsight, it wasn't my finest hour, though it felt good at the time.

Still, my ire was real enough, lingering despite Gallacher's myriad protests and stabs at logic in defending his position. And if you think that I was bothered when I first heard his admission, you should've been there for Leonard's take, hours later, when he found out.

Fireworks are less explosive.

I've used the estate's recording system to provide an exact account of how things shook out, edited only for cohesiveness and tossing out the choicest indecencies that were uttered during the various exchanges, many of which came from me.

Gallacher (after a great deal of verbal dancing and deflection): I appreciate yer willingness to hear me out.

Me: So why do I get the feeling you'll waste my time?

Caeli (ignoring me): Go ahead, Liam. But I trust you to realize you have some serious explaining to do.

Gallacher: Don't I know it, though I'll not apologize for what I ordered regardin' this morning's road encounter. If anything, it saved the professor's life – along with yer missin' bodyguard's.

Me: It's a good thing he's not here. If he knew you were responsible for throwing pipe bombs at him, you'd need more bodyguards of your own.

Elmore: How 'bout I call him – let him know what went down, Professor B? That'd bring him back in a hurry.

Gallacher: Please don't. I'm in Dutch enough with me own government.

Me: Nothing you don't deserve, I'm sure.

Gallacher: Yes, well, as to that, let me give you a taste of what the past 48 hours 'ave been like from my perspective – not just for me but for most of my team as well. You can judge for yerself whether I warrant a bloody sacking or somethin' else entirely.

Me: I hope you're not thinking of a medal.

Gallacher: Nothin' of the kind. But I'd appreciate a bit of understandin'.

Caeli: If only you'd tell us something we can evaluate.

Me: And that makes sense.

Caeli: And explains what you were thinking when …

Gallacher (interrupting quickly while waving his wrists in a gesture of what I took for futility): Yes, yes, and yes again – a t'ousand times over. I do understand yer concerns. Please hear me out before ya throw me to the hounds.

Me (after he lingered once more): And once again, get on with it, boyo.

Gallacher (avoiding eye contact, talking to the wall): Right. So hours back, it was, I got short notice from the boys at the head office. I was wanted in Dublin forthwith, with no warnin', ya see. I knew it was serious when they sent a plane and then took me straight off to Phoenix Park. The G2 honchos were there, of course, along with the top lads from the Guards and my supposed contact in government – the same man you met at the warehouse. Also in attendance were a couple of gents from Interpol, a chap from MI-6 who's decent enough, and an insufferable prig from the CIA. Leave it to the Yank to drive the meetin'. It didn't go well for the home team.

Caeli: The home team being …?

Gallacher: Why me, of course, Miss Brown. I wouldn't think you'd need a scorecard after all this time.

Me: You would if you want to tell the good guys with pipe bombs from the bad guys with pipe bombs.

Gallacher (ignoring me): The gatherin' amounted to an execution, the result bein' preordained long a'fore I arrived in Dublin. Everyone had a part to play, I suppose – a line to deliver, a comment to offer, a rebuke to make. Or maybe I should say that most everyone participated. The MI-6 chap told me later that he'd fought the massacre but was little more than one voice alone, shouted down by the CIA.

Caeli: They pulled you from the investigation.

Gallacher: Quite.

Me: So what was the main beef, exactly, that landed you on the sidelines? Taking target practice at your men? Running them off the road with tanks? Forcing them to jump from the Cliffs of Moher at gunpoint?

Gallacher (exhibiting a grim smile): Nothing so dramatic, Professor Blake. The bottom line, ya see, was lack of progress on my part. The French, it seems, dropped a net on much of the operation there. Frog One's in custody as of three hours ago, if all's gone according to plan. (He checked his watch to ensure that his timing was correct.) I'm told a similar operation in Tokyo and another still in New York City is about to be wrapped up as well. That leaves Ireland unaccounted for in what's shaped up to be a bloody four-pronged terrorist extravaganza, all run by the same man. The government toady didn't think that was sportin' of us – "not nearly efficient" were his exact words. With the CIA eejit jerkin' his strings, the bastard pulled the plug on me, along with much of my team and the operation we were after runnin', which places me in a not-too-friendly mood.

He crossed his arms over his chest and pushed his wiry frame deeper into the cushions. I could offer, I suppose, that he appeared to be pouting. But Caeli pointed out, perhaps correctly, that this last observation is a matter of interpretation of his mood and facial appearance and not a solid fact.

Caeli: Four operations at the same time? Seriously?

Gallacher: We suspected as much, but it's just been confirmed.

Caeli: So you were angry. I get it. But why order your men to throw pipe-bombs at Max and Leonard?

Me: Yeah. Explain that. I'm sure you'll make it look good in your report. You are writing a report, right?

Gallacher: Yes, Professor Blake. I'm writing a bloody report, just as I'm obliged to do for all actions taken. As to the situation on the roadway, let me assure you that it was the right call …

Me (interrupting): I've heard all that. Just tell us why.

Gallacher (after a deep sigh that was easily picked up on the recording): Despite bein' sacked, along with the very lads ya see here, plus a handful of others, a good many of those who're loyal to me and accomplished much of the work we've done to date remain in place. They've also continued certain initiatives to battle the threat – keepin' me in the loop, of course – though workin' now with a jointly led international team under, ah, different local leadership. One of the lads, assigned to monitor yer movements, along with Miss Brown's and yer two recent imports, rang me up to advise that yer journey into Limerick this mornin' to collect the armored vehicle for yer man had been compromised by the same bastards who've been after ya since yer first encounter at Bunratty and then again at the parkin' structure on Anne Street.

Caeli and I exchanged glances of true concern here. Despite the precautions we'd taken, not only were we still being monitored by Gallacher's crew (no great surprise, considering the fact that G2 is a world-class spy organization), but we also were being tracked by the terrorists we'd inadvertently encountered.

Not good, I recall thinking.

Caeli: How did your people gather that intel?

Gallacher: Surely, Miss Brown, ya don't expect me to pass along state secrets.

Caeli: That's exactly what I expect, given what's taken place.

Gallacher: Yes, well, let's just say, without puttin' too fine a point on things, that yer mobiles, as well as yer landline, have been put into play – and not just by our people. The lads on the other side figured a way to keep watch on the two of ya. My guess? Their operation involves far more than occasional drive-pasts on the road.

Me (thoroughly perplexed): Wait a minute. Days ago we turned our phones into someone who could wipe them clean, making sure that no trackers and listening devices were in place.

We've yet to get them back and picked up two burner phones in Limerick so we wouldn't have the problem.

Gallacher: That wouldn't 've been necessary had ye seen fit to use the mobiles I'd given ya.

Me: So you could monitor us at every step? That's why we got the burners.

Gallacher: Did ya really think we wouldn't crack that bit of subterfuge after ye made the purchase at CeX in front of our people on the street, with DS Phelan ferrying ya about the city in his own bloody car? Really, Professor Blake.

Me: That's not very sporting.

Caeli: What about the other guys – the terrorists? How did they …

Gallacher: Good question, one I've yet to produce an answer for. Our people are lookin' into it, sure, but so far it's guesses, other than they're damn clever.

Me: That's hardly comforting. And I've yet to hear an explanation as to …

Gallacher: Gettin' there, boyo. Easy does it, eh? We knew ye were plannin' an early-morning run to the Greyhound Stadium to meet with the two lads who'd ferried a rig 'cross the countryside durin' the night. We also knew, and this is the key part, yer friend from Bunratty and his boys were onto it. Ye even saw 'em, ya know. They were inside the …

Me: Don't tell me. They were inside the truck that whizzed past during the commotion.

Gallacher: Good on ya. The fake bombs were the only play we could determine on the fly to keep ya safe – to keep everyone safe. As it turned out, my people forced 'em off the road minutes after they'd rocketed past.

Caeli: So you ran a calculated risk with Max's life at stake, and Leonard's.**Gallacher**: Correct, Miss Brown, though I wouldn't call it a risk of any kind. It was more of a well-planned operation, a chess match, perhaps, that turned out beautifully for all concerned – except, of course, for the tossers in the lorry. It didn't end well for them, ya see.

There was more, of course, with multiple questions on our part and Gallacher holding his own line of delineation while defending his positions and operations and people – and most of all his decisions.

And I'll grant you that, in the moment, it was tough to second-guess him, given that the four roustabouts his people captured in the lorry were now providing information that the spy chief hailed as "crucial to bringin' an end to the whole bloody mess."

If you can believe him, of course …

I wondered about that for a time and found myself distracted from much of the trailing conversation that ensued, with Caeli and Gallacher going back and forth about multiple attack points and the ramifications of his sacking and the current status of the investigation and the people who were now leading the taskforce.

"I'm really not relegated to pasture, ya know – not yet, at least," he said. "It's just that, well, because of the slimy little government weasel and the ham-fisted CIA wanker pullin' strings like some arrogant bloody Wizard of Oz behind a curtain that shouldn't exist, I'm forced to pull a few strings of me own. It gives me no pleasure to tell ya, but if things don't go well in the next 24 hours, I could be on permanent holiday – perhaps lookin' for a job as a gardener on yer estate."

"Do you know anything about planting flats of flowers?" Caeli asked him, which actually made me smother a laugh.

"We've been after keepin' watch on yer place, ya know," he said, shifting the discussion once more. "My people 've been lurkin' nearby, on the road and in the weeds, even by boat."

Caeli asked the obvious question.

"So you still think we're in danger."

"Let's just say our intention's to keep ya safe. If we latch onto a few bad guys along the byway, so much the better."

I couldn't help but argue with his logic.

"If you really wanted to keep us safe, you would've arrested the bastard who killed Mrs. Shedd instead of screwing around out here," I said. "You'd still be employed, and one fewer murderer would be on the streets. Think about it: No more treasure-hunting from clueless tourists, no more dead victims in hotel rooms, no more pipe-bombs terrorizing passing motorists … no, wait. Those were your guys."

Gallacher was growing annoyed at my continued assault. He shot me a quick look that betrayed what he was thinking, though he remained outwardly calm and didn't offer an immediate defense. But I was intrigued by his actions and couldn't stop myself from poking the bear.

"So tell me, Liam, because I need to hear it," I said. "And don't give me that seeking-out-bigger-fish excuse because I'm not buying it. Why didn't you get this guy a long time ago, when you realized what he was up to at Bunratty? You knew he was a thief, mucking up a hotbed of tourism – something the country desperately needs. And if you can't adequately explain that, why not take him out when he killed Mrs. Shedd? Why leave him in the hen house, picking off the flock? Explain it to me."

I got the flash of anger again, deadly and biting, and this time it lasted for a couple of seconds before he exchanged it for an expressive puppy-eyes look, the one where he attempts to convey that he wants to spill everything he knows but just can't do it, for any of a dozen or more national security reasons.

But I remained troubled by his lack of action on Mrs. Shedd's murder, and I pressed ahead, sticking the knife in deeper though I knew he couldn't – or wouldn't – give us a decent answer.

"Come on, Liam. Cough it up," I said. "You knew he was responsible for the thefts, and for the murder. You had his picture up on the warehouse wall. You probably even know his name, rank, and serial number. And yet, you've let him be, doing whatever he pleases while your boys are running around out here. No wonder you got fired."

I got another of his stabbing-dagger frowns, flashing by almost too quickly to register, and a hand wave this time, a gesture indicating helplessness, perhaps. Or maybe it was resignation that I saw in his eyes, or even regret. It was difficult to determine, and I was angry.

Caeli shifted positions, accompanied by a soft sigh that was surely directed my way. But given all that had happened, Gallacher felt obligated to provide an answer, even if it rang hollow.

"Once more, Professor Blake, we were hopin' he'd lead us to bigger things while tryin' our level best to keep the two of ya, and everyone else, out of harm's way," he said. "As to whether ye believe that, it makes no difference in the great scheme o' things – nor in any report I subsequently write."

I was about to go at him again, reminding him that Mrs. Shedd might well be alive if he'd acted quickly to end the robberies at Bunratty, when Leonard barged through the kitchen and into the sitting room with a handcuffed cretin who'd been roughed up to no small degree and was being held tight at the collar.

"There's a rat infestation by the river," Leonard said as Elmore jumped up to help, though we all scrambled from our seats at roughly the same time. "Found this one and a couple others like him. High time somebody cleaned it out."

The cretin was short, no more than 5-foot-4, give or take, and weighed in at what I guessed to be under 120 pounds – a true bantam. The only thing that could be described as fat on him was his lower lip, which apparently had been smacked by Leonard in the scuffle that led to his capture and sudden appearance inside our home.

"Who the hell are ya?" Gallacher asked while appraising Leonard's captured rat.

I felt like barging in, telling Gallacher to back off because Leonard was our man and, in case he hadn't noticed, this was our turf, not his. But I likely would've asked the same question anyway and let it go.

"Are ye the professor then?" the cretin asked.

Gallacher shook his head and indicated with a nod that Leonard's prisoner should look in my direction.

"It's ye then, boyo, is it?" he said, directing the query to me.

"Who the hell are you?" I asked, repeating Gallacher's query. But I added a question the spymaster failed to ask – one, I thought, that was every bit as vital. "And what the hell do you want?"

"I'm here to deliver a message," the cretin said. "Tell yer ape here to back off and I'll give it to ya nicely. He keeps it up and I won't bloody tell ya a fookin' thing."

Terrific, I recall thinking – *a punk with attitude, giving orders. He should join G2 and work for Gallacher.*

THIRTY-NINE

DANCING WITH THE DEVIL

It took some time to get the smug little tosser to sing.

I initially figured that our guest would cave when Leonard cocked the Beretta – unnecessarily, I'd add – and forced him to his knees with a twisting downward yank on his shirt collar that took some of the starch out of his surly disposition.

But it was Caeli who convinced him to warble his message, not like a delicate songbird, exactly, but more like a squawking crow. She and Leonard performed an unscripted version of nice cop/scary cop that eventually produced some insight into his occupation along the riverbank.

While Ian and Gavin slipped out of the room to search for the other two men Leonard had alluded to when he burst into our discussion with his captive, Caeli took over the interrogation.

"Would you like something to drink? Water, perhaps?" she asked.

"Like I can take on a drink with these bloody things on me wrists," the cretin said, displaying plastic zip-ties and jutting his chin in a show of defiance. "An' the last thing I'd be after takin' is water. Bloody Jaysus."

"A beer then. We can do that. Leonard – please take the handcuffs off our guest," Caeli suggested.

The big bodyguard shook his head.

"Not gonna happen," he said. "He's no guest, and he's not exactly what I'd call housebroke."

It dawned on me later that Caeli and Leonard were on their own private wavelength. She was unfazed by Leonard's denial and continued seeking in a pleasant manner whatever information the man possessed.

"I'll make sure you're allowed to leave unscathed," she said, speaking casually, as though this were an everyday occurrence in our home. "I wouldn't want to see any harm come your way."

Liam Gallacher squirmed at the offer but said nothing.

The cretin was quick to reply.

"Too late fer that," he said. "The Yank's already given me a bit of a thrashin'. And what he's done to me mates" – he jerked his head northward, toward the spot where the River Shannon runs along the front of the estate – "ain't fit fer mixed company to hear nor see. Not sure I'll tell ya a thing – not now. I'm as good takin' me chances with me own lot when the time comes."

"Then you've wasted our time and yours, with nothing to show for it except a beating … and a lengthy jail sentence," she said and turned toward Gallacher, who remained fixated on the exchange. "That can be arranged without difficulty, I imagine?"

"Surely," Gallacher said. "The list of charges would be long, indeed."

The cretin squirmed.

"Charges? Are ye daft, man? I'm the one to bloody well press charges here," he said. "I'm the one assaulted by this lumberin' bollox. Look what he's already done to me face." He thrust his chin outward again.

Leonard closed in.

"Just think what I'm gonna do to the rest of you if you don't start squawking," he said.

"Fook off, Yank. Ya don't bloody scare the likes of me."

"Then you're dumber'n you look, and right now you look pretty stupid," Leonard growled.

Caeli intervened once more.

"All right – let's finish up and enjoy the rest of the day, shall we?" she said, again projecting an everything's-fine persona. "Tell us your message and you can leave – no further incidents. We'll even throw in a beer for the road."

This time Gallacher appeared as though he wanted to argue the point. He shuffled his feet but remained quiet, to his considerable credit.

Even then, the cretin was as cocky as he was determined.

"What kind o' beer are ya talkin' then?" he asked.

Caeli smiled.

"Let's see. Guinness, both stout and lager, and Harp or O'Hara's or Murphy's Red. I'd have to check."

"I'll take one of each then."

"You'll take one and like it and thank the lady – after you've spilled what you came for," Leonard said, jerking the cretin's collar again.

"What about me mates, eh?"

"They're in no condition to drink," Leonard said.

"Maybe a pint'll revive 'em."

"Enough," Gallacher nearly shouted. "What's the message?"

"I'm talkin' to the lady, boyo – sure as hell not the likes of you or this wanker behind me."

The room went quiet, with the little man staring at Caeli and the rest of us staring at him.

"Max darling," Caeli said after a long pause. "Would you be a dear and grab three beers from the refrigerator – as a peace offering?"

"Sure," I said. "Delighted. But only after we've heard what he has to say."

Caeli tossed her wrists outward – a gesture that conveyed *It's out of my hands; take it or leave it* – and turned her face away.

The cretin sat expectantly.

I held my ground.

He was inclined to wait us out, it seemed, when Ian and Gavin returned to the house and slipped silently into the corner, watching the standoff with interest. Their faces were blank; it was impossible to determine what they'd seen.

"Tell you what. Cough it up and my friends here" – I nodded toward the new arrivals – "will let you know how your mates are faring."

"Give us the beer first," he said.

Caeli waved at Gallacher and shrugged theatrically.

"We've done our best," she said. "I trust you won't torture him too much."

Gallacher beckoned Ian and Gavin, and they swept in to collar our recalcitrant visitor.

"All right, for bloody sake," the cretin said, swiveling his head to face me. "It's not like the fate of the fookin' world hinges on it. I'm to tell ya yer man is set to meet at Raven's Ridge at 3 in the afternoon tomorrow."

"Raven's Ridge?" I asked. "What's that? Better yet, where's that? And who, exactly, is my man?"

"Right – he knew that bit'd get yer notice well enough," the cretin said, smiling thinly, as though he'd put one over on us. "I'm expected now to fire off a flare. Once that's done, yer man'll explain the works himself. Then ye can sort the details, but only after me and me mates is long gone."

"What kind of flare are we talking about?" I asked.

He began reaching his still-joined hands toward the inside of his jacket but thought better of it as the hovering Ian and Gavin reacted by quickly drawing their pistols. Leonard had already shoved his Beretta into the cretin's back with enough force to warrant his full attention.

"Easy now, Yank," the cretin said. "I'm just after the bloody mobile. Need it to make the fookin' call – send up the flare."

"Hold still," Leonard said, snaking his free hand inside the man's jacket. "I stick this into something sharp, your mother won't recognize the parts they stick in the box."

"Good on ya, Yank – a good stab at it," the cretin said, grinning. "Might try the same line meself."

Leonard growled something indecipherable as he extracted a flip-phone, studied it momentarily, and tossed it to Gavin.

"Here," he said. "Blake tells me you're the expert."

I didn't remember making any such claim, but Gavin seemed pleased with the compliment and examined the phone for a few seconds, pulling it open and peering at the keys before snapping it shut again, feigning indifference, and tossing it back to Leonard.

"Looks clean," he said.

"You sure?"

"Sure enough for you to try it."

The cretin laughed.

"Hand it over," he said.

Leonard shook his head.

"I don't think so. Maybe it's wired to blow us up once you punch in the code."

"Why would I blow meself up, boyo?" the cretin asked.

"Other'n you're dumb as an empty glass? How the hell would I know?" Leonard growled.

The cretin turned sideways, striving for eye contact.

"If ya don't give me the bloody phone, Yank, the flare don't git lit and yer man won't git his call," he said.

I was annoyed at the back and forth.

"Give me the phone," I said, extending my hand.

Leonard tossed it over, and I flipped it open and glanced at the cretin.

"What's the number?"

"It's the first one on the quick-dial," he said.

I dug around in the menu, finally located the proper section, and hit the number, which in turn activated the call sequence.

"That you then, boyo?" the voice said after its owner picked up on the third ring.

It's him, Mister Denmark – no question, I thought, identifying our nemesis from the two encounters at the Folk Park. I covered the phone with my hand and mouthed "Bunratty" in Caeli's and Gallacher's direction before responding.

"Depends on who you're looking for," I said. "If it's your carrier pigeon, letting you know he's all right, you're out of luck – and so is he."

He didn't seem bothered with this turn.

"Well now, if it isn't the famous Professor Blake," he said. "How nice of ya to join me. What've you done with little Michaleen?"

"He's tied up at the moment," I said.

"And his mates?"

"Taking a nap, I'm told."

I got a lengthy pause. Caeli waved at me to activate the phone's speaker so that everyone could hear. But I wasn't sure how to manage it without fishing around in the menu again and possibly losing the connection, and I glanced apologetically in her direction and shrugged my shoulders.

Leonard snatched the phone away and stabbed at the keypad a couple of times.

"For god's sake, Blake," he whispered.

The speaker kicked in an instant later.

"All right," Mister Denmark eventually said. "I don't give a shite about that lot anyway. Did he tell ya to meet me tomorrow at Raven's Ridge?"

"He did. What the hell is …"

"First things first, boyo," he said, interrupting. "I thought you'd enjoy me little turn of phrase in selectin' Raven's Ridge as our meetin' spot. I've been after readin' yer books, ya see, and it's plain enough the word means something to ya – to both of ya. So Raven's Ridge it is then."

"Fine. Give me the directions."

"Yer to bring the archbishop's niece, Blake – just the two of ya," he said. "No coppers, no bloody spies, no blighters from the C-I-fookin'-A, no Interpol bastards, no bodyguards from Oregon, no bleedin' hardware. Just you and the missus – nothing else and nobody else. Got it, Yank?"

I didn't like the sound of that.

"Hell no. I'm not interested in meeting you under those terms," I said. "You've got nothing we want – nothing we need, other than your hide, which we'll get soon enough anyway. It's not like you're holding hostages or threatening …"

"Yer dead wrong, Yank. I'll text the directions," he said, cutting me off again. "Don't be late or ya won't like what comes next – that much I promise."

He clicked off the connection, and I cursed softly and tossed the phone to Gavin, figuring that he could monitor the incoming text.

"So it's the archbishop's niece he's after then," Gallacher said, as though talking to himself. "What's the bloody connection? He wasn't in Ireland for the Mutton Island fiasco. Is it our friend Kathleen MacAmhlaoibh, maybe?"

Good question, I thought.

But the cretin remained focused.

"What about me beers then?" he said. "Ya promised me three of 'em, Yank."

Gallacher called the Limerick *Garda* station, spoke briefly with DCI Declan Abbot, and arranged for the removal of Michaleen the cretin and his two associates, who remained trussed up along the riverbank, several dozen yards from the house.

Caeli and I were immersed in a conversation about the mention of her uncle, the former archbishop who was now under the protection of the church, despite the crimes he'd committed on Irish soil.

"I knew he'd somehow come back to haunt us," she said. "It was too much to think we could come here without Uncle Jack's shadow hovering over our heads."

I did my best to assuage familial guilt.

"We don't know what it means, Caeli," I said. "It might be anything – or nothing at all."

"I don't believe that for a second, and you can't, either, Max. Nor should you," she said. "He was quite specific, and it means something. It's got to. Given Uncle Jack's track record in this part of Ireland, it can't be good."

"Maybe he's a fan and nothing more," I said, referencing the Bunratty mesmerist. "You know – one revolutionary to another."

She shot me a look that would dry winter paint, and I gave up on my make-her-feel-better approach and tried looking at the problem logically, or at least realistically.

Trouble was, nothing sprang easily to mind. I'd been anxious to follow through on the proposed meeting, but I was far less inclined now that he'd dragged Caeli into the bargain.

"The issue isn't Jack," I eventually said. "We're under no obligation to meet this guy, as you've already pointed out. Right now, with you involved, I can't see a good reason to – other than curiosity. And you know what that did to the cat."

Caeli saw another angle.

"Don't you want to get the guy who killed Mrs. Shedd? The Irish government doesn't. They've left it to us. We're the only hope her family has," she said.

Fortunately, Liam Gallacher strolled confidently back into the room with a map in one hand and a fresh cup of coffee in the other.

"Not true, Miss Brown – not true a'tall," he said. "I assure you, the government wants this man brought to justice for his many crimes, including the murder of yer friend. But we still believe he can lead us to others who are central to the terrorist plot, our old friend Kathleen MacAmhlaoibh included. And he can't do that from a bloody jail cell."

"So you won't allow us to meet him?" Caeli asked.

"To the contrary, Miss Brown. I think the two of ya should do whatever it takes to meet up with the bastard and learn what he knows of the greater threat here in Ireland, if anythin' a'tall."

"Easy for you to say," I countered. "He hasn't personally tried to kill you. It's not even likely he knows you exist."

"And I assure you, Professor Blake, he knows all too well who we are and what we want, which is why the two of ya may be our best hope."

Then another ugly truth struck home.

"Wait a minute. I thought you'd been booted off this investigation," I said.

"Indeed I have. But that doesn't mean I'll sit twiddlin' off to the side while me two favorite Yanks are threatened on the one hand and enticed into a trap on the other," he said, and he generated a quick snort of laughter that was over as quickly as it began. "Let's see if we can find the location of this Raven's Ridge he's mentioned, shall we? Then we can lay out a plan to guarantee yer safety while allowin' us to keep an eye on the man. Maybe – just maybe – he'll show his hand."

We spent the next hour looking at topographical maps that Gallacher's people accessed, along with computer printouts that Caeli made from the coordinates we'd been given via text message. It wasn't long before we determined that the name *Raven's Ridge* was little more than a concoction bestowed on a remote area along the River Shannon estuary, miles west of our estate, by the demented bastard who'd robbed DS Phelan's aunt, killed Joan Shedd, and god knows what else while parading around Bunratty, preying on the unsuspecting, waiting for the perceived terrorist plot to begin.

DCI Declan Abbot himself arrived to collect the three punks who'd been sent to our home to deliver a message and left us, not with a bottle of beer but rather with their hands secured in the back of a paddy wagon. Gallacher spent a moment with Abbot before the thugs were hauled off, and the G2 operative seemed satisfied that everything was in order when he joined us once more in the study to continue planning what he called "a strategic operation to bring down this bastard and his mates, once and for all."

"Who knows?" he said of the departed thugs. "Maybe one of that lot can cough up somethin' of importance. I've sent Gavin and Ian along to see what they can learn. With any luck, we'll have items to work with – things that'll help."

Gallacher's mobile rang 20 minutes later. He checked the caller ID, frowned, and opened the connection.

"Jaysus," he said seconds later as his face screwed up into a look of seething anger and betrayal and disbelief. I figured that it was the home office in Dublin, shutting him down once more after learning that he was again poking around in the investigation. He did little more than grunt a time or two as the one-sided discussion unfolded, although our recording system indicated that at one point he whispered a single word: "Explain."

When he clicked off, he drew a couple of deep breaths to calm himself.

"That was Gavin," he said. "Abbot was speedin' back to the Limerick station when he took a sudden turn – off the track. By the time my lads backtracked and found the rig, Abbot's man was secured in back, with Abbot himself and the three messengers long gone."

"No. That makes no sense – something's off," I said.

"Yer instincts are good, Professor Blake," he said. "Abbot's man said the little one, Michaleen, somehow broke free from the back and commandeered the wagon with a pistol, forcing them off the road, where they tied him up, took Abbot hostage, and were collected by a waiting van."

"Horseshit," Leonard said. "I checked him myself – twice. He wasn't armed when he left here."

"Yes – something's off," Caeli said.

"Agreed," Gallacher said. He was pensive and brooding as he spoke. "There's no way the little shite could've broken loose, let alone made it from the back of the wagon to the cab – not unless he freed himself from the chains he was in, pushed out the gate, which was padlocked on the exterior, and climbed along the side or up and over the top and entered the cab through a side window, all the while unseen. No, that didn't happen – not without help, anyway."

He shook his head and snapped on his phone, calling in favors to assist with the manhunt.

Caeli was quicker to conclusions that seemed obvious on their face, however.

"You know that mole you were looking for, Liam?" she said. "Looks like you've found a candidate."

"Abbot?" he barked, holding his hand over the face of his mobile. "Ye can't be serious."

"Wake up," Leonard said. "No wonder you got tossed."

FORTY

SOME TECHNICAL SUPPORT

But we were wrong about Abbot.

Hell, we were wrong about so much then.

Let me explain.

We spent the next tension-filled hour trying to determine a logical assault plan for Raven's Ridge (so-called), attempting to discern what had happened to Michaleen and his battered band of escaped river thugs, and determinedly striving to learn what DCI Declan Abbot was up to, if anything at all.

Gavin and Ian returned to the estate 30 minutes into our discussions, shocked by what had taken place on the road and angry enough about it to do some serious damage to those responsible for the treachery. They immediately huddled with Liam Gallacher and spent a few minutes howling at the moon. I suspect that the venting was at least cathartic.

"Good thing Abbot's not here for this," I whispered to Caeli. "He'd be lucky to talk his way out of it, even with a good explanation."

"I'd sure like to know what happened," she replied.

Gavin and Ian had a theory.

"The wanker set us up," Gavin griped, slamming his hand onto the kitchen counter with enough force to rattle the coffee cups. "He set the whole bloody business up. He's the reason we've been playin' catch-up all this time."

We kicked it around again: the timing, the necessary steps for the cretin and his minions to escape their binds and secure the rig, the logical conclusion that they'd had help, a healthy suspicion that Abbot was behind the escape (masterminding his own convenient disappearance in the mayhem that ensued), and much speculation regarding Abbot's previous behavior, with Gavin and Ian relating conversations they'd had inside the warehouse with the missing copper that made him sound slippery.

Oddly, I found myself sticking up for the guy. I recounted his passionate reaction to DS Alan Phelan's friendship with us when we met the pair inside the Henry Street station and relayed what I thought were a handful of pertinent facts rather than speculation and after-the-fact puzzle-fitting that attempted – poorly, I'd add – to hammer the pieces into preordained slots.

"I could be wrong, but that doesn't sound like a man who was playing for the other side," I said.

"To the contrary – sounds exactly like it fits the bill," Gallacher counter-punched. "He'd want us to believe he'd fight hard – do whatever it took to make the situation right. Little more than play-actin', I'd say."

"I don't know," I said. "He was a martinet, all right, but I saw his conviction first-hand. It wasn't something you could easily fake."

"Depends on the strength of yer actin' skills," Gallacher muttered.

But nobody was happy with the back and forth, and few of those who were in the room were buying Abbot's innocence for what had just happened – even when the suggestion was forcefully made rather than merely danced around.

"Maybe he truly was kidnapped, is it," Danny O'Herlihy said. "Maybe we've got it all bolloxed up, eh? Maybe Abbot's little more than a victim – set up to look the part of the mole."

"If that's the case, boyo, dinner's on me for the next year," Ian said.

Leonard and Elmore were quiet during the exchanges, and I motioned at them after a few minutes had passed, encouraging them to offer their thoughts.

"We don't know him," Elmore said. "But it doesn't sound good – that's plain enough."

Leonard was far more emphatic.

"He's the duck in the pond, all right," he said.

When the allusion was met with empty stares from the Irish contingent, he growled out an explanation.

"If it waddles and quacks and flies like a damn duck, it's a damn duck and not a goose."

"I don't know," I said. "Bad as it looks, it's a long leap."

But Gallacher again recounted the likely scenarios, ticking them off one at a time, and his men nodded their agreement as the logic hit home once more.

"It's bloody-well impossible the little weasel'd slip the nick without some help," Gavin muttered as though talking to himself, referencing the cretin Michaleen.

"What of the copper who was with Abbot during the transfer?" I asked a moment later. "What's happened to him?"

Ian shook his head in frustration.

"Told us he took a decent knock to the head but was all right otherwise," he said. "We suggested he seek medical aid, but he shrugged it off, indicatin' he'd best help find Abbot."

"So he's gone?" I asked.

"We had no reason to hold 'im, if that's what yer askin'," Gavin said.

"We should talk to him – see if he remembers anything pertinent," I suggested. "Maybe he's got something now that he didn't have then – a tidbit that'll help."

Caeli had perked up at the mention of the accompanying copper.

"Better yet, let's see if we can entice him to have a sit-down with us," she said, and I figured that she'd spotted something the rest of us had not.

"What are you thinking?" I asked.

"Maybe it's not Abbot at all. Maybe it's his toady instead."

The line raised more than a few muttered asides.

With Gallacher's official status as director of the orchestra off the table, I pulled out my burner phone and dialed Spud Phelan's direct line, which he answered on the second ring. I took a moment to let him know that we'd heard rumors of Abbot's abrupt disappearance and then let him talk.

"Jaysus, Professor Blake, but all manner of shite's rainin' down on our heads at present," he said without further prompting. "It's a bloody disaster, it 'tis."

He paused for a second to see if I'd react and launched in again when I gave him space.

"Sorry, but the place is a madhouse an' more to come, I'd wager," he said. "You two all right then? It's all over the station, ya know – the two of ya bein' right in the thick of it again with the spy lords."

When I waved off the concern, he recounted the circumstances that surrounded the cretin's escape from the paddy wagon, Abbot's disappearance – "our lads found a trail of blood leadin' down the lane to where an auto was parked, apparently, and waitin' for the lot of 'em" – and the search that was currently under way to find not only Abbot but the missing river crew and the thugs behind the abduction.

"Everybody here's runnin' 'round with little sense of order a'tall," he said. "Abbot may be a right bollox, 'tis true, but he's our bloody bollox and we're after doin' our level best to bring 'im home so we can despise the wanker all over again."

I let him ramble on for a time, having activated the phone's speaker early on so that everyone could hear, and cut him off only when Gallacher began spinning his index finger in the air – an indication to hurry it along.

"Spud," I said during a hesitation as he gulped in some air. "I'm interested in the Guard who was with Abbot during the attack. Can you …"

"That would be DS Mahoney."

"Right. DS Mahoney. Have you talked with him? Is he …"

"Mahoney's in hospital, I'm told – sent off by the G2 lads who were nearby as Abbot brought the three eejits in," he said. "I'd like to be after havin' a word with the two of 'em, I would."

"Mahoney went to the hospital," I said, ignoring his jab at Ian and Gavin. "Are you sure?"

"That's what he told our boys on the scene," Spud said. "They wanted to take 'im in for a quick check, but he drove himself – didn't want to waste anyone's time or pull 'em away from the search for Abbot."

"And you're certain that's what happened?"

"I'm not certain of anything," he admitted. "But that's what's goin' 'round here regardin' Mahoney. He borrowed a car at the scene an' left."

I tried another angle.

"How well do you know Mahoney?"

"Not all that, I suppose. He's a recent transfer from Dublin, ya see – brought on when yer man at G2 set up shop," he said. "Not sure why Abbot took him on this run – hell, I'm less sure why Abbot took it upon himself to make the bloody trip. That's not the type of thing a DCI normally does, ya know. But I'll bet Mahoney wishes he'd stayed put. Then again, I'd wager Abbot does, too."

"Which hospital? Do you know where he went, exactly?"

"No – not a'tall. I can ask around and get back to ya, I suppose. I'm fairly sittin' here doin' little more 'n answerin' the bloody phones at present."

"Sure," I said. "Give me a call if you learn where he went. I'd like to talk with him."

I signed off, and Gallacher offered some choice words about muddled *Garda* operations in Limerick while Ian and Gavin both sputtered on about Abbot's treachery and the fact that Mahoney was a filthy liar. Caeli dug into her phone to obtain a listing of the closest medical centers that would be likely places for Mahoney to go ... *if, in fact, that's what he was up to when he bolted.*

I had my suspicions – I think we all did by then – and worked with Caeli on a list of numbers to call to see if we could find the missing detective sergeant.

But Spud called me back minutes later, after I'd made contact with one of the hospitals on Caeli's list, posing as a family member before striking out.

"Abbot's dead," Phelan fairly shouted into the phone. "They found him in the street, shot to bloody pieces three miles from where the hijack occurred. They just called it in. And never mind lookin' for Mahoney. They found him, too, shot twice in the head, six blocks from St. John's."

And yeah, we spent a hell of a long time kicking that around as well.

"Maybe they were on the right side of things after all," Gavin offered.

"And maybe their mates turned on 'em," Gallacher said. "And maybe we'll never know which is which."

With one theory down and little else to do but plan ahead for the confrontation at Raven's Ridge – *whatever and wherever that is, exactly*, I continued thinking as the words spun through my head – we spent our time looking for any advantage we could think of to end the muddle.

Elmore and Leonard disappeared into the security room early on, indicating that they wanted to pour over Google Earth and Irish topographical maps that they'd located online. I hadn't truly realized that Elmore was so adept with a mouse and keyboard, but he'd apparently been modest in describing his newly acquired skills. While he wasn't exactly hacker-efficient – "Not yet, anyway," he said – we soon learned that he was damn good.

He emerged 20 minutes or so into his internal prowlings to inform us that he had evidence – "Pretty solid, I'd call it; maybe 90-10" – that our security system had not only been hacked days earlier but, even worse, was still being monitored.

"Just kinda stumbled onto it while looking into the other thing," he said. "Can't tell who's watching yet, but they've taken over a couple of the cameras pointing out toward the road and another that's facing toward the river. They've also got monitoring capabilities inside the estate, including the master bedroom."

"What the hell does that mean?" I asked.

"It means they can see what's going on. Not sure about voice, but it's possible – maybe even probable."

I turned a baleful eye on Gallacher.

"You know anything about this?"

"No – well, maybe," he said quickly. "I had my people look for flaws in yer system a day or two back – turned it on and off a time or two in the dead of night. All they did was look for glitches – a quick in and out. We thought of it as a favor, to help keep ya safe."

Caeli was furious at the revelation.

"Are you serious? I'm still waiting for a tech crew to make time to come out here and fix it."

"Don't bother – that was us," Gallacher said. "I don't see what the …"

"Can you guarantee that your people didn't leave some surprises behind?" she asked, cutting him off.

"Absolutely," he said immediately, and I couldn't detect a hint of dishonesty in the reply. "I had them run a sweep to ensure it was up to snuff – capable of alerting ya to an outside attack. I promise ya, we were being proactive, tryin' our level best to keep ya out of the soup."

"Sure you were," she said.

"I assure you, Miss Brown, that was our intent – nothin' nefarious a'tall. This isn't my first trip through the smorgasbord, ya know. I knew you'd …"

"Save it, Liam."

Her tone made him wary, but she instantly switched gears – a technique that made Caeli such an effective investigative reporter during her newspaper days.

"How tight are you with the head tech on your warehouse team?" she asked. "You know the one – Aedan, I believe: 20s, baldish, Belfast accent …"

"Yes, of course," Gallacher said. "He's actually the very man I sent into your system – to check to see it was workin' properly."

"I might've guessed," Caeli said. "Is he loyal to you? Would he help if asked?"

"He is, and he'd help, I think. But he's sure to be tied up with this other business and a new boss and wouldn't be at liberty to bolt," Gallacher said. He turned inward for a moment, his eyes finding a distant corner of the room as he thought it through.

"Still, I'll ask if he'll lend us a hand when the timing's right," he eventually said. "What is it ya want him to do, exactly?"

"Find us an opening – something we can use to take the fight to them instead of the other way around," she said.

"I'm not sure I follow," Gallacher said.

"The best we've got right now is a demand for us to show up at this Raven's Ridge," Caeli said. "That's not a good …"

"We'll of course protect ya, make sure yer in no …"

"But it's a dangerous situation, regardless of how many people you stake out in the brush with rifles," she said. "If we can find the location where they're monitoring our system, we could get the jump on them there …"

"… instead of out in the hinterlands, on their timeline," Gallacher said, finishing the thought. "Yes. I like it – bloody brilliant, in fact."

"If we can pull it off."

"Let me see what I can do, Miss Brown," he said and pulled out his phone.

Elmore, who'd followed the back-and-forth, offered to do what he could to help and returned to the security system. He wasn't gone but three minutes when Leonard appeared and sought out Ian and Gavin for a quick word in a corner of the kitchen, well away from the rest of us. I had no idea what he said, but it wasn't long before Gavin and Leonard left the house, with Ian rejoining us at the table.

"What's that about then?" Danny O'Herlihy, Gallacher's driver, asked.

"The usual stuff," Ian said easily. "It's all good."

He whispered in my direction a few seconds later.

"Yer man says to tell ya he's off then," he said. "If ya need him, yer to give him a ring on his mobile – says ya have the number."

"Sure," I said. "What'd he need from your partner?"

"Just a loan of some equipment," Ian said, and he turned away, making it clear that he had nothing more to offer.

Gallacher was off the phone a couple of minutes later, rewarding us with the first genuine smile I'd seen from the guy since he'd surprised us at *Garda* headquarters on Henry Street.

"Aedan'll join us in three hours or so – 'fraid I had to insist. Threatened to send Gavin and Ian after him, in fact," he said. "Might as well put the time to good use and plot strategies for this Raven's Ridge encounter, should worse come to worse and Aedan gives us nothin'."

He returned to the notes that he'd been taking throughout our discussions, looking for answers, and began muttering to himself, though the words were spoken too softly to be heard clearly.

I decided to ask anyway.

"How's that again?"

He glanced up as though he'd been caught at something embarrassing.

"It's just that I've long thought it strange. As ya know, a gatherin' of crows is called a murder," he said. "Not a bevy or a flock or a collection, mind ya, but a murder. I wonder if the same applies to ravens."

I didn't bother parsing the origins of associating crows with murder. But I thought a great deal about where Leonard had gone and what he'd secured from Gavin before leaving the estate. And I thought, for just a fleeting moment, about the late Tommy McNevin and his equally dead brother-in-law and what the two of them had been up to.

FORTY-ONE

A BITE IN THE BYTE

Aedan O'Duinn arrived four hours later, with Elmore, who was watching from the monitors, giving us a heads-up that he'd entered the grounds.

Danny O'Herlihy waited as the computer wizard pulled into the long winding driveway and ushered him inside a secondary oversized garage, detached from the house, so that his car couldn't be spotted from the road.

For what it's worth, we took a great many precautions at that stage, hoping to minimize the risk to everyone who was attached to Liam Gallacher's band.

O'Duinn was noticeably nervous when he entered. I wrote it off to his reluctance to switch masters … *or maybe he thinks he'll get caught associating with Gallacher and thrown off the anti-terrorist team entirely.* But he perked up when he spied Caeli. The look on his face reminded me of the one he'd flashed at her, unbidden, when Gallacher first invited us to view the technicians' expansive workstation inside the spy warehouse. It was filled with lust and longing and greed, I think, and a hunger that seemed ferocious, if only for an instant – like the sound of snapping fingers, razor sharp and then instantly gone.

I shrugged it off at the time, rationalizing that Caeli's natural beauty often drew this type of reaction. I've seen similar gazes at airports, in restaurants, and from passing strangers on the street.

But I also thought that the look O'Duinn flashed at Caeli days earlier, when we'd first met him, was inadvertent, not meant to be seen. It reminded me of an escaping animal that had been penned in a cage and, given an unexpected opportunity, bolted at its chance at freedom, well before it could consider the dangers that lay beyond.

Back then, he hadn't noticed that I'd been watching.

This time, however, he spotted me intently eyeing his every move and flushed with recognition, his face turning from pink to flaming red in an instant.

As I read the signs, he did his best to recover. He cleared his throat and blinked his eyes several times, as though shedding them of dust, and mustered up a smile that was as innocent and as chaste as a father gazing down at his first-born. He nodded toward the others in the room, making eye contact, offering his hand a couple of times when it was expected, muttering words of greeting.

But the fact that I'd noticed his unguarded moment of lechery made him edgy as he greeted his old boss and apologized for his late arrival.

"Sorry," he muttered, to me and Gallacher both, as we were standing near one another. "Tried to get on earlier, but it's a fright back there, with everybody needin' this an' that an' straight away."

Gallacher waved off the apology, but the tech wasn't done.

"It's grand to see ya, sir," he said, and his eyes inadvertently shifted from the top spy to Caeli and back again. "Wish it were under better circumstances. It's all a bloody disaster, it 'tis."

I couldn't tell whether he was saying what was expected or whether he actually was happy to see Gallacher and this time figured that it was stress, the result of a long day spent under trying conditions.

He spent a minute bringing us up to date on the probe into the deaths of DCI Abbot and DS Mahoney, prodded by questions that came mostly from Gallacher and his driver. At one point, he glanced toward the kitchen's far corner and spotted Ian and Gavin.

"Ah – there ye are. Lots of bollox bein' asked 'bout the two of ya," he said. "Some of 'em think yer up to yer eyeballs in it and wonderin' where ya buggered off to. Wondered a bit meself, listenin' in."

But Gallacher cut short the awkwardness with a muttered curse and words of support for his men before introducing Elmore.

"This one's ready to show ya the security bits," the spy chief said. "See if ya can dig into the thing and tell us who's been pokin' about – might give us a look into who killed Abbot and his man and save us all from a long night of it. But what I really want straight-up is the location of the blighters. Find it for me, lad."

O'Duinn bobbed his head up and down in tacit agreement, though his eyes shifted repeatedly toward Caeli and then back to Gallacher. I couldn't tell what was driving his steady attention and was about to ask him, but Elmore indicated that he'd lead the way, the tech offered a muffled reply, and they headed down the lengthy corridor.

"Interesting lad," Gallacher said softly. "What he lacks in social graces, which is a gob-full, he makes up for in mad skills. We're damn lucky to have him."

"Not sure I'd take a road trip with him, especially with Caeli along," I said.

"Let's just see what he can pull together," Gallacher said.

Caeli, who'd been half-heartedly listening, had her mind on other issues.

"Tell us who he is, Liam," she said.

"O'Duinn? You already know. He's …"

"Not O'Duinn. We'll make time for him soon enough. Tell us what you know about Joan Shedd's killer – every detail, starting with his name."

He stared at her for a long time.

"It's not a matter of trust," he eventually said. "There's still much we don't know, ya see: his full military record, for example, the time he spent on the continent after his discharge, and …"

His voice trailed off, and he shook his head from side to side, displaying a sadness that I found myself questioning: Was it authentic, or was it merely a contrivance to put Caeli off the scent?

But she, too, wasn't buying it.

"This again?" she said, boring in, moving close to where he sat at the kitchen counter. "Do you really expect us to blindly follow along, asking no questions, while you give us nothing in return?"

"It's not like that."

"Yes – it's exactly like that," she said, stopping him before he could mount another defense. "We've played this game for too long."

"I honestly don't think you're …"

"So it's honesty you want? I'll give you honesty. I honestly don't think you've been straight with us from the beginning," she said. "I've been monitoring news sites for days and haven't seen a single reference to coordinated terrorist plots, here or elsewhere. I'd like to know what's going on – the truth this time."

I detected the glint in his eye, as though he found Caeli's passion to be amusing.

"Ya really don't expect Interpol to give out details of the Paris operation, do ya?" he said. "Publicity only encourages more terrorism. Ye should know that from yer days as a professional gossip."

"It doesn't pay to insult us," Caeli said. "It's beneath you. Why not try something new and give us the truth, starting with what you know about the lunatic who's playing games with our lives. A name would be nice – for starters."

I'll give Gallacher credit. He wasn't used to being confronted in this manner, though he'd previously witnessed Caeli's dogged determination and perhaps wasn't all that surprised. He waved his hands in a sign of surrender and smiled faintly.

"Go ahead, Miss Brown. Ask yer questions. I'll tell ya what I can – an' what I can't. It's the best I can do. You'll have to trust me when I split the line."

"We're back to trust again," she said.

"Surely, fer better or worse," he replied. "Ye must decide who the true monster is, and who among us is yer friend."

For purposes of accuracy, I used the estate's voice-activated monitoring system to record the exchange. Outside of a few muttered asides and areas that weren't pertinent to Gallacher's investigation – requests for coffee; a bathroom break – it's presented here exactly as it shook out.

Caeli: I want his name.

Gallacher: It's of little importance. Don't ya think we should start with the plot to attack Shannon International?

Caeli: The airport? That's the end game – not Bunratty?

Gallacher: Bunratty's little more than a sideshow, we think —
a spot for a handful of 'em to blow off steam.

Caeli: Security at the airport is …

Gallacher: Yeah. It's top-rate — always has been, or at least
since late 2001. Why they thought it a soft target is beyond me,
but that's where the intel leads us. What they hope to accomplish
is another matter entirely.

Caeli: What if you're wrong about Shannon? What if it's
about …

Gallacher: Our people are confident, Miss Brown.

Caeli: Your people have been wrong all along.

Gallacher: And yet, here we are.

Caeli (after a lengthy pause): Start at the beginning. And I
want a name.

Gallacher: Yes, of course. It began with the Americans.
These things always do, what with their vigilance after 9/11.
They ferreted out a multi-nation plot to attack tourist-friendly
symbols: the Eiffel Tower in Paris, the Tokyo Skytree, the Empire
State Building in New York, Shannon International here. The
mastermind's a Frenchman, Jean-Claude Daimallier by name,
with a penchant for money and mayhem going back two decades
or more. He also has a taste for the ladies, gamblin' on the ponies,
livin' the good life in the French and Italian rivieras, and payin' for
his extravagances via Ponzi schemes that cross borders. According
to yer CIA friends — and, I suppose, the NSA — he planned these
attacks as a way to extort money from the various governments, a
decidedly bad idea. The Yanks tell the world they don't negotiate
with terrorists. Neither do the rest of us. The result was a rather
haphazard operation that was eventually shut down — except, of
course, for here. Daimallier, ya see, recruited in Ireland a true
believer, I suppose you'd call her: the woman ya met in the car
park on Anne Street, a former compatriot of yer uncle. She, in
turn, recruited the man we believe killed yer friend Mrs. Shedd.

Caeli: Tell us about him.

Gallacher: What, exactly, do ya wish to know?

Caeli: Is it really so difficult to give up his name?

Gallacher (smiling grimly): His family name is McMahon,
which should tell ya a great deal. McMahon, as ya might know, is
a storied appellation when it comes to Irish terrorists. Think of the

bastard who murdered Lord Mountbatten. Whether they're related, of course, is anyone's guess, though it's possible. Accounts vary on his given name, and the number of aliases he's taken through the years borders on the tens of dozens, which further complicates things – that and a fire of suspicious origins that wiped out the files at the orphanage where he spent his formative years under the care of the nuns.

Caeli: Plenty of crackpot loons are running around this island, thanks to the IRA and its offshoots – my uncle included. What makes this guy special?

Gallacher: For starters, he's as hard a case as you'll find. We tracked down one of the nuns who served at the orphanage lo those many years ago, ya see, and she remembered Master McMahon vividly, though the number of children who slunk through the system numbered in the thousands.

Me: She doesn't recall his given name?

Gallacher: They were called by surname only, just as they were whipped for their transgressions, however slight. Things were different then – not that I'm dismissin' what took place. But none of the children had it easy, and McMahon was always first in line for the punishments that filled each day, day after day. He eventually escaped, was caught, escaped a second time and then a third, and on his fourth attempt, at the tender age of 12, they didn't bother goin' after him. He was on his own and has been, for the most part, since. We don't have much on him during the next decade, though there's evidence he fell in with tinkers, gypsies – what you'd likely call the carnival crowd. That's where we think he learned his skills at hypnotism – and from all accounts, he's quite good.

Caeli: Surely he didn't pop up on your radar because he was talking people out of their possessions at traveling tent shows.

Gallacher: No, indeed, Miss Brown. He first came under our purview during an increased period of IRA activity in the west: Limerick, Galway, Tralee, Ennis. He was identified early on as a particularly adept recruit, and it wasn't long before he was suspected in the deaths of more than a dozen combatants. Just as we were gettin' close, he vanished, overnight, as though he hadn't existed a'tall – as though he'd been advised of our interest. We eventually learned he'd signed on with the British Army and, after a bit of seasoning, was sent to a sniper's unit and shipped off to the first Middle East conflict, the one the Yanks called Desert Shield – or was it Desert Storm? I can't for the life of me separate the two. Our boy, it seems, had a penchant for death and destruction from a half-mile out, though how he managed to enlist given his background remains a puzzle.

Caeli: How long was he in?

Gallacher: Close to three years, we believe. The Brits are rather tight-lipped on the whole thing. Much of the paperwork surrounding his enlistment, training, the details of his deployments, his service record in general – gone, destroyed a-purpose, we believe. It's difficult to ascertain fully, and even my contacts over there – people I know and mostly trust – haven't shed much light. I'd speculate it's a matter of embarrassment rather than deception. Just a guess, though.

Caeli: How did he get involved in this business?

Gallacher: Happenstance, we believe, given the timing of his appearance on Irish soil after years of bein' away. He was released from British service under restricted circumstances, we're told, and returned to London, where he stayed for half-a-year or so before vanishin' entirely. The lads monitorin' his whereabouts for a handful of Army generals indicated, and this should sound familiar, that it was like he was there one day and gone the next, without a shred of evidence that he'd ever existed. We think he wandered the continent under a variety of assumed names. There's evidence he was in Berlin for a time, Athens, Rome at some point. We've seen fuzzy CCTV footage and surveillance tapes of suspects in a dozen crimes that all look similar and might be our man – and then again, it might be someone else entirely. But he crossed the Irish Sea three months ago on the mail boat from Holyhead. We know this because a sister agency was running a joint operation with Interpol in tracking *Monsieur* Daimallier – not that they knew who he was at the time or what he was up to, exactly. In Frog One's company was a striking redhead with eyes that were as green as the Irish hills. When G2 learned of this and examined the footage, long after the fact, our boy popped up, though it was another week before he was singled out and another still before we finally connected the dots. Time wasted, 'tis true, but it put us on the scent at last. Trouble was, he was already long gone from

Dublin and didn't actually show up again 'til we were well into our operation here – short days before the two of ya stumbled on the scene, which forced me to accommodate yer arrival.

Caeli: You weren't forced into anything.

Gallacher: Perhaps. I know you've chafed under the bit of G2 – you've made that clear enough. But even early on, when ya turned up in hospital to visit Mrs. Shedd and we invited ye on to the station in Limerick, all I've ever had in mind was to keep ya free from the certain destruction that follows in the wake of our leading players.

Caeli: So you keep saying. If you really wanted to keep us safe, you'd reel this guy in, given everything he's done.

Gallacher: Let's just say we've a difference of opinion on the matter. We've had our eye on him for some time, as ya know. We've complied a long list of what he's been up to during the time he's been in Ireland – far more extensive than the incidents ya know of: the likely murder of yer Mrs. Shedd, of course, and the theft from DS Phelan's aunt and a dozen others at Bunratty. He's responsible, we think, for the death of one of my best operatives in Dublin. I believe I've mentioned the details. There's more, of course – a great deal more. But he has few weaknesses, if any. The only thing we're sure of is a soft spot for orphans, which is not somethin' we can easily exploit. Still, we trust he'll lead us to the key player in the Irish game: Kathleen MacAmhlaoibh, yer garage shooter. But they're both quite good, quite elusive, and it's taken longer than anticipated. Now, with Frog One's other cells shut down, the pressure's on to tie the knot here.

Caeli: So why don't you?

Gallacher: Because I'm no longer in charge, Miss Brown, and because, to be blunt, we'd lost track of McMahon and the redhead. The two of ya seem to be the only true lead at present. That trace we ran off yer phone earlier – the one we all hoped would give us quick results? It led to a toss-away mobile propped up on a window ledge next to a wheelie-bin in a Limerick alleyway. That's why I'm here yet again. I need yer help, even if I'm not officially assigned.

Caeli: I suppose we should be flattered, were it not so pathetic.

Gallacher: That's one way to look at it. Another is to do what's needed to bring yer friend's killer to justice. God knows he won't be after findin' it on his own.

They went back and forth in similar fashion for a time, with Gallacher continuing to play coy and Caeli digging in. But the conversation ended when Elmore unexpectedly appeared.

"Professor B – got a minute?" he asked softly, trying not to attract attention.

"Sure," I said. "But feel free to speak your mind. You're among friends."

"That's just it. I'm not so sure."

Gallacher perked up at that disclosure.

"What's up, lad?" he asked.

Elmore hesitated, glancing back and forth between Caeli and me, flat-out ignoring Gallacher and his men, all of whom were seated nearby, interested onlookers.

"Is it Leonard? Is he all right?" I asked.

"No – why?"

"Because he's not here."

"Right," he said. "He's close, though – if you need him."

"All right, so go ahead, Elmore," Caeli said. "What's up?"

He squirmed uncomfortably, and I couldn't determine whether it was Gallacher's presence that troubled him or something that he and Aedan found in our security system.

Whatever it is can't be good, I thought.

But he surprised us entirely, or at least he surprised me, when he cleared his throat and forged ahead.

"I've picked up some skills on the computer, as you know," he said. "I'm not as good as I'd like, and not as good as the guy they brought in to help" – he gestured toward Gallacher. "But I know when something's fishy, and right now something stinks in the way he's prowling around."

"And by he, you mean …"

"Aedan – Gallacher's guy," Elmore said. "I think he's trying to tank the search, muddy the waters, cover tracks instead of expose them. I don't like what he's doing, and I thought you should know."

That's not good, I recall thinking. *Not good at all.*

But it dawned on me later that Caeli wasn't surprised at all.

FORTY-TWO

WIZARDRY OF ANOTHER SORT

Gallacher was up instantly, charging toward the safe room that contained our security system, with Elmore chasing him down and Caeli and me a couple of steps behind. His men followed us, doing their best to keep up – no doubt wondering what the hell was going on.

Then again, they'd have to stand in line for that.

"If it's mischief he's up to, why'd ya leave him alone in there?" Gallacher rasped as he pressed ahead, turning his head so that Elmore could hear.

"Didn't want him to know I knew," Elmore said, and he reached out and grabbed Gallacher's arm, tugging it to slow him down. "If I give him enough rope, I figure he'll hang himself."

"You think he's doing that now?"

"Yeah. Most likely. No need to rush."

Gallacher shook loose, but Elmore grabbed him again, bringing the spy to a halt. Danny O'Herlihy hustled forward to protect his boss but was waved off, and I got the feeling as I viewed the pair that Gallacher was taking Elmore's measure for the first time. Sure, they'd talked during our last visit, when we were his guests at Castle Ballygarvan and again on the tarmac as we were leaving Ireland in a rush and Gallacher revealed himself as a spy lord. It's also likely that he'd ordered his team to do a full workup on our bodyguards back then, assessing their strengths before we'd arrived on Irish soil.

But you could see as well as sense the tug of war that was taking place between them now, with Gallacher anxious to confront his computer tech – if only to discover that this was all a colossal misunderstanding – and Elmore equally anxious to delay a nasty confrontation.

"I want to see what's after takin' place in there," Gallacher said.

"The more time he has, the more we'll learn," Elmore replied, speaking the words softly, even soothingly.

"Learn what, exactly?"

"What he's up to – and if we're lucky, who he's helping."

Gallacher still looked as though he wanted to bolt, forcing his way down the hall. I thought for a second that he might motion to Danny to lend a hand, in the event that Elmore grabbed him again to keep him in place. But he paused, as though a switch had been flicked inside his head, and I figured then that he'd at last begun to grasp Elmore's strategy.

"You want him to stretch his own neck."

"Don't you?"

"Sure I do, lad – if it's a hangin' he needs. But if he's up to somethin', as ya say, I sure as hell don't want the little tosser wrenchin' the works while the lot of us are out here, whistlin' tunes in the corridor."

"No worries," Elmore said. "It's under control."

"All I ever do is worry, boyo. It's what makes me good at this. Tell me then: How are ya able to find what he's up to if yer out here and he's after bangin' away inside?"

Elmore had a ready answer for that, too, one that made me smile.

"I said he was better than me. He is. But I didn't say I wasn't any good."

"Yer sure about this?" Gallacher asked.

"Yeah. I laid a trap," Elmore said. "It'll be easy enough to follow."

Gallacher wasn't convinced. He shook his head and muttered words I couldn't hear, despite our proximity. Then he tried again with additional conviction.

"It's all mucked up, this is. Aedan's been a godsend to the taskforce," he said, addressing us all. "He's helped any number o' times, with odds and ends and keepin' things straight and gleanin' the wee insights that can tip a case in yer favor."

But it was Caeli who got to the heart of it, likely because she wasn't invested in the same way that Gallacher was with one of his own.

"It's understandable you'd feel that way, Liam. But has he given you anything that's truly mattered?" she asked. "Or has he delivered instead the obvious, confirming items you already knew or suspected – like the day we were at the warehouse and he tracked the plumber's van well enough but didn't offer significant help: the location of the sniper, for example, or the holes in camera coverage around the warehouse."

Before he could respond, she provided a more damning observation.

"And when you decided to hack into our security system – for our own protection, as you put it – wasn't it Aedan who poked around?"

Gallacher took a long moment, searching his memory for past conversations or interactions, running them through his filters as a spy instead of the techie's boss.

"It's hard to venture, comes to that," he eventually said. "I'd like to think he was helpin', but it might be little more than wishful thinkin' at this stage."

"I've never like the bastard," Danny muttered. "Wouldn't surprise me a lick to learn he's dirty."

I whispered in Caeli's ear.

"You knew – didn't you?"

"I suspected, after the Abbot theory went out the window," she said. "The fact that he was prowling around, even with Liam's blessing, was a good indication."

Gallacher smiled grimly at a sudden memory.

"Days ago, when I first mentioned a mole, ya told me to watch the techs 'cause they did things the rest of us didn't understand," he said. "Should 've listened to ya – right then."

Caeli didn't respond.

Elmore held us in place for another minute before he nudged his way past Gallacher and entered the security room, though only after tapping a couple of times on the outer door. I was surprised that he'd provided his quarry with a heads-up before he entered, but Elmore clearly had a plan.

After a word to his aides to remain in the hallway, Gallacher trailed Elmore inside while Caeli and I followed, more curious than angry.

I'll give O'Duinn this much: If he suspected anything, he was at least outwardly adept at covering his emotions, even with the four of us now carefully watching. He sat stoically in front of the monitors, tapping relentlessly at the keyboard, as though it were a living thing, glancing up for just an instant.

"Wasn't expectin' a bloody convention," he muttered, returning his focus to the screen. "Jaysus."

Elmore was ready to spring his trap; you could see it in his eyes. But Gallacher subtly grabbed his wrist, deciding on an opening gambit that opted for allowing things to play out, without hinting at suspicions that something was amiss.

Then again, maybe he was still hoping against hope that his boy was clean.

"Any luck then, lad?" he asked.

"I'm havin' a spot o' trouble gettin' a fix on the tosser," O'Duinn said. "Whoever it 'tis, he's good at coverin' tracks."

"You're certain it's a man?" Caeli asked.

He grinned as he glanced at her, and you could see the unchecked hunger flit for an instant in his eyes, which were darker than I'd remembered – and far more dangerous.

"No – just a guess. Most of the skilled hackers I know are men, ya see. Comes as automatic."

Gallacher wanted another go, but Elmore wasn't inclined to wait.

"How 'bout showing us what you found?" he said. "You were making decent progress when I left."

"Not much there," O'Duinn said. "Things 'ave taken a countermarch, ya see. Thought I was on to somethin' early on, but it turned into a bit o' nothin' instead."

"Show me," Elmore said, and he plopped into the unoccupied swivel chair that fronted the monitors and wheeled it close to where the *Garda* tech was hunched.

O'Duinn didn't bother hiding his disinterest.

"Sorry, Yank," he said, "but I'm afraid it's all past ya."

"Take your time," Elmore insisted. "Step by step, maybe. It'll help me learn."

O'Duinn cranked up a 60-watt smile and glanced at Elmore benevolently, as though humoring a youngster who'd asked a busy scientist to explain the inner workings of astrophysics.

"Love to, boyo. But there's no time now to show the ropes," he said. "We've an investigation to run, ya know."

Gallacher stepped in, gently prodding.

"No – it's fine. Go ahead and show him," he said. "Better yet, show us all."

O'Duinn didn't see that coming. His eyes couldn't contain the distrust that he must have felt, though he kept his grin intact.

"I don't think it's helpful to …"

"I insist," Gallacher pressed.

The smile slowly drained from the tech's expressive face, and he seemed to shrink into himself, as though withering on a vine that was attached to multiple computers and big-screen monitors and a single plastic mouse.

"I don't see the git as helpin'," he said. "Can't he poke about on his own time – without gettin' in me way?"

"Forget the Yank. I want to see it," Gallacher said, and he edged in closer and nudged O'Duinn with his hip.

It was a curious move, I thought, designed to intrude on the techie's space, and it worked. O'Duinn reacted as though he'd been slapped – or, more to the point, had just been discovered with his hands in someone else's code book.

"It's far beyond ya, boss," he muttered. "But I'll tell ya what I found, which is pretty much nothin' a'tall. Whoever's been muckin' about is damn crafty. I can't get a lock on the trail for the life of me. It's throwin' me sideways."

"So tell me what ya found, boyo," Gallacher said patiently. He looped his hand behind O'Duinn's back and gave Elmore a *I've got this* gesture.

Our bodyguard remained silent, but he didn't appreciate the intervention.

"Only that somebody's been thrashin' about," O'Duinn said. "Who he is, or where he's come from, is anybody's guess. I might get it in time, but …"

"Maybe ya need some help then," Gallacher said. "Shall I put out a call to one of yer lads – somebody ya trust?"

O'Duinn flashed his biggest smile, but you could again see the wariness creeping into his eyes.

"No need," he said. "I'm on it."

Elmore couldn't contain himself.

"Maybe I can dig him out," he said, and his fingers, like thick sausages, began pecking at the keyboard with surprising dexterity.

"Don't bother," O'Duinn said dismissively. "If I can't find him, yer sure as hell …"

His mouth dropped open when the monitors lit up with material that the techie didn't mean for any of us to see, starting with a two-way conversation that opened with a derogatory slap at Gallacher and his team, followed by a few lines of derision about Yanks in general, and concluding with Elmore's lack of computer skills.

The time stamp indicated that the back-and-forth had taken place during the period when Elmore left the room.

"Hey," O'Duinn said without thinking. "How'd ya get in there and …"

As Elmore continued tapping, Gallacher nudged his aide.

"How 'bout tellin' us who ya were just talkin' to – and why?"

He motioned for me to open the door and gestured at Danny O'Herlihy once I'd complied. Ian and Gavin framed the doorway, their hands now covering the butts of their holstered pistols, as Danny entered and stationed himself next to his boss.

Additional information scrolled onto the screen, including the locations of the security cameras and microphones within our system that had been hijacked.

"Look like something of interest?" Elmore asked Gallacher.

O'Duinn shook his head, mumbling a feeble protest, as Gallacher clamped his hand on the tech's shoulder.

"Or this?" Elmore asked, striking the Enter key with a flourish. A minutes-old video appeared, showing O'Duinn furiously carrying on the keyboard-to-keyboard conversation he'd just reviewed. You could follow each word that he typed and the responses that instantly flowed in.

"Who is it yer talkin' to, lad?" Gallacher pressed. "Let's have it 'fore I set the dogs loose."

"It's not what it looks like," O'Duinn said, in full panic mode. He attempted to stand, but Danny pushed him roughly back into the chair.

"It surely is, boyo," Gallacher said.

The terror in the techie's eyes turned to hardened resignation once he'd glanced at the door and realized that there was no way out.

"I'm not sayin' another word," he snapped. "I demand a solicitor."

Gallacher barked out a laugh.

"A solicitor, is it? You'll get no bloody lawyer on my watch. What you'll get is a box full of bollox and years in the nick, doin' porridge with blokes who'll have ya for breakfast – and again for late-night. It won't be pretty, boyo – that much I promise."

He waved at Ian and Gavin, who were watching the proceedings with dark eyes that betrayed nothing.

"How 'bout takin him down to the river an' dunkin' his head in the muck 'til he talks?"

"Good on ya boss," Gavin said, and I had the healthy suspicion that they'd played this game before. "If he won't give it up, what then?"

Gallacher grinned, exposing his teeth, which gleamed white in the harsh glare of the monitors that crowded the room.

"If he refuses to talk, give 'im to the Yank – the big one, the one outside. No paperwork, an' no trail back to us."

But we never got to play out Gallacher's bluff – or at least I choose to believe that a River Shannon waterboarding was a bluff. The monitors jumped to life again, this time without Elmore's urging.

"Looks like yer mate's back," Gallacher said as the cursor pulsed to life and Elmore pulled his fingers off the keyboard. "Tell us who he is."

"Bugger off," O'Duinn said. "You'll get nothin' from me."

"I don't think we need ya, boyo," Gallacher said.

A message typed in an ugly bold font crawled its way across the monitors with military precision, leaving no doubt that we'd been thoroughly compromised.

>>I can see you, hear you too, wait til you see what happens next

"Where's it comin' from?" Gallacher asked, looking to Elmore for the answer.

O'Duinn barked out a laugh.

"Yer fooked now – the lot of ya," he said.

"Maybe we should pull the plug," Gallacher muttered, nudging Elmore's shoulder.

The traitorous techie was suddenly enjoying himself.

"Good luck with that, boyo," he said.

FORTY-THREE

KEYBOARD COMMUNICATION

The demands began streaming across the monitors, one after another, long before anyone could pull the plug – and once they started, nobody wanted to.

>>Keep O'Duinn at the computer

>>Clear the room except for Blake and the lady

>>Listen carefully, I don't like repeating myself

>>I want money, lots of money, and safe passage to someplace where it doesn't bloody rain all the time

>>I want guns too, lots of guns, enough to fill up a suitcase or maybe a lorry

>>And women, lots and lots of women Ha ha

>>Just kidding, I want Blake and the lady

>>Tomorrow, 1500 hours, Ravens Ridge

>>We'll settle our differences then

The stream-of-consciousness assault was both frightening and amusing, although it also greatly offended my notion of what constitutes correct punctuation.

Gallacher directed Ian and Gavin to remove Aedan O'Duinn from the room. He whispered into Ian's ear, fearing that anything he said aloud would be picked up by the microphones that had been compromised during the hack of our system.

O'Duinn continued to shout grade-school invective as he was pulled away, which was difficult to ignore – especially when the keyboard artist at the other end kicked out a string of fresh lines ordering us to keep the tech in play, threatening additional mayhem if we didn't agree.

>>These aren't idol demands

>> You don't want to cross me

>>I'll show you real fire and fury, not some fat egomaniac's blusster

>>Get O'Duinn back in the room NOW!

"What do you think? McMahon?" I whispered to Caeli.

"Has to be – who else? He doesn't know idle from an idol."

"Nor how to spell bluster."

"And the slammer is so Old School."

Gallacher was flummoxed.

"Slammer? What the hell's that then?"

"An exclamation point," we both replied.

The messages continued in a similar vein, with varied threats interspersed with hints of humor and playfulness. Under normal circumstances, I would've questioned the guy's mental state, but we already figured that he was nuts.

Hell, you'd be crazy not to see it.

"He's been reading political news from the States," Caeli said as she absorbed the "fire and fury" line on the monitors. It was a casual observation, bringing to mind Mister Denmark's earlier comments about American presidents.

"Yeah. The early back-and-forth with North Korea," I said. "A former student, one of the good ones, sent me a note a couple of weeks ago. A newspaper in Maine put that story on the front page and made a hell of a gaffe in the headline. It read 'fire and furry' – f-u-r-r-y – in 72-point type."

"Seriously?"

"You can't make it up. The editor issued a blanket apology the next day, saying she was mortified."

"We worked for editors who would've rolled heads for that," she said, and we both laughed.

If you got the sense that we weren't taking the situation seriously, you'd be wrong. But we've learned in times of stress to share a laugh when we can, and the chaos that we were in seemed ripe just then for a lighter touch.

Our efforts were unappreciated, however.

"Knock it off, you two," Gallacher said, covering his mouth to disguise his words. "If we're gonna get somethin' decent out of this fiasco, we need to talk to this wanker – posthaste. Who wants the honors?"

Elmore was already positioned at one of the keyboards and volunteered with a simple question.

"What do you want me to say?"

"Ask him who he is," Gallacher suggested.

"But we already …"

"Let's be sure," the spy chief interrupted. "Go ahead – type it in."

Elmore did as he was instructed. We waited all of four seconds for the reply.

>>Don't waste my time

>>Get O'Duinn back oin the room

>>I want him there now

"Tell him we aren't interested in his demands and don't negotiate with terrorists," Gallacher said, snapping out the words crisply. "If he can hear me, as he says, fine. But spell it out for him, in case it's another bloody lie."

When Elmore duly typed the message, I volunteered another before a response was returned.

"Tell him to watch for typos and to add periods to the end of his sentences," I said. "I don't want to deal with anyone who can't write proper English."

"Seriously?" Elmore asked.

"Yeah – go ahead and type it up," I said.

"OK. Run it by me again so I get it right."

I repeated the message, and Elmore banged in the words, stiffly but effectively.

"Wait. Make that 'full-stops' – hyphenated – instead of periods," Caeli said. She took the time to spell it out for him.

Gallacher figured that we weren't yet on the same page, and he wasn't happy.

"What is it with you lot?" he said, firing off a vicious scowl. "We can't be after actin' the fool here."

"It's important to set a tone," Caeli said as Elmore finished typing, then took a moment to correct a typo of his own before sending it off to the ether.

"Yer gonna anger the twit, worse than ye already have with that bloody Wanted poster," Gallacher said. The needle on his exasperation meter was in the red zone and climbing.

"Good," we both said in unison.

"I don't think it's in anyone's best …"

"Nobody says we have to keep him happy," Caeli interrupted. "Plus, we don't negotiate with terrorists. You said it yourself."

"So what are ya doin' then?"

But the conversation was interrupted as another couple of lines crawled across the monitors.

>>You think this is funny then

>>I'll give you something to laugh about

"He missed the question mark," Elmore said. "You want me to let him know we noticed?"

"Sure," Caeli said. "Go ahead."

As Elmore began typing, two additional lines lit up the screen.

>>There's a bomb in your house

>>Laugh that off

"Jaysus," Gallacher muttered. "You've done it now."

Caeli, at least, wasn't fazed.

"He's bluffing," she said with confidence. "He had help hacking the system, and there's no way O'Duinn could have wired a bomb into the security feed. It's physically impossible."

"He was alone in here for a few minutes," Elmore said. "Maybe he did it when I came out to let you know what was going on. Nobody frisked him when he came in, you know."

"There was no need," Gallacher said. He began a quick search of the room, checking under the chairs and behind the bank of monitors. He poked at Elmore at one point, urging him to pull the back cover off the three computer towers that powered the system.

"It's a bluff," Caeli repeated. "He could start an electrical fire in the wiring, I suppose, but then he'd have no way to talk with us. And he seems to want to do that."

She said this last part slowly and deliberately, staring up at the rack of monitors that lined the wall in front of us. We'd figured that he was continuing to watch us through the setup that O'Duinn had patched into our system, and we soon got confirmation that he was listening in as well.

>>I can always ring up your mobile

"And spoil all the fun?" Caeli said, again addressing the monitors. "What do you really want? You've no leverage, and your face is on every BOLO alert in Ireland, in the UK and throughout Europe, plus every entry port in the U.S. It's even been given to the appropriate authorities in the Middle East and Africa. You're a man without a country, Mister McMahon. Once they track you down, and they will, along with your girlfriend, you'll either rot in prison or die bloody and forgotten in some Irish bog."

I damn near burst out laughing when Elmore waited for a beat and then asked, his tone deadly serious, "You want me to type that out, Caeli?"

"No. I think he got the message," she said.

We waited then, with seconds turning to minutes and dragging on. I was tempted to count out the time in my head but let it go. Gallacher continued searching for a bomb, Elmore began tapping his index finger on the desktop beside the keyboard, and Caeli and I both stared at the monitors.

My guess is that three minutes passed before he provided a response.

>>Ravens Ridge. Tomorrow. Be there. Both of you. Hope you like the full-stops. Might be the last you ever see

>>Then again, get ready for a surprise, one you won't see coming

This time Caeli tapped Elmore on the shoulder and whispered.

"Tell him no. Nothing more ... just no."

"Got it," he said and tapped in the single word.

His response came seconds later.

>>Tomorrow

>>Both of you

>>Don't be late

>>I'll show you who's a liar and thief

"Shut it down, Elmore," Caeli said. "Turn the whole thing off."

Gallacher, clearly angry, was shaking his head.

"So what's it gonna be then? What's yer grand plan?" he asked.

"Good question," Caeli said. "I don't even know that we need one."

Gallacher disagreed.

"I think we do. This lunatic won't leave the two of ya be just 'cause you've pulled the plug on yer computers," he said, though he was pointing up toward the ceiling, confident that the mics were activated and McMahon – who else could it be? – was still listening. "He's gonna come at ya. I think it's best to make plans, though we should do it out-of-doors, as he's sure to listen in."

We huddled in the corridor, well away from the microphones that McMahon was able to monitor, at least according to Elmore's assessment. I wasn't sure that we knew the full extent of his reach and was anxious to get out of the house entirely. I'll confess that our earlier experiences with the guy left me jittery.

The task, as I saw it, was twofold: neutralize McMahon and the redhead, first and foremost, which would shut down the terrorist operation, and then clear everybody out of the house and get back to prepping for our wedding, which would make Caeli decidedly happy. We could always debug our hacked security system after the fact.

Caeli agreed, as did Elmore.

Gallacher's priority focused on a take-down of McMahon at the one time and place where we knew he'd eventually be: the spot he'd called Raven's Ridge.

Caeli was quick to reject the idea.

"I'm not letting Max walk into a trap," she said.

Gallacher held his ground.

"You forget, my dear, that our enemy's requested both of ya," he said.

Caeli wasn't buying that, either.

"But Max will insist on going alone. I won't let that happen," she said. She was talking to Gallacher, but she shot a sideways glance at me – just to let me know that I'd lose whatever argument I might propose.

When Gallacher attempted to reassure her that good planning would work in our favor, she cut him off.

"I don't care how many spooks you send out there, or how good your logic seems," she said. "We're not walking into a trap."

Gallacher paused – an indication, I think, that he knew Caeli wouldn't budge. Then again, who could blame her? Kicking an angry terrorist in the shin is always a bad idea. Hell, even I knew that much.

"All right," he said a moment later. "Let's wrestle with the other part then, shall we? I don't see know of place for us to meet that's as bloody convenient as yer house, and yer security's a mess. We can't allow McMahon to use it to monitor us here."

"Agreed," Caeli and I said in unison, something we seem to do often.

"I can likely persuade one of the techs from the taskforce to make it right – lend us a hand," he said.

"No – bad idea," Caeli said. "How do we know O'Duinn didn't have help? We need to bring in someone we trust, and you need to look at your entire team to see who's playing nice."

It dawned on me that perhaps we didn't need to go far afield.

"How about it, Elmore?" I said. "Is this something you can do?"

He shook his head.

"I can help. But I can't guarantee I'd get it all."

"What about one of Phelan's people?" Caeli suggested. "He seems to know or is related to anyone and everyone locally who's handy."

"I can call him," I said and fished in my pockets for the burner.

"No, don't bother," Elmore said. "I'll call the guy I know in Salem. We can get him here in a day or two and have him revamp the entire system: make sure it's clean, make sure it can't be hacked again."

Gallacher was dismayed.

"So it's all the way to the States then, boyo? It'll be far easier to get somebody local," he said.

"We can trust my guy," Elmore said. "And right now, I don't trust anybody over here, you included – no offense."

Caeli and I exchanged glances.

"Sure," she said. "Make the call. Whatever it takes."

Elmore pulled out his phone and wandered down the hall.

"All right then – let's get at the rest of it," Gallacher said. "If ya both refuse to meet the man tomorrow, which I think is a mistake, we still need to take these two off the board before additional mischief takes place. That requires a foolproof plan."

"Agreed," I said. "It's well past time."

Gallacher was at last moving in the right direction, it seemed, but he remained cautious.

"We can't figure it out here, with the bastard listenin' in, watchin' us," he said. "Even Henry Street is out, given me status and doubts as to who we can trust."

"I've got an idea," Caeli said. "It's not much of one, but it'll buy us time."

FORTY-FOUR

A VISIT FROM THE MAGI

Caeli's plan was stop-gap at best, but it was all that we had, based on the certainty that we needed to abandon the estate until the security system was thoroughly checked, the compromised microphones and monitoring cameras were deactivated, and all computer bugs and viruses were removed.

And that was going to take time.

We ended up in the garage, sans monitors of any kind, loading up the Range Rover with a laptop, the shotgun, the police batons, an extra emergency first-aid kit that we kept in the kitchen, our burners and the phones that Gallacher had given to us, and additional odds and ends, including bottled water and a bag of homemade cookies that Caeli pulled from the freezer.

We both carried the Berettas from G2.

We'd already taken a few minutes to collect Mitts and stash him in the laundry room with a fresh litter box, water, and two bowls full of food, just in case it took us a day or two to return home. We stockpiled extra food and water for Koko as well and gave her the run of the place, but only because it was easier to catch and control Mitts. He'd already been cowering in a corner, a result of the activity in and out of the house.

Gallacher and his driver offered a hand before heading out to their own SUV to lead a small convoy away from the estate. We figured that Leonard would join us along the way, or at least keep a watchful eye on us, but we had yet to contact him. Too many other issues needed our attention.

"And yer sure there're no mics and whatnot in here?" Gallacher asked Elmore as we scurried about the spacious garage.

Our bodyguard shrugged.

"Sure as I can be."

"That's not comfortin', lad," Gallacher said.

"It's as good as I got – 95 percent, maybe," Elmore said.

"So we keep things quiet and make it quick," the spy chief said, glancing about as though seeking out cameras, microphones, or other hidden baggage – including, I suppose, the redhead and her traveling companion.

At Gallacher's urging – "Makin' sure we're on the same page" are his exact words – Caeli outlined the operation once more, this time in whispers.

"We drive to Bunratty, we take over a suite at one of the hotels, we regroup, we call in Elmore's computer genius to debug the house, and we determine what to do about McMahon and the woman – along with his proposed meeting at Raven's Ridge," she said.

"Don't forget Leonard," Elmore offered.

"Right. We contact Leonard," Caeli agreed.

"How long ya think it'll be 'til yer computer man shows?" Gallacher asked.

"They're working on it now," Elmore said. "We'll know more in an hour or two, but we should see him sometime late tomorrow."

"So we're stuck 'til then in some fleabag hotel amongst all the bloody tourists," Gallacher muttered.

"You can stay in a fleabag hotel if you want, Liam," Caeli replied. "I won't."

"I'm with Caeli," I said.

"I'm with them," Elmore added.

Caeli remained concerned about the welfare of her cats, and I was thinking of the logistics of leaving the estate, and Elmore was mentally assessing the computer/security nonsense, and the three of us were still capable of trying to keep the mood light.

That's the way I looked at it, anyway.

Then Gallacher's mobile jangled a tune that sounded suspiciously like an Irish reel. He grabbed it from his belt, grunted into the glass, cursed softly and pulled it away from his ear when he realized that he hadn't actually accepted the call, used a finger to swipe the screen, and grunted a greeting in Irish as he moved off to a corner so that we couldn't hear the conversation.

We'd just finished packing the last of our supplies into the SUV – three overnight bags plus Caeli's satchel containing battery chargers for the phones, extra pairs of shoes, and her makeup needs – when Gallacher returned.

"Not sure how to break this, exactly," he said as he approached. "It appears as though we're not leavin' quite so fast as we'd hoped."

"Oh. And why is that?" Caeli asked. She'd been paying no attention to the spy and hadn't noticed the phone call interruption.

"It seems yer about to be paid a visit by people who claim a connection of sorts to Miss Brown," Gallacher said, and I couldn't tell whether this was a good thing or a bad thing … *or something in between, perhaps*. "Understand, I'm only speculatin', but that's my belief, at least. A contingent, for want of a better word, landed at Shannon no more than 30 minutes ago in a private jet, flying in from *Leonardo da Vinci Fiumicino* in Rome. The jet belongs to …"

"No," Caeli said sharply, and he had her full attention now. "Don't even say it."

She stared daggers at Gallacher, but he merely shrugged it off with a *Don't shoot the messenger* look.

"I'm sorry, Miss Brown, but I've been given a courtesy heads-up because of my involvement with yer uncle a year ago, on Mutton Island and then again in its aftermath," he said. "It seems that influential people at the Vatican learned of yer encounter with Kathleen MacAmhlaoibh, and three papal agents and a couple of aides are on their way here to … well, I'm not exactly certain why they're comin'. All I know is the five of 'em are headed out here right now, representin' what I'm told is the highest authority in the church."

Surely it can't be Uncle Jack, I recall thinking, but I didn't dare speak the words for fear that mentioning his name would somehow make him appear.

I couldn't tell whether Caeli was more angry than surprised, more disappointed than annoyed, more appalled than resigned, though I had a decent hunch that irritation was the driving emotion.

Then again, maybe none of those sentiments fit. God knows her uncle had been a constant cause of concern for much of the past two years, once he'd gone missing from his role as the archbishop of Armagh and then resurfaced, weeks later, as a full-blown revolutionary intent on overthrowing British rule in Ulster.

We'd thought that he'd been killed on Mutton Island, of course. But the spectacle of his death, an event we'd actually witnessed, was greatly exaggerated, thanks to magic from Gallacher and his team, and Jack ended up in Rome, working at the Vatican while atoning for his sins. We'd even tracked him down, exposing an ugly clutch at power by a demented church insider named Father Pietro Angelus and at least some of the mysteries of the Secret Archives Building, where Jack was assigned.

Still, we'd thought that he was out of lives for good ... *until now*.

Caeli seemed dumbstruck, or at least flabbergasted, at the revelation that papal gadflies were on their way.

I decided to get to the heart of the matter – the one thing we cared about.

"Does one of these so-called priests answer to the name of Jack O'Lennox?"

"Right now, the answer is no – and I asked that very question," Gallacher said. "According to my contact in at the customs house, the names are DuCharme, Shannon, and Rottach – French, Irish, and maybe German from the sounds of it. They're traveling with two unnamed bag-totters, apparently. Then again, he could well be among the lot and travelin' under an alias."

"You mean my uncle," Caeli said.

"Who else might ya be expectin' from Rome?" Gallacher asked.

"I'd expect the Pope ahead of Uncle Jack," Caeli said quickly. "We have an understanding – one insisted on by the church, as I've already explained. We aren't to make contact with one another until, well, until some considerable time passes, if even then."

Gallacher bored in.

"Do ya have reason to believe these priests might be representin' yer uncle, or his interests?" he asked.

"I've no idea – nor do I know what my uncle's interests, as you call them, might be at present," Caeli said. "As indicated, we've had no contact since our time in Rome, which was precious little anyway, and that's been months ago."

"That's been my understandin' as well," Gallacher said, and he seemed equally puzzled by this turn.

I continued looking at the bigger picture.

"Without making assumptions, or getting ahead of ourselves, it seems apparent that someone in Rome learned that we had a run-in with the woman who used to hang with Jack," I said. "But I'm also guessing that news of our encounter was withheld from broad circulation. Is that correct?"

"Yes. Of course," he said. "Outside of the people on the taskforce, along with a few higher-ups in G2 and the *Garda*, that information's need-to-know."

"So how do you suppose it got to the Vatican and, much as I hate to think it, to Caeli's uncle, who seems to be the only logical connection?"

"I've no bloody clue," Gallacher said. "It sure as hell didn't come from me."

"Your people then?"

"Absolutely not," he said. "Not even the little bastard we just hauled away would make the connection to the shooter and the church, I'd guess. We've had no contact with the archbishop – not since he ended up in Vatican hands after the tussle on Mutton Island."

The word caught Caeli's attention.

"Tussle? That's what you think? Some good people died during that tussle," she said. "A good many more came close to dying in that tussle. Max was wounded during that tussle."

"I don't mean to make light of it," Gallacher insisted. "It's just that …"

"Days ago, you asked me to contact my uncle and get him involved," Caeli said, cutting him off. "I find it terribly convenient that three Vatican priests suddenly appear, demanding an audience. Is this something you've set up – an attempt to bring Jack into play?"

"Absolutely not. I just learned of it, and only as a courtesy. Without that, I, too, would've been caught unawares."

"Maybe we should just leave," Elmore said. "If we aren't here, we won't have to worry about who they are or what they want."

"Good idea," I said.

"No – it's a terrible idea," Gallacher insisted. "What if they possess information that can help?"

"What if they don't?" Elmore pressed. "Five minutes ago we were anxious to get out of here, with good reason. The security's a mess. Who knows what might happen?"

We argued back and forth for a couple of additional minutes, but the discussion became moot when we heard a vehicle approaching.

"Looks like we've got company whether we want it or not," Caeli said.

She reached for the button to activate the overhead garage door, but Gallacher warned her off.

"We don't know who's there, and we can't risk using the security monitors," he said. "Danny – go take a look and …"

"I'll do it," Elmore said. "It's my job."

But Danny joined Elmore, and they both drew their sidearms and started for the side door that afforded a view of the long, winding driveway leading up to the estate. Elmore's phone dinged as he reached for the knob, and he pulled it from his belt, checked the caller ID, and answered, motioning for Danny to wait.

"Yeah," he said.

He paused for a moment, grunted a couple of terse asides, and returned the phone to his belt.

"It's the priests," he said. "Five in all, according to Leonard."

Leonard? I thought. *Where the hell is Leonard?*

Caeli hit the button on the access door, and it rolled up, offering us a look at our guests.

She didn't react, or at least not outwardly.

Then again, Jack wasn't front and center with a warm greeting, either.

It took me a moment to recognize him, standing off to the side with a black clerical robe and a Biretta, the familiar hat of the priesthood, adorned on the top of his head. He'd grown a full beard since we'd last seen him, making him look as much like a lumberjack as it did a man of the church, which is likely why Leonard hadn't tipped us off that we knew at least one of our guests.

"Caeli, my dear," her uncle said after a long moment of awkward silence. "Can you explain to me why you've a sniper stationed on the roof of yer bloody house?"

For a moment, she didn't say a word – nor did anyone else. We stared at Caeli's uncle as though he were a space alien, beamed down from a distant planet to experiment on us in gruesome ways.

For his part, Jack was as stoic as I'd ever seen him, as though his time under Vatican protection had somehow bestowed a sense of inner peace that you'd expect from a Buddhist monk … *or maybe from a former archbishop*, I thought.

But the idea gave me no pleasure, no smile, no sense that levity was in play. Just the opposite, in fact. To say that it was a shock to see him again, standing in front of us, betraying no emotion whatsoever, is among the greatest of understatements, akin to Apollo 13 astronaut Jim Lovell's "Houston, we've had a problem here."

Yeah. The movie folks got it wrong.

Had we really been thinking that Jack was among the priests who'd just arrived at Shannon International and informed customs officials that they were heading our way? I can't speak for Caeli, but I can damn well guarantee that I didn't. She was correct when she told Gallacher that she'd expect the Pope to show up at our doorstep before her rebellious uncle made an appearance.

And yet, there he was, anticipating a reply from his niece to his tendered question.

Liam Gallacher broke the silence.

"I'd say it's nice to see ya again, Archbishop O'Lennox," he said. "But then, I've never been much for stretchin' the truth."

"I no longer hold that title, though I expect ye already know as much," Jack said. "Still, I appreciate yer honesty – such as it is."

He again directed his attention to Caeli, unable to hide a look that was now filled with concern and irritation and also immense pride, I thought, and maybe even relief that the woman he'd so admired – long before his folly and incredible downfall – was safe from harm, at least temporarily.

"So let me ask it again, Caeli darlin', dear to me heart that ye are. Why's a sniper stationed on yer rooftop? Humor an old man and tell me, if ya would, for I fear it's the reason we've come."

Caeli's response was calm and even, giving away none of the emotion that she must have felt.

"I thought we were supposed to keep our distance – and yet here you are, asking questions that make no sense," she said. "What are you doing here? What do you want?"

"I heard ye were in need of a simple parish priest to officiate at yer pending nuptials," he said, his eyes twinkling. "And you've not answered me question, dearheart."

She looked on blankly.

"The sniper? On yer roof?" he repeated.

"I've no idea what you're talking about," she said in a whisper.

His eyes betrayed the fact that he didn't believe her but also that he didn't want to press her. He looked to me instead.

"That scar doesn't make ya any more endearin', Max Blake," he said.

"No thanks to you," I replied. "So which one are you? Father Rottach, maybe? DuCarme? Or are you Shannon – after the river or the airport?"

He laughed, his face crinkling with mirth.

"Allow me to introduce fathers Rottach" (he pointed toward a grizzled man in his mid- to late-60s, I guessed), "DuCharme" (another finger wag indicated a priest in his early 40s, handsome in a bookish way), "and Shannon" (and a hooked thumb directed us to a third priest who, while well into his 60s, was as dashing as a Hollywood leading man). "They were kind enough to travel with me, along with me *aide de camp* at the Archives Building, *Padre* Giuseppe Blinstrub. We've worked together on some glorious finds while pokin' 'round the place – haven't we, *padre*?"

Blinstrub, as with the other priests, remained silent.

I didn't, however.

"Don't tell me you located more nonsense supporting your JFK assassination fantasy," I said, harkening back to Jack's so-called discovery during the *Melia Ridge* affair. "Or have you unlocked the secrets of the Loch Ness Monster, or alien takeovers of Skellig Michael, or – hell, I don't know, confirmation that the Shroud of Turin was bought at the Five and Dime in Ennis?"

"Mock me if ye will, Maxwell, but it's no laughin' matter, I assure ya," he said. "Why do ya have a sniper on yer roof? And why haven't ya yet asked us inside yer humble home?"

"The sniper belongs to me," Gallacher said, edging around Danny O'Herlihy to better assess our visitors. "And it's because of you that a sniper's needed here a'tall."

"Ach, and don't I know it," Jack said, shaking his head slowly from side to side. "Ya don't have to tell me: Kathleen MacAmhlaoibh herself – I know all about it. Come now, ask us in and we'll see if we can figure a path out of the madness."

His eyes shifted to Caeli again, and I detected pride and sadness and regret this time.

"Ya look glorious – like Blessed Mary herself," he said.

"Cut the crap, Jack."

She swung about and hurried inside without so much as a backward glance.

FORTY-FIVE

ANGELS AND OTHER SPIRITS

We didn't get far into the foyer before Caeli confronted Liam Gallacher, the easiest target in the place, and the verb is carefully chosen here.

"Would you care to tell me what a sniper is doing on top of our home?" she said.

Her voice, at least, remained calm, though I knew that she was churning inside.

Gallacher avoided her eyes but answered the question.

"It seemed like the logical thing to do," he said. "Still does."

"Are you expecting an assault on the place – on us? Or are you more concerned about your own government coming after you?" she persisted.

Gallacher shrugged his shoulders, and his mouth and eyes betrayed a grin.

"Maybe both," he said. "It never hurts to prepare for every eventuality – though I'll confess I didn't see *that* coming," and he nodded at Jack and his entourage.

I figured that Caeli would continue pressing him, if only to avoid a second go-round with her uncle, who was shaping up to be the proverbial trumpeting elephant stomping through the manor. But Jack, carrying an agenda that he was anxious to share, grew impatient with the back and forth.

"So it's not Kathleen MacAmhlaoibh who has ya worried then," he said, more a statement than a question, addressing the spy chief.

"Of course she has me worried," Gallacher said. "All of G2's concerned, along with the *Garda* and Interpol. The Americans'd love to get their hands on her, and I hear the Brits have a bounty on her pretty hide."

Jack smiled thinly, pursing his lips.

"What makes ya think she'll be after showin' up here then?" he asked.

"You, for one thing," Gallacher said. "With you here, on Irish soil again, can fair Kathleen be far behind – eh, *padre*?"

"She's no friend of mine – not even back then, God help me, when the world was far younger and fervent rebellion was in the air," Jack said, and his eyes took on a wistful look as he glanced about the room, taking the measure of the place. "Kathleen always had a mind of her own, ya see. Ya couldn't tell her a bloody thing, nor convince her that wrong was right and the way of things. If she'd made up her mind the sky was green and the floor of the earth instead of its ceiling, well now, there was no turnin' her away from the notion."

He redirected his energy toward Caeli, serving up a warm smile, turning on the charm.

"I see you've done all right for yerself, Caeli darlin'," he said.

"I see you haven't changed," she said, and the words came out as pointed as a spear. "What are you doing here, Uncle Jack? Why would you risk the wrath of the Pope, as well as the Irish authorities, to be here now?"

"I've already told ya, my dear," he said. "This whole mess yer in is a product of me own makin', I'm ashamed to admit. But I've every intention of fixin' it in the best way I know – with the Holy Father's blessing, I'd add. It's the reason I brought me friends along."

He waved a hand toward his silent traveling companions.

Caeli was unmoved.

"Do you think that offering a mass or two will make things right?"

"I think it's unwise to bring a dull blade to a gunfight," he said. "In this case, I've with me three of the pontiff's special security detail. They know their way 'round a good battle, and I suspect that with green-eyed Kathleen involved, a fight's the very thing comin' yer way, Caeli dear. Or should I say our way?"

Caeli shook her head in disbelief, giving the impression that no matter how hard she tried, it was impossible to keep up with her uncle.

Jack grinned again, broadly, as though proud of himself, and stared this time at Gallacher. You could tell that they shared a mutual respect … *far more than passing acquaintances*, and I recalled our time on Mutton Island and the deception that was necessary on the part of G2 to pull off Jack's supposed death and sell it to the world.

Gallacher was smack in the thick of it then, just as he is now, I thought.

"One thing ye can help us with, boyo. We didn't bring any weapons to the fight," Jack said. "I somehow didn't think we'd get through customs with machine guns in tow, ya see. But I'll wager ye can lend us a hand, eh?"

Gallacher was incredulous. Hell, we all were.

"Have ye lost the little sense ye were born with?"

"Hardly," Jack shot back. "If anything, the time I've spent at the Vatican these past long months has given me a chance to right the ledger, to cleanse me soul of its previous misdeeds, as it were – to rectify the many wrongs that haunt my niece and her wounded mate. And for those after keepin' score, we're more than capable. All we need is the proper accompaniment."

"I'd no more hand out firearms to yer lot than I would to Kathleen bloody MacAmhlaoibh herself," Gallacher said, more loudly than was necessary. "I'm not sure what they're puttin' in the collection plate in Rome these days, *padre*, but it won't pass inspection here."

The response and its harsh delivery didn't bother Jack. He spread his arms wide, as though ready to serve up a sermon to the non-believers.

"We can talk, once I learn what's taken place these past 12 hours and whatever plans you've set in motion to keep Caeli from harm," he said. "But first, a cup of tea, perhaps – if it's not too much trouble. Coffee, too – and the jacks, of course, if you'd be so kind to point the way. It's been some time in the plane, ya see, and they rushed us through customs as though we carried the plague."

Elmore, who'd watched the exchanges with interest, reminded us once again that our task was made more difficult because of the compromised security system. At Uncle Jack's urging, he explained in detail the treachery of Gallacher's mole, what he'd found in the computer, and the dangers that lurked inside if we remained in the house, all the while speaking in low whispers, though we believed that the foyer was safe from prying eyes and ears.

"Before you showed up, we were on our way to Bunratty so we wouldn't be snooped on," he said.

Jack had an answer for that as well.

"Nonsense, lad," he said. "If the enemy's listenin' in, take advantage: Feed him the things ya want him to hear, keep him from what's vital, nudge him along on the path ye want him to travel. Deception, done correctly, is a fine art, indeed."

"And yer the expert then?" Gallacher said, clearly a non-believer.

Jack grinned.

"If me last few years in Armagh taught me anything, boyo, it was navigatin' in one direction while makin' it seem I was after headed in another still," he said. "A bit of misdirection could be just the thing for catchin' the charmin' Miss MacAmhlaoibh and her lackey foot soldiers."

Gallacher's aide whispered in the spy master's ear, prompting a hushed exchange that took place out of earshot. Jack, meanwhile, repeated his plea for drinks and directions to the restrooms – "Some common courtesy," as he called it.

To save time and the possibility that we'd be ambushed while on the road, we decided to set up shop in the garage while our guests used the jacks. I made a fresh pot of coffee and heated a sauce pan filled with water for the tea. I also dug out a serving tray from one of the cupboards, topped it with cups and sugar packets and artificial sweeteners and a selection of teas, and delivered that to the garage before fetching the coffee pot.

"Any biscuits about?" Jack asked as we gathered around the built-in workbench, which was well-stocked with an assortment of tools and homeowner necessities. "Plottin' strategy can kick up an appetite."

Caeli directed Elmore and Giuseppe Blinstrub to secure a folding table and metal chairs while I hustled back to the kitchen for an assortment of cookies, cold cuts and bread, and sliced cheese and peppers, raiding the refrigerator, and we were soon huddled in what could be described as a fact-finding mission of questions, explanations, muttered asides, and raw emotions that often defied a good explanation.

Jack fancied himself the leader of the orchestra, Gallacher established himself as the go-to answer man, and Caeli and I sat back and watched the two spar with light jabs and occasional haymakers while the priests silently looked on and Elmore and Danny O'Herlihy stood off to the side, their hands hovering by their holstered pistols.

I got up at one point and asked Elmore if he knew something that I didn't.

"Something how?" he asked.

"As in trouble coming our way," I said, pointing toward his itchy trigger finger.

"Yeah," he said. "I'm surprised you'd ask, given what's going on."

His response made me laugh.

"Good point, though I feel like the cavalry has shown up, for some reason," I said. "Not Jack so much, but the company he keeps."

"You really think those guys are security for the Pope? At least two of 'em look old enough to be the Pope's father."

I laughed again, though he had a point.

"Why not? Jack may be a lot of things, but he's never been much of a liar – not on something like this."

Elmore's phone lit up, and he waved an apology as he held it to his ear.

"Sure," he eventually said into the device. "Bet you didn't even notice Caeli's uncle." He paused, muttered an acknowledgement of some sort, and added, "Yeah. He brought along some help from the Vatican, of all places."

He laughed then, grunted a sign-off, and returned the phone to his belt.

"That was Leonard, checking in," he said.

"Where the hell is he?"

"He's on top of the building," Elmore said. "Leonard's our sniper."

Didn't see that coming, either …

"Does he need anything? Something to eat or drink, maybe?"

"No. He's good," Elmore said. "He took a sack with him."

"How'd he even get up there?"

"You know Leonard," he said.

"Yeah – well enough to know he probably flew."

He laughed, and Elmore explained that Don Vincenzo had designed the sniper's nest himself, with a hidden stairway through a bedroom closet providing access. He was about to tell me where to find it when we were called back to the table by Jack, who seemed to have come to an arrangement with Gallacher.

"It's mostly settled then," Jack said as we approached. "But there's something else ya need to know."

I didn't like the sound of that and said so, though Jack waved off my concern as being of little importance.

"This Raven's Ridge spot yer to meet at tomorrow," he said. "I know the place, though nobody's ever called it that – not in me lifetime. It's the very spot we used a year ago when we were armin' up against the Brits. We had a weapons cache on the land, in a bunker buried deep and properly fortified. If memory serves, we had guns enough inside to – well, to start a bloody revolution."

He laughed, as though he'd shared a joke, grinning as he glanced at his audience.

"Plenty of C-4 in there back then – enough to take out a city block or two," he said. "Could be the reason they're drawin' ya in to that spot. Fair Kathleen, ya see, knew of the place."

Terrific, I recall thinking. *It just gets better and better.*

But there was more.

We spent another hour plotting strategy to deal with Kathleen MacAmhlaoibh and her goon, the one-time soldier we suspected of killing Joan Shedd. Much of that time involved writing a script of fantasy lines that we intended to share in whispers inside the house, where compromised microphones would pick them up. We had no way of knowing whether this tactic would work, or gain us any advantage, or even whether anyone was still listening. But Jack insisted that it was worth the attempt, and he took great delight in devising dialogue to hoodwink his one-time ally.

When Gallacher pressed him to talk about his relationship with MacAmhlaoibh, he gave up little and talked in circles.

"Come on, Uncle Jack," a frustrated Caeli eventually said. "Give us something we can work with."

"I don't know that I can," he said. "You already know she's right dangerous."

"How'd you meet?" Gallacher asked.

Jack remained coy.

"I can't say exactly when she drifted to the cause," he said. "She was detached, never showin' much, though she knew her way 'round a fight – that much was plain. She could handle a rifle better than any man in the crew and was as committed as any of us, I think – likely more so. But she also was … aloof, I suppose you'd call her. She didn't rattle or get distracted, but she wasn't exactly forthcomin', either."

"Why wasn't she on Mutton Island with the rest of yer rebels?" Gallacher asked.

"I sent her on another task entirely," Jack replied. "Truth be told, I knew it was a suicide venture all along, and she bein' such a rare thing of beauty, I didn't want to see her clubbed and booted to the side of the road like some dead possum. She was more hawk than songbird, it's true, but Mutton Island was a place marked for death, and we all knew it … even if we did our best to pretend otherwise."

He paused, sipping at his coffee.

"Surely she wasn't happy when she heard the freedom strike we'd planned flew away in the bloody wind," he eventually said. "Then again, all she knows is I'm bloody well dead – just as the rest of 'em believe."

"Ah, but you don't know that for sure," Gallacher said. "Something's dragged her into this nonsense. Why not the idea of gettin' back at the likes of you?"

Jack found it unlikely.

"The only way she'd know I was still on this side of things is divine intervention, boyo, and I no longer find that credible," he said. "If she's truly involved, it's to finish things – things she couldn't put an end to the last time we had a go. Still, she won't be pleased to see me when the time comes."

"Maybe she read Max's book?" Elmore suggested.

"Kathleen read a book? Hardly."

"But her partner's been reading Max's books, at least," Caeli suggested. "Maybe he's passing things along."

"And maybe storks are snortin' off in the sty and the slobberin' pigs are deliverin' wee Irish babies, is it," Jack said.

He barked out a laugh and refilled his coffee cup.

"No – I don't think it's possible … not for a second," he eventually whispered.

I thought it strange that we knew so little about the woman who, along with her cohort, had brought so much turmoil into our lives, and I wondered again about the driving forces that kept her motivated and on such a destructive path. Had it not been for the parking garage incident, we never would've known of her existence at all.

How she knew of ours was another matter entirely, one that was wrapped up in her association with Caeli's uncle – and he claimed to have no insider's knowledge. I wasn't certain that I believed him, of course. But I didn't believe a lot of things back then, which didn't help with what happened next.

FORTY-SIX

A STITCH IN TIME

Leonard eventually wandered in, eyed Uncle Jack suspiciously while paying no attention whatsoever to his delegation, and abruptly left for the kitchen without a word. Elmore doggedly followed after him, no doubt hoping for an update on what he'd seen from the sniper's lair atop the house.

I figured that if Leonard had spotted anything worth sharing, he'd spill it without prompting. I also figured that someone had taken his place during his current walkabout – Ian or Gavin, perhaps; maybe even both of them – but I had no way of knowing for sure.

For his part, Jack smiled at our bodyguard as he passed through and whispered something to Father DuCharme that made the man laugh, the first utterance of any kind from the traveling retinue of papal fighters that I'd detected.

I decided to see if could determine what made these guys tick.

"Something funny there, *padre*?" I asked DuCharme.

He sobered quickly, shook his head, but said nothing.

I glanced at Father Shannon and then at Father Rottach and made a show of including them in the conversation.

"What about you august gentlemen?" I asked. "Anything to offer as we consider the end of the world as we know it?"

Their expressions didn't change, though you could tell if you looked long enough, hard enough, that all three had opinions to offer.

"Perhaps English isn't your mother tongue," I offered. "Would you like me to give it a try in Italian, maybe?"

But even that produced nothing but blank stares.

They must be on a short leash, I thought, which of course led me back to Caeli's uncle.

"How 'bout it, Jack?" I said with a bit more force. "You're somehow finding this craziness to be amusing, I take it – right up your alley."

"I'm findin' things to be more than troublin', Maxwell," he said, waving a hand sideways, a show of disgust. "But if I've learned anything a'tall in the past year, it's that you should enjoy the delights of each day that come yer way 'cause ya never know when you'll breathe yer last."

Even that line rang hollow.

"If you find a flower's delight in Leonard's scowl, I'd like to know what you're smoking, or drinking," I said. "How about telling us something about your traveling companions: Why you picked them, how you got access to them, skills and hobbies? – you know, full disclosure. We'd all appreciate the insight."

Jack grinned at me, or maybe he was flashing a thinly disguised frown, and he glanced about the room, studying Gallacher for a moment before moving on to Caeli, skipping me and Danny O'Herlihy entirely, nodding sagely at the three priests, one after the other, and eventually alighting on his aide, Giuseppe Blinstrub, who remained as enigmatic as a Mount Rushmore carving.

"My companions, as you call 'em, are just that: fellow priests with a shared goal, which is puttin' an end to the trouble that's come yer way. If given a chance, you'll find they can more than hold their own in a fight – guns, knives, fists, gin rummy. I dearly wish I'd access to their lot during that dreadful day on Mutton Island when this one" – he eyed Gallacher – "killed me off and then shipped me on to Rome."

He laughed heartily and smiled, beaming at all of us. But he cut it off as quickly as you'd turn a page on a book, serious once more.

"Wish I'd better news to pass along," he said. "But I'll tell ya this much, for whatever it's worth to ya: The view from this end isn't all that encouragin', much as I wish it were otherwise."

"Care to elaborate?" Gallacher asked.

But Jack just shook his head and spouted instead the opening verse of the Hughes Mearns poem *Antigonish*:

Yesterday, upon the stair,
I met a man who wasn't there.
He wasn't there again today.
I wish, I wish, he'd go away.

"There's some significance to that, is there, archbishop?" Gallacher, who was unamused, asked.

"I'm no longer an archbishop, as ya know – not that it matters," Jack said. "What matters is gettin' a plan in play to end this madness and allow me niece to move on with her wedding day, minus nutters with blazin' guns … much as I was meself when we first crossed paths."

Caeli, who was following the conversation with increasing alarm, likely because she recognized the same traits that her uncle exhibited during his revolutionary days, couldn't contain herself.

"You worry me, Jack. I thought you were over it, but here you are again, talking of crazed killers as though it's an everyday occurrence in your world," she said.

"Sadly, my dear, is seems to be just as common in yer own world as it once was in mine," he said. "It tears me heart out to think it's true, and yet … here we are. You've stirred a hornet's nest o' trouble, and it's on me to fix it so ye can pass it by – so we both can pass it all by. As to that, I've some thoughts on this soldier who killed yer friend. If we can neutralize him, ya see, this whole thing might just blow over, a wind along the coast that huffs itself out."

Caeli shook her head.

"And what of the crazy woman who tried to kill us in the parking garage?" she asked. "Is she going to blow herself out, too?"

"Not likely," Jack said. "She's a force of nature, our Kathleen. Her storm is as wide as a continent, as steady and as certain as the ocean itself. Still, if we can manage to take out her mate, she might just reconsider her path – and make a mistake based on rage. If she does that, we all win. If not, it'll take more than plans from the lot of us to bring her to heel. And I'm fresh out of armies to command, as ye can see."

"So it's an army then we need?" Gallacher asked.

"Maybe two, just to be safe," Jack said. He didn't bother this time with a smile, a grin, a light-hearted look of any kind. He was deadly serious – just as he'd been during our visit to the Vatican, when he was drinking hard and ranting even harder.

"Two armies, is it?" Gallacher said, his voice now mocking his old adversary. "Are ya sure we shouldn't call in NATO? Or maybe ask the Yanks to loan us a nuke or two?"

"Mock me all ye want, boyo," Jack replied. "But I know things ye don't – things that'd make ya feel far different about Kathleen were ya to hear 'em."

"Pray tell, your former eminence," Gallacher said, sweeping his hand to the side in a gesture of *Let's have it*.

Jack's response was typical. He served up another verse of *Antigonish* in a sing-song voice that would've amused a class of elementary students.

When I came home last night at three,
The man was waiting there for me.
But when I looked around the hall,
I couldn't see him there at all!

"I bloody well think you've lost it entirely," Gallacher said.

"An' I think you've underestimated yer foe," Jack shot back.

"Do ya now?" Gallacher replied. "Tell me what ya know then, *padre*, that should have me quakin' in me boots."

"I'm just suggestin' that if we take out her man, she'll find herself stretched thin and might decide to reorder things a bit, which'd buy ya time to move in for the kill, as it were."

"You really think she'd reconsider … or blunder?" Gallacher asked.

But before Jack could elaborate, Leonard was back in play with a water bottle in one hand, a sandwich in the other, and a deep-seated frown covering his face. This was a look that I knew well.

"Hate to interrupt," he said, "but we're running out of time. We're being watched – on the road and from the river."

"Yer sure?" Gallacher asked.

Leonard scowled.

"Then we'd best hurry," Gallacher said. He'd been staring at Jack since Leonard entered the room, and his eyes didn't stray now. "And we'd best get it right 'cause I doubt we'll get a second chance – unless you disagree, Father O'Lennox."

Jack's expression didn't change.

"It's comin', ya know," he said. "Like a bloody freight train on a greased track."

In short order, Gallacher, his bodyguard, and Ian and Gavin took control of the discussion and quickly made several command decisions. Among them:

-We'd all get bulletproof vests, compliments of G2. (How Gallacher was going to arrange that, exactly, given his status as a sidelined performer, we had no idea and, when we asked him, he shrugged it off with a terse comment: "Let me worry about that, lads");

-Jack and his fellow priests would be armed, again by G2, which I found to be an extraordinary concession on Gallacher's part, given the risk;

-Leonard, Elmore, and Danny O'Herlihy would be issued sniper's rifles and would set up well ahead of the 3 p.m. Raven's Ridge showdown at strategic locations they'd decide on long before the planned meeting;

-Ian and Gavin also would arrive early and prowl the grounds, looking for the same sort of hidden gunmen that we were inserting into the landscape;

-Gallacher would accompany Caeli and me in the Range Rover, hiding in the back seat;

-Jack and fathers DuCharme, Shannon, and Rottach would act as a second greeting contingent, arriving no more than 30 seconds after our SUV, driving the armored vehicle that Leonard had secured from Fierro Enterprises in Dublin, with orders to take on any trouble they encountered or observed;

-A misdirect via conversations whispered into our compromised security system would lead our adversary into false beliefs about our plans.

I'll confess to having my doubts about much of this, especially the part where Caeli would be present at Raven's Ridge, just as the thug we'd once called Mister Denmark demanded. I'd expressed my reservations more than once during the back-and-forth, only to have them brushed aside by everyone in the room, Caeli especially.

Her uncle also was a valiant supporter.

"For God's sake, boyo, but would ya let it go?" Jack spouted at one point. "She's a big girl, ya know, fully capable of handlin' herself in a tight spot. Ye should know that better'n most. Things are not always as they seem."

But it was his last line that caught my attention – akin to a building's unexpected collapse on a crowded street. For reasons that I can't explain, it became a true Eureka moment of lightbulbs flashing and bells ringing, pinball-style, with sirens singing in the background, and I was struck by the notion that had it not been for Jack's presence and his off-hand comment just now, the whole thing would have most likely slipped by me – a breath on the wind.

"Hey. Hang on a minute," I said and then waited for the voices that filled the garage to slowly grind to a halt.

It took a moment, but I remained silent until every eye in the room was staring at me.

"I'll bet money – big money – that they're running a bluff on us, a misdirect, if you will," I said. "He's trying to force us in one direction while the two of them will be going in …"

"… in another direction entirely," Caeli said, picking up the thought. "Of course. He wants us out of the way by sending us out to the boonies …"

"… so he can do whatever they've been planning all along, without the need to worry about our interference," I finished.

A calm settled over the room as the pieces clicked into place.

"Not him alone," Jack said. "It's the woman ya need to be concerned with. With the Frog now behind bars, she's the brains behind whatever's goin' on – likely has been all along. At least here, in Ireland."

Surprisingly, Gallacher nodded his agreement.

"Yer right – both of ya. God knows I've been swallowin' it whole, like a damn trout, thanks to the many lines I was fed by Aedan bloody O'Duinn," he said after a long moment passed. "But what're they up to then? Where will they strike? Is it the airport at Shannon, do ya think?"

"No," I said, feeling as confident as I sounded. "Think of where he's been all this time, week after week, scouting. The airport's vital to the national economy, but it's no landmark – sure as hell not like the Eiffel Tower. They're going after Bunratty and the tourists who flood the place. Tell me that wouldn't make a hell of a statement."

FORTY-SEVEN

ORDERS FROM HEADQUARTERS

After throwing our initial strategy on the scrapheap, we damn near overplanned the subsequent operation, and that's saying something.

Then again, the slightest miscalculation could end up getting somebody killed, and nobody wanted that — not even the professional soldiers among Liam Gallacher's team who otherwise might factor so-called acceptable casualty rates into their thinking.

Within minutes, Gallacher called in reinforcements, including the full taskforce that had been redirected to combat the threat after he was sidelined. He accomplished this with strategic calls to the top brass in Dublin, advising of the mole's outing, our contact with Mister Denmark, the proposed Raven's Ridge meeting, and our conclusion that Bunratty, not the airport, was the terrorist's true and immediate target.

That last bit got their attention, and it no doubt drove the decision to allow him back in. I got the feeling, as did Caeli, that the folks in Dublin, now out of earshot of the CIA, were actually relieved to have their man back in the saddle. He was soon riding herd on the operation once more, with willing assistance from the obtuse hard-liner who'd temporarily replaced him, a man we came to know as McGibbon: no courtesy title or honorific, no rank, no given name.

It became apparent if you listened closely that McGibbon never really wanted the job.

It also was readily obvious that nobody wanted to work with him, either, given some of the salutations that came Gallacher's way after the announcement that he was again in command made the rounds via email, text, tweet, and carrier pigeon for all we knew.

We were told later that the CIA dimwit who'd demanded Gallacher's head vehemently protested the decision but was cut out of the loop for what followed. My take was that this was the same bozo who'd confronted me in the warehouse when we'd first arrived with Gallacher and his men, but the spy chief would only smile when I asked him about it, long after the fact.

The first decision that came through the command pipeline was a surprise. We were ordered to remain at the estate, despite the security issues, maintaining a low profile until the heavy lifting began. This applied to Gallacher and his men, Uncle Jack and his priests, Caeli and me, and of course Elmore and Leonard. In time, a handful of additional G2 agents joined us.

Elmore protested vigorously but to no avail.

"If the security's bein' monitored, lad," he was told by a G2 muckety-muck who seemed to be parroting Caeli's uncle, "we'll make the most of it – keep 'em guessin'. This is a good thing; it's not bad a'tall."

In short order, working through the magic of Skype and a laptop belonging to Danny O'Herlihy in a three-way connection with Dublin and Garda headquarters in Limerick, where McGibbon had set up his operation, the big shots determined that they'd flood Bunratty with well-armed G2 agents and local coppers, both uniformed and in disguise, to aggressively seek out any and all activity related to terrorism at the castle and Folk Park. In addition, they'd create road blocks, establish perimeters leading into and out of the grounds, erect show-of-force impediments in the area immediately surrounding the castle itself, and broadcast alerts from moving vehicles asking visitors to report anything suspicious, beginning at noon the following day – 3 hours ahead of the meeting at Raven's Ridge.

Bomb technicians and trained dogs would immediately be assigned to sweep the grounds and stay at it until the danger was past. Armed personnel also would blanket the area, watching for anyone or anything looking remotely suspicious.

"It's all serious business now," one of the Dublin fat cats told Gallacher. "Ye see 'em, ye either lock 'em up or shoot 'em 'til they don't get back up. *Tuiscint?*"

I thought that many parts of the plan were ridiculous and said so – more than once, each time more fervently than the last.

"All you'll do with that show of force is drive them elsewhere – maybe even to the airport," I argued. "Right now you know where they're going to strike. But when you pull this armed-men-on-every-corner stunt, with megaphoned town-criers scaring the hell out of everybody with a pulse, your terrorists will disappear, and you won't know where they'll end up until the casualty reports start pouring in."

It seemed obvious enough, and I think that Gallacher, at least, understood my objection. But the Dublin boys had taken over at that point, even after Caeli pointed out the potential media fallout that could make them all look like circus clowns.

In short, we were ignored.

It never once dawned on me that they might be right. But then, I wasn't in the terrorist-fighting business, either.

Our reward for being vocal was swift. The Dublin brass wanted us out of the way entirely, while McGibbon, Gallacher's operational counterpart, suggested instead that we march to a tune of his calling as a ruse of sorts while the Bunratty operation proceeded.

"Here's the way I see it. The Yanks are civilians with no reason a'tall to be at the center of this mess, other than the insistence of the actual bloody terrorists – and like the Americans, we don't negotiate with their lot," he said emphatically, whacking his hand on the table and jarring his computer, which in turn caused us to see only half of his face via Skype when he started in again. "Even so, let's serve 'em up on a platter at this Raven's Ridge spot and trust they don't get themselves killed. That wouldn't look good in the newspapers, either here or in the States."

I thought he was nuts and said so.

Caeli was even less happy.

"You know that no one will be at the meeting site," she said, pushing closer to the laptop so that she could be seen on the monitor. "It's a waste of time and resources."

"Exactly, Miss Brown," McGibbon said, smiling as he made a slight adjustment to his monitor. "But it's only a waste of yer time, ya see – and yer resources, comes to that, as you'd be expected to drive yer own vehicle. The fact that no one'll be there to greet ya is its own reward – unless, of course, someone actually is there to greet ya. In that event, I'd encourage ya to run – to get away as fast as ye can manage. Best take yer bodyguards along. I understand you've a couple of beefy Yanks on standby."

Caeli jumped from frustrated to furious.

"You're kidding – right?" she said. "Tell me this is a joke."

"On the contrary. Short of keeping ya under house arrest, I can think of no better way to …"

She reached out and snapped the computer's cover shut, cutting the bastard off. Gallacher cursed softly, frowned at Caeli, and opened the laptop again, calling for assistance from Danny O'Herlihy to restore the connection.

We slept poorly that night, no doubt because a contingent of agents milling were about the house. Most of them had orders to remain silent, communicating by text or scribbling messages on sheets of paper well away from the cameras affected by our squirrely security system, though you could still hear them as they shuffled around. Whatever scripted subterfuge Gallacher deemed appropriate to whisper into the walls would be handled by his men alone, we were told, which left us hanging once again.

And OK, I'll admit it now, but Caeli and I had every intention of blowing off even the appearance of driving to Raven's Ridge that afternoon, as ordered. Our intention was to head straight to Bunratty to help stop whatever terrorist attack the lunatics had in mind, catching Mister Denmark at the same time.

We knew his game, after all, far better than anyone on the taskforce, Gallacher included. A little payback for what he'd done to Joan Shedd would be reason enough to cover that base without hesitation or fear of reprisal from the G2 crowd in either Dublin or Limerick.

If we ran into Kathleen MacAmhlaoibh along the way and were fortunate enough to settle that score – well, so much the better.

But things don't always work out the way you envision. For starters, we hadn't taken into account Leonard's stubborn streak and his insistence on checking under every rug and inside every cupboard before moving on. The trait makes him an effective bodyguard, which is why he and Elmore insisted on checking out Raven's Ridge in the early morning hours, well ahead of our 3 o'clock appointment. But it also can be maddening as it plays out in real time.

We chafed at our forced inactivity (at a minimum, I wanted to catch the dolts Leonard had spotted who'd been spying on us from the river, a move that Gallacher nixed) and left the estate nearly two hours ahead of our scheduled meeting time, supposedly to carry out our directive to thoroughly scope out Raven's Ridge. We were convinced, of course, that we were simply being shuttled off to pasture – and we weren't happy about it.

Caeli was driving, I was riding shotgun, and Leonard was in the back seat. Elmore was curled up in the space reserved for luggage, watching our backs, because the two of them couldn't be in the same seat and also remain out of sight as we approached our meeting spot. Gallacher and McGibbon had insisted on the arrangement because they determined, correctly, I'm sure, that we would need the help if we actually ran into armed opposition.

That discussion, of course, brought Jack and his crew back into play. Initially, Gallacher had checked the talents of the Pope's security detail with Vatican officials and, learning of their legitimacy and peculiar fighting skills, embraced the foursome, assigning them to a detail sweeping the Bunratty grounds. But when Jack confirmed our role at Raven's Ridge, which would take place out of his purview, he demanded the right to accompany Caeli, railing at Gallacher.

It wasn't the spy lord who'd overruled him, however.

"I don't want you with me, Jack," Caeli said sharply.

"But I've come to keep ya safe, sweet girl," he protested. "Surely ya know that, despite me many mistakes, the only thing I still want in this life is to see to yer happiness."

"No. You need to stay away from me."

You could see that he was hurt by her words, so much so that Caeli softened her refusal, at least a bit.

"The truth is, I don't want to worry about Max and you, too – not after Mutton Island and what we thought happened to you there. I won't allow it. I won't see you killed again," she said, and I wasn't sure whether she was telling him the truth or simply feeding him a line that he might accept.

This time he bowed his head and said nothing more as we headed out for Raven's Ridge.

Leonard was unhappy with the seating arrangement and groused repeatedly. As was typical, he wanted to drive, though in this case it made no sense. Elmore was uncomfortable but stoic, thankful that our assigned destination was a relatively short distance away. Caeli and I were anxious to get out of sight of the minders who remained at our estate and on the way to Bunratty. But we didn't even make it to the highway before the disagreements began.

"All right – we're off to Bunratty then," Caeli said as we reached the end of our lengthy driveway.

"No – turn right," Leonard said. "We stick to the plan."

"Why bother?" she asked. "We need to catch the guy who killed Joan Shedd, and we can't do that out in the boonies."

"No. We need to go to Raven's Ridge first. They'll be watching," Leonard said.

"Who's they, exactly?" I asked. "Most of Gallacher's people are long gone, and the ones still here likely won't care. Neither should you. Or are you referring to the bastards we're out to hunt down?"

"Just turn right so they'll at least think we're following the plan," Leonard said, referencing Gallacher's people. "Besides, I want to check the place out – make sure Blake's right and nothing's going on out there."

"It doesn't matter," Caeli insisted, though she kept the SUV stationary. "The only script we're following today is our own."

"No. What if Blake's wrong? What if your guy is out there, waiting for you right now? We need to check the site first – cross it off the list," Leonard said, and you could tell that he was digging in for a fight.

"If we do that, we'll miss whatever's happening at Bunratty," Caeli said. "The woman will coordinate her attack with the time we're supposed to meet. Leaving now gives us a shot at stopping her."

"And we're leaving early enough to do both," Leonard said. "Maybe all the action's at Bunratty, but maybe not. Let's scope out the meeting site – see if they've left any of their people behind. Then we go to the castle if this other doesn't pan out. Won't take long – especially if I drive."

"We're wasting time," I argued. "Terrorists don't make statements by blowing up marsh grass. They make statements by blowing up landmarks. If they take out a bunch of tourists at the same time, the headlines are bigger and the TV coverage goes global. They'll be at the castle."

"So you keep saying," Leonard countered. "What if all they want is revenge, which they'd get by taking out the two busybodies who've been a pain in their ass since you first stepped into this mess? If you buy that, and I do, nothing's gonna happen at that castle. We need to go to Raven's Ridge."

We were silent for a moment, contemplating Leonard's reasoning and insistence, when Caeli glanced in the rearview mirror and caught Elmore's attention. He looked uncomfortable, a Dill pickle stuffed into a jar that was two sizes too small.

"What do you think we should do, Marcus?" she asked.

"Whatever we do, I hope we do it quick," he said. "This isn't the best place to hatch plots. My back's already sore."

The phone that Gallacher had given to me began jangling, and I silently cursed when I spotted his name on the screen and swiped the accept button and then activated the speaker so that all of us could hear him.

"What's going on, Professor Blake?" he said before I could offer a greeting. "My people tell me yer sittin' at the end of the drive and haven't moved in some time."

I shushed Leonard when he began to automatically advise the G2 spymaster to stuff it sideways and tried the non-committal approach.

"Just making sure we have everything we need," I said.

"Is that so?" he asked, clearly not buying what I was peddling. "Get on with it, lad. Make certain yer careful and thorough both. I doubt you'll run into anything a'tall out there, but be cautious nonetheless. Call me once you've secured the area."

"We've been over this," I said. "What do you really want?"

"I want to make sure yer off to this Raven's Ridge and not to Bunratty. That hero's streak ya carry will land ya in a world o' trouble one day, but it won't be this day. Show up at Bunratty in any form, and me orders are to arrest the lot of ya on sight and toss ya inside for a week or two. I trust that's clear enough for the lot of ya."

When Caeli protested, he cut her off.

"Just go to the site and do the job you've been given," he said. "That's all I ask."

"You want a hell of a lot more than that," Leonard snarled. But Caeli jumped in before Gallacher could respond.

"How's my uncle holding up?" – and I'll admit that her words surprised me. "You'd better keep him safe."

"Had ye agreed to let him accompany you instead of me, you'd already know," he said.

"A straight answer, Liam. How is he?" she pressed.

"We've been over this as well, Miss Brown," Gallacher said. "Yer uncle and his mates are fine – even helpful. I again promise ya, we'll do our best to ensure their safety. I wouldn't want to answer to the Pope on that count, ya know."

"You won't want to answer to me, either, should your plan go sideways and something happens to him," she said. "I'll hold you to your word."

"As well ya should, though understand, yer uncle decides things for himself. Little enough I can do – or you, comes to that – to keep him from whatever path he chooses. Consider his folly on Mutton Island."

Leonard leaned over the seat and snatched the phone from my hand.

"Get on with it, Gallacher," he growled. "Leave us the hell alone."

He snapped the phone shut, tossed it back in my lap, and waved a hand at Caeli.

"Let's get moving," he said. "Turn right – we're burning daylight."

He was right about that much, anyway.

I ignored the phone when it immediately began ringing.

FORTY-EIGHT

RAVEN'S RIDGE

We arrived at Raven's Ridge a full 90 minutes ahead of schedule. We were still running late by my own internal clock, or at least for what I'd calculated to be sufficient time to prepare for the unexpected – just in case Mister Denmark actually showed. But it couldn't be helped, given all of the oversight that had gone on once the G2 brass got involved in the planning. Everyone, it seemed, was on a taut leash.

We'd studied the area, of course, using Google maps and satellite images that Gallacher obtained from the G2 vaults, and we also took advantage of the foray that Leonard and Elmore, Gavin and Ian, and two other operatives made to the site in the early-morning hours.

In short, we knew the general layout, though Caeli and I had yet to set foot on the land, which was little more than scrub brush and wind-swept sand and hardscrabble rock and swaying reeds and a couple of seemingly insignificant dunes that backed up to the broad River Shannon Estuary.

Elmore crawled into the back seat once Leonard quietly exited the Range Rover a quarter-mile or so away from the site, carrying his sniper's rifle and god only knows what else in a rucksack that he slung over his shoulder. I had to laugh at Elmore's long sigh as he uncoiled himself into the plush leather bench, which must have seemed like a king-sized bed with satin sheets compared to what he'd been tolerating.

"Make sure you stay down," Caeli cautioned as she edged the SUV closer to the specific coordinates we'd been given via text the previous day. "We don't want to spook him if he's here."

"I know," Elmore said. "Just don't get close 'til Leonard sets up. It'll take him a few minutes."

We sat quietly, with the Range Rover idling and the three of us alert for an attack that could come at us from any direction, the river included – even if we didn't believe that we'd see anyone at all.

"You think we should wait 'til 3 on the button?" I asked Caeli long minutes later.

"I don't think we should be here at all," she said.

I spotted a spark of reflecting sunlight off in the distance and shouted a warning, certain that it was the glint of a rifle scope. Elmore, who'd also seen the flash, assured us that it was Leonard.

"I'm tracking him on GPS," he said, holding up his phone.

"Good thing, too, because a bullet from a good sniper's rifle with the right ammo would punch though our plating like a nail hammered through a sardine can," Caeli said.

"That's hardly reassuring," I said.

"She's right," Elmore said. He swapped his phone for the compact binoculars he'd brought along and began scanning the area.

Caeli was restless, which I seldom saw in her demeanor, and she returned to a familiar theme.

"So tell me again why we're out here like sitting ducks when we should be at Bunratty with Gallacher."

Elmore felt obligated to respond.

"Because your uncle's there, and you don't want to spend time with him," he said. "Besides, Gallacher threatened to arrest us if we're spotted at the castle. We'd be spotted straight off, given all the boots he's got on the ground."

He spoke softly, sincere in the assessment. And while I smiled at the Uncle Jack barb, his words made me, at least, feel better about our current task, which in truth had reminded me of spinning tires on hot asphalt, getting us nowhere.

Caeli had been steadily drumming her fingers on the steering wheel, but she stopped in mid-beat.

"Didn't Jack say this place served as a cache for guns to supply his revolution?" she asked.

"Yes – but he didn't elaborate, which is typical," I said.

I shifted positions so that I could see Elmore.

"Did you find anything when you were wandering around this morning?" I asked.

"No, though we weren't really hunting for them, either," he said. "Looking the place over, my guess would be somewhere around the dunes, or maybe a cave along the river – if anything's still around or Jack wasn't just blowing smoke."

He considered it for a few seconds more as his gaze shifted north.

"Most likely the dunes," he said. "The river's too damp for storing anything made of metal for long."

"So if he's here, maybe he's hiding in whatever place they'd used for stashing weapons," Caeli said. "Maybe he's out there right now, watching us."

"Yeah. Could be," Elmore agreed. "Then again, maybe he's in the Caribbean, sunning himself on a beach and drinking a mai-tai from a gallon jug. That's what I'd do – no question."

I found either scenario unlikely and said as much, but our bodyguard was persistent.

"I don't know," he replied. "Self-preservation is strong in a military man, and he's got to know time's running …"

He abruptly stopped talking, and I wondered why until I shifted my position again and followed his eyes across the desolate stretch of ground toward the river.

They appeared as an apparition might, materializing from the dunes: two small children, a boy and a girl, 5 or 6 at most, holding hands and walking slowly, tentatively, toward us, as if afraid of what they would find inside the Range Rover were they to open a door. They were dressed in school uniforms that had been neatly pressed, and a look of uncertainty – not quite fear but not nearly comfortable, either – registered on their cherubic faces.

"What the hell?" I muttered. "What's he up to?"

Caeli's hand automatically reached for the door handle, but she halted as two more children, and then two more after that, appeared from nowhere and began making their way toward us.

They all wore the same tidy uniform, and they all exhibited the same expectant, puzzled stare.

"Who are they? Where are they coming from?" Elmore muttered.

Three more children appeared, girls this time, and then two additional boys followed them, all in the same age group, all headed our way. Elmore was scanning with the binoculars, looking for signs of snipers who would attack once we opened the SUV's doors – or at least that's what I thought he was doing. But he cursed aloud, something he seldom does, and nudged my arm, handing the glasses over the seat.

"He's there, to the right of the dune nearest the river – the guy in Caeli's Wanted poster," Elmore said. "He's with a bunch of other kids – eight or nine, maybe. Might be more – hard to get an exact count."

I peered through the binoculars for a moment before handing them to Caeli.

The two children who'd first appeared were maybe 25 yards away, and they stopped as though they'd hit an invisible barrier and waited for the others to catch up. Moments later a line of inquisitive faces stared at us as though demanding answers to a mystery they couldn't quite fathom.

They weren't alone.

"He's on the move," Elmore said.

Sure enough, Mister Denmark was walking slowly toward our SUV, surrounded by a dozen more youngsters, all sharing the same look of doubt and hope and expectation that we'd previously noted. He held the hands of two of the children and had drawn them in close – a shield of sorts.

The sight was so odd, so otherworldly, that you couldn't pull your eyes away.

"Do you think he hypnotized them?" Caeli whispered. "Is that even possible?"

A sharp rap on the Range Rover's rear quarter-panel startled us. The door behind Caeli opened, and Leonard stuck his head inside. Where he came from, exactly, I had no idea, but he seemed as mystified as the rest of us.

"What the hell's going on?" he asked.

"Good question," Elmore said. "Anyone else out there?"

"Doubtful. There's a school bus a half-mile down the road –
likely how the kids got here."

"Yeah," Elmore said. "But why – what's he doing?"

"Don't know, but I don't like it," Leonard said, and he silently
closed the door and disappeared.

"I hope to hell he wasn't seen," I muttered.

"Nobody sees Leonard unless he wants them to," Elmore
muttered.

I counted 24 children now, milling about as their eyes searched
the vast open estuary for help, for guidance, for some logical
answer or solution to whatever plight had befallen them.

Behind them, the man we'd called Mister Denmark grinned
and waved a hand, beckoning us to leave the SUV.

Another Ahab, I thought.

"They must be frightened to death," Caeli said, and she
scrambled outside. I followed, as did Elmore. Hell, what choice
did we have? We all used the still-open doors of the Range Rover
for cover, and we all had our hands on the butts of our pistols,
though we kept them holstered to avoid additionally upsetting the
children.

I drew comfort in the fact that Leonard was close by with
his rifle trained on the bastard, though I didn't see our bodyguard
when I glanced about. I took that as a good sign, however. If I
couldn't see him, neither could Mister Denmark.

"And a fine, glorious day it 'tis," McMahon called out. "Nice
of ye to join me – and yer early … well ahead of schedule, though
expected all the same. Good on ya. Thanks fer playin' along then."

"What are you up to?" Caeli called.

"I was just showin' the youngsters a good time: a little freedom
from the rigors of the classroom, a stop at the ice cream parlor, a
trip to see the birds along the river. I call that a fine day, indeed –
am I right, chiselers?"

The children said nothing, and you could see it in their eyes
now: distrust, anxiety, an uneasy dread, the knowledge that
something was far off kilter.

"Those children are afraid of you," Caeli called to him.

But McMahon shook his head, feigning surprise.

"Not a'tall," he said. "We've had a grand time – haven't we,
kids? Answer me now."

A handful of them – six or seven, perhaps – mustered up a sing-song response: "Yes, lance corporal."

Geez – he's turning them into little soldiers, I recall thinking.

I stared at him, trying to determine what was behind those dark eyes, and spotted a splotch of red on his left shoulder – definitely blood.

He's wounded, I thought. *Somebody's shot him ...*

"So what'd you do – raid an orphanage to provide cover?" I yelled, recalling a detail that Gallacher provided about his background.

"An orphanage? Hardly," he said. "There are no orphanages in the traditional sense left in Ireland, ya see – not after what happened at Tuam and dozens of places like it was finally exposed and the many graves discovered. These little tykes are from the nearby National School. Their bus driver was kind enough to allow me to take 'em for a jaunt a'fore headin' home."

"Will the driver agree with that assessment?" Caeli asked.

"Ye can ask her, of course – once she wakes up," he said, waving his arm toward the distant school bus that Leonard had spotted. "What else do ya want to know then?"

"Why Raven's Ridge?" I called out.

When he looked on blankly, I expanded the question.

"Why call this place Raven's Ridge? It doesn't exist – not on the map, not on the internet, nowhere in Ireland. Why pick that name?"

"Ah, Jaysus, man – easy enough. Yer fond of the word. It's in all yer books, isn't it now? You should be proud of the name – feel right at home."

He grinned.

"Besides, I saw a gatherin' of crows here, days back – along the river bank, ya see," he said. "They call that a murder, ya know – a murder of crows, though why they bloody well call it that I'll likely never know."

"So why not call it Crow's Ridge?"

His smile widened.

"Crow's Ridge doesn't deliver the same sound now, does it? Crow's Canyon, maybe, or Crow's Corridor. But Raven's Ridge sounds bloody perfect, the right name to git yer attention, boyo, which is all I was after doin'."

"He's nuttier than we thought," I whispered to Caeli.

"Either that or he's damn clever because – here we are," she whispered.

I went at him again.

"What's your end game, lance corporal?"

"End game? What makes ya think there's an end game a'tall?"

"That hole in your shoulder, for starters," I called.

What he shouted next was a shock – a line that none of us saw coming.

"Yeah, well, there's that now, is it. Much as I hate to say it, boyo, I know me time's short on this little venture," he yelled. "I've been watchin' it, feelin' it, fer days now, and it's chasin' after me, closin' in. I'm fond of Kathleen, it's true. That much ya know. But what she's after sellin'? Let's just say it's not for the likes o' me. I only took this business on as a lark, ya see. Well, that and a bit of lust."

He laughed, perhaps waiting for us to acknowledge his discretion in front of the youngsters. But we didn't bite, and the burner phone that Gallacher had given me began jingling loudly from its resting spot inside my pocket. I ignored it, fumbling blindly until I shut it off.

McMahon seemed amused.

"Wanna get that, mate?" he asked.

"No," I called. "Keep talking. You've got a lot to answer for."

He waved that off, expanding his grin, though you could see the occasional flicker of pain in his eyes … *likely from being shot*.

"Someday, maybe. Not today, though – sure as hell not today. We'll settle our business another time, Max Blake and Caeli Brown. Count on it, ya can. I will."

Caeli pressed the issue.

"You're covered, you know," she said. "One word and our man takes you out. End of story. End of threat."

"Nae. Ye wouldn't do that in front of the little ones," he yelled. "Think of the trauma. Years from now and they still wouldn't get it out of their heads. Ye wouldn't want that on yer conscience, would ya now?"

"Maybe," Caeli called. "After what you did to Joan Shedd, it's a fate you deserve."

"Ah, the woman at Dromoland, the one I was after helpin'
meself to her jewelry at the Folk Park when ya first came along,"
he called. "Sure – heard all about it, though far too late, ya see.
That wasn't me. That was dear Kathleen who saw fit to visit the
poor woman at her hotel room."

"I don't believe you," Caeli called.

"Maybe so, but it won't change the facts. I was on the road
just then, followin' the pair of ya to yer lovely estate in the country
… getting' the lay of the land, as it were."

His words registered. I instantly thought back to our return
trip from Bunratty after we'd left Mrs. Shedd at the taxi stand,
recalling Caeli's suspicion that we were being followed.

"So if not her, how many others?" Caeli called.

"Well now, Caeli Brown, soon to be Mrs. Max Blake – if ever
ya live so long. That's between me and me own gods, along with
the bloody British Army," he said.

"Not good enough," I yelled.

"It'll have to do, boyo. That all ya got then?"

"Why Denmark?" I asked him, changing the loop, figuring
that the question might keep him talking long enough to let
something vital slip out.

"Why bloody Denmark?" he repeated. "What's that mean
exactly?"

"Your hat with the DK on it – the one you wore that first day
at the folk park. What's the connection?"

"Ah, Jaysus, man. Sometimes a hat is just a hat – ya know?"

He made a show of glancing at his wristwatch, momentarily
shaking loose from the children to spread his arms wide. He
winced from the pain but toughed it out.

"It's been grand an' all, but I'm runnin' late," he said. "I'll
mostly leave the kids in yer hands as I've other places to be. But
in case yer man in the weeds is the twitchy sort, I'll be after takin'
a couple of 'em along with me – just 'til I'm off. Follow me and
ya won't like what happens to 'em. Nor, I suspect, will they. Leave
me go in peace and they'll all be home in time for snacks with
mater."

I called out to him then, insistent, holding him in check for a
final instant, at least – defying him to answer.

"Tell us about that bullet hole in your shoulder, lance corporal. Trouble on the home front, maybe? No longer getting along, the two of you? Bet you didn't see that coming. The best-laid plans and all that – what? … up in smoke?"

His face clouded in anger for just an instant. But he caught himself, offered nothing, and smiled once more, though grimly this time. He held out his hands, and the children nearest him, a boy and a girl on either side, latched on, and he slowly back-peddled away from us, grinning the whole time, mindful to keep the frightened youngsters upright. He was around the edge of the far dune before we could develop a further plan, and we heard an outboard engine sputter to life moments later.

"I don't think things were supposed to shake out like this," I muttered. "He had something else in mind for us on this day."

Caeli heard me, despite the wind that had kicked up off the water.

"Agreed, though I'm still amazed he was here at all," she said. "I was certain it was all a ruse."

I looked around for Leonard, figuring that whatever we did next would have to include him. But the two children McMahon had taken were soon running toward their classmates, who'd remained in a line in front of us, and Caeli called to them, assuring them that they were safe. We began walking ahead when Leonard abruptly appeared from whatever rock he'd been under.

"I can still take him out," he said. "Just say the word."

Caeli shook her head.

"No. Hide the rifle, Leonard," she said, her eyes sweeping the line of youngsters. "You'll scare them even more than they are right now."

My phone began ringing again, and I grabbed it this time and saw Gallacher's name on the screen.

"Yeah," I said after activating the connecting. "You won't believe what's going on out here."

But Gallacher didn't inquire.

"I was about to say the same," he said, and you could hear the excitement in his voice. "We found explosives wired to the castle, enough to take it all down. Our lads have it mostly dismantled, though we think there might be more still and have teams with dogs clearin' the grounds 'round the Folk Park."

He took in a gulp of air but pressed on before I could give him an update about what we'd discovered.

"No need to ask, but we've yet to get our hands on Kathleen MacAmhlaoibh or McMahon. We saw her well enough, thick in the fight, early on, but she's slipped the bloody noose again – thus far, anyway. Haven't seen McMahon yet a'tall, though it seems likely he's lurkin' nearby. Still, I suggest ya keep yer eye out for 'em both – just in case."

Caeli was collecting the children, with help from Elmore as Leonard looked on, and I couldn't shake the image of Lance Corporal McMahon back-peddling his way toward the river with the two youngsters in his clutches, once again avoiding capture and comeuppance, although this time he'd moved with the hesitant steps of a man in who was no longer certain of his place in the world.

"Blake – are ye still there?" Gallacher asked.

"I can't talk," I said. "We've got a bunch of scared kids to look after."

"How's that again?"

I cut the connection and joined Caeli, doing what I could to help.

I dismissed what sounded vaguely like a couple of distant gunshots moments later, seconds apart, after glancing about and determining that no one else reacted.

FORTY-NINE

SA TÍR SEO TRÍNA CHÉILE

While Leonard ran down the road to check on the bus driver's condition, Elmore pulled his phone and alerted the *Garda* station in Limerick.

Thinking quickly, he referred all questions to Liam Gallacher when the hardball stuff – "Who are you again, sir? And what exactly are ya after doin' with a bus filled with children that aren't yer own?" – began in earnest.

"Gallacher doesn't know what's happened here," I said when Elmore abruptly ended the call. "He had his hands full – didn't seem interested."

"He'll need to catch up fast – us, too," he replied. "You can bet they're already on the way."

He was right. Five police sedans with sirens wailing, stuffed with suspicious coppers, arrived quickly at our position. The one-sided grilling didn't end until DS Alan Phelan rolled up in his Mini Cooper minutes later and took charge – or he at least took charge of keeping the heat off the four of us who were doing our level best to tend to and comfort the frightened children left behind by Lance Corporal McMahon's sudden exit.

Even Leonard, god bless him, had pitched in by that time.

A woozy, goose-egged bus driver eventually provided corroboration with a detailed accounting of what had taken place on the road before our arrival, painting an ugly picture of squealing tires and a pistol-whipping, which helped considerably.

My phone continued to ring while we remained in the grilling stage. Gallacher's name appeared each time I checked the screen. I was in no hurry to talk with him – not, at least, until the children were accounted for and individually asked whether they'd been harmed in any way – though I finally heeded Spud's advice.

"You'd best talk to him, ya know," he said. "Given the inquiries he's already after gettin' from this lot" – he waved his hand toward the dozen officers who were milling officiously about – "he needs to hear directly from you or Caeli as to what went on."

He grinned, pausing for just an instant.

"Hope ya don't mind if I listen in," he said.

It was only after the headmaster, three teachers, and a number of frantic parents who'd been alerted to the situation showed up to embrace the children that I opened the door to the Range Rover, climbed inside to get out of the constant wind, and punched in Gallacher's direct line.

"From what I'm told, ye were forced to trade the safety of the kids for the bastard who took 'em," he said when he picked up. "Is that a fair representation?"

"Close enough," I said. "The children are in good hands, but we didn't have much of a shot at getting McMahon – not after he pulled this stunt. Why he did it – any of it – is another matter entirely."

"He didn't hurt them, anyway," Gallacher said, "which is more than I can say for the situation out here. I've issued a nationwide alert."

"For McMahon."

"And Kathleen bloody MacAmhlaoibh. Jaysus, man, but the mere sight of her …" He paused momentarily, drinking in the image, I suppose, before continuing. "We had her in our sights, ya know, but she bolted. Odd thing is, she'd been wounded, well before we first spotted her, skulkin' about plantin' fuses into the castle's framework."

"McMahon was shot as well," I said. "Shoulder."

"Huh. Sounds like they went at one another then, which maybe prompted the way this all came together," he eventually said. "Still, I wish I had that part of it to play over again. She was here one minute and gone the next. The how of it's a mystery, even now. We had eyes on her – hell, I had eyes on her for an instant.

A half-dozen of me best men insisted it was impossible for her to do a runner, which is exactly what she did. We've teams about, of course, searchin' the grounds, turnin' over rocks, knockin' on doors and windows and panel vans and most every place else that moves or doesn't, tryin' our best to turn her up again. And yet …"

He let the thought drift away, which told me everything I needed to hear about the battle we'd missed at Bunratty.

"Watch out for her, lad," he added a moment later. "I've no reason to believe she'll come for ya, of course – but I've no reason to think she won't, either."

Then he did something that I found peculiar: He began reciting a poem in Irish, his voice and diction almost singsong, the way a school boy would learn the words by rote at an early age.

"I don't follow," I said, interrupting him at the third stanza. "Caeli can handle the language all right, but I'm not there yet."

"Ach – it's all right. Just something I picked up a long time ago, from me learnin' days, is it. There's a line in there – in the Irish, *Sa tír seo trína chéile* – that translates to 'Where chaos is the heart of rule.' This whole bloody disaster just reminded me of it, somehow."

His voice trailed off, and I thought it best to change the subject.

"Caeli wants to know if her uncle's OK."

"I've no bloody idea a'tall," he said, and I could sense the sudden tension in his response. "Like the woman, he was here, and then he was gone, and we've not set eyes on him nor the others in nearly three hours now. I've got a call out to the airport to keep an eye on their jet, but it's still on the tarmac. You sure you've not seen him?"

"That's not a thing I'd hide," I said. "If Jack were here, I'd rat him out quick enough. You think he's in league with the woman?"

He paused, thinking it over.

"Lord help 'em both if true, but it's something we'll need to assess if and when the archbishop turns up, or doesn't. God a'mighty – what a mess."

I got the long pause again and waited him out.

"If he shows up out yer way," he finally said, "give us a ring, eh – especially if he brings the woman in tow. Then again, maybe they'll kill each other off – two less things to worry about."

"I'll be sure to pass that on to Caeli."

"Bollox. Thinkin' aloud is all," he said quickly. "Just let me know if he wheels himself into yer orbit."

"Sure, though I can't imagine what would draw him out here."

"Beyond seeing his niece, ya mean, or the idea the spot yer now standin' in was used at one time to store his guns for the grand revolution? – somethin' else we'll have to check on."

"You think he wants to start another uprising?"

"I wouldn't put it past the old goat," Gallacher said – and just like that, he let it go. "Yer sure the lot of ya are all right?"

"Yeah. We're good. We're available for your people whenever you're ready. I'm sure you'll want a debrief."

"Not me so much, but yeah. You'll get plenty of questions because of the kids," he said. "It'll be some time, though. We're still securin' the grounds here, lookin' for Kathleen, makin' sure we haven't missed anything else."

He paused, sucking in air in a hesitant manner that I could detect through the wireless connection and across the miles, and I pictured him as weary but content, anxious but fulfilled nonetheless.

"She's a clever woman, our Kathleen," he said at last. "And she damn near pulled this off. Had it not been for the two of ya and a few lucky breaks along the way ..."

"No such thing as luck," I told him. "You were a terrier, and your efforts paid off for all of Ireland."

"Kind of ya to say, Professor Blake, but we both know better. My dawdlin' damn near ruined us. And now, with both the redhead and McMahon in the bloody wind, I'll be after catchin' all manner of shite from the front office. Might be time to dust off my CV after all."

"You'll look good in my report, at least," I said. "That much I can promise."

He laughed and hung up after once again issuing a stern reminder of necessary diligence. I relayed the information that he'd shared with Caeli, Elmore and Leonard, and Spud Phelan only after the children were returned to their school bus, a fresh chauffeur was secured, and an ambulance arrived to take the battered driver off for a medical check.

Six police vehicles, with lights flashing, along with a parade of parents and staff, accompanied the bus as it left the site.

"So yer off to yer place then," Spud said.

"Sure. Care to join us?" I said.

"If it's not too much trouble," he said. "I've actually been asked to tag along 'til DCI McNeill can make it out for the talk-through – keep an eye on things, ya know. But I don't want to impose on ya – truly."

"So they're sending you to spy on us until the big guns arrive," Caeli said.

"Something like that. I don't know what they think you'd do if I wasn't around, but I'm happy enough to keep ya company if yer good with it."

"At least you're honest about it," she said.

"Wouldn't occur to me to be anything but."

Our return to the estate seemed overly long. We remained on high alert, vigilantly watching Phelan's tailing Mini Cooper along with everything else on the road – especially approaching vehicles. Leonard insisted on driving, and he kept his pistol in his lap, as did Elmore, who was riding in the front passenger seat. I had the feeling that Leonard, at least, was expecting an attack at any second, similar to the one we'd experienced the previous day. He seemed edgy, and he didn't respond to the comments or a couple of questions directed his way.

But we'd seen this sort of behavior previously, many times over, and I wrote it off to his general dislike of Ireland, along with being called in to once again help us. I was in a celebratory mood, after all, looking forward to easier days ahead, which got me thinking about the wedding, which in turn got me thinking about Caeli and what a treasure she is and my own good fortune. I reached out and took her hand and smiled at her, a smile that she returned, and I was certain that we'd put the dark encounters of the past several days behind us.

The miles slipped by without incident, either because of or despite our attentiveness, and we soon gathered at our kitchen counter. I put on a fresh pot of coffee and offered up whatever goodies I could find, including the cookies that Caeli had pulled from the freezer to take on our aborted dash to Bunratty, just before her uncle arrived and altered our plans. I figured that we could unwind before McNeill showed up for the mandatory police debriefing, after which we'd make dinner for our guests – salmon and chops came to mind – and I began foraging through the freezer to see what was available.

Caeli must have been thinking along similar lines because she swept in to help, and we soon had the necessary ingredients for a superb meal set aside.

I noticed after several minutes that Leonard wasn't around and asked Elmore where he'd gone.

"He's on the roof," he said casually.

"Why? It's over," I said. "The good guys won, and all is right with the world – at least until it's not again, which I trust will be a long way off and far away from our little corner of Ireland."

Elmore shook his head, a subtle chiding.

"No, Professor B – wishful thinking," he said. "McMahon escaped in a boat. What's to keep him from paddling it straight down the river and showing up here? Besides, the woman's still on the loose, and so are the punks Leonard caught – the ones that killed the cops. There's a whole bunch we don't know and no reason to relax until … well, 'til we know more than we do right now."

His logic was sound enough, to be sure, but I wasn't buying in. I'd mentally shelved the entire episode – the Bunratty thefts, Joan Shedd's murder, the terrorist threat, the road attacks, the bizarre encounter at Raven's Ridge – and did little more than thank Elmore for his good cheer and friendship and continued attention to detail and our safety. I'll also confess that I was in a party mood, and I even offered to get him a beer, along with Caeli and Spud, and was thinking about whether I wanted a Guinness or a Beamish, trusting that we had both on hand.

I hadn't quite made it to the spare refrigerator when Elmore's phone crackled to life. He answered it with a quick swipe, grunted something unintelligible after a moment passed, then waved at us with a deep concern fully registering on his face.

This, too, was a look that I knew well.

"That was Leonard. A boat just tucked in along the river, a couple of hundred yards to the west," he said, pointing before securing his phone.

I was stunned. Hell, we all were.

"So he's come to finish it then," I muttered.

"No – it's not McMahon. It's the woman ... Kathleen whatever her name is."

She approached from the river in a low crouch, perhaps unaware that she'd already been spotted, or that we already were watching her every movement from the vantage point of our covered and extended porch overlooking the river, or that Leonard had her in the crosshairs of his sniper's rifle from his lair on the rooftop of the estate.

Then again, you never know with an adversary like Kathleen MacAmhlaoibh.

One thing was certain: She was no longer the old shopper wearing shabby church clothing and a gray wig and dowdy hat. Her hair, trimmed in a cut that reminded me of Louise Brooks in her cinematic heyday, was flaming red, just as her eyes shone like sparkling emeralds through the lenses of the binoculars that I'd zeroed in to follow her approach. She wore dark jeans, a hooded pullover that was slate grey, and black hiking boots. She carried two SIG Sauer pistols, one in each hand, and she wore a backpack that looked as though it was stuffed with ... *something*.

Something unpleasant, I recall thinking.

She also had a patch of dark red on the outside of her left thigh, which reminded me of Gallacher's comment that she'd been wounded before showing up at the castle. It accounted for the slightest of hitches in her step, though her face gave no indication that she was in pain as she moved along, glancing back over her shoulder at least twice ...

... as though looking for something ... or someone ...

I was packing the Beretta 92 that was on loan from Liam Gallacher. Caeli had retrieved the shotgun that we kept at the estate for emergencies, and she'd given Spud Phelan her own Beretta-on-loan so that he, too, would be armed – just in case.

If he was surprised that we had so many weapons on hand, he didn't mention it or react in any way.

Elmore had cautioned us to be careful before he ducked into the garage so that he could monitor the opposite end of the estate in the event that a secondary attack featuring McMahon, little Michaleen and his river cretins, or their assorted minions approached from the road.

"Keep your heads down and your phones on," he'd said and scurried away.

I'd made certain that we had adequate cover on the porch before producing the binoculars. What I saw provided no assurance that our trials were over, and I whispered a "Hey" and passed Caeli the lenses so that she could get a better look.

"What do you think?" I asked.

"She means business," she whispered. "Something's in that backpack – ammo or guns, maybe … or worse."

"But she can't think it'll be this easy," I said, thinking aloud. "She can't just waltz in and do whatever she wants."

Caeli's response rang so true that I recall thinking, for just an instant, that she was absolutely correct. But it also occurred to me that perhaps we were in over our heads – just as we'd been warned.

"Maybe it's not her first trip here," Caeli said. "Maybe she's been back and forth a dozen times."

As scary as that sounded, and it was chilling, what MacAmhlaoibh did next was even more frightening. She abruptly stopped and smiled at us, as though she had accessed a window into our soul and knew that we were watching.

She's known that we've been following her all along …

I recall ducking, though I understood there was no way that she could see any of us from where she stood. I also vividly recall uttering a solitary expletive, the kind of word Americans have come to expect from their current president.

What I didn't anticipate was Leonard's reaction.

Then again, neither did the smiling terrorist.

"Take another step and it'll be your last," he yelled, as clearly as a ringing church bell summoning the faithful ahead of Sunday service.

But she didn't give much away beyond a glint of annoyance in her eyes, at least not outwardly. She had the foresight to keep her hands, and the pistols that she carried, fully extended downward, at least momentarily. I could envision her raising them in a sudden explosion of violence and fury and blasting away, but I doubted that she knew exactly where Leonard was stationed. She continued staring at the porch where Caeli, Spud, and I were ensconced, her face now twisted in anger.

Incredibly, she remained stationary.

"Drop the guns – then raise your hands," Leonard hollered. "Do it now."

I was tempted to text Elmore and fill him in on what was taking place. But his caution resonated: The woman's appearance might be little more than a diversion, with our bodyguard the only line of defense from a road attack. That, of course, posed a second dilemma: Should I send him reinforcements – Spud, perhaps? Or should I let Elmore hold the line himself while the rest of us faced what was an obvious threat, even if we seemed to hold the upper hand at least momentarily?

"What do you think?" I whispered to Caeli, the second time I'd muttered the same question.

She didn't respond, nor did our uninvited visitor. The terrorist remained in place, guns in hand, eyes fastened to the porch that was perhaps 40 yards from her current position, searching for the unseen enemy … *searching for us.*

We were startled by the sudden crash of gunfire from Leonard's sniper rifle, two rounds fired in quick succession, which kicked up dirt at the woman's feet. I jumped at the sound, and I'm fairly certain that Caeli did as well – an involuntary flinch as the shots registered, as you often see bystanders react during a 21-gun salute.

I was amazed that the redhead was rooted in place, unmoving and unbending except for her eyes, which now drifted up to the top of the estate, trying to locate the threat.

She flashed a smile, just for an instant, and made a show of spreading her arms perhaps a foot from her body before dropping the SIGs. But as our eyes remained with the downward arc of the abandoned pistols, her right hand snaked to her belt and grabbed a dead-man's switch that apparently had been within easy reach. Her fingers latched around the device, with her thumb settling over the red button that adorned the top like a cherry on a sundae.

"Stalemate," she yelled. "I've wired the place with explosives, just like what's in the rucksack. One slip and the whole bloody place blows."

A deathly quiet settled over the estate. Even the birds were stilled.

Kathleen grinned as she held the switch aloft.

I glanced past Caeli, who remained transfixed on the woman, and hissed at Spud, trying to get his attention. When my initial effort didn't register, I tried again, calling his name this time to break whatever spell he, too, was under.

"Spud. Hey – Spud."

He glanced over, his eyes wide.

"Call your people. Let 'em know what's going on – tell 'em to get out here right away," I whispered. "Then call Gallacher."

"Gallacher? I don't have his bloody number," he said.

I reached inside my pocket, found the phone that the spy lord's driver gave me while we were in the restaurant in Limerick, and tossed it over.

"Speed dial one," I said. "Go check on Elmore. Make the calls on the way."

When he continued to stare at me, waiting for more, I gave him one more prompt.

"Move it, Spud. Now."

He nodded then and crab-walked awkwardly toward the side door, repeatedly glancing over his shoulder, mindful to keep his head down.

I noticed that Caeli was working her phone, sending out a text message.

"Elmore?"

"No – Leonard," she said while her fingers worked the keypad.

I focused again on the terrorist once Spud was through the door.

"Stalemate, hell," I muttered.

I was determined to fix the situation, figuring that Leonard would be eager to take the shot, which would eliminate our chance to get at a dozen questions – chief among whether she'd actually killed Joan Shedd, as McMahon had told us. I also didn't want to witness an angry Caeli confronting the redhead because no one could say what other devices or tricks the woman might pull from thin air. And I understood intuitively that I couldn't count on Elmore, who was guarding our back, nor Spud.

I was about to call out to the woman when Caeli latched onto my arm with surprising force.

"I've got this, Max," she said, calmly and efficiently.

She rose from her hiding spot with a confidence that was considerable given the circumstances and pocketed her phone – before I could register a protest. The best I could do was to jump up and stand with her, locking the Beretta on target.

"Hey," Caeli called. "Over here."

Kathleen's eyes shifted from the roofline, which she'd been assiduously studying, and she smiled in recognition when she spotted Caeli, ignoring me entirely.

"Ah, there ye are – just as the archbishop described ya, long ago," she yelled. "I'd say it's a pleasure to meet at last – but then, that'd be a lie."

"I'd say you've been lying about a great many things," Caeli called back. "That switch in your hand, for instance."

Kathleen smiled, but she remained focused.

"And what would ye know about me a'tall then? Surely yer sainted uncle wasn't after tellin' tales out of school? Or is it out of church?"

"I know a liar well enough," Caeli said. "I also know a bluff when I hear one."

"A bluff, is it? Nae – it's all real enough, ya silly cow," Kathleen said. "So here's how it plays out, now that you've come home ahead of schedule to interrupt me plans. I walk away, back to the river, while the lot of ye get out of the house, if ya like. Or not. Your call, as the Yanks might say. I'll still blow the place, mind ya, along with yer man on the roof. Too bad he can't get off his perch, but who'd stay in place to maintain the standoff? Still, I'm givin' the rest of ya the chance to get out, seein' as me own life's under threat an' I've still much to do. But after that, well then, the two of us can settle up, eh? – though at another time, another place. It's somethin' I look forward to – the only reason I'll let ya walk away now."

Geez. She's crazier than McMahon, I thought.

"Sorry," Caeli said. "It's not going to happen."

She glanced at me for an instant and smiled before calling out to our sniper.

"Go, Leonard."

A single gunshot shattered the silence, and the dead-man's switch that Kathleen held up as a threat disintegrated from the force of the well-placed round from Leonard's rifle. As she clasped her now-bleeding hand to her body, enfolding it with her free arm, she sank to her knees and screamed, no doubt realizing that her revolutionary dreams, like her mentor's before her, were lost with a crash from a single bullet.

I bounded off the porch, racing ahead despite the risk, certain that she needed to be stopped before she could reach for the two SIGs and begin shooting: at Caeli, at Leonard, at anything that moved.

I never considered that she might fire at me.

I also figured that the shock of what had just happened had taken the fight out of her – a decided mistake.

As I approached her inert form, which seemed to be huddled into a ball, my eyes were focused primarily on the pistols that she'd abandoned at Leonard's first call-out. I kicked the closest one away and was headed for the second when she lashed out, spinning sideways with a gymnast's move and extending a leg in a sweeping motion that caught my left ankle. It hurt like hell and damn near took me down, but I managed to pivot with my right leg and turn away, catching my balance in the process, although that was due as much to luck as skill.

I also think that the wound in her leg took some of the snap out of the kick she'd delivered, which also worked in my favor.

Momentum swept me a few feet away from her position, which turned out to be a good thing for a couple of reasons. She couldn't follow up with a second leg-kick – a true plus, given the pain that already was shooting through my ankle – and Leonard fired a shot at the abandoned pistol closest to her, hitting it directly on the slide and sending parts of it flying into the air. He repeated the feat an instant later with the second pistol, the one I'd originally kicked aside, and then drilled two additional rounds into the ground no more than a foot from Kathleen's leg.

"The next one's in your ear," he yelled. "Try me."

I stared up at the roof where Leonard was stationed. He was lining up the shot through the rifle's telescopic sight, unwavering. Why he didn't shoot her when she first kicked out at me is a mystery that only Leonard can answer. It's also one that I'll never ask him because … well, I can hear his answer, even now:

"What? Stop her from giving you an ass-whooping, Blake? Yeah, right."

When I glanced away from Leonard, Caeli was standing immediately behind me, her shotgun trained on the emerald-eyed terrorist. I can't say that I've ever seen her look more beautiful.

Seconds later, or perhaps it was hours, we could hear the steady bleating of police sirens, whooping their mournful cry in the distance.

DCI Thomas McNeill, accompanied by a dozen well-armed and well-armored coppers, personally slapped the cuffs on our captured terrorist inside a minute of his arrival. Steered to the scene by Elmore, he didn't ask us a single question, nor even inquire if everyone was all right. I can't recall that he uttered a single word.

That's likely a good thing. I was still holding the Beretta while Caeli retained a firm grasp on the shotgun. Leonard remained on the roof with the sniper's rifle in hand, his cheek pressed to the stock, his right eye fixed on the telescopic sight. Spud Phelan, thinking quickly when his boss arrived up, abandoned Caeli's Beretta on the porch and hurried over to help. McNeill acknowledged his presence with a nod before pulling the redhead to her feet. Spud gingerly removed the woman's backpack and issued a verbal caution, the Irish equivalent of reading her rights, and three members of McNeill's team quickly marched her away.

Surprisingly, she hadn't uttered a sound, although she continued to glance over her shoulder at times, as though expecting a rescue from the river – one that somehow never came.

When Spud peeked inside the liberated backpack, he gasped audibly and held it open so that we could take a look.

"C-4," Caeli observed, and she somehow remained calm, which is more than I can say for my own reaction to the sight of what amounted, we learned later, to more than 10 pounds of the explosive. "Pretty much a worst-case scenario."

Elmore whistled to us from a spot along the porch foundation.

"Plenty more of it here," he called. "She wasn't lying after all. How'd she get all this stuff in here, do ya think?"

"We haven't exactly been around much the past few days," Caeli said.

"It's yet another reason they messed with the security system," I added, though needlessly.

Liam Gallacher showed up minutes later, accompanied by Danny O'Herlihy and the ever-present Ian and Gavin. He'd already called in the bomb techs and advised us to stay well clear until the entire estate was swept for explosives.

"Get yerself a place for a day or three, though not in Bunratty," he said, and I'm sure that it was this suggestion that kept Caeli's mind off her uncle's whereabouts for the next couple of hours, anyway.

"Nonsense," she said. "That woman isn't going to run me out of my house – not with the wedding so close."

"Hey – ya never know who might turn up next out this way. Remember that yer pal McMahon's still on the lam."

Caeli was adamant.

"No – not gonna happen," she said. "I won't drag the cats out again. We've lost enough time to this madness."

They argued back and forth for a couple of minutes before Gallacher conceded and called in four additional bomb teams, flying them in from Dublin after I suggested that we'd happily pay all expenses, including the cost of the flight.

Even then Gallacher wasn't through with us.

"Damn lucky ye spotted her when ya did," he said. "She might well 've brought the whole place down on yer heads, which would've ruined me plans for the lot of ya."

"Plans? What plans?" Caeli and I said in near unison.

"Turnin' ya into national heroes, of course. What else?"

"Absolutely not," Caeli said. "The less said about what's happened here, and our role in it, the better. Our wedding is days away."

Gallacher laughed.

"Ya don't understand, Miss Brown. Mention of Kathleen would only bring up talk of yer supposedly dead uncle, and we can't have that – can we now? No, I've somethin' else entirely in mind for the pair of ya in the days ahead."

I'll say this about the days that occupied our time ahead of the wedding: Getting a handle on the terrorist plot that sucked us into an exasperating vortex was like picking up sand at the beach. The more grains we grabbed, the more it seemed that they slipped through our fingers and eventually ran back into the vast and unforgiving ocean.

EPILOGUE

A DIARY OF DELIGHTS

Newspaper stories and television reports were filled with at least parts of the story in the weeks that followed the events recounted here.

Typically, they concentrated on the singular item guaranteed to reel in readers and viewers alike: the rescue of the children at the remote spot on the River Shannon, far to the west of Limerick, that everyone was now calling Raven's Ridge.

Thanks to Liam Gallacher, who understands media manipulation as well as anyone I've encountered in law enforcement or the spy game, Caeli and I became folk heroes of a sort – the kind who willingly stepped into harm's way to save a school bus packed with youngsters who'd been kidnapped by an "unknown offender with an unknown agenda."

As my journalism students used to say, "Yeah, well, whatever."

But it's hard to ignore the raw power that modern media exert, even when your natural instinct is to change channels or switch off the power or cancel your subscription.

The radio and TV broadcasts that first evening and well through the following week, along with the newspaper headlines both in print and on the internet, didn't follow my suggested script, which was to say nothing at all of our involvement in the children's rescue and even less about our role in helping to ferret out the Bunratty terrorist attack.

But hell, we had no control over the way that Gallacher let it play out. He had his reasons, apparently, and all he did was grin at us when we asked him, politely at first and then with more energy, to knock it off.

"Ex-reporters should know what it feels like on the other side o' things," he said.

It was all malarkey, of course. But what can you do when malarkey is presented as fact and then swallowed whole?

"You've no idea what a well-timed story can do to change the manner of things," Gallacher told us after the initial onslaught of stories. "Then again, given yer background, maybe ya do."

Speaking of stories, we'd been disappointed in the lack of global coverage of the four terrorist incidents that we knew about – in Paris, Tokyo, New York, and of course the west of Ireland. It was as though nobody wanted to talk about what had taken place, even locally, as the reports close to home concentrated primarily on the rescue of the kidnapped youngsters rather than the events that had shut down the Castle. We saw next to nothing from the other hotspots. It wasn't a cover-up, exactly, but it wasn't an outpouring of unbridled truth, either.

But Caeli's persistence in reading the news paid off days later when she spotted a small item in the *International Herald Tribune*, which is edited and printed in Paris.

"Check it out," she said, turning the laptop so that I'd get a better view. "Looks like portions of the unthinkable cat are starting to emerge from the bag."

The story, seven paragraphs in all, described an Interpol operation that resulted in the capture of an extortion ring tied to a terrorist plot to blow up the Eiffel Tower unless a substantial ransom was paid.

Credited with assisting in capturing Jean-Claude Daimallier and a cadre of hired help were officials with the Paris Police Prefecture, the *Direction générale de la sécurité extérieure* (France's external intelligence agency, a CIA equivalent), and select members of the *Commandement de la force d'action terrestre* (the Land Forces Action Command, a Seals/Rangers-style fighting force).

There was no mention of similar plots in New York City, Tokyo, or Bunratty, although the story quoted an unnamed source as saying that the threat was thought to have been wider than what was uncovered in France.

"How can they miss the connection?" I wondered aloud.

"How can the local media mostly ignore what happened at Bunratty, even with the blockades and police cars driving through the streets, warning tourists to stay away? Then again, given the clampdown on what's actually released, I'm amazed that anyone got this much," she said.

A few days later, National School officials invited us out for a celebratory thank-you moment, an enjoyable if unnecessary touch. Parents and grandparents of the kidnapped students gathered for the brief ceremony, joining teachers and children from all of grades at the school, and additional media coverage resulted. Caeli offered brief remarks, speaking in Irish as well as English, and we shook hands and smiled a great deal as the heartfelt cheers of dozens of people poured in, especially when five of the shanghaied youngsters joined their recovering bus driver in singing an Irish ballad to praise our efforts.

"I feel like a fraud," I muttered.

"You're an honest fraud, Max," Caeli said.

I don't pretend to understand all of what took place during that time – not in and around Limerick and Bunratty, and certainly not in the other global points of interest. My efforts to obtain documents and details were rebuffed many times over, as were the official requests of dozens of working journalists from around the globe, we later learned, who tried valiantly to pull back the veil of secrecy and get at the truth.

I can offer with certainty that the terrorist plots, and the planning that put them into motion, were triggered more by money than by dogma. When captured, Frog One was little more than a common crook, albeit a stoic one. Gallacher's people could find no ideological connection between the Frenchman and Kathleen MacAmhlaoibh.

Perhaps their union, like the one she'd apparently maintained with Lance Corporal McMahon, also was driven by lust.

Rumors, steady yet unconfirmed to this day, persist that similar plots in Spain and in Mexico City also were foiled in or around the same time, but journalists have yet to connect the dots – and again, no one in officialdom is talking.

It may be that the American president's relentless attacks on traditional media as a strategy to lather up his snarling horde of yapping supporters has started to wear down the Fourth Estate to the point that it no longer functions with the same zeal and commitment that it once did, in saner times. But that's speculation and applicable only to what's reported in the USA.

Gallacher and I spent a great deal of time talking about what I could mention in this report regarding the involvement of his team. The given names of at least some of his taskforce members, for example, were altered to comply with Irish national security and secrecy laws, and specific details about how the Bunratty takedown was accomplished have been omitted. Politicians and lawyers eventually got involved, slicing pounds of facts from the text while extending the length of the discussions to fatten their own wallets.

I eventually called a halt to the back-and-forth and told one smug law-degreed member of the *Oireachtas* that I was done talking and, further, was done editing to satisfy him and his equally smug cronies. When he protested vehemently that he'd not yet begin to parse, I served up a typically American phrase that at least allowed me to find the door:

"So sue me, bozo. And note: That's bozo, with a zed, not boyo, with a y."

I dutifully check the mail when it arrives each day, waiting for legal documents demanding my head or other applicable parts of my anatomy. My own attorney, Michael J. Parker, is salivating.

We weren't exactly enthusiastic about the resolution to our involvement in the Bunratty/Raven's Ridge mess. Joan Shedd was dead, after all; Lance Corporal whatever his first name was McMahon remained on the lam, so far as we knew; and Kathleen MacAmhlaoibh had been whisked away with no explanation of what her end game at Bunratty was supposed to be or why she'd seemed so obsessed with meddling in our lives.

Gallacher, for his part, has refused to confirm whether the green-eyed terrorist actually killed Mrs. Shedd, nor will he reveal her current fate, contending that – as with most everything else connected with the events that we experienced – it all falls within matters of national security. He did, however, confirm that she was responsible for the deaths of DCI Declan Abbot and DS Sean Mahoney. He also was fairly certain that Mahoney, along with the already-outed Aedan O'Duinn, was involved in the plot in some as-yet undetermined way.

O'Duinn, at least, was in it for the money, we were told.

"The mop-up operation at Bunratty netted a half-dozen tossers in all," Gallacher said in the aftermath. "But I've a feelin' that more 'n a few got away clean, and likely the most committed of the lot – the ones who'd take cyanide rather than be caught and forced to talk."

"Like little Michaleen and his crew from the river that Leonard nabbed," I said.

"Exactly, along with the lads who broke 'em out of the paddy wagon and killed Abbot and one of their own – for reasons we'll likely never know. They're out there somewhere, god knows," he said. "Still, we did our best."

That's an assessment of probabilities, of course, though I'll grudgingly admit that it was the best we could hope for under trying circumstances and certainly better than some of the scenarios we'd envisioned, especially after Caeli's uncle arrived.

More on Jack in a minute.

When I asked Caeli, by the way, what she'd texted to Leonard when he was stationed atop our roof in the sniper's lair, she pulled out her phone, scrolled through her messages, and showed me.

Don't kill her. We need answers. Kill the device.

Leonard didn't bother replying.

One surprise that's worth reporting: At least some of the jewelry that McMahon took during the weeks preceding the planned attack at Bunratty was left in the school bus, including items belonging to Joan Shedd and to Spud Phelan's aunt and mother. The one-time British Army sniper actually attached a note that was found inside the jeweler's sack he left on the driver's seat.

I believe you were looking for these baubles, boyo.

We'll square up later. Count on it.

Caeli logically wondered how he'd reacquired the items that were stolen from Mrs. Shedd if Kathleen MacAmhlaoibh had truly been responsible for killing her friend, but I suspect that it's a question we'll never be able to answer with certainty.

Elmore's computer tech buddy from faraway Oregon arrived late on the day after our Raven's Ridge adventure ended and was hustled out to the estate by our bodyguard, who was anxious to talk shop about the massive project ahead of them.

In all, it took four days to sort through the elaborate system of traps and viruses that Gallacher's man Aedan O'Duinn wriggled into our security setup and another full day of counter-measures to ensure that nothing similar would happen again. Elmore also showed me how to turn off the voice-activated recording device that Don Vincenzo had installed at the estate. At Caeli's insistence, it's shut down for now.

We didn't see much of either Elmore or his pal during that period, though we all had other tasks occupying our time.

We didn't see Leonard, either. He took a commercial flight out of Shannon International on the same day that the computer geek arrived.

"Screw it," he said. "I hate Ireland — absolutely hate coming back here."

"But we'll see you in a couple of weeks — right?" Caeli asked.

When he looked puzzled, she added, "You know … for the wedding."

"Sure you will. Can't wait," he lied.

Elmore told us later that Leonard's shoulder wound, sustained while he was protecting us during his previous visit to Ireland, during the *Emerald Ridge* affair, was not fully healed and continued to trouble him.

"That doesn't account for all of the way he acts — you know how he is," he said. "But maybe it explains some of it."

Uncle Jack and his retinue of traveling Magi turned up an hour or so after Kathleen MacAmhlaoibh was arrested and hauled away to her fate, putting to rest Liam Gallacher's concerns that the former archbishop had somehow reverted to his revolutionary ways. But our papal visitors quickly disappeared into Limerick proper without expressing much interest in what had just happened at our estate or providing an explanation of their sudden absence from the fight at Bunratty. Jack said they were tired after the battle and had booked rooms for the evening at a modest downtown hotel because he didn't want to put us out, and that was that.

I suspect that he feared being told by Caeli to take a hike had he asked her for an overnight accommodation, but that's mere speculation.

The four priests didn't hang around for long, either, and were on a flight out of Shannon on the same day that Leonard left us. I'd like to say that their visit was fulfilling in some way, but that would stretch the truth.

We didn't learn until we met them at the airport to see them off that Father Rottach had been knifed during a nasty scuffle with one of the terrorists recruited by MacAmhlaoibh and McMahon in the early going of the Bunratty siege, shortly before he and his fellow priests mysteriously disappeared.

"Ah, it's but a scratch," Jack explained when we asked about the extensive bandaging that covered the priest's forearm, none of which we'd seen the previous evening. "Only two dozen stitches or more, it 'tis, which is hardly worth the price of admission to a good fight."

"Is that why Gallacher couldn't find you?" I asked. "You were at the hospital getting your man put back together?"

"Not a'tall," he said. "Father Shannon is quite skilled at field dressings."

"They couldn't find you? How come? Where were you?" Caeli asked – and full confession here, I hadn't told her of Jack's absence or Gallacher's concerns because, well, why toss that pipe bomb onto the road?

"It was nothing a'tall – just that we had many things to tend to," he replied quickly, looking away.

His cryptic reply made me nervous, and I changed the topic for Caeli's sake.

"Still trying to save the world then, Jack?" I asked him.

"The world? No – just me own little corner of it. I'm merely tryin' to make up for the past year and the horrible mess I made of things for the two of ya," he said. "All I can tell ye is ya won't have to worry about that lot – ever again."

Geez ... what the hell does that mean? I recall thinking.

But I never got the chance to press him. He nodded at me, gave Caeli an awkward hug, and called out to her in Irish as he climbed the steps leading into the waiting *Alitalia*-run private jet. I asked her later what he'd said, but she just shook her head.

We didn't know what to make of Gallacher's late-night phone call a few days later when he told us that a 14-foot inflatable boat with an outboard motor attached had been discovered on the rocks near Barley Harbour, close to Shannon International.

The location was due north of the spot that Lance Corporal McMahon had christened Raven's Ridge, almost directly across the wide expanse of the River Shannon.

"We think it's the one yer man used to make his escape once he set the kids free," Gallacher said. "No way of knowin' for sure, of course, as the two of ya never got a look at the bloody thing. We'll ask the youngsters he tugged along as a shield, but it's unlikely they'll be of any help. Still, we think it's his well enough."

"So he traveled close to the airport and had a car waiting. Or maybe he caught a plane, or even a cab or a bus," Caeli said. "Makes sense if you're looking to disappear in a hurry."

"It's a good bet, sure. We're rechecking the CCTV footage, of course, along with taxi and bus logs and records from the car rental operations," Gallacher said. "I don't hold out much hope, but ya never know."

He paused, and you could sense that something was troubling him.

"Go ahead, Liam," Caeli offered. "Let's have the rest of it."

"Ah, ya see, there's one bit that has us flummoxed," he said. "We turned up a bullet hole in the motor and a decent tear in the skin of the raft. I find that most peculiar."

"Why?" I asked. "It would make sense to sink the boat once he got ashore."

"True – no craft bobbin' about means no questions from those that might see it," he said. "But why put a bullet in the motor? And why one so destructive – far beyond what a round from a handgun would produce, even up close? It makes no sense – unless, of course, he was carryin' a rifle. Was he carryin' a rifle when he left yer sight?"

"No."

"Yeah. I thought not."

"What are you thinking – or suspecting?" Caeli asked.

"I don't know what to think," he said. "All I can offer is we've had no sightings since McMahon buggered off, despite the alerts. I find that most peculiar, too."

The wedding was fast approaching, and the nonsense with media coverage of the National School rescue was ratcheting up daily, it seemed, and I forgot about the conversation in all of the hub-bub.

It didn't occur to me until much later, in fact, that Gallacher was likely correct: A bullet hole through the 18-horsepower Tohatsu outboard that powered the inflatable made no sense.

It was something that warranted additional attention.

We gave the insurance claim for securing clan Phelan's stolen heirlooms to the family of the G2 agent who was killed during the investigation, a tragedy that had hit Liam Gallacher particularly hard. We quietly added a substantial amount to the sum so that the man's two children would be assured of a college education.

We also welcomed Joan Shedd's offspring to Ireland after Gallacher's people finally broke through the perplexing diplomatic impasse and got word to them about what had happened. We met them at the airport and took them on a tour around Bunratty, talking about their mother and the role that she played in helping to bring down the terrorist organization. We didn't embellish the story in any way, nor did we need to, and I think that our words of comfort, Caeli's in particular, were appreciated.

They left the following morning after Gallacher helped with the paperwork and made a surprise appearance to personally thank them for their mother's contributions toward keeping all of Ireland safe.

He provided one other fitting touch. Before the casket was loaded onto an *Aer Lingus* jet, a crack team of Irish cadets performed the near-silent military funeral ritual known as the Queen Anne, the same somber but stunningly beautiful rifle drill that a similar Irish team performed at JFK's service almost 55 years previous.

Then as now, everyone who witnessed the ceremony shed a tear – even Liam Gallacher. To cover his emotions, he asked if we'd ever heard of pyrotol. We didn't make the connection to the Bath schools disaster until days later.

DS Alan Phelan was among the first to arrive on the day of our wedding. He brought with him, as promised, two women: his mother, and his aunt from America. He proudly escorted them around the estate, introducing them, along with himself, to everyone he didn't know – and he knew, or at least knew of, a great many people who were there.

A half-dozen of his fellow Guards arrived in uniform to provide extra security in case Lance Corporal McMahon decided to make an appearance – silent sentries to our celebration.

Spud's cousins, in-laws, and no doubt a few outlaws as well did a bang-up job on the wedding details, supplying copious amounts of food and drink, ensuring that no one went hungry or thirsty and that everyone had a grand time of it. We remain in their debt.

The priest he supplied, another relation on his mother's side, was a handsome man in his early 70s, I'd guess, with an easy smile and warm words, most of which were delivered in Irish, including during the actual ceremony. He enjoyed himself afterward, dancing along with his relatives, and he took a moment during a lull to sit at the piano and offer a tune to the bride and groom. He wasn't the last person to leave that night, but he was among them.

Caeli's vows, which she'd written the night before, were conveyed in the old language. Mine, consisting of three sentences, were in English, though I offered a coda in Italian that Caeli, at least, understood. The details aren't important, other than to the two of us. But the heartfelt applause we received, and the smile on Caeli's face at the end, was worth the long wait to get there.

Her dress was white, though tinged with a blue that was the color of the Irish Sea. Her ring was Claddagh with added diamonds, a creation I'd sketched on paper and turned over to yet another of Spud's many connections. How he pulled it off in two short weeks is beyond me.

A small silver horseshoe with a dozen tiny silver bells, Caeli's most treasured possession – one that was handed down from relatives on her mother's side, years before – was tucked into her bouquet.

Caeli insisted on outfitting me in a stylish tux and told me that I looked rakish – "a modern-day pirate" were her exact words. I stuck with the get-up through the short service and greeting line but soon swapped it out for Dockers and a sweater vest over a blue polo shirt, which far better suited my comfort level.

Despite our admonitions for no gifts, Spud gave us a proper teakettle, made in Ireland.

Liam Gallacher, who attended with a handful of his trusted G2 compatriots, Danny and Ian and Gavin among them, gave us two gifts. The first also was a teakettle, although it had a British stamp. I don't know what to make of that, exactly, but I pass it along. The second was a matched pair of Walther P99s with extra magazines, several boxes of ammo, and signed permits to legally carry them during the course of our official duties as Interpol agents working in Ireland.

Yeah. Go figure.

Leonard returned for the event, along with Elmore and Don Fredo, of course, sweeping in on the big corporate jet. They brought with them a contingent of our American friends: Floyd and Barbara Strand; Michael J. Parker and his stylish secretary, Effie Smith; Bill and Skyla Kohlmeyer, of course; Troutdale neighbors Nora, Laura, Martin, Rich, Darcy, and Peyton; former Salem neighbors Julie and Kimmi; newspaper pals Steve Jackson, Jay Silverbird, and David Doucette; Jerry Berger, the longtime president of the college where I taught journalism for so many years, and his wife, Victoria; Terry Rohse, another longtime college pal; and John and Bonnie Hawkins, dear friends who worked at the college during my tenure, although I'd first met John when he was a fellow reporter at an Oregon daily, years earlier.

A number of our Irish acquaintances also accepted invitations.

The *ceili* band was terrific and kept most everyone on their feet for hours – except, of course, for Leonard, who was having none of it. Spud was a big hit here as well, laughing and singing and providing instructions and telling jokes and drinking copious amounts of alcoholic beverages for far longer than I could ever manage, or even keep track of, given all the craziness and all the love that surrounded us on that day.

There was more, of course, but those memories are our own.

Let's just say that we danced, well into the wee morning hours.

POST SCRIPT

AROUND WE GO

It was only as I was completing the initial draft detailing the events that occupied our time during the Raven's Ridge affair that I remembered Liam Gallacher's late-night telephone call regarding the inflatable boat that had washed up on the rocks at Barley Harbour.

The story he relayed had a bad stink then, and the details continued to smell fishy, weeks after our wedding. I'd too easily dismissed what had sounded like faint gunshots on the afternoon that Lance Corporal McMahon kidnapped the busload of youngsters to use as leverage during his escape. But that was before I knew about the inflatable with the bullet-shattered outboard motor and began connecting the dots during our two-month honeymoon cruise of the Greek islands.

I didn't mention my suspicions to Caeli. Instead, I spent some time trying to determine a way to contact her uncle, the one-time archbishop who was again ensconced at the Vatican's Secret Archives Building in the heart of the Italian capital after briefly forcing his way back into our lives.

For what it's worth, the church edict that required Jack and Caeli to refrain from contact was again in place, although the way that I saw things, it didn't apply to me. Still, unless you've got a direct number that jangles the cell phone in the man's pocket, reaching Jack or anyone else at the secretive archives operation is a difficult undertaking at best – deemed by many, insiders especially, as next to impossible.

Fortunately, I had a contact – someone I was able to reach after a game of cat and mouse and a bit of deception borrowed from my investigative reporter days.

Fredo Fierro's Uncle Roberto was at one time a *consigliere* for the sitting Pope. Things had gone south for him when he was supposed to provide us with assistance during our *Melia Ridge* adventure and instead sided with a bully, Father Pietro Angelus, who had designs on taking over the church treasury and proclaiming himself the new pontiff in the process. Angelus ended up in the CIA's hands, and Roberto Fierro was forced into hiding when his brother (and Fredo's father), Don Vincenzo, learned of his treachery.

But a man can't hide forever, and Roberto crawled out of the ancient woodwork shortly after his brother's death.

I took a flyer and, using a satellite phone to disguise the international dialing code for Ireland, called the main number at *Castello Fierro* in the heart of Rome and dusted off my Italian, along with my radio voice, when a butler answered on the fifth ring.

"I'm calling for His Holiness, I said, clipping each word to sound authoritative and officious. "His Excellency requires a word with Don Roberto."

A slight hesitation followed. I could almost picture the man, puzzling at the message before his brain engaged.

"I am terribly sorry, sir. Don Roberto is unavailable," he said. "I am instructed to refer all of his telephone calls to …"

"Tell him to call me at this number within the hour," I snapped, interrupting what was no doubt a well-rehearsed dismissal of all inquiries as to his master's whereabouts. I dished out the digits and added, "His Holiness does not like to be kept waiting," then cut the connection.

That ought to get his attention, I thought.

The return call came 12 minutes later.

"*Boun giorno*," he said, and there was no mistaking the voice, which oozed charm and sophistication and a certain oiliness that his years in the Vatican had polished to an exacting sheen. "*Sto riconsegnando la chiamata del Santo Padre.*"

"Or so you thought," I said, purposefully switching to English. "You are, in fact, returning my call, Don Roberto, not the Holy Father's."

"Max Blake," he said, hissing the words. "Why are you wasting my time with your nonsense?"

"There's the Bobby I know and love to despise," I said. "And before you even think about hanging up, I need a favor – one that may put you in good stead with your nephew Don Fredo."

"I don't believe you," he countered instantly. "When last you were in Rome, you ruined my reputation, both with my brother and my nephew. You also cost me my position in the church and …"

"Save it," I said. "You brought all that on yourself when you backed the wrong horse, and you damn well know it. But I might just put in a good word for you with Fredo – when the time is right, of course – if you get me a working number for Caeli's uncle, the former archbishop, at the Secret Archives Building. Failing that, you can get word to him to give me a call."

I could hear his intake of breath, which in turn led to a pause that lasted for six long seconds.

"Why would I agree to this?" he asked. "Fredo no longer mentions my name, and I do not believe you have the power to make a difference in how he views me."

"You're wrong – something you make a habit of," I said. "But I'll go you one better. Make this happen, and I'll ask Caeli to put in a word for you with the Pope. They're on a first-name basis, you know."

"So I have heard," he said, and the anger that dripped from his voice was tangible. "It does not please me, I assure you."

"So fix it – make this happen. Who knows how your fortunes can change?"

The hesitation this time lasted close to 30 seconds. I was concerned that I'd overplayed my hand, which was damn thin to begin with, and he would simply hang up. But he surprised me – something I no longer thought was possible.

"I will do what I can," he finally said. "As to the other, a word to Don Fredo or even one to His Excellency, is beyond my expectation and a thing I do not expect, nor ask for. I will do this for you because you were kind to my late brother, may he rest in peace."

He cut the connection, and I stared at the dead phone for a moment, wondering about fate and time and redemption and the quirks of the ever-whirling universe.

A day went by, and then another, and soon a week had passed and then two more and I no longer thought about when the telephone would ring again, or even if. I was too occupied with other passions as Caeli and I fell into the easy rhythm of married life: lazy afternoons on the porch overlooking the river; trips into Limerick to shop; an overnight to Dublin to catch a play at the Abbey Theatre; jaunts to Galway and Lahinch to sample Ireland's special beauty, employing the services of a local cat nanny recommended by Spud Phelan to watch Mitts and Koko during our absences. Caeli had recently bought me a Nikon D500 digital camera, and I was experimenting with a variety of lenses, determined to hone my photographic skills while working on the manuscript for *Raven's Ridge*, the very book you're now holding.

And then Jack was on the phone, 23 days after I'd spoken with Don Roberto, on a morning that unveiled gray skies and gusting winds and a lashing rain that discouraged all but the heartiest adventurers from braving the elements. That short list included Caeli, who was at the cat groomer's, giving Mitts the full treatment, while I was running some recent pictures of a glorious sunset over the River Shannon through the latest photo-editing software program when the call came through.

It wasn't Don Roberto passing along a phone number, however.

It was Jack himself.

"I've been after wonderin' whether to ring ya up or let it go entirely, Max Blake," he said when I picked up.

"Jack," I replied. "What made you decide?"

"Yer wife, of course," he said. "I figured the only reason you'd have for tryin' to reach me was Caeli – that maybe somethin' terrible had happened to her, or even somethin' grand, I suppose, though I'm guessin' yer long in the tooth for fatherhood, boyo."

"Caeli's fine, thank you – and I wouldn't put my prospects of becoming a father in those exact terms."

"Ye can run from the truth, lad, but ya can't hide from it," he said. "What is it that prompts yer call then, especially one brokered by that thievin' Roman lawyer?"

"I've a question – one the whole world doesn't need to hear," I said.

"A question, is it – and ya don't want herself to know yer askin'. I don't like the sounds of that. A man shouldn't keep secrets from his wife, after all. I'm startin' to be sorry I rang ya back a'tall."

"Humor me, Jack. You don't even need to answer. But it's a question I have to ask as I put the Raven's Ridge affair to bed for good."

He didn't like the sounds of that, either.

"Ah, Jaysus, man," he said. "Take off yer journalist's cap and then leave it off for good. Ya don't have to insist on God's given truth every minute of every day, ya know. Give it a rest. It's allowed."

"Sure it is, though not today, Jack – not in this case anyway. Tell me where you were on the day of the take-down at Bunratty Castle, just before 3 o'clock, when Gallacher was looking for you and your friends and didn't have a clue as to where you'd scarpered off to."

"That's yer question then?"

"It is."

"It's not much of a question, is it?"

"It's the one I need to ask."

"But that's not true, either," he said. "What ya really want to know is whether I was after spendin' time along the banks of the River Shannon just then, nearby to the place ye were to meet with fair Kathleen's mercenary, keepin' watch on me niece and her intended, it bein' so close to the wedding day, after all, studiously avoidin' discovery by yer own sniper, which proved easy enough."

He laughed, giving me a chance to react.

But I chose to let it play out.

He jumped back in seconds later.

"And yer far too discreet to ask whether we put the cur down so he'd never bother Caeli again, nor to confirm if two shots were fired at the bastard 'cause the first one missed, killin' his bloody boat engine instead of the man himself. Isn't that what ye really want to ask me, Max Blake? 'Cause I have to say that, if it is, if that's what ya truly want to know, then I'm not a'tall sure I'd be after wantin' to tell ye a precious thing about what I was doin' or where I was exactly at that precise moment."

I considered a half-dozen replies and another dozen questions to draw additional details from him, but in the end I chose to let it go.

"I think, Uncle Jack, that you've given me more than enough," I said.

"Good, though I'll deny havin' mentioned a thing, should it come to that," he said. "Still, I'm happy enough to help, I suppose. Are ye needin' anythin' else 'fore I return to the glorious drudgery of the archives?"

"No. Not a thing. Thanks."

"Really now? Are ya tellin' me ya never wondered why Kathleen came to yer place that day without any backup – not so much as a single man or woman to help her along in the event that she'd be waylaid as she drew near with a sack full of explosives? I have to say, I find that hard to believe, given yer credentials as a man who's said to be thorough in his pursuit of the awful bloody truth."

"Are you trying to tell me something, Jack?"

"Me? No – not a'tall. Nice of ya to reach out, boyo," he said. "Pass along me best to Caeli – unless, of course, ya don't want her to know we spoke."

The connection died, and I put on a jacket and took the new Nikon to the porch overlooking the river and spent a half-hour shooting photos of the geese and black-backed gulls that flew low and fast above the water.

Caeli returned home two hours later with a bedraggled Mitts in tow and a radiant smile covering her face.

"Doesn't he look handsome?" she asked as she freed the surly beast from his carrier, which is large enough to accommodate a good-sized dog.

"He does," I said. "Was he amenable?"

The tones of her laughter were musical.

"Mitts? Amenable? At the groomer's? Hardly."

The big cat stomped angrily to the cupboard that contains his food bowl and began thumping at the door, using both paws as though he were throwing punches.

"Looks like he's hungry," I said and moved in for the rescue. "Then again, he's always hungry."

Caeli seemed content.

"What's going on?" she asked. "Anything new?"

"New? Can't think of a thing."

ABOUT THE AUTHOR

William Florence is a former newspaper reporter/editor. He worked at dailies in Michigan, Washington, D.C., South Dakota, Indiana, and Oregon for almost 25 years before heading the Chemeketa Community College journalism department for 22 years. He retired in 2015.

During his initial career, he was widely published in individual newspapers and wire services and in industry magazines such as *The Bulletin* for the American Society of Newspaper Editors and *APME News* for the Associated Press Managing Editors group, as well as noted travel publications such as *Arizona Highways* and *Michigan Living*.

He was honored with writing awards in four states.

In addition to living in the West, he has traveled extensively throughout the region to gain an understanding of the land and its inhabitants. He studies Western lore, is knowledgeable about the customs and history of the Old West. In his spare time, he writes the Max Blake Westerns series (available at www.amazon.com).

Florence attended colleges in Michigan and Ireland. He is a voracious reader and movie buff. He is married with two adult children. His wife, Linda, a public schools administrator, is his toughest critic and best friend.

and then determining the fate of the archbishop, a complicated man who believes that British-held Ulster should be returned to the Irish Republic by any means necessary.

EMERALD RIDGE is a thrill-a-minute sleigh-ride that features unforgettable characters, sleight-of-hand twists and turns providing surprise after revelation after bombshell. Toss in a love story and you have what it takes for a riveting Max Blake Mystery.

http://wbp.bz/era

well hold the key to determining who actually shot American President John F. Kennedy in 1963.

This gut-wrenching tale will surprise you, and then it will surprise you again as you embrace the eccentric, adventurous, at times humorous and other times deadly serious characters in this edition to the Max Blake Mystery series.

Readers and fans of the Max Blake Mystery series have their say:

"William Florence's latest effort, Melia Ridge, has surpassed his previous works. This time his intrepid protagonists, Max Blake and Caeli Brown, find themselves in Italy fighting against a rogue prelate who works in the Vatican. Florence's knowledge of the Italian geography as well as the language makes for an exciting read. I can hardly wait for his next!"

"This is a fast-paced, enjoyable read, especially by fans of Max and Caeli. Leonard and Elmore remind us why we love them as characters. The intrigue of the Vatican plays a central role."

"Without question the best book yet in the series, and that says a lot because all of the novels are wonderful reads, containing everything that a good story, well told, should tell."

http://wbp.bz/wfmra

The trail winds through the incredible mansion called Raptor's Ridge, through the streets and alleyways of Oregon's state capitol, and it eventually spills into the state's beautiful but deadly High Desert near the town of John Day.

When the killer is eventually cornered and violence explodes in unexpected ways, Max must use all of his wits and daring, plus a little bit of luck, to remain alive during a deadly night of terror ... and eventual reckoning.

Fans of the author's Max Blake Westerns series will rejoice in discovering this new and thoroughly modern Max, the great-great grandson and namesake of the legendary federal marshal that forms the basis of five novels from the same author.

http://wbp.bz/raptorsa